A FINAL ENCHANTMENT

"She's evil, Charles. Can't you remember when you were little? You and Merlain?"

"A little. She controlled us, all right. It was fun stealing and it was fun doing naughty things. She never let us feel guilt."

"That's what she would do to the kings."

"She did it when they were younger. They as much as my sister and I. Why didn't she now?"

"I don't know, Charles. I'm as puzzled as Helbah."

"Could it be that she's changed? After all, I did cut her head off. I deflated her old body with my father's sword and dipped you into her blood and disenchanted you."

"You broke the spell, Charles, but no, my love, I don't think Zady can have changed. Witches' natures don't change."

"You feel it too, then. What about my father? He acted strange. He could be under a spell, but wouldn't Helbah know about it?"

"It depends on the spell. If Zady got to Kelvin…"

"But he's the hero. He's the one in the prophecy. Mouvar's prophecy…."

TOR BOOKS BY PIERS ANTHONY

Alien Plot
Anthonology
But What of Earth?
Demons Don't Dream
Ghost
Hasan
*Letters to Jenny**
Prostho Plus
Race Against Time
Shade of the Tree
Steppe
Triple Detente

WITH ROBERT E. MARGROFF:

Dragon's Gold
The E.S.P. Worm
Serpent's Silver
Chimaera's Copper
Mouvar's Magic
Orc's Opal
The Ring

WITH FRANCES HALL:

Pretender

*Forthcoming

PIERS ANTHONY AND ROBERT E. MARGROFF

Mouvar's Magic

TOR®
fantasy

A TOM DOHERTY ASSOCIATES BOOK
NEW YORK

MOUVAR'S MAGIC

Cover art by Darrell K. Sweet

A Tor Book
Published by Tom Doherty Associates, Inc.
175 Fifth Avenue
New York, N.Y. 10010

Tor ® is a registered trademark of Tom Doherty Associates, Inc.

ISBN: 0-812-51982-5
Library of Congress Catalog Card Number: 92-6921

First edition: August 1992
First mass market printing: May 1993

Printed in the United States of America

0 9 8 7 6 5 4 3 2 1

Contents

Introduction

This is the fifth and concluding novel in the fantasy series beginning with *Dragon's Gold*, continuing with *Serpent's Silver*, *Chimaera's Copper*, and *Orc's Opal*. Since there are more than fifty characters here, and a good deal of prior adventure, the reader who starts with this volume could have a problem getting his bearings. This novel can, however, stand by itself. To allay confusion, here is a summary of the major characters and their relation to each other. The minor ones should fall into place, as they normally are in scenes with one or more of the major ones.

Professor Devale is the evil magician, with a taste for power and young female flesh. His chief tool is *Zady*, a malignant witch who was almost killed in the last novel. His opponent is the good magician *Mouvar*, offstage. The benign witch *Helbah* leads the forces of good.

John Knight came originally from Earth by a weird accident. He married the evil *Zoanna*, but later escaped her and married the good *Charlain*. Their children are *Kelvin*, who became the unlikely Roundear of Prophecy, and *Jon*, his feisty little sister. John Knight later disappeared and was presumed dead, so Charlain married *Hal Hackleberry*. Then Hal strayed and John reappeared, so the couple was reunited, leaving the last names of their children somewhat in doubt. Kelvin married *Heln*, the daughter of *St. Helens*, one of John Knight's Earthly companions, and they had telepathic triplets: *Charles*, *Merlain*, and *Dragon Horace*. Jon married the son of *Mor Crumb*, *Lester*, and had *Kathy Jon* and three younger boys: *Alvin*, *Teddy*, and *Joey*.

Glow was once enchanted into a sword, but she has been restored and is now Charles' girlfriend. She, too, is telepathic. She is looking for her brother *Glint*. There are also two perpetually juvenile kings, *Kildom* and *Kildee*, whom Glow helps watch. And *Krassnose*, *Phenoblee*, and *Brudalous*, who are huge fishlike orcs. Also the *chimaera*, whose three heads are named *Mervania*, *Mertin*, and *Grumpus*.

Now hang on; this is a wild novel!

PROLOGUE

Night

*T*he ugly old witch's face did not match her lusciously curved body. Midway up the neck the firm smooth throat became wrinkled chicken skin. There were warts on the beaked face, and gray hairs that contrasted sharply with the smooth nude body. She smelled bad, as if from twenty years of soaking in bird droppings.

She stood in Professor Devale's study, there before his desk, glaring at him with just the right amount of malignancy.

Professor Devale did not seem to be surprised or disturbed to find such a creature in his study. He looked up from his papers as if slightly bored. "Zady, I understand you lost your head," he said conversationally. He admired her beauty even beneath its accumulation of filth; of course he found other areas of her anatomy to be of far more interest than her face. Head bowed slightly, carefully repolishing his ever-polished horns, he was as pleased with her as was possible. What displeased him was her failure to conquer the dragon frame and bring him the master key opal.

"You," Zady spat, producing a smoking drop of spittle, "didn't come to my rescue! For twenty years I nourished my strength and grew back my body. Now I'm back, I'm strong, and I want your attention."

"Why, certainly, Zady." What a spitfire she was! Appropriately, as that red-haired niece of hers had been. He shouldn't allow such impudence in his office, but there were compensations he would soon extract.

"I want to go back! I want this time to conquer. I want your help!"

"Certainly, Zady. Otherwise you'd not be present."

"You didn't help me before!" Zady accused him. "You allowed me to be defeated by those brats! Twenty years in the dragon frame is a long time! Twenty years of sheltering under a louse-infested bird's rump! Twenty years gradually growing arms and legs and all the rest! Why, Professor, didn't you help?"

"Because, my dear Zady," he said with just a hint of annoyance, "that would have taught you nothing. You were to conquer, you were to bring me the opal. I provided the means. My participating in your revenge was not in our agreement."

"But you—" The old hag face frowned in frustration. "You wanted—"

"Yes, and now you have a younger body without resort to shape changing. All you'll need to change for me is your face. Possibly not always that."

"You—! You—!" the old hag head mouthed, managing to produce some more smoking spittle.

"Temper, temper, Zady!" the professor admonished. "Remember that I am the teacher. You want to conquer, you must conquer. As before I will provide you with the means. In return, of course, for compensation."

"You mean—" Smooth hands gestured at smooth body, warm and now virginal. In this respect they understood each other perfectly; their words were mere games.

"Of course, of course. As you say, twenty years in the dragon frame is a long time. But you must not assume, my malignant friend, that I will depart from custom."

"Why not? Doesn't Mouvar?"

"Oh, Zady, Zady, how little you know. And with all your centuries! Mouvar only appeared to appear. The real Mouvar is not a green dwarf. The real Mouvar was not ignominiously defeated by that frame's inept magician. All was of a fabric—a pretense for the purpose of creating a legend and a hero to work to his final purpose."

"And that purpose is?" Zady demanded.

"Oh, Zady, I was afraid you'd ask. I do not know; I have been who I am for too long. All I know is that neither—neither Mouvar nor I—interfere directly. To do so would bring us into direct confrontation with each other, and that would be out of form."

"You are saying," Zady grated through ugly teeth, "that a green dwarf shape is not Mouvar's true form?"

"Correct, Zady."

"But he was there, several times. And elsewhere. Setting up John Knight and Charlain to become parents of Kelvin. Providing Kelvin with weapons. Arranging for the creation and birth of his brats."

"Correct again, Zady, as far as you go. Mouvar is always indirect. I have to be also."

"That doesn't make sense to me. I interfere as much as I can."

"That is because you are a tool instead of a prime mover. I am the one who must be indirect."

"Then it's you and Mouvar as much as malignant magic practitioners against benign magic practitioners? As much as Kelvin and prophecy against an otherwise established fate?"

"Your grasp is quite astonishing. It's only through Mouvar's indirect interference that Kelvin's kind has triumphed as much as it has."

"Then I wait your interference!" Zady said. "Direct or indirect, there's no difference."

"Ah, but Zady, there is. Mouvar took centuries in the dragon frame to set up what you will now knock down. He foresees events but cannot always control them. I foresee less clearly but just as certainly. If I take direct action in human affairs I risk more than you can know. A draw is the most I can hope for from this particular contest, with just a chance for personal victory."

"Mouvar's defeat?"

"Yes."

"I don't believe any such thing," Zady said. "If you wanted to you could destroy my enemies and Mouvar."

"It's proper that you think so. You are supposed to think so. Mouvar and I are both too powerful ever to meet in open conflict. If we did the contested world would be destroyed along with its inhabitants. Mouvar and I in mortal combat would send frame after frame crashing."

"Then you won't come out? Won't battle directly?"

"Not directly. But indirectly, perhaps, as necessary."

"You want my kind victorious?"

"Always. It's like the game the humans play called chess. Mouvar moves and I move, but neither of us moves ourselves upon the board."

"Like chess but with more pieces."

"Exactly. But with pieces of more varied and unequal powers."

The beautiful young witch with the old, ugly face stared at the handsome, horned professor from her rheumy yellow eyes. He could imagine her thinking, turning over and over what she had only just learned. Thinking now not about Kelvin or the hoped-for victory. Rather she would be considering the larger implications.

Zady, he thought, standing, ready to take her shapely body into his scaly arms, *this time you'll win. When this is over the goody-goodies will be gone; your kind, my favorite kind, will throughout the dragon frame predominate. There will be no Kelvin Hackleberry left alive and Mouvar will have wasted centuries.*

"Zady," he said aloud, "come to your professor. Come now and we will dance."

She held back, but not, he knew, from coyness. "You will give me your help, Professor?"

"All that is necessary," he promised. "All that you will need to make Kelvin Knight Hackleberry's world a world ruled by malignant magic."

He grabbed her quickly, to claim his reward.

Morning

Glow was lovelier than she had ever been, thought young Charles Knight. He sat contentedly on the riverbank, watching her disrobe for an early swim. Her curves were just perfect, and her face—what a lovely, glowing countenance!

It had been twenty years, he thought, remembering as she dived. He watched the water splash, the ripple rings form. Twenty years ago she had been an enchanted sword. Though but a child he had disenchanted her, with Helbah's help. Their father, Kelvin, had saved his sister's life, and he, scared little Charles, had somehow found the courage to kick Zady's severed head from off the high precipice. In his mind's eye he saw it turning over and over, wailing as it fell. It was after that that he had performed the magic and brought Glow out of his dreams and into his life. Twenty years later and they still only planned.

"And what are you doing, as if I don't know?" He turned to see Merlain, his coppery-haired sister, emerge from the woods. A real beauty, she, and like himself still unmarried. Being telepathic, the three of them shared an intimacy that was more than body and sometimes seemed more than mind. They had decided long ago that when Merlain had a suitable mate the four of them would wed. Alas, finding another telepath, or even a nontelepath of the right quality, was taking time. But time was what he and his sister most had. The tiny bit of chimaera powder that had allowed them to be born had at the same time given them all indefinitely extended lifetimes. But Glow still had the nightmares in which her gleaming sharp edge was being used against those she loved and cherished.

"Well?" Merlain persisted.

He shrugged. "You know quite well. Did you find Horace?"

"No!" She looked a little worried. "But I think I know

where he's gone. Darn dragon, you'd think that he could wait."

"Yes," he said absently, "dragons do live for centuries, but dragons are dragons."

"He's our brother!"

"Yes." He and Merlain were not twins; they were two of triplets, and the third was the dragon. Without the chimaera's intervention they would have been a chimaera: a woman's head, a man's head, and a dragon's head on one giant scorpio-crab body complete with long, copper sting. Though separate, they were closer than triplets, because of an incidental legacy of the chimaera: telepathy.

"Do you think we should call him? Before he's out of range?" She meant with their minds, for Horace had the same mental power. The young dragon was keeper of the magic opal and overking of the Alliance. Unlike normal dragons Horace had copper scales instead of gold. The three of them had been affectionate friends and playmates all their lives, but spring was spring and the dragon was the carrier of an ancient urge. The same urge Charles had when he gazed at naked Glow, and so became vulnerable to his sister's teasing.

"No," Charles said, ruminating, "we shouldn't bother him."

"But he might get in trouble!" the beautiful copper-haired girl said. "He's never been with other dragons. He won't know how to behave."

"That's why he's going. You know he's smarter than dragons he'll find. He needs to find his own kind, as you do too."

Merlain frowned, seemingly from distaste. She plunked her pretty bottom down on their favorite boulder. She studied her reflection. "At least he's got dragon territory to go to. Sometimes I wish there was a telepath territory."

"Some chance!" They'd searched everywhere and asked everyone. Even Helbah couldn't help. Yet somewhere there had to be some male deserving of and deserved by his sister.

"Oh, there you are!" Glow called. She came dripping wet in all her beauty. She was oblivious of her nudity except when her brattling charges were around. Hers was an enormous responsibility. Kildom and Kildee were kings who aged only one year for a normal human's four. The extended childhood was supposed to make for expanded learning, but the terrible twins rarely displayed that. In their case it seemed to mean expanded time for mischief. Now an apparent twelve years old—never mind that they were in their mid-thirties in actual years—they were curious boys slowly developing into arrogant men.

Charles took off his leatherskin jacket and positioned it on the boulder, hoping Glow would perch there. Instead the lovely girl put on her correct underclothes and her neatly starched white nannydress. Then she joined them. She knew his hope, of course. She wasn't teasing him; she just preferred not to tempt him.

"Kildom, Kildee, and Helbah have some business with your parents. That's why I have the day off. We might just as well enjoy the spring while they spend the day in talk."

"I can't imagine those brats discussing anything seriously," Charles said. "Mom and Dad, perhaps."

"Well, they are. Your granddad and grandma will be with them. I don't know what it's about. It's certainly Helbah doing it."

"I wonder if it could have something to do with Dad's prophecy?" Merlain asked. "You know." She recited the lines that always made Charles wince:

> A Roundear there Shall Surely be
> Born to be Strong, Raised to be Free
> Fighting Dragons in his Youth
> Leading Armies, Nothing Loth
> Ridding his Country of a Sore
> Joining Two, then uniting Four
> Until from Seven there be one
> Only then will his Task be Done
> Honored by many, cursed by Few
> All will know what Roundear can Do.

"Most likely," Charles said when the recital was done, "it's to do with Zady. Helbah has always insisted she'd be coming back. Twenty years ago Dad struck her head off and I kicked it off the cliff. Then you, Merlain, claimed you saw an eagawk carrying it."

"I did!" Merlain insisted. "Proof of that is that the head was never recovered. Helbah thinks there's some counter-magic that prevented her finding it."

"Most likely the eagawk dropped it," Charles said. "You two believe what you want, but I don't think she's coming back."

The two girls looked as if on a worse day they might have argued. They might believe him wrong, but it was too nice a day to be bickering with those you knew were your very best friends. Besides, had either of them looked into his mind, Charles knew they would have gleaned his uncertainty.

Story Time

*T*he big, gray-haired, gray-bearded man with the gnarled face definitely had round ears. He sat there in Charles Lomax's Wine and Chess House, sipping a short mug of dark red. He was toying with a king, in the meantime joking it up with Danceye Nellie, the serving maid all men swore had to have the biggest jugs in town.

"That him?" The tall, bronzed man had the mark of an adventurer. He nodded now at the table, as Charlie had expected him to do.

Charlie wiped at the bar where the noon patrons had spilt. He prided himself on reading types. This man was the sort he had soldiered with when he was young and idolized the man at the table. But the questioner was a stranger.

"I'm Charlie Lomax. I own this place. Introduce yourself and I might tell you."

"You might?" The stranger seemed amused at this middle-aged man's near challenge. It was as though he knew perfectly well that he could get the information without troubling himself. "I'm Dack. Tim Dack. I've been poking around dragon territory, looking for scale."

"Dangerous business." Charlie gripped Dack's firm, rough hand in his decidedly pudgier one. It had been a long time since he had been soldiering. "You there long?"

"Better than half a year."

"You bring back a lot of scale?"

Dack shook his head. "They shed 'em but I didn't find many. Mostly I escaped with my life."

"Good practice. You want to know about that gentleman?"

Dack nodded. "He's not John Knight, Kelvin's father?"

"Nope. He's Kelvin's father-in-law. Sean Reilly, commonly known as St. Helens."

"I've heard of him." Dack seemed about to walk over.

"Wait until she comes back. He's still got his temper. He might think it's her you want to see."

Nellie whooped suddenly and pretended to brain the roundear with her serving tray. St. Helens made a slap at her seating arrangement. When she got back to the bar the tips of her pointed ears were red. "That man!" she said to her employer, dark eyes dancing. "If he doesn't quit joking me he'll be the death of me."

"More likely the life of you if he has his lecherous way." He took her tray, observing again that she really was pretty, top-heaviness aside. Sometimes St. Helens called her "Dolly," though he hadn't worked out why.

"I'll tell you what, Dack. I'll introduce you. But then you'll have to buy a round of wine."

"Fair enough." Dack was halfway across the room in long strides before he caught up with him. St. Helens looked up from the chessboard, probably wondering if this were an autograph seeker or some scribe intent on getting an article.

"St. Helens, this is Tim Dack. He says he's a man back fresh from dragon territory."

St. Helens nodded, looking first at Dack's pointed ears. Four times in recent years men had come in who were descendants of John Knight's company from Earth; without exception they had wanted to meet someone who had known their father. He held out his hand and they shook.

"Dack wants to talk with you and he asked me to sit in. He's buying a round of red when Nel gets back. New keg of the dark to be tapped."

St. Helens belched. Dack pulled out a chair and sat down across from him. Charlie took the empty chair to the side.

St. Helens waited, toying with the chess piece. He and his business partner, Phillip Blastmore, onetime king of the former kingdom of Aratex, had made money on the game they had introduced. Everyone knew about St. Helens' business, and most knew his history. St. Helens, as many, many people had discovered, generally liked to talk.

"General Reilly," Dack began. Like most people the respect he felt made him hesitant.

"St. Helens," St. Helens said. If he had not had an immediate favorable impression of the man he would not have corrected him.

"St. Helens, I've read and heard about your exploits all my life. I know how you and John Knight and a company of roundears, all soldiers from some place called Earth, arrived in our world by magic. You and he and the other roundears—"

"Army unit, and it wasn't magic, or at least my old commander, John Knight, always claimed it wasn't. Science, he always said, as if it made any difference. I used to agree with him because he was the commander, but these days I sort of lean to the majority."

"You think, then, that it was magic?"

St. Helens nodded. He looked away, as from a painful subject, giving the studied impression that he was not about to elaborate. "So you want my story?" he asked in a way he supposed was unexpected.

Dack nodded. Poor fellow, he didn't know the former general of local troops.

"Well, sir, I was born on Earth, a world like this except that Earth was in some ways nicer and in some ways worse. No magic on Earth to run things—none at all. Instead we had science, and with that we accomplished things that here are accomplished by magic."

As he always did at this point, St. Helens paused and took a sip of wine. He rinsed it around in his mouth, savoring its distinctive spicy flavor. He swallowed, then continued.

"I was in the North American army along with my commander, then Captain John Knight. I volunteered, as did the rest who were with us. 'We want twelve volunteers. Reilly, you've just volunteered.' "

Dack chuckled appreciatively. Evidently he knew about armies.

"This big deal was to test an atomic missile that was clean. That meant it only killed people and did nothing disastrous like poisoning valuable territory. We weren't supposed to any of us have been hit, but somehow we were. The missile came in low and we all ducked and threw ourselves flat with our eyes shut. The next thing any of us knew we were at the edge of the Flaw, that big, incredible crack in reality you have here. We didn't any of us have any idea what had happened. Then we figured out that we really were in a different world. Well, sir, we talked it over like regular fellows and not army men, and—"

On and on, telling his familiar story. Dack could have been an unusual type of scholar and author, but Charlie doubted that he was. No matter; he liked hearing his old friend's tale as told by his old friend. If it hadn't been for his business of making chessmen and boards—none of the work actually done by himself, of course, or Phillip Blastmore—he could have made money lecturing.

". . . and so there the kid was, stuck with his prophecy!" St. Helens was saying much later. "My old commander's son, and him in the Rud Queen's prison and me in the Aratex palace with very young Phillip. Kelvin wasn't the sort to believe in prophecy, but thanks to his father he had the ears, and now he had the gauntlet. Well, after the kid whipped the big guardsman in the public park, there was no doubt in anyone's mind that he was genuine. All this time Jon, his pointed-ear little sister—and let me tell you she was a pretty good man with that sling of hers—was in that terrible auction place. My own dear daughter, Heln, was there too. Now I guess you know how guards used to be at those places. Poor little Heln, as delicate a lass as you ever saw, was ravished. You see, she had the ears, thanks to me, and no prophecy. When the filthy guardsman had finished with her, all she could think to do was die. But little Jon was there, and she had some dragonberries. Those things are poison to you with pointed ears, but in us roundears they work different. Jon didn't mean any harm with the berries, but Heln grabbed them and swallowed them. Instead of dying as she wanted, Heln had this strange experience. Let me tell you, what happened to her then took away all thoughts of dying."

Nellie brought a fresh jug. She put it down by the chessboard and seated herself midway between her employer and the storyteller. Her sharp ears were tuned, obviously. In the process of telling his own story St. Helens was, as always, telling of adventures he had shared—a delight to the proprietor's ears. Most of what he told had to be about Kelvin Knight Hackleberry, the fabled Roundear, but St. Helens assigned everyone he could a role of importance. As always St. Helens did not omit his own bravery and accomplishments.

Tick tick tick went the big clock above the wine barrels, counting off the narrative. As always Charlie was spellbound, and Nellie and the stranger seemed to be as well.

"And so young Charles—not your good host, though he was probably named for him—kicked the old witch's head. It wailed in midair, and it fell off the cliff in the wake of his sister. In the meantime, Kelvin, young Charles' father, was moving like a blur. He saw his only daughter falling to her certain death, and acting without a moment's hesitation, he—"

Inevitably the long story reached its satisfying end. Dack, like many a listener before him, had kept enthralled. Nellie, though she knew the big roundear well, had the look of full hero worship and the eye-gleam that said how much she could love him. For long moments they simply sat, each of them aglow in separate ways.

"Is that enough for you, young fellow? That fill in the gaps?"

Dack took a swig of wine, not quite looking at them. He was coming slowly back from the adventures that had held his attention. He wiped his mouth, making a purple streak on his sleeve. Like most adventurers, Dack's table manners weren't the best.

"St. Helens, General Reilly, sir, I wouldn't have interrupted you for all the loose scales in dragon territory! I could never top your experiences or equal them. But I've had a recent experience—"

"Say on, young fellow," St. Helens said amiably.

"Well, sir, I've heard from childhood about how young Kelvin killed a dragon when he was still a boy, then used the golden scales to buy an army. It was my favorite story, and interesting adventure looked to be more interesting than work. I thought if I could find enough dragon scales, work would thereafter be no problem. So after I inherited my father's horse and sword and few gold coins, I set off for dragon territory."

Charlie sipped his wine, marveling at how good his merchandise had become. This promised to be another story, newer than the one before. Of course no story could top St. Helens', but it was only polite to listen to a potential good customer.

"And so," Dack was saying later as Charlie's head buzzed pleasantly, "I lay trapped beneath the big tree branch as the two dragons fought over which would eat me. I gave up all thoughts of becoming rich or living to return home. Then suddenly there was this tickling again—the strange head-sensation I described before. It made me think of the way I felt after several mugs of wine, and yet at the same time it was as though something were sharing my thoughts. I looked up, past the two dragons, and I swear it was just as though my eyes were drawn out. There, coming out from the forest, was a third dragon!"

"Gods help us!" Charlie exclaimed. Even Kelvin had

never faced three dragons with no weapon better than a sword. Furthermore Dack couldn't even have reached his sword. Dack's weapon had been flung to the side by a casual tail-whip that had killed his horse.

"What did you do?" St. Helens prompted.

"I could do nothing," Dack admitted. "But then I saw this body on the body of the new dragon. It was a human man, very dirty, with long yellow, almost golden hair. He rode there between the two tiny wings, and he hadn't anything on at all. All he did was sit there on that smaller dragon. He just sat there, bare naked, and he thought."

"Thought?" St. Helens was incredulous. "It would seem to me, young fellow, that the time for thinking was past."

"Ordinarily, yes. But this was thinking too. I know because he thought to me afterwards. What he did at first was think to the fighters that they should quit fighting and go. And you know what? Those battle-scarred old veterans, both of them streaming blood, did just as he and I wanted! They turned tail and lumbered off, and that left just the smaller dragon, the thinker, and myself."

"Mouvar on a picnic!" Charlie said. Lately he had adopted this meaningless oath that had doubtless been invented by rebellious youngsters. Considering the freedom kids had these days Charlie would sometimes have liked to be a kid himself.

"He stood there, atop the dragon, squarely between the wings, St. Helens. He was as tall as you, with muscles to match his sense of balance. When he stood up, it was just like he grew right up out of the spine of the dragon. He fixed me with a stare, a little accusing. Then that dragon came close, and I started screaming and cursing. But instead of the dragon eating me, it lifted the branch and let me free. The blond man didn't say anything—he just pointed back the way I had come. Back out of the mountains, back out of dragon territory. I knew what he meant as surely as if he had spoken. I went, believe me I went, and I didn't even bother to retrieve my sword or to pick up the bloody scales. All I wanted was to get home."

"And now you're home," St. Helens said, "and you're thinking you'd like to know about that man. I can't say I blame you. I'd like to know myself."

"I'll bet he was a sorcerer!" Charlie said. "Like Zatanas. He controlled dragons for a time, though through sympathetic magic. I don't recall that he ever rode around on one."

"I don't think he was a magician," St. Helens said. "Sounds more like a wild man with extra brainpower. Like Heln's kids, maybe. If he could think into your head and the dragons' heads, he had a power."

"I'll say he had a power! You should have seen those dragons get!"

"I would have liked to. I wish I could have been there."

"I'm going back! I'm going to find out! St. Helens, can you go with me? There's no one better to lead an expedition! No one I'd rather have in charge!"

St. Helens sighed, and Charlie knew his frustration was real. "I'd like nothing better, young fellow. Even though I'm not as young as I once was or in the shape I was when I was younger. But the fact is I may have a responsibility here. According to good witch Helbah, old Zady is going to come back. I don't know that I believe her and I don't know that I don't. My son-in-law still has some prophecy to fulfill, and maybe Zady will make him fulfill it. Gods know I couldn't talk sense into him! But the point is, if there's trouble, I may have to put on a uniform."

"You really think there may be?" Dack asked.

"I'll tell you, young fellow. I'm almost but not quite sure of it."

Charlie exchanged meaningful if wine-blurred glances with his number-one serving wench. Both knew that the big man was really agonized. For Sean Reilly, missing an opportunity for an adventure just wasn't natural.

Dack stood up, said his good-byes, shook hands all around, only a little bit hesitantly with Nellie. It had been a long, pleasant afternoon storytelling.

Scary Time

*K*elvin Knight Hackleberry sat his middle-aged self down in the comfortable chair between his mother and father. It seemed strange to him to be in one of the twin palaces with them and Helbah and the twins terrible, as Merlain and Charles called them. The young scamps were slicked up with their official robes on and brightly polished crowns on their red heads. Even Katbah, Helbah's familiar, shone, if anything, blacker than usual.

"As you know," Helbah said, facing the tight little circle, "it's been twenty years. That's how long it should have taken for Zady to grow a new body on her head. As you also know, my magician, warlock, and witch friends and I have searched. The head has not been located, and that means a powerful protective spell was placed on it. Zady has an ally who wants her back."

Kelvin tried to look impressed. He had decided years back that Helbah, though with the best of intentions, had to be judged more than a little inept. The same had to go for her friends, many of whom he had met at the convention. The head could just have disappeared when his son deflated the body with the point of his father's sword. Then it had been only Merlain who saw the eagawk carrying the head. Merlain was his beloved daughter and unnaturally smart, but at the time she was six years old and had just been subjected to what had to be the shock of her young life.

"Kelvin," Helbah said abruptly, interrupting his far more interesting thoughts, "you've gotten fat! You're in no shape to fight battles! When's the last time you exercised?"

"Uh . . ." Kelvin said, exerting his brilliance. It was true he hadn't been weight lifting or jousting or even riding horses much. But then why should he? He couldn't believe that Zady was coming back, and if she did, he had help. His gauntlets, his boots, the chimaera's sting, and Mouvar's antimagic weapon, not to mention the levitation belt, would handle everything. If he couldn't wear them these days he'd gladly let someone else use them.

"What kind of a hero are you, anyway?" Helbah stormed. She was poking him in the middle with an aged forefinger. Strong old woman that she was, the finger went through his buffer area and hurt.

"And you, Charlain!" Helbah said, turning on his unoffending mother. "When's the last time you practiced those spells?"

Charlain blushed. "Really, Helbah, I'm not a witch. I know you wanted me to be your apprentice, and we did work together that once, but I haven't really practiced."

"You belittle yourself. You have natural talent. It isn't your fault that you were born human. Your daughter also has talent."

"Only because you and Katbah used us. All I ever tried to do before meeting you was to predict with the cards. Really, there's no use in arguing, it's you who are the witch."

Helbah turned to Kelvin's father, who was quietly examining his own waist. He had put on weight too, though unlike his son he still often exercised.

"Each of you is going to get into shape. And Charlain, you're going to practice spells. I'll help with magic, but you men are going to do what is necessary."

"You mean"—Kelvin choked on the thought—"dieting, and—"

"Of course! You won't suffer nearly as much as you might; my spells will ease your pain. But that body of yours is going to smooth and harden and do it fast."

"Maybe just a temporary spell—"

"No! Magic can be reversed, as you well know! You are going to be a hero again and you are going to be in shape!"

"Does that mean no more of my wife's pies?"

"No pies! No cooakes. No cakies, holenuts, or kudge! No peajelnutly sandwiches! None of that fattening stuff—at least for the duration."

"The duration of what?"

"The duration of the danger, of course!"

"You really think she's coming back?" The idea still seemed absurd to him.

"Yes! Charlain, you tell them what you see in the cards."

Charlain fidgeted in a manner totally unlike herself. Clearly Helbah's question was one she would rather not answer.

"My ability's not what it once was," she said. "It's grown weaker and weaker, and for the past year I haven't even practiced."

"What did you see last time you consulted them?"

The beautiful woman of advancing years swallowed visibly. There was no resisting Helbah's stare.

"The cards told me nothing," she finally said. "Everyone I consulted about. Every question I asked. Uncertainty and danger is all the cards show. Helbah, it may be the end of our world is coming!"

"Don't talk foolish!" her husband said, putting an arm around her.

Kelvin felt a cold chill traveling from the base of his backbone. This was his mother talking! His mother who had always been so optimistic and so hopeful that the cards could bring the answer to anything.

"There you are," Helbah said. "That's why we have to get ready. Why we have to prepare to meet destiny head on."

"Meow," her familiar said, stretching his midnight blackness. It was a sound of total agreement. In the past when danger beckoned he had bared his claws and spat defiance at the universe. The cat recognized that something worse was coming, and that was scary.

Kelvin wondered just what could threaten their very existence. His mother's cards should have shown her something.

He looked at the apparent twelve-year-olds and they were sitting still like perfect little kings.

Something, Kelvin decided with an uncontrollable shiver, definitely wasn't shaping up well in his universe.

Kiddy Time

Jon, Kelvin's little sister, crossed her arms over her properly mature bosom and glared a mother's disapproval at her youngest son. Joey was muddy and slimed with green pond scum. More clothes washing, and she had just finished a batch!

"Well?" she demanded.

The boy pointed back along the rail fence to the froog pond. "Kathy. She splashed me."

Jon groaned. Not "he" but "she"! Never a brother, always the older sister. What kind of an incorrigible was she raising? Girls were supposed to help their mothers. Kathy Jon should be here helping with the wash. Instead she was down at the froog pond slinging stones.

"I'll warm her bottom!" Jon promised, grabbing her favorite whipwillow stick and heading for the pond.

"Can I watch, Mom? Can I?"

"No! You stay here and get those muddy clothes off!"

Mentally Jon delivered a thorough thrashing to her firstborn every step to the pond. It wasn't going to work and she knew it. Kathy Jon was too much the way she had been and not enough as girls were supposed to be. Her gestures with the whipwillow hadn't worked when Kathy was five. They certainly didn't now that she was the age Jon was when she and Kelvin had gone adventuring. The only time she actually had used the whipwillow the only result had been that Kathy looked at her accusingly and made her cry.

SPLASH!

Muddy water with algae greening it geysered up at her, splashing on her face and sprinkling her heavily from head to foot. At the same time a boat with a sail made of a girl's unmentionable bounced on a stone-created wave. Kathy Jon, it seemed, was bombarding a pretend warship.

Jon wiped mud and slime from her face with her apron. What a brat! Where was she?

There she was! Hanging upside down from the big oaple tree. All that saved her from exposing herself were the newfangled jeans she wore; not that that would have stopped her for long. Kathy's idea was that boys who looked where they shouldn't should get a knot on the head. Worse, once her mother had had the same attitude.

"Kathy Jon, you get yourself right side up! Kathy Jon, you get your butt over here!"

"Right, Mom."

The girl swung up, grabbed the tree limb without letting loose of her sling, and dropped. She spoiled her athletic performance by slipping where she landed, falling in a rain puddle. She got up, appropriately filthy, laughing.

Jon said things to herself that she wouldn't have wanted her three sons to hear. By the time she had finished Kathy Jon was standing in front of her, all muddied but sweet innocence.

"What is it, Mom? You want something?"

The brat! The incredible brat!

"Kathy Jon, Alvin and Teddy are helping their father cut wood. What are you doing to help your family?"

"Keeping out of the way while you wash?"

"How about *helping* with the wash?"

"Aw, Mom! Do I have to?"

"Yes! Starting with that mud plaster you've got on!"

Halfway back to the house she remembered that she still held the whipwillow and hadn't raised it to Kathy once. But how could she? As Kelvin and her husband Lester were both always saying, the girl was exactly the way Jon used to be!

Dragon Time

*H*orace was as moody as he had ever been. A handsome young dragon with beautifully polished copper scales, he was feeling the natural dragon urge. Bothersome business, this. Not the least of it was this long journey.

He took a small opal-hop to the nearest clear spot. Immediately he was there where he decided he should be; that was the nature of opaling, a process he had grown quite accustomed to. Instinctively, and also because he had been given the information by Merlain, he knew that having passed the end of the worn road he was now in dragon territory.

He paused, looking at a nearby stream, sniffing the air for scent, not really thinking. His innards rumbled hungry. Was that the scent of a meer? If he saw a meer he would opal onto it, dine, then sleep for the rest of the day. Tomorrow could be a new start.

"GGGGRRRROOOOTHMHHH! HISSSSSSSSS!"

Success so soon? He hadn't expected it. Good! He'd get the mating done and then he'd be free to do something interesting—like eating.

Tree limbs snapped. A very large dragon's head emerged from two splintering trunks and gave a loud snort from a giant golden snout. No female this!

"GWOOTHHH!" he said, showing his teeth. Actually he felt silly doing it, but Merlain had assured him that this was the way male dragons expected other males to act.

"GGGRRRHISSSS!" said his soon-to-be opponent. Most dragons were not part human and hadn't doubts. This one's teeth were bigger than Horace's.

Thinking as he thought Merlain would have him think, Horace wanted across the river. Immediately the opal put him there. Here he was safe from the bigger dragon, unless—

Rising up from a patch of weeds was the prettiest, golden-scaled girl dragon he had ever dreamed! He was all set to stroll over to her, pay his respects, and request that they mate. But then he saw the other. The second dragon, rising up behind the first, was if anything bigger and meaner looking than the bully across the river.

This newcomer did a mad tail lash. He started a dragon charge, wriggling from side to side as his short legs carried him over rocks at the speed of a fast horse.

Horace decided he wasn't going to chicuck out this time. Instead he braced himself on his four clawed feet and waited the other's charge.

CHAPTER 1

Heroic Preparations

*U*h, uh, uh," Kelvin puffed, his middle-aged feet now encased in ordinary boots pounding the turf. His breath was wheezing between his fortunately still-good teeth. His feet were smarting, his leg muscles aching, and his stomach hurting from the pressure of an unmagical belt.

"Me too, Son," his father gasped beside him. "It's just too much!"

Three times around the horse track, she'd said. Three times to induce a little magically assisted hardening of the muscles and reduction of the forms. Three times, puff, puff, puff, and it would be as though they had trained and exercised and starved for weeks or months. Three times today, and then tomorrow, and then the next day. Three days in a row and they'd be finished, if not dead of exhaustion first.

"We have to keep going, Dad." Kelvin couldn't afford the breaths, but wasted them anyhow. "Otherwise she'll start us over again."

"I know." Puff, puff, gasp.

They really could die doing this, Kelvin thought. What would Helbah do then? Enchant their hearts into resuming beating, their chests into heaving again? Probably. Helbah was a very demanding trainer who would consider their dying of overload to be but a bothersome delay.

Ahead, perched comfortably on the railing, were three young boys who to all appearances had more of the makings

of heroes than these two aging men. Blond of hair, ruddy of
cheeks, they were actually enjoying this.

"Faster! Faster!" Joey, the youngest, insisted.

"Get ahead of him, Gramps!" Teddy, the next oldest,
now positioned between his brothers, called as John managed
to wave. For reasons that Kelvin had never penetrated Teddy
was Grandfather Knight's favorite of the Crumb boys.

Kelvin thought some not very nice things about children
with nothing better to do than watch their elders. He forced
his feet forward and down, step after step, aware that athletics
were not his true calling. He glanced at his father's red face,
and knew that he too was running full out. If only he had the
damned Mouvar boots! One step with them and he'd be to the
finish. Three steps and he'd be three times around the track.
Why couldn't Helbah work her magic that way and save them
embarrassment?

The Crumb boys vanished behind, waiting for them to do
their next lap. If they were capable of it. It would serve Helbah
right when she had to revive them.

Puff, puff, puff. Hurt, hurt, hurt. Ahead, standing just
back of the railing, were Jon and Lester Crumb. Jon held a
picnic basket that was probably overflowing with fried chicuck, greasy goober chips, cooakes, pies, and magically cold,
tangy oranglemime aid. Trust his sister to bring along everything he and his father were strictly forbidden to eat!

Jon waved and Kelvin hadn't strength to wave back.
Where was the girl of the brood? Oh, there she was, a little way
ahead. Kathy Jon, pretty as Jon herself had been, and just as
much of a boy. Why was she twirling that sling as they ran by?
No!

Kelvin leaped ahead of his father as the track exploded in
a puff of dust right at his heel. The girl's aim had been fault-
less; the stone wouldn't have struck him though it had seemed
that it would. A pretty girl, but she lacked discipline. In every
way that he could see she was just as her mother had been at
that age.

"Move them big feet, Unc!" the pretty girl called. "Put some oomph into it!"

They were rounding the curve like two aging racehorses. Just ahead were the bleachers, now occupied by a few onlookers. Two figures in the front row caught his eye. As they grew nearer he saw that they were Helbah and his mother. His mother was making gestures while Helbah watched. He hoped that she was having a mother's fit, telling Helbah that it was too much for them and that it was wrong of her to have ordered it.

As his feet started to slow in anticipation he saw that the two kinglets were there beside Helbah. Properly dressed as they had been the other day, they sat again like statues. Beside the two young redheads sat golden-haired Glow, the girl his boy should soon marry. Beside Glow, the nursemaid to kings, were his own copper-haired son and daughter. And there—off just a bit with his attendants and an attractive and inappropriately young girl—King Rufurt of the waistline and ruddy complexion, officially king of Rud. With the king's group he thought he saw St. Helens and that barmaid. And there, most definitely, were Charlie Lomax and a stranger, and St. Helens' business partner, Phillip Blastmore, onetime king of Aratex.

Kelvin tried to catch his mother's eye as he drew close. She was doing something with her arms as Helbah watched, and now, between her raised hands, glowing letters that seemed composed of fire stood and blazed for attention. Unmistakably, the letters read: "GO HEROES! RUN!"

So much for motherly understanding, he thought. It seemed impossible to him that he and his father could make a second lap, let alone a third. As he looked at Helbah's wrinkled face he saw nothing but an expression of disgust. Even Katbah, crouched on her shoulder, looked away as though embarrassed by their performance.

"You have to try harder!" Helbah advised in a loud, only slightly crackly voice. She now had a small ball of fire between her fingertips. Suddenly the fireball was flying like an arrow and hovering just slightly above the turf. The fireball danced up and down, then rolled in midair ahead of them up the track.

Kelvin put his eyes on the speck of witch's fire and concentrated on his feet: lifting, moving forward, putting down. He heard his father gasp something, and several footfalls later he guessed that he had said: "It helps." His father was right: watching the spark did help. Better to think of the witch's fire than of dying or failing this preliminary test.

Thump, thump, thump. Gasp, gasp, gasp. Thinking of nothing now, now that the bleachers were passed. The speck of fire was leading them like a magical squirbet might lead a pack of racing houcats. He could think of nothing else. He dared think of nothing else.

He was going full out, he knew that he was, while beside him his father worked away, amazingly fast. Was it becoming just a little less certain that they were about to die? Might they make it around a second time, despite all the body-racking and reasonable doubts?

"Go Grandpa! Go Uncle!" the Crumb boys shouted. On the curve was their sister, readying another stone. This time Kelvin did not mind nearly so much when she hurled it: her aim was ever true and her eyes were on Helbah's magically created spark.

Jon and Lester, having moved up the track a way, now seated on a blanket, waving hands, calling encouragement as they passed.

Ahead were the bleachers, somehow appearing darker than they had before. As he pounded near Kelvin saw the seats were rapidly filling as villagers and country dwellers got the word. A free show was a free show, and there was no show to beat a famous person making a complete ass of himself.

Pant, pant, pant. Stumble, stumble, stumble. The track blurring and then refocusing. His mother's hand raised, the letters formed again: "GO HEROES! RUN!" The letters blinked and re-formed into: "YOU'RE DOING FINE!"

Kelvin couldn't question it. He was still alive, trying. Helbah's hands produced a second spark as the first vanished. This time she and the cat both looked him in the face as he plodded past. "Keep your eyes on the lure," Helbah said, and he determined to do so, even as he looked past the spark and saw people he recognized.

"Go Kelvin! Go Kelvin!" St. Helens' barmaid friend called. Nice to have a woman cheering, but where was his wife? Did she expect that he would be humiliated?

"Kelvin! Kelvin!" There she was, waving madly, not bouncing as much in front as the barmaid. Still somehow beautiful, still his beloved wife.

Heln, what terrible things I've put you through. In rapid succession he remembered her as his young bride, then being swollen in pregnancy and dying of magic, and of his flight to save her and their magical children. She had endured all, recovered from all—even giving birth to a dragon. That had been something of a shock at the time, but the passage of years had helped them adjust.

Heln called to him again and somehow he found the strength to wave. Then she was past, along with all their faces, and there was only the track and his body and the dancing, beckoning spark.

Agony unlooked at is still noticed. Yet the mind has its powers, it own near-magical ability to hold back and keep in place. By thinking only of doing and plodding step by pain-racked step, chest heave by chest heave, leg thrust by leg thrust, Kelvin was able to make the impossibility become less and less obvious. *I will take this breath. I will take this step.* On and on, thinking not of certain failure or depressing consequences. Somehow on, and then on again, and again, stumbling, sweating, paining ever and ever on.

His nephews, his niece, his sister, and her husband. They seemed scarcely to exist as his ears, his round ears, heard their calls of encouragement. His father was still with him, still panting, now wheezing a little, still nearly dying as he, like his son, plodded on and on and on.

The bend. The wide, long, never ending curve. The bleachers ahead, far ahead. The spark dancing, urging, pleading them on.

Now his mother with her arms raised and fiery letters

embraced by them. Helbah, her familiar on her shoulder, its shiny blackness visible in a way that the greenness of the grass, the bright and dark colors of the clothing, the multicolored hairs on the heads of pointed-eared folk were not. Leg swing, foot fall, breath in, breath out. One step, one step, one.

Cheering and gasping and trembling, and then they were stopped, amazingly stopped, light snapped off in front of them, well-filled bleachers at their right. His mother's bright sign: "YOU DID IT!" Then his mother embracing his father, his Heln embracing him, Helbah making passes with her hands, doing magic so that he and his father would not die from the effect of the punishment.

As light faded around him he heard her aged voice. "Today was easy. You slackers can't even imagine what tomorrow will be like. Tomorrow it's going to be hard!"

Kelvin awoke with light in his eyes. He blinked, saw that it was indeed the sun shining through his own bedroom window, assaulting him. Heln stood there holding the pull string of the shade.

"Ohhhh," he said, feeling that he was near death, "pull it down."

"You have to get up, Kelvin. You are going to run again."

He stretched under the covers and every muscle and joint screamed a protest. Run! He'd be lucky if he could walk. If he could even get out of bed!

"I'm not going to run today, Heln. I'm going to rest."

"You are not! Helbah said—"

"Helbah's an old woman," he argued logically. "She doesn't know more than Mother. Mother reads cards; Helbah just guesses because she can't really see the future any more than Mother. Zady isn't going to return to life with her head cut off, and if she ever does I'll sic Horace on her. Huh, I'd like to see even a two-headed witch escape a dragon!"

"You might do that. Get up!"

"No, I said."

"Your sister and brother-in-law are here."

"They are not."

"They are. I told them to come."

"Let them in, then." He knew a bluff when he heard it. Wives were always doing that to their husbands.

Heln left the bedroom. Kelvin closed his eyes with a sigh. He could sleep for a week, if not an eternity.

"Morning, hero!"

"Don't call me that!" He spoke before realizing that it wasn't Heln's voice. He sat up, hurting his back. There she was in the doorway, just whom he didn't want to see.

"That's what you are, Kelvin, like it or not."

"Sister Wart—"

"You promised eleven million times ago not to call me that!"

"Uh, yes, sorry, I'm reverting to childhood. Your beloved brother is an old man and about to die. Have some respect for the soon-to-be-dead. Close the door when you leave."

"See, I told you, Heln," Jon said to his wife. "I've known him longer than you have."

"Oh, I know him too, Jon, but I was hoping he wouldn't be quite this balky. Do you think the two of us can handle him, or will we need Lester?"

"By the looks of him we may need Lester and the boys."

"What are you two talking about?" Kelvin demanded, annoyed.

"We're talking about you getting up," his wife said. "Helbah gave me an oil to rub on your muscles. After we massage you you'll feel great."

"I will not," Kelvin predicted. "Out, you two. I want to get dressed."

"I'll stay," Heln said. "You start the coftea, Jon, and make it strong."

His sister disappeared from the doorway. Kelvin thought he heard Jon and Lester talking in the kitchen. He might as well give it up. He put his feet out of bed. Pain lanced from his hips all the way up to his shoulders. "Ohhhh," he said, unable even to work up a decent groan.

Heln was holding a large green bottle. She put it on the

night table and rubbed her hands briskly together, warming
them.

There was no putting it off further. He stood, with difficulty, and pulled off the nightdress. Everything, absolutely
everything, hurt.

"We'll start with the arms," Heln said, grabbing his aching biceps as gently as a torturer. Her hands moved briskly,
cupping the muscles, smoothing. The oil felt tingly and warm,
but the soreness was still there.

"Now on your belly! I'm told that's the best way for this."

"The sheets will get oily."

"I'll wash them. Belly flop, hero."

He submitted as graciously as he could. Now and then an
"uhh" or an "ouch" escaped him, but for the most part he
suffered her ministrations without sound. When she was finished he felt a little bit human and was ready though by no
means eager to get dressed. Especially since he knew she would
not allow him to return to sleep.

He grabbed a fresh pair of undershorts Heln had laid out,
put his legs in them, and stopped. Something wasn't right.

"Heln, these aren't my shorts. They must be your father's
or Mor Crumb's."

"Look in the mirror."

He did, astonished at a new flatness. His belly, his enormous troublesome belly, was gone! Furthermore, his flesh,
though he hadn't realized it until now, was firmer than it had
been in years.

"Gods, Heln," he said, using one of Mor's favorite expressions, "the old witch really does know a little magic!"

She smiled. "I had come to that conclusion myself. You
look great, Kelvin."

He would have been pleased if he still didn't hurt so
much.

After a too short breakfast and a short drive with sister
and brother-in-law and wife in the Crumb family buggy, he
was again at the track. Clad now in new running shorts Lester
had brought, Kelvin had to admit to himself that he could

possibly feel worse. The new slimness was nice, though it was sweat-making just to think about the way he had earned it.

"Ready, Kel," his father said.

John Knight, similarly clad, looked flatter and more solid than he had appeared in years. He had just buggied in from his Rud farm with Kelvin's mother, Charlain. The two buggies were now side by side, their horses tied to hitching posts.

Kelvin had to adjust his thoughts. His father had really changed in appearance! To think, all of that through their combined incredible effort. To think, all of that from just one running session. Maybe, just maybe, the effort would be worth it. *Bite your tongue, Kelvin!* a part of him said.

"I still ache," Kelvin confessed. "I don't know if I can—"

"I ache too, Son. Helbah says the ache will disappear once we're running."

"Do you believe it?"

"No, somehow I don't."

It was, Kelvin knew, going to be agonizing. But Helbah had as much as promised that it would be worse. He wondered about that, and then he saw the twin backpacks Mor Crumb was struggling to remove from Helbah's buggy. Lose a few pounds in front and gain a few in back. Helbah had her ways, and her ways involved, as with so many old people, tried and true methods of making life difficult.

Mor helped first his father and then Kelvin on with the packs. Even Mor had a little difficulty. Kelvin's was so heavy that he felt he'd kiss the dirt. No way was he going to get around the track wearing this—not unless he crawled. And three times!

Then, before he knew it, he was out on the track with his father and there was that bobbing, dancing witch light. He knew it was impossible and that Helbah would see that for herself. Then he was half shuffling, half leaping after the light. It was as though he hadn't shed any weight or gained any strength. Somewhere on the eventual curve Kathy Jon almost nicked him with a rock, and then it seemed that he was so angry with her that he forgot completely the pain he was in. An eternity later he and his father both crossed the final line for the third time this day, and both immediately dropped at Helbah's feet. Track dust in mouth, tongue longing for the cooling drink Heln had ready, Kelvin heard his benefactress say:

"Not bad for has-beens! But tomorrow, I warn you, it's going to be hard."

Next morning Kelvin just knew that there was no way he was going to get out of bed—ever. But then Lester Crumb came with his fiendishly smiling face and knelt on him while Heln rubbed his legs and shoulders and back. His muscles, he was pleased to notice, had gotten fuller and harder. More dead than alive he let Lester dress him, then drag him to a powerful cup of coftea, the buggy, and finally the track.

This time Helbah was waiting for them. As he and his father approached she pointed to two pairs of heavy-soled boots in the back of her buggy. "Put these on," she ordered.

Kelvin watched his father put his on with a grimace. What could be so bad about Helbah's boots? Unless they were stiff, and these didn't appear to be, they could actually make running easier. It would be nice if these were magic, or at least magic enough to make their feet feel light.

Kelvin picked up his pair and knew immediately the cause of the expression on his father's face. The boots were heavy, really heavy, and possibly loaded with metal.

He pulled the boots on. They felt as heavy as he had guessed. To wear these at a fast walk would be difficult; to wear them at a run impossible. He looked to Helbah for signs of pity, and saw none. He knew he couldn't do it; he'd be lucky if he could even walk.

"On your marks," Helbah ordered.

Somehow Kelvin got his feet set by his father's. Helbah's fireball left her hands and began its compelling dance.

Somehow, someway, they were running.

"Keep it up, Grandpa! Faster, Kelvin!"

Spectators, always spectators. He felt as if he were running with heavy weights on his feet through thick, sticky mud.

No sooner had he thought this than lightning cracked and rain began to pour.

In three strides he was wet, in twelve strides soaked. The track grew muddier and muddier. He slipped, stumbled, and fell. He placed his face contentedly in the mud, prepared to lie there forever, but his father, running in place now, was telling him to get up.

SPLASH: A large stone fell almost on his head. Any closer and he'd have been hit! Curse the girl anyhow! A good hiding, that's what his father-in-law would recommend. He got his hands down, and he pushed himself upright. A moment later he was running again.

"Go, Unc!" The saucy girl brat was a soaked chicuck dancing in the rain. He hoped she'd slip and fall on her shapely young butt. The same one that needed the hiding. Then the light was compelling him and he was running on.

Three times around. Could he do it? Could his father? It seemed impossible. He slowed. Another rock splashed. He dragged himself back up to speed.

Nothing to do but think about the light. Think of moving after it. Of lifting feet, then bringing them down.

"ONE" his mother's astonishingly flaming sign proclaimed.

It was dry in the bleachers and in front of the empty judge's stand to the left. No one was getting soaked here. The rain was on the track and the grass beside the track. Could he ever possibly come around a second time?

He slogged on and on, forever plus a few hours.

"TWO" the letters blazed. But that was it; he could never, ever get around again. But still there was that accursed dancing light.

"RUN, HEROES, RUN!" his mother's sign urged.

Some chance! He could hardly move one weighted foot past the other. He was going to quit. Stop. Right now. They could bury him right here on the track. He probably wouldn't even stink, because all of his body had been destroyed by the awful run.

Then he looked into Heln's dark, excited eyes and he knew that he couldn't—not on completion of the second lap. One more time around the track. One more, and then he'd be comfortably dead. One more and Heln wouldn't have to be ashamed.

Plod, plod, plod. Hurt, hurt, hurt. Pain, pain, pain.

SPLASH! A mud drop caught him on one of his famous round ears and he drove himself at what he knew had to be a fatal pace. It was seemingly taking hours, if not days. This long, long curve, rain spitting in his face. Was he running or was he staggering? Was his father?

"THREE" the sign blazed through the rain.

SPLASH, SPLASH. He and his father dropped down on the dry track. Dry? The rain had been illusory? Insult on top of injury!

Helbah looked down at them. Their wives came and slobbered over them. For his part Kelvin couldn't move as much as a muscle without Heln's lifting hands.

"I do proclaim," Helbah said loudly, "that the two of you are now physically and heroically fit."

Kelvin let his face fall from Heln's opening hands. He didn't feel the shock when it hit in fluffy, soft, nose-filling dust.

CHAPTER 2

Unmated Dragon

*H*orace barely escaped the other dragon's charge by opaling himself to the side. The big aggressor, his rival for the lovely young creature batting scaled eyelids at him, came to a teetery halt at the very edge of the river. The big dragon turned its head toward him. Quickly Horace pivoted on his hind legs and smacked his tail across the other's snout.

"Woof! Grunt, glump!" said the big lizard.

That was, of course, an insult not to be countenanced.

Horace opal-hopped over its back and from behind raked his sharp claws across a battle-scarred flank. There was a screeching sound as his nails failed to do more than make scratched furrows on gold plate. The next instant there was a loud whipcrack. Horace was flung sideways by a blow that, had it been delivered at a different angle, could readily have broken his back.

Horace gasped, choked, and tried to clear his head as the other roared. He was up against some tree trunks that hadn't splintered because of his small size. The other was bearing down on him, and his scaleless belly was exposed. In a moment those great teeth would flash and penetrate and—

Horace opaled as the other dragon finished its charge with a tremendous pounce. Without time to choose where he would rather be, Horace had thought of the riverbank. Dirt was crumbling beneath his scaled feet and he fell with the weakened bank into the water. Back where he had been there was a great crash as dragon collided with tree trunk.

Horace choked as water closed over him, then shut his

nostrils, flipped with his tail, and came to the surface. Current propelled him downstream. He felt himself float a way, then scrambled out onto a tree trunk extending into the river. He rested there, choked up some muddy water he had swallowed, and thought of what he should do next. The big dragon was a tough opponent and Horace wasn't certain he wanted to kill him even if he could. Yet killing was the dragon's way and Horace instinctively recognized it. What slowed Horace at times, and made life difficult, was the human part of him that demanded he think.

The waters swirled by and Horace knew he had either to opal back or wriggle back. No more than other dragons could he use his tiny wings to fly. Merlain had once explained flying to him, reading from a book. Once dragons might have been able to fly, but that was long ago, before the air had become too thin and dragons far too heavy. Of course there was magic, Merlain had said, but few magicians or witches had experimented with making dragons fly.

The day was getting on. So must Horace. He thought of the big tree he had been against and of the female, and the opal put him where he wanted to be, right at her feet. The big tree had fallen, and under it he could see the big dragon's golden tail. The tree had fallen on his opponent, possibly crushing him, so that made Horace the winner of the fight.

The female, only a little larger than he, looked down at him. She batted her eyelids. What a beautiful golden creature she was! What a pleasure it would be to grasp her from behind, and—

Her tail slap stung! So did the spot on his throat where she had instantly ripped off his scales with one vicious bite.

Horace sidestepped, and then, as her attack continued, opaled far to the side. What was the matter with her? But then he remembered Merlain warning him: "Male dragons subdue their females. The males and the females fight. Only I suspect not every female fights to her death. If you must mate, pick a female who is smaller."

"SNORT! SNORT! GRUMP!" said the object of his would-be affections. She was charging him, wriggling from side to side in dragon fashion, intent on grabbing him and not giving delight. Horace opaled himself to where he had been, appalled at her ferocity. He could opal himself right onto her back and accomplish his mission that way, but he knew what Merlain would say: "That's naughty, Horace! That's not fair! That's not even nice!"

He shook his head, wondering just what to do if the female would not let him mount. He was too human to want to hurt her; too much like his brother Charles and his sister Merlain. He would fight if he had to, but not just so he could take; Merlain, he knew, had the same problem. Dragons might mate and forget, but humans were different from dragons. Horace, dragon though he was, had been instilled with Merlain's idea that affection should precede and persist after the mating. He could not have explained why this made sense to him and not to other dragons, or even to all humans. Horace was different, just as his sister said.

The female turned, batted her eyelids. Why didn't he come on, her manner suggested. Horace didn't know why, but the burning in his loins grew less, not greater, when he did battle. His late opponent—

The golden tail under the tree branches wriggled. Horace wrinkled his nostrils. The other was still alive. He might be capable of reviving and attacking him again, possibly while Horace was accomplishing what they had both been intent on accomplishing.

The dragon's tail flipped and flopped, somehow forlornly. Horace drew close. He could see that the big male had heavy tree limbs pinning both his front and one rear leg. There was no way the golden one could get up unless the tree was moved.

The dragon raised his head. "Wheez, hisss," he said. Less of a challenge, but still not exactly a plea for help. Horace eyed the branches, considering how they lay. If he were to give the trapped dragon his help, possibly the dragon would then be his friend. Horace had never had a dragon friend; before today he had never seen another dragon.

As Horace turned the matter over and over in his mind,

the female approached at a leisurely walk. She gave a loud sniff, then pushed her snout under the branches. So she was going to help! Should he let her, or should he use his tail to slap her across the snout and get her moved away?

"GWROOTH!" the pinned dragon cried, not seeming to appreciate her effort. The female lifted her face, bloody golden scales and torn dragon hide between her teeth. She spat these to the ground, darted out her forked tongue, and opened her toothy mouth for a really big, tearing bite.

She was going to devour him! Horace had heard from Merlain that dragons did such things, and Merlain had also expressed the opinion that eating your own kind was "bad." Horace wasn't quite certain what bad was, but he knew that Merlain did. If she were here she'd tell him to stop it.

"GWROOMPTH," Horace said, batting the female on the side of the head. His claws were retracted but he instantly got her attention. She turned her head, hissing, long, pointed teeth showing, prepared to battle him.

This time Horace wasn't gentle. He slapped her with his tail, opaled past her head to her rear, held her tail down, and delivered a really healthy bite.

"OWOOOOOO!" the female responded. That hurt and she didn't like it. Her language was in fact rather unladylike.

Horace opaled back so that she could not get at him and raised himself halfway up on his hind legs in a defensive fighter's stance.

The female was temporarily concerned with the pain in her posterior. She swished her tail through the air, and ran back to the river. She dipped her tail in the water. She squatted there, looking back at him.

Horace knew that there was no time to mate, if he wanted to rescue the other dragon. He pushed his snout, then his head, then his back under the tree limb pinning the golden male's hindquarters. He levered himself up, heaving with his young and powerful dragon strength.

The tree limb lifted. Branches poked Horace in the face. The other dragon reared his back, lifting with both hind legs and the strength of his body. He grumbled, growled, hissed, and spat. His front legs were still held.

Horace eased himself out from under the branch as the other's tail flashed. He took a brutal slap across the face, but pushed himself free. The female was still on the bank, the male still unable to lift the branch pinning its front feet.

Horace moved around to the side of the tree. The other glared hatred at him. Ignoring the glare in those eyes Horace wriggled himself under the big branch. By levering upward with the strength of his back, he might take the pressure from his late opponent's trapped feet.

He tried. Feet gripping the loam, claws digging in, he lifted. The other let out a "GWWORTH!" and heaved back. Wood splintered and the tree shook, and Horace found he was pressed down by the branch, now that the golden dragon was free.

"GWOORTH, OROOMIFF!" The big dragon was suddenly on top of the branch, reaching down a clawed foot, intent on harming Horace. A forked tongue darted down. The dragon shifted his weight and descended on Horace with all his considerable weight. It was apparent that gratitude was not the dragon's strong point.

Horace had had enough! He wasn't about to let the freed dragon tear into him as he obviously intended. He thought of the female on the riverbank and there he was, crouched beside her as though still pressed down.

Her eyes looked into his. Her mouth flashed, biting him painfully on his already stinging snout. Her claws snapped out and she raked him, loosening scales that fell copper and red. Then she was on him, intent on destruction. He felt the pain and smelled her reptile stench perfumed with olfactory-stimulating carrion. He tried to crawl out of her embrace. She nipped his tail as he opaled to the tree from which he had escaped.

"GROOMTH!" The male was charging him. Clearly this was no place for a mild-mannered copper-sheathed dragon! Horace opaled himself up past the tree-covered slope to the crumbly ledge and its rocky trail. From here he could look down on the two dragons. Far below he saw them, though not very clearly. They were fighting, going at it tail over head. Should he go back and fight some more himself? No, he thought, considering how the big dragon was now on the smaller. The female was getting mated, as was the custom and expectation. For his part he wanted to crawl off with his smarting hide and forget that any of it had happened.

He could opal, but the trail was empty and he wasn't yet ready to go home to his Rud forest. He had come to dragon territory for a purpose. As he crept gradually upward, clawed feet scrabbling at the rock, his loins and his appetite for food were both urging that he go on.

The small golden-scaled dragon was beautiful, Glint thought. He had always thought so, back as far as he could remember, and that had been long, long ago. He had seen dragons come and he had seen dragons go by the normal birthing and killing processes. Leaning against the wide stone shelf of their cave, he could see her sunning herself by the entrance. Alas, she seemed sad, really forlorn, and he thought he knew why.

Glint was a telepath. He had always been a telepath, from the early days when he had learned to be alert for hostile thoughts. When he had had to urge his dragon mother to hunt food for him and not to destroy him. The young female he thought of as his sister. Yet Glint was not himself a dragon or in any way part of one.

Looking at his reflection in the dark pools of the river, he had long known himself to be of human form, with light, bright hair, blue eyes, pointed ears, and a skin that was almost golden. He had lived among dragons, and only dragons, for so long that he scarcely felt human. When a young man had come hunting the cast-off and torn-off scales, Glint had seen him as more alien than his foster sister and mother. Yet the intruder's form had been human, not dragon.

Ember, Glint's sister, was thinking sad. He felt her sadness and it hurt. She was of a mateable age, yet had no interest in the suitors who had come up from the valley. Partially this was his fault. He knew his sister, or felt that he did, and the minds of the males were coarser and less delicate in sensibilities. His sister had never been hurt; certainly never violated in a mating ritual. He could have mated with her himself had he been a dragon, but apart from their sensibilities there was the matter of size. Had Glint wanted to mount her, and had she let him, there was no way a mating could be accomplished.

On the ledge Ember let out a long-drawn sigh. She felt a need in her loins, yet was reluctant to seek a male to satisfy it. She had never fought another dragon, though she had carried her brother about and accepted the thoughts he directed at her. She was a dragon, all dragon, and because of her strange upbringing she was unlikely to mate. Glint, though only he knew it, had much to answer for concerning his sister's life.

Glint shook himself, hating the way his thoughts were tending. Possibly he should nudge his sister into action. Get her mated to one of the suitors and then she would lose her sadness and get on with her life. The problem was that Glint felt protective of his sister. A normal dragon suitor would slap her around and bite her, forcing her to give in and submit to his attentions. Glint accepted the necessity in other dragons of mating age, but his sister was, after all, his sister. Glint, though he might deplore it, had a brotherly attachment that was not even remotely dragonesque.

Glint's sister held a white dragonberry in her cupped right claw and was preparing to swallow it. When he had been younger Glint had learned that dragons who ate such berries entered a dream state where they traveled afar and yet remained right where they were. He had wanted to share these astral experiences directly and not just through the unsensitive minds of dragons. Very young Glint had himself taken such a berry and had immediately gotten sick and very nearly died. The dragon he thought of as his mother had carried him into the cave, brought him water in her mouth, and cared for him far more tenderly than unknowing humans would have believed. If Ember swallowed the berry it would simply be another trip she would take. He could join her, through their mind link.

Glint squatted down against the cool stone walls of their cave and joined more fully in Ember's thoughts. At first there was only the sensation of swallowing, an uncomfortable pebble under her left haunch, and a bit of discarded stick poking against her tail. Then a swirling and a dizzying, and—

She could see her body lying there on the ledge, and inside the cave entrance, crouched against the wall, her two-legged brother with his scaleless skin. She wondered why he had not crept out to embrace her around the throat and lie against her belly as he had on other trips. Possibly he too was feeling a mating urge and feared to be so close. She was much stronger than he, though she knew that he was older. She could not remember her birth, but she remembered him playing with her when she was small, tossing sticks for her to bring, polishing her scales, rolling with her on the grass and the cave floor. He was her brother and he was not as other dragons were. Alas, she wanted a mate not unlike him, and she knew that was impossible.

She drifted down the mountain and into the valley. The trees were leafing out, the flowers showing in bright patches of orange, red, blue, and lavender. There were dark heaps of flood debris along the riverbanks; tossed-up tree trunks were settling back into the drying ground. Birds were singing, animals scampering. There below was a dragon of about her size. She moved her thoughts close and saw that the dragon was of a lighter yellow than she, very clean, very alert, with the slightly flared nostrils of a rutting male.

Ember moved along with the male. There was no way for him to know that she was there. She watched without surprise as he fought for a female. She watched him vanish and then reappear further away. She didn't wonder how he had been one place and then suddenly was at another; yet she saw it happen. Into her mind came her brother's thoughts:

Sister, Sister, this is something strange!

You thought it strange the first time we traveled together.

That copper-scaled dragon is strange.

Yes. She had no curiosity other than whether this dragon could become her mate.

Sister, this dragon is from far away. Perhaps from where that human originated.

The scale hunter. Yes, we should have eaten him.

I couldn't have, Sister. It had two hind legs and two forelegs exactly like mine.

A head like yours too, Brother.

Yes, but it did not speak with its mind.

Nevertheless you would not eat it.

No. It could have been my kind.

Dragons eat dragons. Why humans not eat humans?

Mentally, his shrugging sensation. It meant to her that he did not know. When she and he were together she sometimes asked him if something should be dug out or eaten and he replied with a lifting and lowering of his shoulders. Strange creature, her brother Glint. Dragons seldom lacked certainty in anything and would not want another to know if they did.

Sister, stay with this dragon as long as the berry allows. I want to see what it does and decide what it is.

I too, Brother. I too.

You would mate with it?

I might submit.

After a battle?

Yes.

It might not take you. It took not the other. It saved its opponent's life.

As you say, Brother, strange. Undragonlike.

Yes. Sister, when it nears our cave I want to think to it.

To kill? To eat? Her more normal appetite stirred.

No. To find out what it is. To converse with it as I do with you.

It would not. It could not. Only you and I can.

Perhaps.

It could eat you.

You could save me.

Yes.

The copper-scaled dragon slowed. It looked ahead, up the mountain, and was suddenly at the higher point. Such vanishing and reappearing could save a lot of walking.

How does he do that?

Don't you know, Glint?

No, Ember, I don't.

If you could you would vanish from here and reappear elsewhere?

Yes. Wouldn't you?

She thought of what an advantage that would be in catching food or escaping danger. Vanish from a place of concealment and be immediately on a meer's toothsome back. Vanish from beneath a male who had pinned you and was mounting your back. How surprised the meer would be. How disappointed the rutting male.

Brother, can you find out how?

Maybe. Possibly with your help.

How help? Through fighting, she supposed. Fighting was the usual way of giving help.

I'll tell you when and how. You will protect me with your strength. The dragon is much closer. Perhaps now.

You will think to it?

Yes.

Now? Anticipation tinged her thought.

Now.

Unsuspecting, the subject of their discussion wriggled around the bend of the trail as their trip ended.

Glint blinked in his cave. Outside on the ledge his sister scratched her ear with her hind foot and yawned.

Their visitor was not far away.

CHAPTER 3

Snoops

Y ou're doing it again!" Merlain said accusingly.

"Doing what?" Charles was all innocence, but his hypocrisy showed. Sitting there on the creek bank, idly fishing with hooks and lines, he might have been just another peasant lad out to stock the larder. Yet the two of them were not ordinary. Having a dragon brother was part of it, and the other was being telepaths.

"I know perfectly well you've been reaching out for him!" Merlain flipped her line to another spot, angered despite herself. It was bad enough that Horace had to have these urges, but worse for Charles to spy on him!

"You mean I was trying to mind-call a bigger fish?"

"No!" He did that constantly, and that too annoyed her. In compensation Merlain used her own mind to direct the fish away from her brother's hook. They always caught enough fish to eat and sometimes to give to Horace. Mind-calling fish, Merlain felt, was cheating.

"You mean Horace."

"Yes."

"I'm curious."

"I know you are. But how would you like it if you and Glow were doing it and—"

"We never have! You know that. We're waiting until we marry."

"Yes, but you think about it a lot. You think so detailed that you might as well be married."

"Now how do you know that?"

Oh. Charles had caught her again. True, she did mind-peek a little now and then, but she didn't snoop.

Ha!

Charles, I didn't invite you!

No, but your shield was down. You left yourself open for it.

I did not! But suppose I did? What's that got to do with your invading Horace's privacy?

Everything. I'm showing that you do it too. Mind-peek, that is. In other words, snoop.

Merlain looked at bubbles near her line and deftly warned the turtle off before it took the bait. Sometimes that little trick saved a bait-stealer a minor bit of pain.

Merlain!

Oh, all right, I admit there's little difference. We're both tempted to snoop, but we don't have to. We have a choice.

But you think it's wrong.

It is with Horace. He's not even like us.

He's our brother.

You know what I mean, she thought. *He's a dragon, not a human. He might enjoy what we shouldn't.*

You told him not to often enough.

I haven't! I told him about love. About commitment.

Which you've learned about from books, he thought smugly.

So?

So he's a dragon. He shouldn't have to do things our way. Dragons don't have to think about it. Dragons just hump.

You think they shouldn't? There, that'd get him!

Merlain . . . Her brother's thought trailed away, a procedure that involved peripheral and semiformed thoughts agglutinating. *Well, Merlain, I certainly don't try to judge. Dragons are dragons and humans are humans.*

So why, Charles, are you invading Horace's privacy?

I'm not invading his privacy. At least I haven't yet.

But you're trying to!

Charles shut her out. He frowned, staring at their fishing floats resting on the water. He might have been an ordinary fisherman thinking of nothing but the impending catch. In fact she knew he was thinking of their brother.

"All right, Merlain. All right," Charles said aloud. "You've got me. I want to snoop, to find out what Horace experiences. But there's a reason, besides the voyeurism."

"Of course there is." Try to lie to her, would he!

"Right! Horace just might get in trouble! He's never been with wild dragons, never even seen one."

"But he's got the opal in his gizzard, Brother dear. With that he can pop away from trouble fast."

"Right, but can we know? You know what Helbah and our parents and our grandparents are talking about. Maybe old Zady really is alive. Maybe—"

"She'd hardly be in dragon territory!"

"We don't know. Her head was never found, even using magic. Suppose she's there? Suppose Horace wanders on to her?"

"He'd destroy her and let us know."

"Well, maybe, but—"

"Charles, go ahead and peek." They had had this conversation for days now, with her first trying to convince Charles and then him trying to convince her. They had switched sides in the argument at least twice.

"Huh?"

"See what he's up to, then butt out."

"Well, if you think I should."

"Go, Charles."

Charles' face wrinkled up as he concentrated. She waited.

"Got him, Merlain. He's enjoying a sensation. He's . . ."

"What, Charles? What?" Merlain tried but couldn't suppress her enthusiasm.

"Eating something long dead with maggots on it. He's enjoying it. Ulp!"

Merlain watched her brother heaving, again suffering one of the consequences of mind-peeking a dragon. She felt a little sorry that she had urged him into this. A little, but only a little.

After his own dinner was gone, Charles wiped his mouth and looked at her with a miserable, sick expression.

"Merlain, if you want to snoop, go ahead. I'm fishing." With those words he snapped up his pole and a good-sized trass flew green and silver through the air. The fish came off the hook in midflight and fell flopping high on the bank where Charles humanely extinguished its simple pain. The fish would taste very good, suitably grilled, once he had control of his stomach.

Merlain smiled and flipped out a nearly identical fish but a size half again as large. Her stomach, she knew, could easily handle it.

Except for Horace being missing, this was turning out to be a beautiful spring day.

"What do you think, Kildom?"

"I don't know, Kildee." Kildom, titular head of Klingland, spoke earnestly to his look-alike twin. Though both appeared to be age twelve, both had lived a total of forty-eight years. Both imagined they had achieved maturity.

Below their hiding place in the rocks on the hill, the pretty girl stood disrobed and golden in the sun. Smooth young arms raised high, she swelled out her torso with its pink-tipped breasts. Her hands came together like mating birds, her blond head lowered, and she dived. She slipped cleanly through the water. She disappeared among a widening ring of silvery ripples, then surfaced. She raised her head high on her slender neck and sucked in more air. Her head went back, all the way back, and she backstroked the length of the pool.

"I think if I were Charles I'd be here," Kildee persisted. "Why should he not be since he intends to marry her?"

"I think Helbah would turn him into a frog," Kildom remarked. "Besides, he's done better than seen her naked."

"You think?" Kildee could play at dumb idleness sometimes. Both knew perfectly well that the two were in love and had more than an inkling of what that meant.

"Of course. We know they swam together naked. We

heard them laugh. We saw them go into the tall grass and the old abandoned house."

"But we don't know they did anything."

"No, but only because we're not telepaths. If I were Charles I know I would have."

"Even if she said no?"

"Uh, she wouldn't have, I think. Anyway, why aren't they married? They're old enough."

"Yeah, and grown-up enough too. Kildom, you think she knows we watch her?"

"If she does she hasn't told Helbah. If Helbah knew we watched she'd probably strike us blind."

"Really?"

"Naw. But you know Helbah. Just because she's a witch and our guardian she thinks she has to keep us from learning things."

"But she always says we should learn."

"Book learnin', yeah. Ruler wisdom and court protocol and all that junk. But lookin' at naked babes and actually doing it—"

"Yeah, I 'spect you're right. But someday we'll be grown enough."

"Yeah."

Helbah contemplated the healthy, lust-filled faces of the boy kings a moment longer and then blanked the crystal. As darkness closed out the pleasant outdoor scene in the smoothly faceted viewing rock, she reached absently across the table to stroke the head of her familiar.

She rubbed the smooth back, so very black that it shone with a sheen of its own making.

"Katbah, the boys are aging. But for all of that they still want to see what they shouldn't. In that way they're just as they were twenty years back at the witch's convention."

"Meow," Katbah agreed, arching his back to her hand. In many ways they were extensions of each other, the familiar and herself. When Katbah needed a scratch Helbah found the place without direct telepathy. Likewise when the feline creature sensed something out of the old woman's sight there was no need for further warning. Until Helbah had restocked her supply of crystals her familiar had been her royalty sitter. Watching the young scamps with sharp eyes, Katbah had informed on them as necessary.

"You know I suggested Glow take a nice swim this morning and I knew where they'd go. They thought they were smart shutting you in the pantry. We have to let them think that. Kinglets they may be, but someday they will rule without our help."

Katbah yawned and scratched a flea off his ear. An ordinary cat would have bitten it, but Katbah was almost too gentle at times. Of course an enemy such as they were to face again was a different matter. Tooth to tooth, claw to claw, the fearless feline had battled Witch Zady that time in their hotel room. In human terms that had been a long time back—twenty years back—but to their kind, hardly a few finger snaps.

Thinking of the past, of young Kelvin going off that high cliff without his levitation belt, of Zady's horrid head sailing off after him, only to be snatched by a passing eagawk, Helbah had to sigh. Work, work, work. Mortals might work fifty years or so and then rest, but a true witch, witch-born and not apprenticed talent, might easily work century after century. To Kelvin and his father and his talented mother, the twenty years was as long an interval as they could possibly imagine. To Helbah, and to Zady, her enemy of centuries, it was a coftea break in the middle of a workday.

Katbah walked silently across the table and stopped with his front paws on the big, open book. The book had scintillating letters on its pages that sparked at her, getting her attention.

"Yes, Katbah," Helbah sighed, "it is indeed time that I proceed with the magic. Kelvin, his father, his mother, his wife, all the children, and you and I—all need the protection of benign magic."

Katbah curled up by the book, waiting confidently for

her to cast her spells. In her witch's heart Helbah tried to draw strength from her familiar, knowing that in their last meeting Zady had come close to triumphing. This time she would not underestimate the enemy. This time she would do everything she could to prepare.

The scintillating letters swam into her mind, telling her of tried and true ways to battle malignants. She would do what she could but she was not certain that this would be sufficient to save them.

Krassnose, resident wizard of Ophal, worked his neck-gills in increased agitation as a fish swam past his orc face. Phenoblee, wife of Brudalous, their king, was frowning at the great yellow crystal in front of them. In the crystal the human witch-creature known as Helbah was perusing a book of magic with her familiar, one black-as-black-can-be feline.

"I don't know, Your Ladyship," Krassnose remarked. "She seems not to be doing magic that you and I have not long ago learned."

"True enough," Phenoblee said, splashing an air bubble on the fish, swerving it and causing it to dart away. "She is but a *human* witch, though longer lived than mortal humans. You and I, Krassnose, being orcs, have the superior art."

"Quite true." He raised his head crest and lowered it, mindful of the bit of current the fish had raised as it swam past. To not meet the king's wife, on the occasion of her concern, would have been dangerous, even for a resident wizard. Phenoblee knew her art, though she softened it with an egg-layer's gentleness; thus she had seen fit to not destroy the enemy humans. Because of Phenoblee and her soft ways orcs did not totally own this frame and all within it. Because of her femininity and her power over Brudalous, that copper-scaled dragon was acknowledged by them as well as humans as overking. True, orcs did govern orcs, totally and solely, and humans governed humans; both orcs and humans pretended that the holder of the phrasing opal had the final say. To Krassnose it was stupid, knowing that they could have had full control at the cost of the young dragon's life.

"I see that she is concerned, Resident Wizard, and that she perhaps has cause."

"How can you say that, Phenoblee? We both have searched for the witch Zady and found her not in existence."

"Not in *our* existence, Krassnose. Perhaps in another."

"If we still possessed the opal we could search."

"True. We may have to. But we do have the opal, though lodged in the overking's gizzard."

"You would want the human child known as Merlain to search with the dragon?"

"She's no longer a child," Phenoblee explained. "Yes, Wizard Krassnose, I think that King Brudalous should now, on our combined advice, issue to her that request."

"It will be honored, Phenoblee?"

"It will be. Even if they believe the danger long past, the humans dare not break the alliance."

"Lest we destroy them?"

"That, Resident Wizard, is but Ophal's possibility of last resort."

"Yet we were allies of this Zady creature."

"Not really, Krassnose. She used us, orcs and humans. She would have had us destroy each other."

"The humans would not have lasted."

"With the hero they have, perhaps they would have. At least long enough to have ruined Ophal."

Krassnose rubbed at the scales on his forehead where he had lately discovered a colony of waterlice. He knew she was right, as royalty always had to be. He knew also that if the opportunity came he would back the witch Zady over the humans. Twenty years it might have been, but Krassnose still smarted from the insult the Roundear's tads had done Ophal. Single-handed, using only magic, they had snatched the priceless opal from its resting place, pulled down an ancient landmark, wrecked an undersea prison, and in effect flirted their impudent tails. Deep down in his predatory heart Krassnose resented what those human tads had done and vowed that someday, should the opportunity arise, he'd demonstrate to them the power of orc magic.

Phenoblee, fortunately, did not know what was in the resident wizard's revenge-hungry mind.

Kathy Jon Crumb smiled to what she considered to be her own sweet self as she carefully changed position behind the big oaple tree in front of her uncle's cottage. Her dumb old brothers hadn't stopped her going, and Mama, though she'd be having a fit about now, hadn't known her intent. Midmorning and just the right time of day to get a look at what magic had wrought.

In great good time the front door opened and her uncle staggered outside, thinner and trimmer than she remembered him ever in her life, but definitely Kelvin. A hero born, she'd always heard, and never once believed it. Now, watching him make his trip to the outhouse, she was less certain. He did look younger, thanks to Helbah's magic and her own little help with a few stones, but he still was old. There were a few white hairs on that golden head, and she doubted that the bristles on his face could make a young beard. How in the world could someone pushing fifty be heroic? With all Helbah's magic and her help it just wasn't possible. Do everything though they might, there was just no way to make an old man young.

Kathy sighed. She had this yearning that was almost akin to sex. What she wanted was to be heroic. Why not? Her mom had often claimed she herself had been. Was Jon Hackleberry twirling her sling at age fourteen really any different from Kathy? She knew that she was as good with her sling as her mom had been, and her uncle and father had told her. She was qualified by age and temperament to be heroic. If anyone around here was.

Kelvin stepped back out of the outhouse, letting the door swing shut. He stood there, adjusting the new, trim slacks—not the old worn pantaloons he had worn for so many years—and looked about. His eyes, never very strong, she had always heard, could not spot her behind the tree bole, but then he wasn't looking for her. A smile was on his face, an almost boyish smile. He raised his arms above his head, clenched his fists, and gave a yell such as she had never heard him give before: "YAHHHHHOOOOOO!"

"Kelvin!" Aunt Heln was in the doorway, glaring disapproval at him, apron around waist, mixing bowl in hand. "Kelvin, did you have to do that? What will the neighbors think? People must have heard that in the next kingdom!" Then her eyes darted to the oaple. "Oh, hello, Kathy Jon. What brings you out this morning?"

Kathy stepped around the tree, caught easily by her aunt's better eyes. Did all women in this family have sharper eyesight? Her daddy's eyesight was better than Kelvin's, but Mama's had to be the best.

'   "Good morning, Aunt Heln, Uncle Kelvin. I was just, ah, out to sling a few stones."

"Nice day for it!" her uncle said enthusiastically. "I may get a little breakfast and join you. Maybe we'll go squirbet hunting."

"Kelvin, you know you don't hunt in the spring! You don't even hunt in the fall!" his wife reproved him. "Besides, you can't sling a stone accurately enough to hit the broadest side of the broadest barn."

"Says who? Today I'm a new man." He made a rush at Heln, then switched directions and snatched up Kathy instead. He twirled her around, then raised her high, showing off his new strength. A week ago fat old Kelvin had grunted when he lifted a small bag of horse feed.

"Come on in the house, Kathy Jon. Heln's making wafflecakes. We'll eat and I'll tell you about my adventures. Did your mom ever tell you—"

Kathy was glad enough for the invitation, though she had eaten fast and early. She didn't mind hearing oft-told family tales again, but it was the new Kelvin and the new adventure she thought might be coming that interested her.

This time, she told herself, it would not be her gray-haired old mother who would do the stone-slinging the better to get bumbling Kel out of trouble. This time it would be darling little Kathy's turn.

She smiled to herself, vowing to hang around her uncle night and day and keep the sling and stones always ready to help him.

CHAPTER 4

Hot Water

Glint strove to reach out his thoughts to the copper-scaled dragon. So soon after the dragonberry trip it was difficult. Through Ember's dragon eyes he had watched the copper-scaled young male on his ramblings. Now the stranger was almost to his cave, and now he would keep his word to Ember and try to think to him.

Ember, I'll mind-talk to the stranger if he'll let me. Watch over me.

Brother, you know I will always watch over you. Didn't we hatch from the same egg clutch?

Yes, she did think that. It had only been that he had been a shiny object found buried in the dirt. To a dragon mother a sword was a perfect object for the newly hatched to fix their eyes upon. Mother had stuck him point down at the edge of the nest, never dreaming that the sword too would hatch. When Golden Mom looked in the nest and saw two instead of one, she did not question it, never having learned to count. Originally there had been five eggs, but as was usually the case with nests, four had been spirited away by hungry beasts. He had become a young boy-child only after the four had been taken.

Glint ached, having been uncomfortable propped against the cave wall. He blinked his eyes, rubbed his arm muscles, and walked out of the entrance. He patted his sister on the neck.

I want up on your back, Ember. There was nothing

unusual about his request. Just so had he asked her many times.

Why? Her thought had a snappishness to it. Her forelegs quivered. She stretched, much as he had stretched.

To carry me to the stranger. I want him to see me before I mind-talk to him. See me on your back.

Ember made a grumbling sound, but crouched. Glint knew it was strange behavior on her part, but for all his centuries, most spent in a dream state as a sword, he hadn't learned to understand females. Golden Mom had moods that he had witnessed during the time of his growing up, so why shouldn't his sister?

He climbed up on her, held her small, otherwise unused wings in his hands, and put the seat of his inadequately padded posterior on the hard, interlaced golden scales. Kings had never had a throne to equal it.

She stood up, lifting him as easily as though he were a bird. She had a formidable strength that he knew he would never have, which was why he utilized it. There was nothing he knew of that could stand up to the strength of a dragon—except another dragon.

"GWOORTH!" Ember said. It didn't sound friendly and it didn't sound ladylike. Glint almost lost his hold and went head over her side. What was the matter?

Sister, that's no way to act! The stranger will think you unfriendly.

Beat copper! Beat copper! she thought back.

Now that didn't seem friendly and it wasn't what he'd thought she'd have in mind. Had the dragonberry caused her mood swing? Quite possibly it had. Dragons lived on the edge of emotions anyway, mostly covered by hunger. They didn't ponder and wonder and sift their thoughts.

Rage! Rage!

No mating thought this! If anything, the opposite. Yet he had been certain she wanted a mate. Before she took the berry it had seemed all that she could think about. Dragons, especially the females, were a total mystery!

The strange dragon had not seen them. Like most dragons its eyesight probably was not of the best. Glint readily reached into its mind.

Claw hurts! Rock bruise. What got into big female? She wanted to mate. Then she whacked me with her tail. Then she drove me off. Then she mated with my rival! Strange beings are females!

I'm with you, friend! Glint mind-talked before he could stop himself. That wasn't what he had planned to say.

Who that? You Charles?

Not Charles. Charles human?

Charles brother. Merlain sister. Both human.

A dragon with human siblings? Possibly no stranger than having been a sword, Glint had to think but not mind-communicate. Now he had to mind-communicate.

I am Glint. I am human. I have dragon sister.

Sister have mate?

No.

I will mate with her.

Possibly, whoever you are. Why are you copper?

Chimaera's hatching help. Three of us. Charles, Merlain, me. Should have been one body, three heads. Should have been chimaera. Mother would die: father not want. Chimaera help.

That's very interesting. And it was, though Glint didn't understand it. Dimly he knew that once he had had a sister, so possibly once he had had a dragon sibling as well.

Charles, Merlain name me Horace. Dragon Horace, as in once-upon-a-time, child-time picture book.

Glad to meet you, Horace. What could it mean by "picture book"? He had been far too young when enchanted to have learned much of what children learn. Besides, that had been long ago, probably before there were picture books.

Horace, be gentle with my sister. I named her Ember because she's warm. She's young and inexperienced with males. She knows me, her brother, better than any dragon other than our mother.

Horace began running. Wriggling from side to side in typical dragon or lizard fashion, he forgot his hurt claw and recent rejection. He wanted to meet Ember, but strangely his thoughts were of gazing on her and daintily touching his forked tongue to hers, rather than actual mating. Glint felt that this was right, but it hardly fitted what he knew about dragons.

"GRWRRRROUTH!" Ember said, and leaped forward. She trembled for her full length on both sides. Glint almost lost his hold.

Easy, Ember! He just wants to talk. To get to know you. He's like me. He can mind-talk.

Ember halted, warily eying the approaching stranger. The male dragon really did have copper scales; it hadn't just been an illusion of light. Glint marveled—dragons with copper scales seemed an absurdity.

Ember, I am Horace. I have traveled far to mate with you and fertilize your eggs. Toss off your brother and assume the position for me.

Male chauvinist man! Ember's gratuitous insult coincided with a vicious tail slap. Glint hung to her wing stubs, more frightened than he had been at any time before riding her back. Always before he had mind-guided her, as he had when they were hatchlings. Today he had elected to let her follow her own will without imposing his; to him it seemed the decent process for mating.

"OOOOMPH!" Horace clutched his bloodied snout with his foreclaws. Big tears rolled from his eyes and splashed down on the ground. *That hurt!*

Of course it did, you big pile of copper! What kind of an upbringing have you had? No biting, no battle, just squat down and you'll climb aboard!

But that's what dragons do, isn't it?

Not this dragon!

Glint felt Horace's injured feelings so intensely that he wilted under them. He tried to transfer what he sensed to Ember, wanting her to know the copper-scaled dragon as a sensitive mate-seeker rather than a crude, rude aggressor.

Easy, Ember! He's a pretty nice guy and you're discouraging him.

Mind your own business, Glint!

But— He had never sensed her so insensitive. All he was trying to do was help.

Out!

She was giving him no choice. She seemed as angry as a jaybin fluffing its feathers and preparing to defend its nest. Why had he gotten into this?

With great difficulty Glint resolved to keep his mind shut. She knew what was right because he had taught her. To grab her mind like the mind of a squirbet or other prey would be ungentlemanly and inappropriate.

Ember, my sweet little tail!

I'm not your sweet little anything! We're strangers, Horace!

But Goldie, I thought we could be friends!

We will be if I want us to be! Ember fumed. *After we get to know each other.*

Right! After we share some good rancid flesh, lap some blood, touch our tongues, rub our tails, then—

Only if I want to!

Of course.

Glint heaved a sigh of relief. The romance was getting off to a shaky start. He had been afraid it was finished with Ember's tail slap. Now all he wanted was to get out of their way and let them proceed or not as was their inclination. He could wish that things could go as well for him.

Ember, can you let me off at the cave?

Why, of course I can. Her manner so sweet that he knew it for unnatural.

Glint rode his sister the few steps back with Horace following. He eyed the copper dragon, decided that it wasn't going to surprise Ember and him by eating him, and slid off. He somersaulted, as he had done since childhood, came up on his feet, and without looking back entered the cave. He thought he'd call up a plump squirbet, cook it over a fire, and eat it wrapped in spintuce leaves. Then he'd drink some cool spring water, eat a few appleberries or perhaps chericotts if those luscious reddish-yellow fruits were ripe. Working at it, he could put in his day. But what, he wondered, would he do when Ember had hatchlings? Would he become just a nurse-maid to the young coals, or would life offer some surprise?

Sighing, he picked up his gourd dipper from its shelf and checked the edge of his skinning knife. It was time for him to start minding his own business again: his business of survival.

Horace was not at all certain that he liked this babe. She had at least one very peculiar friend. Not a brother, he felt certain, though the mind-talk had suggested it. Most likely this was an intruder, which was what most humans were in the existence of dragons.

How had it happened that he, Horace, was so much smarter than other dragons? Because he and his human brother and sister were of one hatch. Because a creature called a chimaera had interfered as a favor to his mother and sire. Somehow he was as he was and this one was as she was, and this one was strange. Not as intelligent as he, no, but every bit as determined. If she wanted mating she would encourage him; if she didn't, she wouldn't. In her nature, then, she was not much different from him.

The spring before them was sparkling clear. Reflected in the water, along with the drooping tree limbs festooned with leaves, tall yellow-stalked weeds and bushes heavy with red and yellow fruits, two perfect dragon faces. She, golden and shining; he, copper and dirty now from the mud he had been in. What a pair they would make! How he would enjoy clutching her with his claws, his long tail scale by scale with hers.

SPLASH!

He blinked as the water rippled away in all directions. Slowly the wavelets smoothed out and the reflection was returned. Her tail was raised, quivering as she was about to slap.

Two could play at that! Horace raised his own tail, pivoted away from her, and brought it up fast and hard. His tail struck hers with a stinging shock.

"OOOMPTH! OWROOTH!" She stopped her downward tail whip, her tail held back by his.

So, you big old piece of copper trash!

She stood up in the water on her hind legs. Suddenly, so quickly that it caught him unprepared, she pivoted on her left hind foot and grabbed him with both front legs around the throat. Her extended claws ripped at his back and hooked into his wings. A moment later he was flipped, his head under water, and she was leaning on him, holding him down.

"Blub, blub," said Horace, appalled at this. Water got into his mouth as he tried to blow it out. *Let me up! Let me up! I'll drown!*

You should have thought of that before! The forefront of her body pressed down on his head, forcing his face against hard river rocks that dented into his scales. This was clearly no way to treat a future mate!

Horace considered that he hadn't really wanted this. The big female who had driven him off and then mated with his rival hadn't been as cute, but Ember was as troublesome. He braced his forefeet against rock, bunched his muscles, and shot his head upwards. His nostrils broke surface, and with their emergence into air his hind feet pushed down and his leg muscles contracted. He lifted her on his head, free of the water. Then, angrily, his forefeet grabbed hers, his neck hunched, and he flopped her down. She went below the water where he had been. He threw his weight against her as they changed places.

Stop! Stop! I'll drown!
You should have thought of that before!

Bubbles of air surfaced, breaking against his snout. His snout was now very near hers, only hers was under water. He counted the bubbles the way Merlain had taught him to count: *one, two, three, four, what in the world are we drowning for?*

Her face drifted prettily beneath the water. He hoped he had not held her there too long. Exploratively his tongue shot down, tickling with forked tip the smooth, golden skin of her nostrils.

"GALOOPTH!" Splash!

Air and water shot upwards into his mouth and face as Ember coughed and choked. She gave a desperate flop and he held her down, watching her eyes widen and then narrow. Quickly, not wanting her to *really* drown, he tightened his hold on her and yanked her head above the surface.

She gasped and spat and choked a while. He considered pushing her down again, holding her longer this time, making her really desperate.

You're killing me, male chauvinist dragon!

Now for that she should go down again. He looked into her eyes, darted his tongue out. Her eyes followed its tip.

I don't really want to hurt you, Ember. That wouldn't be right. Merlain, my sister, would tell me it can't be right.

She strained against him. Her jaws parted and hastily he moved his tongue back, not wanting it bit. Suddenly her tongue was out, touching his, twining with it.

Oh, Horace, what kind of a dragon are you, anyway?

A good dragon, I hope. A dragon with a sister and brother.

A human sister and brother!

Yes, and your brother too is human. Doesn't he want you to do good?

Humans are . . . humans. Dragons aren't. You're supposed to take me, overpower me with your strength, subdue me. Dragons don't question.

You do. I do.

Yes.

It's our siblings' fault. They misfitted us.

Bite all humans!

No!

No?

No, I said. Merlain polished my scales. Charles brought me game. Sometimes it was as if the three of us were one.

Glint fed me meer guts. Glint rubbed plant sap on my baby hurts. Sometimes it was as if Glint and I were from one egg.

Do we have to battle more?

No, Horace. We feel human, though dragon. It is enough.

Enough, Horace's mind echoed. *The bank?*

The water.

It was enough. They plunged deep into the pool, well

beneath the surface. Here, where the water was renewed even in the time of winter, it was the coldest. Here they came together, without pause for breath.

Later in the day the spring water had quite lost its iciness.

CHAPTER 5

Reacquaintances

*H*elbah searched with her magic crystals: first the outhouse, then the swimming pool, then the secret hiding places she wasn't supposed to know about. No sign of the kinglings, no evidence that they or their nursemaid, Glow, had even been about. Where had they gone, anyway?

"Oversleep one morning and everybody's missing," Helbah said to her familiar.

Katbah arched his shiny black back and stared her full in the face. It was as though the animal, really a part of her, was suggesting something.

Helbah felt a chill. "Zady!" she said. "She must have—it wasn't natural, my sleeping so late!"

"Meow," Katbah said. There was unhappiness and fear in the way he said it. Zady had affected Helbah's sleep and could as easily have slain them. But to have overcome Helbah's defense magic would have meant even more power than Helbah had attributed to the evil witch.

Her crystals, all four of them, blinked a rosy shade of pink. Zady's hated face appeared, wrinkled and hideous as ever, on every one.

"Satisfied, Helbah? Satisfied that they're not here?"

"Bag of bones—" Helbah started.

"Oh my, no," the Zadies told her. "Not at all, my dear. Take a look, Helbah. Take a look at what you have done for me."

On all four crystals a woman's lush young body with spectacular ripe curves appeared. It was beautiful and would have been arousing to any male except for one astounding fact: from the neck up it was the old Zady with all her hairy warts.

"What do you want?"

"Why, dearie, I've returned to thank you."

"You're welcome. I'm always glad to help your body separate from your head."

"HISSSSS," Zady said. It was more the hiss of a serpent than a cat. "Perhaps you'll be interested in this!" Her arms gestured in the crystals and in place of herself were the images of two young men and a young woman crouched on a narrow ledge. Below the ledge eagawks flew a magic pattern back and forth, while beneath the eagawks' talons were clouds and a sheer drop into a dark and forbidding crevasse.

"You have them," Helbah said. Illusions were one thing, but she knew this was no illusion.

"Yes."

"What do you really want?"

"Control."

"Over what?"

"Everything this frame holds. Tell your darling princelings they must abdicate. Zady will be your ruler from now on."

"You're twenty years behind the times, Zady. Kildom and Kildee aren't the big rulers."

"No? Then who is?"

"Horace," Helbah said before she could stop herself. "After your defeat the human and orc kingdoms united and placed a member of a third race in nominal command. Horace has the say over all the kingdoms with the exception of Throod and Rotternik."

"Horace? That reptile?"

"Dragon."

"Ridiculous! Where is he?"

"Where he wants to be, of course. If he doesn't want you to find him, you won't."

"Still has the opal in him, does he? I'd have thought an orc would have gutted him for that."

"You don't know orcs, dragons, or humans," Helbah said with satisfaction. "As a matter of fact you don't know witches except for the few you command."

"The frames are full of malignant witches," Zady said.

"The frames are full of those who practice benign magic, as well."

"Where's your Horace?"

"Why, Zady, you have to search. When you find him you'd better be polite. He's all grown-up now and he's fond of politeness. I'd be careful for the welfare of his subjects if I were you. Take care that no harm comes to Kildom and Kildee or their nursemaid."

"Nursemaid! I'll turn her into a sword again!"

"I wouldn't do that, Zady. Horace wouldn't like it, and neither would I."

"Don't you want them returned forthright?"

"You're not going to do that, Zady. Why should I ask it?"

"You're an infuriating witch!"

"I always knew you thought so. Thank you. I relish that respect."

"Respect! For you I have no respect!"

"You should have, Zady. It was I who defeated you."

"You and a great many others! Besides, that was but a skirmish. The real war is coming."

"You mean you can't persuade a dragon to do your bidding?"

"Persuade it? I'll destroy it!"

"Of course you will, Zady. At least you will try."

The imaged Zadies raised right hands and snapped fingers. Instantly the four pinkish crystals grew blood red.

Helbah raised a hand and gestured an invisible wall of impenetrability between her and the crystals.

Zady laughed cruelly. At the end of her laugh the crystals imploded, pulling the simple furnishings of Helbah's palace room inward. A moment later the imploded crystals had left behind a spectacular mess.

Helbah stroked an angry Katbah, smoothing his fur.

"Yes, Katbah, yes, it will take all the art I can muster. I just hope that art will be sufficient."

Katbah dehumped his back. He reached a paw up and touched her lips.

"Yes, Katbah, we have to hope that she will save them. She will want the big triumph, with all around alive to see and suffer. If she ever wins, she will win all. No enemy then will she allow to live unrepentant."

"Meow," said Katbah sadly.

"Yes, yes, of all her enemies you and I and the prophesied hero she will try to hurt the worst. We must stop her completely." She sighed. "I only wish that I knew how. The way to defeat Zady isn't at all clear to me."

Glow shivered on the ledge, feeling the fear of the two kinglets. They were all three terrified by the height, fearful of what their captor planned for them.

"Kildom, I never thought I'd say this, but I wish we had that book again."

"That's stupid, Brother!" the young redhead said to his identical twin. "You know how much trouble we were in."

"Yes, but we were young. Besides, it did get us out of things."

"It got us into trouble as often as out of trouble. I suppose you'd like to call up that big bird again."

"Yeah. It got us to Ophal."

"It also got us into danger, as you-know-who had planned. If Charles hadn't controlled it, it would have eaten all of us."

"Oh, dear," Glow said. "I wasn't with you and Charles and Merlain, but I know how you must have felt."

"You were so!" Kildee insisted. "It's just that you were then a sword."

"Oh yes, and I talked to Charles in his dreams. It was so romantic. I wish we had carefree times like that again."

"The fact remains," Kildee said pedantically, "that it was you-know-who's planning. She got Merlain to steal the book at the convention and then charmed her into using it."

"Which was lucky for us," Kildee said. "Without the book we'd not have escaped the orc prison, or—"

"Without the book and without you-know-who, we'd never have adventured in the first place! The adventure part was fine, but you-know-who had us doing evil. If she'd won out we'd be doing evil still, or we'd be—"

"Dead."

"Or enchanted into something," Glow put in. "She might have turned you into swords."

"That wouldn't have been so bad!" young sovereign Kildee exclaimed. "That might have been fun!"

"You don't know what you're talking about!" Glow snapped. "You boys think it was fun for me all those years? Let me tell you it wasn't! I had no one to talk to! I couldn't eat anything! I couldn't play! I didn't know where I was most of the time or what was happening to me!"

"Besides," Kildom said to his brother, "she might not have made us into swords. She could have made us into jugs or pots. Yes, little fat pots and not the kind you cook in!"

"Boys, boys, this isn't getting us anywhere!" Glow said reprovingly.

"We're going somewhere?" Kildee asked innocently. "Do you suggest down or up?"

Glow looked off the ledge at the eagawks flying their magical patterns, then peered down into the depths. Even with Kelvin's very special boots, courtesy of Mouvar, it was a long way down. "I do know something we can try," she said.

"Try? Try what?" Kildee sounded skeptical.

"I can try to think to Charles and Merlain. If I can mind-talk to them and tell them what has happened, maybe they can help."

"We don't know where they are or where we are!" Kildee protested. "Besides, help how?"

"With Helbah, maybe. With Kelvin, perhaps. Maybe Charles."

"You're dreaming."

"I am not! I've had a lot of experience with dreaming, and this is no dream. Now if you'll both shut up, I have to concentrate."

Glint was tasting a particularly tangy appleberry, which he decided had been picked a little green, when the head buzzing started. Someone trying to reach his thoughts? Horace? He'd have thought the copper-scaled dragon was still involved with Ember. Besides, he doubted that either dragon could mind-speak to him without help. This was a searching thought, a questing thought, a human thought.

Woman. Female. Mind alike.

WHAM!

It was his sister! His sister Glow! Zady had made her forget, and had made him forget. But when her enchantment was broken, so was his. That was what had happened, and it came to him all in a rush. Sister, small and pink and cuddly like him. Learning to walk, learning to play. Taken from their mother, transmuted into swords. Cruel separation. The work of an evil witch, to punish their mother.

She was mind-searching. Reaching out.

Sister! Sister!

Who? What?

Your brother Glint. Remember?

A whir of thoughts. Boy and girl twins not related to them. Red-haired, growing-up king twins, also unrelated. Fight on mountaintop. Switch of sword. Long fall. Zady's head in talons of eagawk.

So much. So very much. Yet he got it. He knew what Glow knew and she knew all that was him. Twin mind-talking was like that. Charles and Merlain and Horace were like that as well.

She's got you again.

Yes.

The evil old witch!

Yes. Help. Please help.

I will. If I can. He did not want to become a sword again. Neither would he abandon his sister.

I don't know where we are. It's high. It's a mountain, but where?

Eagawks flying. Great chasm. Dragon territory, because of strength of your thoughts. He'd seen the eagawks flying, had followed them, had seen a beautiful woman from afar. An eagawk had brought her meat. When the woman had turned in the light, wrinkled face bloody, and he had seen her clearly, he knew it was Zady. He had blocked his thoughts, just in case, knowing then that she was still developing, growing, becoming an apparent human again.

You saw her! You knew she was here, Glint?

Yes.

Why didn't you destroy her when you had the chance?

I was afraid of her. Once I knew it was her I never went near the nesting site again!

Glint, can you help me now?

I can try, Glint thought to his unseen sister. *I know where she has you. It's a long way from here.*

Glint, get Horace. Horace can carry you. Horace has the opal. He can bring you directly here.

Yes, with Horace's help I just may be able to rescue you.

Hurry, Glint! Hurry before she returns!

Kelvin was admiring his newly bulging arm and leg muscles and flat stomach in the reflection in the clear river water. He strutted just a bit, shoulders back, imagining himself a handsome and heroic young adventurer. Except for a bit thinner hair and a reasonably matured face, he was almost the Kelvin who tried to fight against orcs and ended up slicing off Witch Zady's ugly head. Those had been the days—they really had!

"Kelvin, you preening turcock!" Lester had been watching him, a hint of disapproval on his face, instead of his fishing bobber. Now as he spoke a trass took that opportunity to snatch the bait and run with the line, propelling Lester upright.

"That's a big one, Dad!" Kathy Jon exclaimed. As usual she had been the one to come along while her brothers begged their way out of the fishing trip. Though Kathy hadn't the patience of a born fisher, she did take the delight. She was in mannish clothing, as usual: brownberry shirt and shorts. She avoided feminine apparel whenever possible.

"Don't get your line tangled with hers!" Kelvin warned. "Give him line! He'll break your—"

Lester's rambloo pole bent double as he heaved on it. A dark shadow moved up from the depths: a trass of near-record size. "Lester, you're putting too much strain on that!"

"I am not! Get your line back!"

CRACK!

The broken half of Lester's pole splashed its reflection, then made a wake as the trass swam away with it.

"Damn!" Lester swore. "It's your fault, Kelvin! You and your advice!"

"Don't blame me! You're the one who put the pressure on."

"I'll get him, Dad!"

"Kathy, no!"

SPLASH!

Water splashed shockingly cold on Kelvin's sweaty face and his new clothes. He rubbed and shook drops from his eyes and saw a pair of pretty, slim, well-browned legs dipping below the river's surface.

"Lester, she'll drown!"

"Not Kathy," Lester said. "Get him, gal! She's got hold of the line. The fish darted right past her."

Kathy Jon's pretty young head surfaced. Her face was very red and the broken half of Lester's pole she raised was attached to a line wrapped around her neck. The line was cutting into the flesh, pulled taut by the thrashing creature now in midair.

The trass came down with a splash, drenching Kathy's

already wet face and hair. She clung to the line, hauled on it, kicked her heels. She and the fish both disappeared under the water.

"Lester!" Kelvin said, alarmed. He had heard Lester brag that his daughter could swim like a fish; now he believed it.

The water smoothed as the little wavelets ran their lapping course. The sun shone down on glass-smooth water, showing their reflections.

Kelvin looked at his sister's husband and swallowed. If Kathy didn't come up soon he didn't know what he could do about it. Swimming wasn't one of his few accomplishments.

SPLASH! Further downstream Kathy's lovely young face resurfaced. Still very red, she hung onto the line with both hands. She went below the surface and then she popped up again as the fish, as long as her suntanned arm, took to the air and came down short, snubbed by the line. Kathy bobbed under and up and out, a human float with now very red pointed ears. Whether she was playing the fish or the fish was playing her was a question. For a time the contest was in doubt, and then Kathy was struggling upright in the shallows, just above where the riffles started. Her young legs strained to keep her in the current as she stooped down with a darting motion. She shoved one hand in the fish's gills while grabbing its flapping tail with the other.

"I got him, Dad! I got him!"

"Don't drop him, Kathy! Hang on! I'm coming!"

Kelvin watched his brother-in-law run like a man demented. Years dropping from him like bits of shorn shrubbery, he charged through stickery bushes and head-tall weeds as once he had charged other men on horseback. Standing right where he was Kelvin saw it all: father and daughter subduing one large, ornery fish that would bake up well in Jon's brick oven. There'd be a family feast from this one, and he and Heln would surely be invited. Almost he could taste the succulent white flesh steaming and mouth-wateringly fragrant in a delicately browned skin.

"Here, Kathy, here!"

"Take it, Dad, I lost my pants!"

"Kathy, I told you not to talk like that!"

"My button, Dad. The line snagged my button. I couldn't help it."

"I don't care! That's not ladylike! Your mother and I have told you and told you—OUCH!"

"Dad, the hook!"

"The fish, Kathy, the fish!"

SPLASH! The trass hit the water once more, yanking Kathy after it. Not to give up easily, she spread her arms wide as she came down in a sprawling grab.

"I've got it, Dad! I've got it! Help!"

Lester waded into the wet melee and dropped until his hat floated. Now a straw boat with an assortment of hooks and feathers on it, the hat leaped to the current and bobbed up and down, and swiftly, speedily, out of sight. Lester in the meantime had his arms around fish and daughter. Together they struggled ashore, though the flopping fish was not cooperative. Kelvin saw that Kathy had indeed lost some of her apparel, and he felt guilty for noticing that her mud-slick bare legs were nicely proportioned throughout. So was her water-soaked upper torso under the plastered shirt. As with her mother at age fourteen, she might act like a tomboy, but her body had other notions.

Kelvin waited. Eventually a muddy, bloody-handed Lester broke out of the brush and all but shoved the big-mouthed trass in his face.

"What do you think of that, hero? What d'ya think?"

"Nice fish."

"Nice! It's beautiful! Prettiest fish I ever saw!"

It had to be the ugliest, Kelvin thought, gazing into the open mouth with all its pointed teeth. Trass tasted great, but no trass had a beautiful face.

"We're taking it right to the fishodermist!"

"What? You're not going to eat it?"

"No, of course not. We'll have it mounted and displayed in Lomax's place. That way Kathy can show it to her grandchildren."

"Daddy!" a very muddy young lady exclaimed. "Daddy, you know I'm not going to marry."

"You say that now, but someday you'll find a young man every bit as good as your old man. Your mother did."

"Oh, Daddy, you—"

"Come on now, we want to get to the shop while it's open. You coming, Kel?"

Kelvin shook his head. He didn't want to diminish his brother-in-law's happiness, but that trass would certainly have tasted good. "I'll see if I can catch something for Heln to clean. Something we can eat."

"Good! Catch one big enough and we'll all invite ourselves to supper."

Kelvin watched the happy father and daughter squish and splash back to the road carrying their prize. Thoroughly muddied, thoroughly soaked, partly disrobed, he knew that neither had ever had a better time fishing. He envied them the fun and mourned the loss of a gluttonous evening. But maybe, just possibly, he might yet catch—

His float bobbed under and stayed. With a whoop of joy Kelvin yanked on the pole, then rapidly sent coils of line to its darting tip, giving the fish more to pull under. The fishing reel his father had described had not been invented in this frame, though Kelvin, unlooping the line from the base knobs as rapidly as he could, felt that it was time. Though he moved as fast as he was able, the steadily moving fish was faster. If only he had the magic gauntlets on today—then he might have a chance.

SPLASH!

Standing in the water nude, red-haired, curvaceous, and beautiful was no fish. It pointed the pink tips of its full breasts at him, puckered its cherry mouth at him with half a kiss, dimpled prettily in both rosy cheeks, and said:

"Kelvin, heroic mortal, we meet again. Last time was at a convention, and then afterwards briefly on a mountaintop.

You weren't nice to me there. In fact you cut off my head."

"Zady!" Kelvin gasped. Zady, nude and beautiful as she had previously appeared only in his own unheroic, magic-assisted young head.

CHAPTER 6

Helping Hand

*K*elvin swallowed a lump as big as a barn. He wanted to run, but his knees had grown weak. All he could do was stand there by the river as his delectable fish splashed with all her nude beauty to the shore.

"Zady. I—I—"

"You knew I'd be back, sweet boy. You did me a big favor. I'm now not only young again, I'm perfect. I'm sorry for the things I did that caused you to seek to destroy me. I know that you're the hero of prophecy—the Roundear. I know that prophecy has to be serviced."

Serviced! Kelvin could think of only one meaning for that word. Yet he had no use of that kind for any woman other than Heln, the mother of his children; never had, never could. But Zady was so beautiful, and she was coming from the water, little rivulets running down her perfect body. In his mind something whispered that he could find perfect peace and joy in those arms. He wanted so badly to grasp her, to clasp her, to do what his body was urging him to.

What was this, a spell? He had to break it, he had to. Otherwise she would use him and destroy him and—

"I know that there is no fighting the prophecy," she continued in dulcet tones. "I won't try. I want to help you work it out. 'Until from Seven there be One/Only then will his Task be Done.' That can be, Kelvin, that can be."

Her voice was persuasive. Her nude body would be more persuasive. What could he do? What else could he do? He hadn't his Mouvar gauntlets or even a sword.

"We must ally, Kelvin. We must ally. I will prove my worth to you. First we must make love."

"B-but—" he started, shocked despite, or perhaps because of, his sudden desire to do just that.

"Why not? There is no one to see. Love is much better than fighting. The staff, as magical folk keep saying, better than the sword."

He should get out of here. He should flee. If only he had on those distance-spanning boots that had on that distant day enabled him to make the sword swing that took off her head. So long ago, so far in the past, and he so young and vital.

Yet he was young and vital now, to a degree, because of the rejuvenating effect of the magical exercising. That process had restored more than his muscles, he realized. That was the problem.

She was almost to him now, her arms held out invitingly. Her face was not an old face, not an ugly face. She was beautiful and desirable beyond description. She was—she must not be real. She had to be an illusion, a projection of the old witch. But she had said that she had changed, and—

Her hand touched his. It was real and warm. Her full red lips parted. Her eyes, so greenish, so filled with peaceful depths, grew large and near. Tiny golden comets filled the sea-green pools into which he was gazing. She raised herself on her toes. Her lips would soon touch his. They would kiss.

"Daddy!" His daughter's voice, coming from up the path his fellow fishers had taken. For some reason Merlain had come here.

"Bother," said the full lips, pouting prettily. "I will return. Get rid of her! Send her home!"

The beautiful face and body vanished. Kelvin felt just the brush of an invisibility cloak and then he was alone on the

riverbank. Merlain—beautiful, young Merlain—was running
to him on the path.

"Daddy, something's happened! It may be Zady! The
twin kings have vanished and Glow with them. Helbah's viewing crystals have all imploded and she's frantic. She wants you
at the palace."

"I'll come, I'll come," he said, gathering up his fishing
gear. What was that he had just been through—a dream? It
felt so real. He almost wished Merlain had been peeking inside
his head, using her ability as she shouldn't. But Merlain had
given up that naughtiness. Kelvin and Heln now trusted their
son and daughter in a way that long ago they couldn't.

As he followed Merlain he almost forgot what he had
been about. Such a dreamlike experience couldn't have been
real and he didn't want to think on it or to have to tell Helbah.
But suppose it had really been Zady? And suppose she really
had changed?

Later in the day Kelvin heard all from Helbah first-
hand—about the missing young people and Zady's appearance in the crystals. Zady with an ugly face? Magic, he knew,
could do anything. But he didn't want to think her evil. She
had changed, she had said. He didn't want to tell Helbah, but
he would have to if she asked.

"You'll have to do your hero stuff now, Kelvin. Fulfill
Mouvar's prophecy."

"Yes, but suppose it's not what we thought? Suppose
Zady's changed? Suppose that now she's—not evil, maybe
even good?"

"Impossible!" Helbah pronounced firmly. "She's what
she's always been. A lepuar doesn't change its splotches."

Kelvin didn't try to tell her differently. He watched her
get her magical books and paraphernalia assembled. While
she was occupied he took a stroll to the pool where the kings
and their nursemaid were supposed to have been. He looked
down into the water and it rippled, and again he saw that face.

"Zady, you took them, didn't you?"

"Yes, Kelvin." The words were as real as the rest of it.

"You will harm them?"

"No, never. Helbah was my enemy. She's not now, but don't tell her."

"They are on that mountaintop?"

"Not the mountain you remember, Kelvin. This one is in dragon territory. Do you want to see?"

He nodded, unable to speak.

The water rippled. A picture formed, as in Helbah's viewing crystals or the magic smoke conjured for viewing purposes. He saw the young kings and Glow, the beautiful girl who had once been a sword, exactly as Helbah had described them. The girl and the kings were talking but he couldn't hear what they said. Below the cliff edge, just as Helbah had described, eagawks flew their magical cross and crisscross.

"Zady, can you return them?"

"I can."

"You will?"

"To please you. If I do, you will have to help me help you fulfill your prophecy."

"If—if you have no evil intent."

"Done, then!" She gestured with her hands and disappeared in a swirl of underwater smoke.

As the pool water again became placid, Kelvin had to reflect on her last words. The witch had spoken with an inflection of triumph.

Kildom was looking at the royal nursemaid and thinking some improper thoughts that he was thinking more and more often. He knew his brother Kildee was also thinking them. Why not? After all, in terms of growth they were now almost to or just starting the age of adolescence, twelve and a half, or thirteen unroyal growth years. That gave them the right to have such thoughts, didn't it?

"What are you looking so goofy about?" his brother demanded.

"Uh, nothing," Kildom lied. He knew that his brother knew that he lied and moreover knew very well what he was thinking. Even without the telepathic abilities of Glow and the round-eared twins they knew exactly how each other's minds worked.

"She's been standing like that for a long time," Kildee said, nodding at Glow's statuesque form. "You think she's reached him?"

"Charles must be a long way off. I can't see how she can."

"Maybe Horace."

"Horace! You're out of your mind!"

"But she said he was in dragon territory. This could be dragon territory. It's rough enough."

"So is Rotternik. You don't know where we are any more than I do."

"Do too!"

"Do not!"

POP!

Both red-haired kinglets turned an unroyal white and turned to see Dragon Horace occupying the ledge with them. Astride Horace's thick neck, holding his vestigial wings, sat a large, bronzed man neither of them had ever seen. As they stared, he swung a leg over the side of the dragon and slid down.

"Glow! Is it really you?"

"Glint!"

A reanimated Glow took three quick steps and leaped into the stranger's waiting arms. The two young people hugged each other, moaning and rubbing the sides of their faces together.

"Charles isn't going to like this," Kildom whispered to his brother.

"He's kin, stupid!"

"Can't be. Glow was a sword."

"Look at his hair!"

Kildom did and was shocked. Both touching heads were so yellow they appeared to be bathed in bright sunlight. Moreover, both faces were similarly beautifully shaped. If they were not brother and sister, they certainly appeared to be.

"Kildom, Kildee, meet my long-lost brother, Glint," Glow said, leaving his arms. "He mind-talks too. I reached him and he had already reached Horace. So if Horace can take the four of us, we'll go home together. If you royals are ready to travel."

Kildom looked at Kildee, then hastily pushed his brother aside in his rush to get the top, best seat on Horace. He pulled himself up by a wing stub and got his legs astride the big head. In a moment Kildee had hold of his belt. Then Glint helped Glow behind Kildee and she clasped Kildee's middle. Glint settled himself between the wings and then aligned his smooth, bronzed calves to either side of them.

They were ready to go. Ready to return to the twin palaces of Klingland and Kance. Ready now to smooth away what would have to be Helbah's worried looks.

Zady watched Kelvin's image in the pool. "Oh, I have not yet begun to toy with you, my innocent dunce!" she cackled. "Now I have planted the seed, and it will sprout and grow even in my absence. Subtly, at first, so you think it is your own. Oh, how you will pay, idiot hero!" She burst into hideous laughter.

SPLASH!
Kelvin ducked, blinked, and rubbed water from his eyes with a quick wipe of his forearm. There in the pool was his most unusual offspring, Horace. Astride the dragon were the missing royalty with their nursemaid, and with them, seated comfortably on the wingseat, was a tall, bronzed stranger.

Kelvin swallowed. He hadn't expected that the young Zady would make good on his request so quickly.

"Kelvin, this is my long-lost brother, Glint," Glow said. "We met in dragon territory and got Horace to bring us home. I don't know how the kings and I got to be in dragon territory. Maybe Helbah can tell us."

"Helbah!" called one red-haired twin.

The summoned witch stepped out of her war quarters and stared at them. Since she had not yet replaced her shattered crystals and had an aversion to using smoke, Kelvin doubted that she had been viewing either him or the missing kinglets.

She stared at them, and her aged face grew a worried expression.

"This is my brother Glint, Helbah," Glow explained. "Do you know what happened to us? Kildom and Kildee and I didn't wake up this morning in our beds. Instead we were on this cliff together in dragon territory. I don't know how it happened, Helbah, and neither do they. Did you use some magic on us? Was that why we were there, so that Glint and I could find one another?"

Helbah walked slowly to the pool. She motioned with her hands, said some words, and the water parted in a broad path. Her charges and the nursemaid came to her, keeping their feet dry. They joined Kelvin and her and then Horace simply vanished as the pool water returned.

"He's going back to his love," Glow said. "It's so romantic, their finding each other. He'll come home sometime, bringing her with him."

"Nice," Kelvin mumbled, wondering what Horace's bride could possibly be like. Most married men claimed they had a dragon for a mother-in-law, but he had a dragon for a son and probably a dragon for a daughter-in-law.

Helbah said, "I had nothing to do with it. Zady's responsible for your adventure. She took you to the cliff and left you, then allowed you to come home."

"Why?" Kildom or Kildee demanded. Kelvin had to wonder the same thing.

"I'm not certain, precious. I can't imagine what the old nasty had in mind."

"Maybe," Kelvin said hesitantly, "so that Glow and Glint could find each other."

They all looked at him as though he were mad.

"I mean she was responsible for their enchantment. Maybe she's changed. Growing a new body, that had to be a lot like getting a new chance. Maybe she wants to make up for what she did."

Helbah came over to him and felt his forehead with her gnarled hand. "Kelvin, you've been out in the sun too long."

"Maybe. I was fishing, and Lester¯and Kathy Jon caught a big one, so they—"

"Another time, Kelvin. We haven't time to hear of your sporting exploits. This is serious."

"But—"

She made a motion and it was as though his lips were sealed. Kildom and Kildee snickered. Doubtless Helbah had used the same magical pass on them on occasion. Considering their long childhoods, many occasions.

Kelvin pulled at his lips with his fingers and then desisted. Helbah was taking her frustration out on him, and until she wanted him speaking he wasn't. The worst of it was that there was something important he needed to tell her. Something regarding fishing, or was it the swimming pool? His head ached quite suddenly and he couldn't remember.

"As I was saying," Helbah said, "Zady doesn't just do things. She always has a reason and the reason's always malignant. Did any of you actually see her?"

Kildom and Kildee shook their properly crowned heads. Glow frowned a little as though trying to remember. The stranger, Glint, spoke up.

"I saw her once in dragon territory. Once after I became human again and not a sword. When Glow became human I became human."

"Oh, I know how magic works!" Helbah said crossly. "Tell me something useful. When did you see her, and exactly where?"

"When she was growing a new body. Atop one of the really tall spires surrounded by mountain walls on three sides. She had eagawks and buzvuls caring for her. The eagawks sheltered and protected her and the buzvuls fed her."

"That's Zady, all right! Did you think of attacking her? Destroying her while she was helpless?"

Glint looked down at his dirt-encrusted feet and shook his head.

"You should have done something."

"What?" He flushed and looked embarrassed. "I was afraid."

"Of course you were. Anyone with sense would have been. But if you had left dragon territory, come to me—"

"I wasn't in mind contact. I didn't know Glow was alive. Besides, there was my sister."

"Sister?" Helbah demanded sharply. "Isn't Glow your sister?"

"Ember. My dragon sister."

"That explains it! You were thinking as a dragon does. Dragons aren't normally concerned with humans except for eating them."

He nodded miserably while Kelvin watched, actually feeling sorry for him. The poor fellow had been through a lot in his existence and now mean old Helbah was berating him for no good reason. Sometimes he almost wished it was *her* head he had lopped off. What was he thinking! Not Helbah! Helbah was good. Helbah had saved all of them. But what was it he had been thinking about her?

"If I had more experience with humans . . . if I had been less afraid . . ."

"Oh, don't blubber about it!" Helbah snapped. "We all make mistakes. Even I made a few."

That's the truth! Kelvin thought. He didn't mean to project it.

Glint looked into his face. *Really, Kelvin? What were they?*

I'd better not tell. Then something grew in his mind, and changed it. *Oh, I will anyway! She could have been friends with Zady. She could have helped and advised Zady's niece, Zoanna, instead of burning her. She could have had her brat kings surrender to Kelvinia instead of forcing me to surrender.* Then he wondered at his own thought. He hadn't had to surrender!

Kelvin, that's serious!

You'd better believe it, swordboy! The thought, Kelvin realized, was as little his own as it was Glint's. But Glint seemed not to notice this. It was as though he only casually touched Kelvin's mind, fearful of intruding on privacies.

Maybe we can discuss this later? Away from Helbah?

Yes, away from her. Don't let her know what you and I have just now thought.

Kelvin felt a momentary vacancy in his head. What had he been thinking? Glint was looking back at Helbah, squaring his shoulders, like a good private in the presence of a superior officer.

"Oh, for pity's sake, Glint, I'm not going to belabor the obvious! Your mother was a powerful witch, but she taught you and Glow little before your enchantments. It was all Zady's fault! The Sun Witch would have done right by you if she had had time. It wasn't your fault that you and Glow lazed around so long in a state of unknowing enchantment."

"No," Glint agreed. "It wasn't her fault. It wasn't my fault or Glow's."

"Zady's."

"Probably," Glint acknowledged. "I'm not aware of much before the enchantment."

"Glow isn't either. It's called enchantment amnesia. The ability to forget is all that makes the state of enchantment bearable. The after-enchantment amnesia is almost as good."

"If you say so, Helbah."

"I do say so. And take it from me, it was Zady's evil doings at the start. I should have opposed her more, but I was young, inexperienced, not totally smart."

She isn't smart today, either! Kelvin's projected thought was totally unexpected to him, as it was to Glint, its recipient. Kelvin saw his jaw tighten, and he knew that the thought that he hadn't wanted to project had gotten to him. He wondered, without projecting, if he should have sent that thought to him.

"I've a lot to learn about things, Helbah. Both I and my sister."

"Of course you have, dear." Helbah patted the big, bronzed shoulder in friendly, grandmotherly fashion. She turned to the boys.

"Kildom, Kildee, just because you went on a journey doesn't mean you get out of taking lessons."

"No, ma'am."

"No, Helbah."

"Both you boys get your books, and Glow, you see that
they study."

"I will, Helbah. You know that I will."

"And I'll get to work with my magic and try to discover
something. Once I get a crystal that's good for communicating
I'll confer with my orc colleagues. Then maybe I'll get somewhere."

Kelvin, came Glint's thought, *let's you and I go somewhere
and talk.*

"Oh, and here!"

Helbah snapped her fingers. Kelvin's teeth unclenched
and his jaw dropped free of her spell.

CHAPTER 7

Changed?

As soon as they had left the twin palaces behind, Glint
turned to Kelvin in the back of the royal coach and nodded to
the front and their chauffeur.

"He mind-talk, Kelvin?"

"No, and I don't think he can hear us up there, either."
It seemed a safe guess. The old man had shown signs of
deafness and would have no reason to be acting as Helbah's
spy.

"I really don't remember much of my early childhood.
Nor does Glow. I know what she knows, because we shared.
That's the way it is with mind-talkers."

"There can't be many of you. You and Glow are the only

ones I've met, though there may have been some at that convention. I believe we met all kinds of benevolent witches and warlocks and assorted in-betweens. But since with the exception of Helbah none of us were witches, we—"

"Your children mind-talk," Glint reminded him. "Glow knows. She'll marry your son; I'll marry your daughter."

"Oh," Kelvin said, overwhelmed. Mind-talkers could get right to the point! He hadn't even thought about Charles, Merlain, and Horace, but Glint had—especially Merlain.

"I realize I haven't met her, but that's all right. I'll be mind-talking to her before we reach your cottage."

"Yes, I suppose you will." How sure of himself! But mind-talkers, he supposed, had a right to be. He envied them. Even he, great hero of his time, had never, not once, even with all his Mouvar gifts and the prophecy, felt remotely, even passably, self-confident.

"I felt you should know. That's customary, isn't it?"

"It's customary that a parent eventually knows." How true that had been! First the action, then to him for the reaction. Fortunately his children, unusual as they were, had always had sense. From the time at the convention when they had had the wit to steal what they needed and wanted . . .

He stopped his thought, appalled at where it had been taking him. Approve of their stealing? He'd been ready to disown them! If Helbah hadn't uncovered the fact that it had been another witch putting them up to it, he might have. Let's see, who was that witch? She had been old. No, she had been young, and beautiful—heart-renderingly loin-achingly beautiful. If he hadn't been married to Heln . . .

"Mr. Hackleberry?"

"What? Oh, sorry, I was thinking about the past. About when Merlain was little."

"I know all that Glow knows. Merlain and Charles were naughty at age six. It wasn't their fault. They were under the spells and influence of—"

"Yes, yes!" Kelvin said sharply, startling himself. "Talk about Helbah! Talk about Helbah!"

"Helbah? All right. I know what Glow knows of her.

Glow knows only that she's snappish and bossy but has been kind. I was wondering about your thoughts back at the palaces."

So was I, Kelvin thought, but managed not to project. He wanted to say that Helbah was a truly good friend, but somehow an inner vision of a beautiful woman's naked body glistening with translucent drops of water stilled his mouth. His jaw was in fact falling, and he feared that to Glint he appeared unusually stupid.

"You said, 'She isn't smart today, either!'" Glint reminded him.

"Thought. I thought it. I didn't intend to project it. I didn't, in fact, know that I could."

"But you did think it to me. You must have thought hard."

"Angry. She made me angry, sealing my mouth."

"Yes, I understand. What was it you wanted to say?"

"I don't know." It was true, he found.

"About a fish?"

"A—yes, about a fish. Lester and Kathy Jon Crumb caught a big trass. Biggest I've ever seen. They wanted to get it mounted, so they left. I was alone for a while and . . . Merlain, the daughter you say you'll marry, came to me. She'd brought Helbah's message about Glow and the kings. Helbah had sent the coach. Merlain went home. I went to the palaces."

"You said with your thoughts that Helbah could have been friends with Zady. That she could have helped Zoanna, once wed to your father, instead of burning her. That she could have had the twins surrender to you instead of you to them."

"True enough," Kelvin said. Strangely, he felt that it was, though in another way it was confusing.

"I don't really understand that. From what Glow knows about it Zady was not to be reasoned with. She did destroy our mother and turn us into swords."

"But you were young and inexperienced," Kelvin heard himself say. "Neither you nor I nor Glow know that she couldn't have been reasoned with. On that we have only Helbah's word."

"Yes, yes, I see the point. But—"

"I didn't really know Zoanna, but my father knew her and married her. My half-brother in another frame came from that union. If my father had let her govern the kingdom in her own way instead of interfering—"

"That can't be right! Glow told me—"

"Glow wasn't there. I wasn't there. We have only my father's word."

"You think your father lied?"

"Why not? He wanted my mother, and my mother believed in the prophecy and had it memorized. A virile man may twist things where there's a hot and impressionable woman."

Kelvin would have liked to bite off his own tongue. But it was logical, it was—and his own tongue, seemingly with a life of its own, had said it.

"Kelvin, I don't understand. You really think—?"

"I just stated a possibility. I wasn't there, actually, not before I was born. Then there was the war that started when I was away attending my brother's wedding. The twin kings could have surrendered Klingland and Kance to Kelvinia and its ally Hermandy, instead of the other way around."

"But from what I understand—"

"You have to reconsider all the possibilities. Zady may have changed."

"Because she let us escape with Horace's help?"

"Well, she didn't try to stop you, did she? For that matter you don't know how Glow and the kings got there."

"It has to be magic. They just woke up."

"Magic, but not necessarily Zady's. She's not the only witch in all the existences, you know."

"If not her, then who?"

"Possibly Helbah, making a case for herself."

"You think?"

"She wants everyone to think Zady's coming back to destroy us. Let me tell you, I think she's wrong."

"Why do you think that?"

Kelvin felt an inspiration. "I'll show you!" Struggling upright and holding to the front seat, he called to the chauffeur. The man didn't hear him at first, but by reaching outside and slapping the wide seat beside him Kelvin got his attention. The coach slowed as the chauffeur pulled on the reins.

"I don't want to go directly home. Take the third road after the next. Drive to the footpath that leads to the river."

"Kelvin!" Glint said excitedly. "I've got her! Merlain and I are talking to each other! Glow reached her, just as she promised she would! Mr. Hackleberry, whatever it is you have to show me, can't it wait?"

Trust that brat to mess things up! "I suppose it can. Cancel the order, driver."

The chauffeur nodded and drove on at a leisurely pace. Glint had a happy expression on his youthful face as he and Kelvin's daughter mind-talked.

What was it, Kelvin wondered, that he had been about to show the kid? He'd had something, someone, in mind. Then, as had been happening lately, what he had been thinking faded out. Alas, there was no way to recover what had been important. More important than an impending marriage between Glow's brother and his only daughter? Kelvin just couldn't understand the way his own head was working.

"Driver, stop!" Glint was suddenly frantic. Kelvin saw why. Long copper-colored hair streaming behind her, shapely breasts heaving prettily with every breath she took, Merlain was running to the coach.

The coach stopped. Glint got the door open. He ran to meet Merlain. As they neared each other, Merlain opened her arms.

"Driver, a little closer!" Kelvin shouted frantically in the old man's ear. The chauffeur slipped the reins and the horses caught up to where the two young mind-talkers were hugging each other as though they had done so every day for the past twenty years. Glint kissed Merlain and Merlain kissed Glint.

"Oh Glint, Glint, I've waited for you so long!" Merlain said.

Long! Kelvin thought. Until Glow contacted her she didn't even know of Glint's existence!

The two definitely were in need of a wedding. As were, Kelvin well knew, the two other mind-talkers who had waited patiently for Glint's appearance.

Glow! Glow! Glow! he thought.
Charles! Charles! Charles! she thought.

Never had their passions been so intense. Charles felt the vibrations all through his body as his mind reached out to touch and stroke hers. He was in the forest, alone at his private place, clinging to a tree trunk. His fingers felt as if they were touching hers. His mental lips were on her mental lips, his imagined body against hers.

Oh, now we can, Charles! her heart murmured. *Now that my brother is here.*

He's meeting Merlain now. It was an intrusion of fact, but one that it was necessary he convey to her.

Yes, and she knows all about him. All.

We're all of us married, Darling. Starting now.

We were before, Charles, she reminded him. *But now it's different. Now it's like your mother and father.*

We'll have to tell them. The thought was strange to him, though his own.

They'll know.

But they're just people, Glow. No magical heritage.

We'll tell them. They can announce it. We can tell them before Helbah and Katbah at the twin palaces.

Nice. Romantic. But they may want a wedding. Perhaps like the one the uncle I've never met was forced to have.

Do you think so? she thought. *Your parents never had one.*

No, big royal affairs with lots of guests is in that other frame's customs, not in ours.

I'm so glad it's not in ours.

Me too, he thought gratefully. *I wonder about Horace and Ember.*

They're married.

I know. Should that too be announced? Even to him it seemed a bit silly.

By dragons?

Right. Maybe they won't live here. But I hope they do. I'd miss Horace.

They could stay in the forest, couldn't they? she planned. *And then when Ember gets homesick Horace can carry her instantly to dragon territory.*

Yes, I suspect that they can. What a practical girl he had! *As long as Horace has the opal. He'd better keep it in his gizzard, now that Zady's revived.*

We never saw her, Charles.

No, but your brother Glint did. So we know where she's been these past years.

She almost certainly had the royals and me, but she let us go. Isn't that strange?

Very. What's Helbah's explanation?

She hasn't any. She's taken the transporter to get new crystals. She was grumbling that she didn't have Horace to fetch them to her.

Charles smiled mentally. *Horace could hardly have come out of a transporter booth and asked directions of the nearest warlock!*

He wouldn't have had to, silly! Helbah would have been riding him and Helbah knows where to go. They wouldn't have gone near a transporter booth.

But Helbah's not a mind-communicator, he worried. *How would she have given him directions?*

Well, I would have been along. Maybe the terrible royals, too, if they could have persuaded her to let them go.

They didn't try anyway? That didn't seem like them as far as he was concerned.

Of course. But Helbah didn't want them ogling naked girls in the station, and maybe goosing them. You know how their minds work.

Just as they did twenty years ago! They were brats then and they're brats now. Merlain and I were too, but we've matured.

With the help of Helbah and me and the fact that you've grown up four times as fast.

True. Very true, he admitted. *Wouldn't it be cruel to be the royals' twelve and a half physical age instead of what we are?*

We couldn't be married.

No, but we aren't, and we are.

Poor kinglings. And they're so eager too.

All boys of that age think they are, Glow. Grandpa says it's glandular, not magical.

Something all boys experience? Girls too?

You know it. A bug crawled off the tree bark and onto his arm. He saw it but did not disturb it. *It's just that for them it's four times as bad.*

Poor kinglings.

You've said it. Poor Helbah too.

Poor nursemaid? she teased.

Yes. He blew the bug off his arm. *They ever try touching you?*

Kings can do no wrong, they keep telling me. Helbah says not when we don't let them.

They think about it, though, don't they?

Yes.

You tell Helbah?

I have to. It's my job. He considered that, not liking it.

Doesn't seem right. We've thought to each other since we were children. Almost since we first met.

Yes, but Helbah doesn't do anything to them. She says all boys daydream. Kings have to be watched because kings can get away with more.

Not with Helbah they can't, he thought, remembering his ways.

Or with me watching them.

Glow, now that Glint and Merlain have each other and you and I have each other, I have to ask you something.

About Zady?

Yes.

She's evil, Charles. Can't you remember when you were little? You and Merlain?

A little. She controlled us, all right. It was fun stealing and it was fun doing naughty things. Golly, but it was fun! *She never let us feel guilt.*

That's what she would do to the kings.

She did when they were younger. They as much as my sister and I. Why didn't she now?

I don't know, Charles. I'm as puzzled as Helbah.

Could it be that she's changed? After all, I did cut her head off. I deflated her old body with my father's sword and dipped you into her blood and disenchanted you.

You broke the spell, Charles. But no, my love, I don't think she can have changed. Witches' natures don't change.

You feel that too, then. What about my father? He acted strange.

There was something, Glow mused. *I would like to have read his mind.*

Me too. But it wouldn't have been proper.

In this case? Even for a son?

I've wondered too. He could be under a spell. Wouldn't Helbah know about it?

It depends on the spell, but don't spells show? Besides, if Zady got to Kelvin—

She could, he realized, *wearing an invisibility cloak.*

Why would she want to, Charles?

She used to do things just to be malignant. She would have killed my sister if Father hadn't stopped her.

Her thoughts flickered through scenes of incredible cruelty. *All of us, I think.*

Probably, though you she might have kept a sword.

That wasn't living, Charles, that was suspension.

She tormented Father first, he remembered with agony. *Told him she could make Merlain like herself. She offered to save her life and do that.*

But your father refused. He knew her nature then.

Yes, and he didn't know he could save Merlain until his

spanner boots and the magic gauntlets acted. They saved her, I guess, as much as he.

But he's the hero. He's the one in the prophecy. Mouvar's prophecy.

Yes, and he's never liked it. He never wanted it.

Yet he's the hero. Charles, could it be—

That it's he who's changed? That she changed him or is changing him?

Could it, Charles?

I'm afraid it could, love, he thought, and dug his fingernails painfully hard into the bark of the unprotesting tree.

CHAPTER 8

Gather by the River

Zady watched the image again. "I have just begun to torment you, you miserable excuse for a hero," she said. "The seed is growing, and it has many ways to manifest. I shall savor them all, and so shall you, my innocent lout. But you will not enjoy it the way I do."

Kelvin was surprised that his own feet had brought him here. It was almost as though he were wearing the spanner boots again. Somehow he had walked to this beautiful bend in the river concealed by fruiting bushes and flowering trees. He was breathing the good sweet river air, redolent of mud and grass and sand. It had rained and the puddles were reflecting blue sky and treetops and . . .

A face. A beautiful woman's face framed by long red hair that made a perfect setting for eyes so green and bright and all-compelling. He wanted to reach out for that woman, and clasp her and hold her to him. She was there in the mud puddle and then she was there in his arms and there was everything and nothing at all that he could do about it. Such an experience as he was about to enjoy was going to cost him everything he owned and all he had accomplished, but none of that mattered. He stretched his lips to her pulsing red lips, they touched, and he tasted—

Fish! Dry, smelly fish!

He choked, sitting up in bed.

A young girl, almost as beautiful as the one he had been dreaming of, stood at the side of his bed. It was really his bed, in his bedroom, in his cottage. Sunlight streamed through the window onto the impish face of his niece. He remembered how he had seen her legs bare, clothed only in mud and not much of that, and her greenbriar shirt plastered to her body, so that it might as well have been transparent. How suddenly he had seen her change from boyish to womanish, in his awareness!

"Good morning, Uncle. Aunt Heln said I should come in and wake you. She said you were going to sleep away the day. That's right, isn't it?"

Kelvin rubbed his mouth, shuddering. "What's that behind your back, Kathy?"

"Behind my back? Why, nothing, Uncle. Nothing except my pretty little behind. You know what St. Helens says—behind every pretty girl there's a pretty—"

"Young lady, don't you lie to me!" He spoke harshly to cover up his guilty thoughts about that very part of her anatomy. She was his young niece, after all! "Don't get impudent, either!"

"Oh, Uncle, you're such a grouch!" Kathy Jon reached down beside the bed and lifted up a large, ugly, stiff trass with opened mouth. The fishodermist had mounted it to look as alive as possible.

"That's very nice, Kathy, but what are you doing here?" Try as he might, Kelvin couldn't even remember last evening.

After the announcement ceremony at the twin palaces they had gone to the wine house to celebrate, and—

"You said to show you when it was ready. As soon as it was ready, remember?"

"Of course I remember," he lied. Somehow he hadn't used to be able to lie at all. Much had changed for him in recent years. Age and wisdom come to all mortals—especially age.

"Well, Uncle Kelvin," Kathy said, putting her shapely bottom into the nearest chair, "you said bring it over and we'll take it around together. Remember?"

Oddly, he did, and yet it had been as though the little impromptu celebration was elsewhere. They had been celebrating the fish and his daughter's and son's marriages, and—

He sat up in bed, startled by where his whirly head had taken him. He should never drink wine, especially as much wine as he had evidently taken! Everything was so mixed-up he hardly recalled anything in the order in which it had happened.

"Kathy," he said, motioning, "out! I'll get dressed and meet you and Heln for breakfast. Take the fish with you."

Kathy impolitely stuck her tongue out, rose, and exited, fish under arm.

He stared after her. Had she wiggled her pert bottom provocatively as she went out, or had he imagined it? If she had, what was she doing, trying to vamp her uncle? If she hadn't, why had he seemed to see it? Neither notion was acceptable. It must have been a trick of the light.

Kelvin tried to get his thoughts in order as he dressed. He still wasn't used to the nearly new body Helbah had in effect made for him. All that running around the track had been so difficult! He couldn't believe the young firmness, and with it, to his surprise, an increased overloading of a younger man's maturing desires. Last night he had wanted a woman, and it hadn't been Heln. Unbelievingly he recalled the circumstances . . .

St. Helens, looking so much older than he should have, potbellied, wheezing as he reached across his reserved table.

Truly he needed to reduce. Less food, less wine, more hugging from that attractive bar wench. Imagine her interested in this fat old phony, even wanting to marry him! But almost everyone felt that his father-in-law had charm; somehow he, Kelvin, and sometimes he thought Heln, were the exceptions. If the man had stayed with her mother and been a proper father to her, then very possibly the both of them would have felt differently.

"Kelvin!"

He turned at the sharp reprimand, seeing Heln in her housewifely shape and knowing that she had seen him staring at the younger woman, unavoidably comparing her firm arms and legs and quite oversized bosom to his wife's. Being his wife, she knew how he thought. Getting his hero's shape in a manner of days had been great for him, but had done nothing at all for *her* figure. Years of preparing fattening meals to please her husband and then trying to eat a proportion away from him had taken their toll. Maybe she should have joined him in those three hellish days of exercise.

"Uh, dear, I was just, uh, listening to your father." Oops, a lie, first thing. Heln knew as well as he that he never willingly listened to her father.

"I can see that," she said coldly, demanding with her tone that he look at her. Jealous she had never been, but then he had never given her an excuse. All women had the potential to be jealous, he had heard.

He gave Heln his full husbandly attention, clouded just a bit by the wine he had been drinking. "Sit down, dear. I'm certain you'll find this interesting."

"I'm certain," Heln said. She pulled up a chair, her eyes daring Kelvin to stare into that abundant cleavage across the table from them. Kelvin focused on an irregular stain on the tablecloth and set his face in the I'm-really-interested expression. It was a pose he suspected all married men had to learn eventually to insure their own lives and marriages.

True to form, St. Helens talked on while Nellie appeared to give him all her attention. When she shifted her position her blouse gaped wider and wider, and inevitably Kelvin's attention wandered.

"Kelvin," Heln said icily, "I think I'd like a glass of wine."

"Huh? What? Oh, yes." He wrenched his eyes away from enchanting depths. "I was just about to suggest that."

"Oh, I'll get it, Mrs. Hackleberry!" Nellie smiled, stood up, and picked up her tray. "It's what I get paid for."

"And for making things pretty," Kelvin said. Damn, he hadn't intended to say anything like that! It had just slipped out, as thoughts had been doing lately.

"Oh? I had thought perhaps she got paid for something else," Heln said. This time the word "icy" would not suffice to describe the chill.

"It's her big tits," St. Helens said affectionately. "The customers like looking at them."

Nellie smiled wider, lifted the tray higher, and pretended she was going to crown a saint. St. Helens crouched back in pretended alarm, convincing some watchers that she meant it.

"I'll be right back," Nellie said, and left their table.

"She's really very nice," Kelvin said to St. Helens. "When's the announcement?"

"When I can't get out of it," St. Helens said as he had said before. "Not that I want to, of course."

"Then why hesitate?"

"Same reason I should have hesitated more often when I was younger. Marrying is committing."

"More than adventure?" Kelvin was really astonished at the way his words were forming. They seemed to just well up. Almost as though his tongue had a will of its own.

"At least as much as going to war."

"You'd hesitate over that now? You used to be all for it."

"I used to be for glory. I was dumb."

Well, for once St. Helens had said something smart! After all the years he had spent urging Kelvin to fulfill his prophecy! Or was it that his father-in-law was just tired?

"You feel the prophecy will have to be fulfilled?" Kelvin

found himself asking. It was a strange thing to be asking under any circumstances, especially of St. Helens.

St. Helens nodded. "I expect. Only I don't feel as certain. I'm not as anxious as I used to be. Things are good now. The last war almost brought disaster."

"Maybe," Kelvin's tongue suggested, "the prophecy will reverse itself."

"You mean like when Kelvinia surrendered to Helbah and the twins, when the Confederation surrendered to the orcs?"

"Sort of. The prophecy says what's to be accomplished, not how it's to be accomplished."

"If you believe in prophecy," Heln said. "Kelvin, you don't."

"I used to say I didn't. I was younger then."

"Who's the enemy—Rotternik or Throod? Be sort of hard to fight a war without mercenaries, wouldn't it?" St. Helens was definitely interested in his suggestion.

"I think—maybe this is wrong, but it does make a bit of sense—it's not the remaining kingdoms so much as something else. Zady, the witch who opposed us, wanted to govern all the kingdoms. Suppose she comes back the way Helbah insists she will. But suppose she's changed so that ruling will be enough for her?"

"You mean you think she's reformed?" Heln asked with wonder. "How can you suggest that, Kelvin? She tried to destroy our daughter, and you, and in fact all of us!"

"I admit it would be a great change. But so much has worked out so differently than we expected."

"Nothing quite that different," St. Helens said.

His father-in-law finished speaking. Nellie brought the wine and placed it before them. As she leaned over, pouring from the bottle, Kelvin had to admit to himself once again that the girl really did have nice jugs. Finding Heln's eyes were glaring at him, he hastily gulped the fermented graplum—or was it plumape? He never could remember!—and found it refreshing. The rest of the conversation drifted or floated by, and the next he knew he was in bed at home and Kathy, his

niece, was waking him. There had been that dream, and that
fish under his nose, and now he was nearly dressed.

He finished pulling on his bullhide boots, wondering half
seriously if he should get out the spanner ones. The spanner
boots fit perfectly, and like the gauntlets never seemed to
sustain wear, but he felt uncomfortable wearing them. With
his spanner boots, courtesy of Mouvar, he might go places he
hadn't intended. Thus he might step out in the midst of a
casual walk and find himself at a spot he had been thinking
about. It was like that dream of finding himself back at the
river, only in the dream he hadn't been wearing the spanners
or any of his Mouvar gifts.

"Kelvin!" Heln calling to him from the kitchen brought
him all the way back. He could smell the aroma of coftea and
wafflecakes, though he hadn't expected any. Just what had
happened last night at their gathering? Why did he remember
lusting after Nellie and that one pointless conversation? Why
remember what he himself had said as though it were some
sort of revelation?

He stood up from the chair, admired his younger, hand-
somer self in the mirror, and strode out. Heln, disheveled hair
hanging uncombed, worn housedress askew, eyes puffed almost as though from crying, was far from appetizing. He
gulped, having hardly ever thought such a thing in their entire
married life.

"Well, sit down," she snapped.

He pulled out a chair and put his seat in it. He really felt
strange, as though now intoxicated. The wafflecakes were
burned, and the coftea was of a darker and more bilious shade
of green. Again he had to wonder: just what had happened last
night?

"Eat!" she ordered. Definitely he had transgressed in
some fashion and she was letting him know it.

"Where's Kathy?"

"Kathy? How should I know? What are you talking
about?"

He opened his mouth to say that Kathy was here, then
thought about it. His tongue had been getting him into scrapes

lately and he was still confused as to what had happened. He thought that she had been there with him, but possibly it was a dream.

"Are you going to eat that or not?" she demanded.

I'll try, he thought. He lifted a forkful of dry wafflecake, then remembered that he normally drenched that with melted butgen and mappmel syrup. He tried. It still wasn't appetizing. Neither, he thought before he could stop himself, was his wife.

"Well, are you just going to look at that all day?"

The wafflecake tasted like ashes drenched with rancid grease and then dipped into a sickeningly sweet syrup. He retched. He tasted the coftea: bile and dirt mixed. He retched some more.

"I'm not surprised!" Heln said. "A man your age acting like that! And in public!"

Kelvin decided to grasp the animal by the horn. "Just what did I do last night?"

"You don't remember?"

"Only that we were at the tavern, with your father."

"And his bovine girlfriend. You forgot that?"

Kelvin strained his recollection, but nothing came. He shook his head.

"You don't remember what you did that made even that hussy blush?"

He pushed back the plate, determined not to eat. He must have made a fool of himself, but he honestly couldn't remember. Now he didn't *want* to. Strange, he'd never been one to overimbibe.

"Where are you going?" Heln asked.

"To change my boots," he said. "Then I'm going for a walk. Alone."

He strode into the bedroom and went right to the closet. He opened the door, pushed back some clothes, and found them waiting. To all appearances they were as fresh and new as the day he had first acquired them. Dragon-leather boots to match the gauntlets on the shelf. To match, not only in appearance, but also in kind.

He pulled off the bullhide boots and pulled on the

dragon. They felt much better than other footwear he had worn. It was a delight just to feel his toes in them.

He left the bedroom, ignored Heln's hurt look, and walked outside. Deliberately he thought of the riverbank, held the thought, and stepped.

He was there. The trees and the bushes and the river and leaping fish. As in the dream, or as on the day before.

He breathed the air with its flower and fruit and grass smells, looked at his reflection—now not quite so old, now not so fat—and wondered why he should be here. But then why be elsewhere? This was the place to be—the place to live and be alive.

In the water his reflection rippled. It was he, a middle-aged, well-conditioned man who by some stretch of the imagination could be seen as a hero. He had never wanted to be a hero. His sister Jon had wanted to be—energetic, young Jon. So long ago that had been. They had been so young.

His reflection came clearer. He seemed even younger—almost the age when he had found Heln. No lines in his face. No gray in his hair. So young a man, so inexperienced.

A splash where the ripples had formed, and the reflection was not of him now but of a beautiful girl. He gulped. It was Nellie, but not as she was in her thirties but as she might have been when the age of his niece. Her breasts were so big they must have embarrassed her. She was smiling, invitingly, as though to say, "Take me! Take me now!"

He put his toe in the water. He prepared to dive. Then he got hold of himself. The girl was his father-in-law's flame. Besides, she was far too young for him now, and—

The water rippled. The image of Kathy replaced that of Nellie. Smiling impishly, his young niece opened her blouse and gave a lurid wink. Her upper endowment was even better than the prior wet shirt had suggested.

"NO! NO! NO!" he said. He wouldn't have it! He couldn't! Not with his baby sister's daughter!

The water rippled as his heart beat deafeningly. His youthful expectations were rising unbidden by him. It was as if his body were taking over all his will. He gaped open-

mouthed as another woman formed there in the water before
him.

Red-as-dragon-sheen hair. Greenish cat-eyes, with
golden lights flickering compellingly in them. A face, a face,
oh, such a face! And a body—a body so full and ripe and
mature that those of the younger women dimmed and shrank
by comparison. She formed, and then she walked, real and
solid, toward him.

His arms reached out, waiting for her to emerge, nude
and perfect and commanding desire—

"Zady!" he cried, unable to help himself. "Zady, I want
to make love to you!"

"You will, big boy," the red lips promised him.

CHAPTER 9

Skirmish

Kathy Jon was annoyed at her brothers. Alvin, Teddy, and
Joey had begged her to take them fishing, and after that big
trass she'd caught, she wanted to. To see Alvin's young eyes
pop, Teddy yanked almost into the water, Joey screaming with
boyish excitement—what more could a sister ask for? The only
problem was that things were never quite as she imagined they
were going to be. Having rented a boat from Yoke's Boat
Rental, obtained a bucket of squirmy bait, and gathered up
the fishing gear, they were launched, and the brats characteris-
tically misbehaved.

"Was that a froog that jumped, Kathy?"

"No, Joey, that was a fish."

"Ha! Ha! Ha! That was me throwing a rock!"

"Teddy, we do not throw rocks when we're fishing."

"I do!"

"You do not! Not with me you don't. You want to catch a fish, don't you?"

"What fish? I haven't seen any."

"That's because you're making too much noise."

"Phooey! I'll make noise if I want to."

"You do and you won't catch fish."

"I don't want to catch fish. I want to throw rocks."

Kathy stifled an impulse to throw Teddy overboard. The worst of it was that both his older and younger brother thought he was being smart. It was brothers against sister, boys against girl all over again. Having watched her mother and uncle on occasion she knew it was a fight that would never end.

"Look, boys, if you do things right we'll catch fish. You each told me how badly you wanted to catch fish. Well, now is your chance. You can throw rocks at home anytime."

"No we can't!" Alvin shrilled. "Mama won't let us."

"She said she'd warm our butts if we ever threw stones at the side of the house again," Teddy elaborated.

Joey, maybe and maybe not understanding, snickered behind his hand.

"I didn't mean throw rocks at the house—"

"That's what you said!" Alvin reminded her. He looked the most innocent of boys, even of these three, but Alvin had to be the worst.

"Boys, fun is fun, but it's a nice day and we want to catch fish. You don't want to go back empty-handed, do you? People will make fun of you if you do."

"We'll carry the poles," Alvin offered.

"That's very nice of you, Alvin, but I intend to carry fish."

"Phooey, you caught your fish."

"I think Daddy caught it for her."

Kathy stifled an itch to cuff both older brothers as the younger stuck his tongue out. How could they be behaving like this on such a lovely day?

"I'll tell you what, boys," Kathy said, finally inspired. "We'll pull to shore. Then everyone can pop into the bushes—"

"What for?" Joey demanded, pretending that he didn't know.

"She has to pee," Alvin explained. "Girls always hafta go."

"I'd rather pee off the boat," Teddy said.

"Teddy, don't you dare! Now I'm going to row to that big tree trunk and tie us up to the branch that sticks out over the water. We can fish right there; it should be a good spot. Then we can pull up on shore and have lunch."

"I want lunch now," Joey said. He was making his pouty face, daring her by his actions to smack him. The problem was that she really truly wanted to smack him—hard.

"Yeah, let's eat," Teddy agreed with the younger.

"I'm ready," Alvin said.

"It's early morning yet. If we eat it all up we'll get hungry before the day is over."

"We can go home," Joey said.

"No, we'll eat fish," ace troublemaker Alvin corrected.

Well, now I know what Mama goes through every day, Kathy thought. *I'm not going to have any brats. I'm going to spend my life fishing and slinging stones.*

The oarlocks squeaked as she applied herself, rowing expertly as she did most boy-things. Boy-things being mostly rough, fun things as opposed to girl-things which were mostly gentle and quiet and to her mind rather stupid. She didn't really blame boys for looking down on girls. Most girls never got to do anything.

"You're going to hit that log!" Alvin shrieked.

She looked where he was pointing frantically from the bow. Under the water was a long, dark shape. As she watched, it glided out from beneath the tree branches and then lower into deep water until it finally disappeared.

"Dummy, that was a fish!" Teddy cried. "A big fish! Bigger than Kathy's!"

"I told you there were fish, boys. You have to try believing me sometime. Still want to go ashore and eat lunch?"

"No!" Teddy exclaimed. "I want to catch that one!"

"It'd pull you in," Alvin said. "Wouldn't it, Kathy?"

"It might. But if you hang on tight and let out the extra line the fish will take, then don't get panicky—"

"I want to catch that fish!" Joey squealed. "I want to yank hard and pull it right out of the water!"

"You can't!" Teddy explained.

"Can too!"

"Cannot!"

Kathy sighed. Something told her that the finer points of angling would be lost on these three for now and for quite some time to come. Her sympathy for her mother was growing larger and stronger by the minute. Now she understood those frequent retorts of "Just you wait until you're married and have kids of your own! Then you'll see how funny it will be!"

"Poor Mom!" Kathy said aloud, easing the boat up to the side of the tree. "Alvin, get that branch!"

"Mom isn't here. Got it, Kathy!"

Well, for a wonder he had done something right! Now if she could just get them fishing quietly, the day might not turn out to be as hideous as it had been so far.

"Does anyone need to go ashore?"

"I want to fish!"

"Me too!"

"Yeah!"

She helped them with their fishing tackle, starting with Joey. He didn't understand about the winding knobs. His idea was to keep pulling the line out until it was all on the bottom of the boat and ready to grab if a fish should strike.

"See, Joey, you wind it all up, and then when a fish takes your bait and runs with it—"

"Fish can't run. They haven't legs."

"Shut up, sweetie."

"I'm Joey."

"You'll be wet Joey if I toss you out of here."

"You wouldn't dare! Besides, you're my sister."

How, oh how, does Mother stand it! I think I'd drown the lot. Even me, sometimes.

"This worm is yucky!"

"Oh, Alvin, you didn't leave the bait uncovered out in the sun? I told you to put plenty of dirt on them."

"Easier to get if they're all in a bunch," Alvin explained. "Only now they stink and they're not wriggling."

I will never have a brat! I will never have a brat! I will never have a brat! I'll never marry. If a man comes near me I'll stone him.

She handed Joey his pole with a stern admonition not to pull the line out. She untied the boat from the tree limb, not trusting Alvin to do things right twice in a row. In reaching his knot she almost slipped and fell overboard. The boat rocked. Water splashed up in her face and she realized what was causing it.

"All right, boys, get your behinds on those seats and keep them there. I don't want any of you to as much as shift position. No more rocking the boat, you hear?"

"You're not Mom," Teddy said.

Thank heavens I'm not! She crawled back past Alvin, who was now in the lunch basket, wormy hands and all, and getting in the sandwiches.

"Who wants peajelnutly?"

"I do."

"Me too."

"Sorry. There's just one, and that's for me."

"That's not fair!"

"No. Hit him, Kathy."

"I'm not your mother." She pulled on the oars, seeing Alvin stuffing a sandwich into his mouth and wishing he'd choke on it. Oh, how badly she needed to get to shore! To get away from this bunch, even for the time it would take to answer nature, was a necessity. Come to think of it, nature was pressing the issue.

"You're the only one who has to pee!" Joey said, accurately enough. "The rest of us want to fish."

"We can't fish without bait, Joey. We're going to have to find some. Alvin should have to find bait for all of us since it's his fault the bait went bad."

"Isn't either," Alvin said between mouthfuls of worm-stained sandwich. "I did what you told me."

"You did not, Alvin. You let the worms stand in the sun and you didn't put dirt on them."

"So what? Teddy and Joey would have done the same."

"Wouldn't have!"

"No way!"

"Well, boys, someone is going to have to gather bait. Now we haven't a shovel, but maybe if we lift rocks carefully we can find a few worms. Then there are hopgrasses and ketcrits in the bushes and on the trees and in the grass; those are good baits if you can catch them."

"I want worms."

"I want hopgrasses."

"And you can't crush them. You have to have them alive and kicking so the fish will see them and grab them."

"Says who?"

"Says your long-suffering sister, that's who! And Dad would tell you the same thing." Only their father had wisely declined to come along. Kathy's respect for her male parent's judgment went up a notch.

She parked the boat, anchored it firmly to an old log, and got the boys to finding bait. That was all they'd get done today, she thought, if the boys didn't get tired of searching and get into mischief. Her brothers get into mischief? Incredible notion! But wouldn't it be wonderful if while she was absent they found a stinkcat or disturbed a hornee's nest? In her mind she heard them screaming as they got what they had coming to them. She'd better quit thinking this way. She'd better just get by herself—and fast!

"She's going to pee!"

"I'm coming too, Kathy!"

"No! Stay here. All of you stay here and find some bait!" She practically ran into the brush to get away from them.

A little later, having done what was necessary, rubbing the smarting scratches on her arms and legs caused by the thorny bushes, she seriously considered not going back. They were too much of a handful for anyone, especially their sister! She'd just walk down a meer path for a way, hoping to get lost but knowing she wouldn't, ready to tell them later that she had if that would buy her more time. What she had to do was clear her head—get the anger and frustration out. She should have known better than to come here with them. Her mother knew how it would be—that was why she'd put up no argument against the excursion.

The trees opened ahead and she could see water. A different spot, downstream from where she had lost the monsters. If she just kept walking for a while before going back she was certain it would help. She stepped over a tree limb in her path, bent down and picked up a stone. Her sling was over her left shoulder, held there by a thong. A few rocks heaved at something would be pleasant. Let's see, what was there here that would make a target? What was there she could pretend was a brother?

She reached up the rolled-up sleeve of her greenbriar shirt and got the loop off the shoulder. She fitted the rock into the pocket of the sling and walked along the riverbank. A large bird flopped just above the water, but Kathy did not want to scare it or hurt it. A long-eared squirbet ran up a tree and chattered at her, bushy tail moving. She could chuck a stone that way, but she wouldn't. She wanted to wait for just the right thing—something she would not frustrate or hurt.

The meer path paralleled the river and was here heavily strewn with stones. She knew that daily the slick, antlered herbivores would come to the river to drink and to cool off. It was too late in the morning for her to meet a bull or a cow here, but then a living target wasn't needed. Just an interesting chip bobbing in the riffles, or a drifting piece of wood such as a log with a viable knot. Anything that would be a little challenging to her skill.

Mom had had the same skill when she was her age and had used it often. Only at her age Mom hadn't been looking for targets to escape spoiled brats. At her age Jon the heroine had faced a dragon and popped it with a rock. What must that have been like! Of course her uncle had always explained that Jon popping the dragon had been the dumbest thing possible; the dragon had been apparently dead, and from atop the drift pile in dragon territory the two young adventurers had looked down on it. No, no, not quite right. It was Mom who had spotted the beast and decided to see if it was alive. Kelvin, then scarcely older than her mother, had been setting up their camp. Jon had done her brave or foolish deed, then both had hidden from the dragon in the flood pile until Kelvin finally worked out a way of slaying it.

She reached down and picked up several stones that seemed shaped for accuracy. How much more interesting life must have been for her mother and uncle. Jon hadn't any younger siblings to torment her and keep her from doing things of importance. Jon had been lucky.

She stepped around a dried meer pat, pushed through some appleberry bushes, and had a clear view of the river. It looked good. Not too high, just about the way it had been the other day. The contours of the banks looked familiar, and those riffles—she'd been in those riffles trying to subdue her prize fish! This was where she and her father and uncle had fished. If she kept going she'd soon be at the exact spot.

She kept going; she could not have said exactly why. She wasn't expecting to see anybody. Not today. Even with the word spread about her spectacular catch the river wasn't easy to travel or reach. Easier by boat, she'd thought, and without children it might have been. Did she hear something like a voice?

She saw a man by the river with his arms outstretched. A woman, a beautiful woman with long, red hair, was coming from the water. The interesting thing about the man was that it was her Uncle Kelvin. The astonishing thing about the woman was that she wasn't wearing a bathing suit or underwear. The woman, whom she had heard speaking to her uncle as she advanced toward him, wasn't, as her mother would have said, decent.

How dare he! How dare her uncle be like this! He to whom she had always looked up! He whom she had always admired! The old fool, though a slimmer, better-conditioned fool, was plainly doing what he shouldn't. Poor Aunt Heln; this could break her heart. Damn men anyway!

Kathy hardly thought. Her sling was in her hand and then it was raised and twirling. There was just enough clearance here for the sling to circle free without catching anything. As it went round and round, the sling whistled.

Which one? Which head? Which cheating person did she hate the most? Her arm hurled, having selected its target.

SPLASH! Water and mud geysered up on the two people now on the bank. Kathy's stone had struck the water at an angle instead of a head. Even the wicked are not to be casually slain.

Her uncle and another looked at her with dirt on their faces. Under the mud, Kelvin's was very red.

"Kathy! Kathy Jon! What are you doing here?"

But her thoughts were not on her uncle. The woman, not even trying to cover herself, was looking at her. The body of the woman was beautiful in every way that a nude woman could be. But her head! In the instant the rock had splashed, the woman's head had become gray-haired instead of flaming red. Her face, smooth and lovely when the stone had been thrown, was now that of a singularly ugly hag!

Kathy swallowed. Her legs felt weak. She wanted to tremble and lie down, but instead she shouted: "It's the witch, Uncle Kelvin! It's the evil witch!"

Kelvin turned pale as the smooth belly of a kittyfish. He was looking into the beautiful body's ugly face, and clearly the sight of it so near his own had an effect on him, an unnerving effect.

"You brat!" the witch cried. "I'll fix you for this! I'll turn you into—something nasty!" She extended her smooth alabaster arms in Kathy's direction. Her ugly old mouth started reciting some ancient spell.

Kathy was horrified. She wanted to strike the creature on the head, hard. Yet her arms and legs felt wooden, as though she could not raise them of her own accord. Barely she could whisper what she intended to be a shout: "Uncle Kelvin, help me!"

Kelvin seemingly did nothing. His right boot raised, carrying his foot in it; raised and stomped. Down, hard, on a perfectly lovely toe.

The old witch mouth screamed. She tried to dance on her right foot and hold her left foot at the same time. She stepped on a bruising stone, toppled, and fell in the river at what was here its deepest part. Her face came up out of the water and it looked mad as well as ugly.

"Zady, I'm sorry, I'm sorry," Kathy's uncle said. Nothing he might have said could have astonished Kathy more.

She found now that she could move. She flung the second stone, striking precisely the center of the witch's forehead. No mercy this time—she intended the stone to kill. The witch fell back with a groan, disappeared beneath the water, but quickly resurfaced. There was a lurid red mark on the forehead where the stone had struck.

Kathy fumbled for another stone. At first her fingers missed getting it, and then they found it, fitted it to her sling. "Kill her, Uncle! Kill her!"

"Kathy, you stop that now!" It was as if he were scolding her for some infraction. "I don't know what you think you're doing, but I want it stopped."

"I'll get you for this!" the hag face promised, then vanished without sinking below the surface. Kathy could see a depression in the water where the beautiful body had been—a trough without motion. She aimed her rock at the place. Her missile struck where she aimed, and bounced. From the waterless area had come a distinct thump, as of rock striking flesh. A moment later the ugliest bird Kathy had ever seen erupted from the spot and shot out of the water, beating its dark wings. The bird, terrible talons extended, flew straight at her face.

Kathy lifted her sling instinctively and swung. The leather

strap wound itself around the warty bird's neck in midflight. The bird somersaulted and fell in a thorny bush, instantly becoming a woman. "I'll get you for this! I'll get you!" the woman screeched.

Then the woman was gone and the bird was once more there. But as Kathy crouched, ready to strike out with every weapon she had, the bird flew off. She watched it as it flew downriver, then abruptly vanished from the sky.

"Whew," Kathy said.

Her uncle said nothing. He merely dropped to the ground as if dead.

CHAPTER 10

Bratlings

*A*lvin finally got his line in the water. He watched the dark green and bright yellow bobber carefully, focusing on its bright yellow stripes. He was ready to get a fish. Ready to get a bigger fish than Kathy Jon. Ready to be hailed "Big Fisherman."

"You got a worm on there?" Teddy asked, moving up beside him.

"Yeah. Haven't you?"

"Hopgrass. I snuck up on it. Didn't crush it much."

"Yeah." Alvin let the current take his bait, paying line out the way his father had shown him. He wished he had behaved better that day. Daddy had gotten so mad at him and his brothers that he had threatened to leave them.

"You know how to get this thing out?"

"Just take the weight in your hand and toss it out. Don't put your line too close to mine. Keep it closer to shore."

"Uh-huh. Where's Kathy?"

"Peeing."

"She must have drunk a lot."

"You know girls."

"Yeah. Here comes Joey."

"Watch him. Don't let him tangle our lines. He's too young to fish."

Joey came carrying his fishing pole and one slightly squashed worm. He had the worm squeezed on the hook but the hook wasn't tied to his line.

"Can you put this on for me?"

"Yeah. Give it here. You can't tie knots yet, can you, dummy?"

"Don't call me that! Give me back my line!"

"I'll fix it for you. You need a weight to get the hook down. And then you need a float. Kathy put them in the lunch basket."

"The lunch basket?"

"That's what I said, dummy. Why don't you clean out your ears?"

"Give me back my line!"

"No, no, I'll help you. Just get the basket."

"Can't."

"Why not?"

"Basket's gone."

"How'd that happen?"

"I made a boat out of it. But I don't know how to tie knots very well. The basket got away."

"You mean you let our lunch float down the river?"

"Uh-huh." Joey looked at the worn toes of his boots. His shoulders slumped, his fist went to his eyes, and he began crying.

"Idiot!" Teddy said.

Joey sniffled.

"I ought to make you go after it!"

"He really should," Alvin said. "Maybe it's hung up on

a snag or something. Joey, you walk along the bank and see if you see the basket. Leave your fishing pole here. Teddy, you better go with him."

"Uh-uh, I'm going to fish."

"Joey, if you see the basket out in the water, don't try to wade for it. Just come on back. You can't fish until you've got all your equipment. Go now, before the basket floats too far."

"You're mean to me!" Joey said. He threw down his pole with an angry motion. His face reddened. He ran bawling away from them.

"Good riddance!" Teddy said.

"Yeah. Now we can really fish. Maybe he'll chase that basket all day."

"I hope we don't lose our hooks."

"Why should we?"

"Snags."

"Don't get snagged."

"Easy to say."

"Yeah." Alvin decided that his line had floated far enough. He'd gotten so interested in listening to his brothers that he hadn't paid full attention. Most of his line was now in the river.

He wound in the line, the butt of the pole hard against his stomach. Out in the water the distant float started coming home to him; then it disappeared.

"Damn!" Alvin said, using a word he wasn't allowed to use at home. "Snag."

"Told you."

Alvin twitched the line. The line began moving out.

"You've got a fish, dummy!"

"I know it, dummy. Get out of my way!"

"I'm not in your way."

"You will be. Get your line out of the water."

"I want to fish."

"You can after I land this one."

"You aren't going to. It'll get away."

"Shut up! Do as I tell you!"

"You're not Dad!"

"Hurry up! If I lose this one I'll drown you."

Reluctantly, and very slowly it seemed, Alvin's contrary brother wound all his line. He carried the pole a little distance and laid it down on the bank. In the meantime Alvin had a tight hold on his pole and was straining for all he was worth. The fish made the pole bend and bend and bend until its tip almost touched the water. Hurriedly Alvin let loose of his death grip on the line.

Alvin's line shot out, faster than the current. Soon there would be a loud snap and that would be the end of it. Alvin looked around frantically, saw no help in sight. "Kathy!" he called.

His sister did not come running. Running! That was the answer. Taking a firm grip on the pole with both hands Alvin tried running along the bank. If he didn't fall down and the fish didn't get off, he might catch it in time.

"Line's all out?" Teddy called as he passed him.

"Almost. Come help!"

"I'm coming! I'm coming!"

Alvin took the longest strides he could manage. The fish was now pulling him along, having come to the end of the line. Whatever it was, it was a big one. Alvin could think of nothing else but holding on to the pole and running hard as he could go. His eyes blurred, but he couldn't take time to wipe them.

"Alvin, watch out, you're going to—"

He felt something hit his ankle and then he was down. The pole pulled from his fingers and went skidding and sliding through the sand and the mud.

"Teddy! Get that!" Alvin cried.

Teddy threw himself belly down on the pole and grabbed it with both hands. The line tautened, cut through some weeds, and snapped. Out in the water a great fish splashed.

Alvin looked downriver, trying to see something. He pounded a fist on the sand, striking a burr into his hand. The burr bit deep and he howled.

"It wasn't my fault!" Teddy protested.

"Was too."

"Was not!"

"Shut up, I want to swear."

"Swear a good one, Alvin. Swear some for me."

"Damn! Double damn! Triple and more damn!"

"Me too," his brother said, awed by the forbidden power of the outburst.

Alvin wished his education was more complete. There had to be a worse curse that wasn't actually magical. He searched his memory and came up with something. "Mouvar on a picnic!"

"Geeee," Teddy said, even more impressed.

Alvin sat up, pulled the stickleburr from his hand, and rubbed the bleeding, smarting place against his pant leg. He had done his duty now, he felt. He walked over to Teddy.

"You can't fish now," Teddy said.

"Why can't I?"

"No equipment."

"Uh-oh." He reached in his rear pocket and pulled out a small round box of metal. He took the lid off and there were the hooks. "Gee, Alvin." Teddy's eyes were wide. "I didn't know you had those."

Alvin reached into his shirt pocket and brought out a spool of extra line. Then back into the pocket that had held the hooks, and he had a small bag of lead weights with the copper eyelets on them. Finally, into his left front pocket for a green and yellow float.

"Gee, Alvin, you thought of everything. But I told Joey they were in the basket."

"They were once. What Joey doesn't know won't hurt him, will it?"

Pleased with his foresight but not his luck, Alvin set to work fishing and trying to think up another really powerful curse.

Joey was panting and crying and stumbling as he ran. He'd spotted the basket caught in some riffles, but then as he got close it slipped off a rock and whirled down the river. It rode out the rapids and then was in the deep, and Joey, who could not yet swim, could only run after it.

If I get the basket they won't be so mad at me, he thought. He had been thinking that ever since he first spied the basket caught on an overhanging branch. He had crawled out on the branch, fallen in, but held on while the basket went floating on its way. Now muddy from head to toe, soaked to the skin, scratched from bushes and weeds and with stickleburrs in his hair, Joey was desperate. He had never tried so hard to do anything, or failed so many times in a row. He wished he knew magic. With magic he would get the basket, get cleaned, and get home. Let his dumb brothers and sister stay and fish if they wanted—there weren't any fish anyway. Joey wanted home, way home, and his mama and the warm bath and dinner she would have for him. Thinking of the dinner he was missing and fresh corbeans in the pod made him want to cry all the more. But Joey knew that he was a man and that men weren't supposed to cry.

He stopped running to sit and pant on a tree root, then got up, wiped his eyes, and looked downstream for the basket. It was bobbing way ahead, maybe caught in some riffles. He had to start running, but his sides ached and his scratches hurt. He wished he had Alvin to swear for him—Alvin swore so beautifully.

Flop! Flop! Flop!

Joey raised his eyes to the skies. It was a bird flying high above the river, and it was just about the ugliest if not quite the biggest bird he had ever seen. It lowered its height as it neared, then passed him on the bank, and speeding its wing-beats, caught up with the basket.

"No! No, bird, no!" Joey cried, but the ugly feathered creature was dropping from the sky. It lit on the upright handle of the basket, then shot back into the sky carrying it. Joey's mouth opened. He had never imagined this happening.

Instead of flying off with its prize, the big bird made a half-circle and started back the way it had come. Maybe it had young birds to feed. Maybe it was just tormenting him the way his brothers liked to do. Joey shook a fist at it: "Bad bird! Bad bird! You give that back!"

To his astonishment the bird swerved directly toward

him. Almost skimming the water with the basket, it flopped over to shore and dropped all the way down until it and the basket were hardly a jump in front of him. The basket settled to the sand. The bird opened its beak, squawked, and hopped off the handle.

Joey opened and closed his mouth. "It's all right, bird, you can keep the basket. I'm sorry I shook my fist at you. I'm just a little boy. Please don't eat me. You don't eat little boys, do you?"

The big bird opened and closed its beak. Joey was reminded of what he had just done. "Well, you don't have to be insulting about it!"

The bird blurred before his eyes, changing to a thick, dark smoke. The smoke roiled and came together and disappeared. In place of the bird there was now a woman who had no clothes on. The woman had everything that Mama had but hers was more smooth and firmed and tight. Joey could imagine what Daddy would say. Then he looked above the rosy-tipped breasts and the smooth, milk-white throat. Her face shocked him. The face was old, and ugly, with wrinkles and lines streaked with what seemed to be handfuls of grease and dirt. The woman's eyes were yellow and rheumy and unpleasant.

"Were you the bird?" Joey felt strange asking it, and also fearful.

"Yes, darling boy, I was that bird." She reached out a hand to him—a beautiful, smooth hand unlike his mother's. Clearly this person never had washed dishes and labored at scrubbing floors.

Joey backed up a step.

"I won't hurt you," the croaking voice said. It was just such a voice as the bird would have had.

"I—I don't like your face."

"Oh, bother! Here!" There was a poof of smoke around her, and when the smoke cleared Joey saw the woman had a face as lovely, if not lovelier, than his mother's. Not only was her skin smooth and white, but her hair was a really pretty red and fell down to her shoulders and full round breasts. Her eyes

were greenish—greener than he had thought human eyes
could be. Now she was beautiful; now she should be nice.

The face smiled, making Joey know she was nice. The
hand reached his shoulder, patted it, touched his hair, and
stroked his cheeks in the way his grandma did.

"You have the basket." Her voice, too, was now smooth
and soft and pretty. "I brought it back for you. The river
didn't want you to have it."

"Y-yes. B-but the food will be spoiled."

"Look at it."

Hesitantly he walked over to the basket. Though it had
been in the river it appeared to be dry. He reached out to it and
opened the lid. Delicious aromas rose from the basket's inte-
rior. Inside, and he could hardly accept this, was a lunch such
as his sister and mother had surely not prepared: whole
roasted chicucks, their wings crisp and brown; dark and light,
pink and red cooakes; covered dishes of several kinds; even a
bottle of what appeared to be a dark red wine.

Joey swallowed. "It's the wrong basket."

"No, dear boy. It's yours. Yours after a little magic."

"You want me to take it?"

"It's yours."

"But—"

"Don't you think your brothers will be happy when you
take this to them?"

"Y-yes."

"There's enough food here for a very good picnic. Can
you lift the basket?"

Joey tried. He strained and strained but the basket remained grounded. How could it have floated?

"I will carry your basket. I will be your guest."

Joey swallowed. "My brothers—"

"Oh yes, mustn't shock them." The smooth hands made
a butterfly ripple. Smoke puffed and cleared, revealing gradually a beautiful red gown. The material of the gown was what
Joey had learned was "satiny," and it seemed to him that every
part of her was not so much covered as drenched in the color
red. As the wisps of smoke vanished he still saw her milk-white

breasts; the gown came up to them, but the nipples were now barely covered with the wonderful red.

Joey looked at the contours and wondered what was hidden, or if anything was supposed to be. He wasn't much interested in what the woman had, except for the picnic basket.

"Take my hand, Joey."

He did, and it was cool, almost clammy, in fact. He was going to ask her why, but with the other hand she made a gesture.

Smoke puffed around them but did not get in Joey's nose or eyes. The smoke cleared and there were his brothers, both with glum expressions, holding on to their fishing poles. They looked up, saw them, and their mouths opened as Joey's had recently done.

"I brought us the basket and a picnic," Joey said. "She got it for me. Her name's—" What was her name, anyway?

"Shady," the beautiful red-gowned creature said. "Shady as in shady under the trees when the sun is beating down on you. Shady, cool and comforting."

Joey thought it a nice name, but somehow it reminded him of another. He was just about to say when he saw her sprinkling a sparkling powder from her fingertips. The powder went to his face and his brothers' faces; then it vanished and everything was very pretty and very right.

Looking at his brothers' smiling faces Joey knew how it would be: in Shady they had a grown-up who, unlike most, was a generous and good friend.

CHAPTER 11

Family Connections

Kelvin opened his eyes and saw a really beautiful girl. She was young, fresh, pretty—everything a young man could want. She was leaning over him where he lay on the ground. Her face was so close to his that he didn't even think about his actions; he simply lifted his head and pressed his lips up against the girl's lips, kissing her.

A moment later the young girl was standing back, color drained from her cheeks, the pointed tips of her ears red with embarrassment. When she spoke it was with shock: "Uncle Hackleberry, how could you!"

"What? What?" In a moment it came to him who she was. She was Kathy Jon, his niece. He got to his feet, knowing himself for an old man.

"I found you here with that—that woman. No, that witch! She was naked and you were going to—going to—"

"Oh, gods!" It came back to him in a rush, bringing a headache. "I was—I was bewitched."

"Of course you were. You had to have been."

"I didn't know who you were just now. I didn't even know who I was. There was this pretty girl's face almost touching mine, and—"

"Pretty?" Kathy seemed genuinely surprised at the notion. "You think I'm pretty?"

"Everyone does. You're as pretty as any girl I've ever seen, and not just in the face."

Kathy's entire head and neck flushed. She still seemed puzzled but pleased. "You—you really think that?"

"I said it, didn't I? Would your uncle lie to you?"

"Pretty as that, that—you know?"

"Pretty as Zady? You saw her face."

"Pretty as her when she hadn't her own face? When she seemed all beautiful . . . all over?"

Kelvin hesitated. He didn't want to lie to his sister's child. To tell her that her beauty was human and Zady's not human might not be right. On the other hand to say she was just as pretty could cause trouble. She was, after all, only fourteen. Whatever he said, it had to be appropriate.

"Zady's a seductress, Kathy."

"And a witch."

"Right. So there's really no proper comparison between the two of you."

"Evil. You mean she's evil."

"And you are good."

"Oh, I wouldn't want to be like her!" But it was evident that she was flushed with the compliments to her appearance and her nature. "I'm sorry I thought—I know you would never—not with an evil witch—"

He hesitated. He wasn't certain any longer. Had his niece not appeared when she had, he didn't know what might have happened. He didn't think that he would betray Heln, and yet—

Yet here was his lovely, attentive, and impressionable niece, and somehow he wanted to— No! How could he even think such a thing?

"You look sick, Uncle."

"The, eh, spell." Was he lying? He couldn't have said.

"Maybe you'd better sit down. Gather your strength."

"Yes, yes, I'd better."

He sat down on the bank and Kathy slowly moved over and sat down beside him, close.

She reached over and trustingly patted his hand. It was almost motherly but awoke thoughts that he didn't the least want to have. *Think different!* he told himself. *Talk about something!*

"Kathy, how did you happen to be here?"

"Fishing. I found out about the new boat rentals and my rotten little brothers pestered me to take them. Mother said 'Go, get them out of the house!' She was getting back at me. She knew how they'd act."

"Boys will be boys," he said automatically. As a girl his sister Jon had been the most boisterous boy-child imaginable; he wondered if Kathy knew that. "You didn't drown them, did you?"

"No, though believe me I felt like it! They simply would not mind me, and I don't know which of them was worse. Teddy threw rocks in the water, Alvin ruined the bait and lunch, Joey wouldn't mind me on anything—"

"Typical," Kelvin said.

"Typical brats."

"Boys just don't mind their sisters. They have to try bossing them and making themselves feel superior."

"You've got that right, Unc. Mom always said the same thing."

That's where I heard it, Kelvin thought. He knew that part of it had come to her by way of St. Helens when he was talking about Earth's women's liberation movement to help instill a bit of self-confidence in Heln.

"Where are the boys?"

"Back a way. I left them to fish or eat what there was left to eat, or fight or do whatever they wanted. I was going back."

"Just had to get away from them, eh? Reminds me of the children's suite at that grand hotel at the Benign Witches and Warlocks Convention. The witches and warlocks left their offspring there, as did Heln and I, but ours got into trouble."

"But yours were telepaths, and it was all that old witch's fault."

"Yes," he said reminiscently. "Though they should have known better. Of course the twin kings were there too. They all should have known better."

A flydragon the size of Kathy's hand buzzed in front of Kelvin, reminding him of the giant flydragons those offspring and the kings had encountered in Rotternik. One sign of growing old, he supposed, was this constant remembering.

"I suppose you should be getting back. To see that they haven't drowned or something. I should walk back with you."

"Unc, how did you ever get here?"

He showed her the boots. With their bright sheen they might easily have just been made. The mud and the sand didn't in the least put a mark on them.

"Uncle Kelvin, I always wanted to see those boots! They're famous."

He was foolishly flattered, knowing that the merit of the boots was their own, owing nothing to him. Yet there was something about the interest of a pretty girl that dulled this distinction. "You can see them now."

"Could you? Could you show me?"

"Certainly. See that tree on the other bank?"

"Yes."

"Watch." Kelvin thought he'd like to be standing by the tree under the big branch. He took a step and the river blurred to his eyesight, and then he was standing there under the big tree limb. He miscalculated and struck his head a resounding crack.

"Ouch!" he said, holding his forehead where the limb had struck. That's what he got for trying to show off! He turned around and waved at his niece across the river. Then he stepped back.

"Uncle, that's the most incredible thing I ever saw!" she exclaimed, her bosom heaving. "Even when Zady made her face beautiful or turned herself into a bird it was less amazing. Why haven't you been wearing them?"

Kelvin rubbed the bruise on his brow. "Maybe because they can be dangerous. Maybe because I thought I was keeping them for a purpose."

"Yes, to fight Zady with. They did a nice job stomping her toe."

"I didn't think at them to do that," Kelvin said, and the thought bothered him.

"Well, it worked! Saved me from that spell she was casting. Oh, Uncle, I'm so grateful!"

"Uh," he said, trying to suppress forbidden thoughts. What was the matter with him? "Shouldn't we get back?"

"Uncle, I'd like to try those boots. Put them on and step in them. I know they adjust to any foot just as the gauntlets adjust to every hand."

Kelvin hesitated. He wanted to please her, but distrusted his own motive. "What would you—"

"I just want to try them," she said, in a wheedling manner that seemed to come naturally to the female species. "Just to the top of that rock."

Kelvin looked at the great, flat river boulder. It would give her delight, he thought. What was the harm? She was such a nice girl. Let her have her thrill; then they could go home. He pulled off both boots and handed them to her.

"Thanks, Unc." She slipped off her own thick-soled farming boots and pulled on the Mouvar boots with ease. He could see her wriggling her toes under the soft leather, smiling. "Here I go!"

She stepped, and the step carried her all the distance. She waved from the rock. "Now I'm going to check on my brothers."

"No, no, don't! You have to think very carefully, and—"

Abruptly she had stepped. Her stride took her up, up, over the treetops and, he supposed, to wherever it was she had left the boys.

That's what he got for his foolishness. He had allowed himself to forget that the girl was a tomboy like his sister of yore, in her mind, and eager for adventure.

Kelvin stood up, stepped on a stickleburr, danced, tripped over a tree root, and fell on his back. And he had allowed himself to forget that he was a blundering old man!

He hoped Kathy Jon was less clumsy this morning than he.

Kathy held the thought of the spot where the boys had been searching for bait. In no more time than it took to take a normal stride she was putting her foot down precisely where she had visualized. There was no perceptible jar to her foot and ankle. She had taken one step and moved far upstream.

The rocks were the ones the boys had been moving in search of daycrawlers, the big version of the fishing worms. The boat was downhill, tied up to the tree as she had left it. The boys were nowhere in sight. Now where would they go? Possibly they were fishing from the riverbank. That high hill—she could see much from up there.

She took her second step since leaving her uncle, and the scenery changed. She stood on a rock outcropping high above the river bend. She looked down, dizzy, and searched the banks. There they were! But who was that with them?

Two more steps and she was on the hillside behind them. Quickly she darted around a tree and then looked down at them. She had to slip closer. There was another tree ahead, behind which she would be concealed and could look out and see. She stepped.

"Hoo hoo, Alvin!" Teddy's voice, but overly boisterous. "You ain't ever going to get that down!"

"Will too!" Alvin insisted.

Kathy frowned in incomprehension. She knew those sandwiches would all have been gone by now, given the natural order of things. She looked between branches and saw her two oldest brothers munching on full-sized roasted chicucks. Both had very red faces and between Alvin's knees was what seemed to be a wine bottle.

Kathy felt properly shocked. Those little boys, drinking wine! Mom would never allow it. And where was Joey and that other person she had seen? Maybe she'd better go back to her uncle. Uncle Kelvin was, after all, the hero of the family.

"Shady, Shady, you can't get me!" Joey sing-sang, running and looking over his shoulder. In a moment a woman in a red gown, far too flimsy to be worn in the woods, emerged from behind another tree. The woman grabbed Joey, lifted him high, twirled him. As she twirled her long red hair flew in a cloud around her face, tickling Joey's nose and ears.

Kathy gasped. It was Zady, as she had seen her with her Uncle Kelvin. Did she dare challenge her again? Last time she had been lucky, but now she had the boots. What should she do? Go over there and kick the creature? Lob more stones at the witch? Could she be fast enough to avoid Zady's spells?

"Oh, come, Kathy Jon," the beautiful woman called, spying her. "You can see I'm not hurting anyone. I'm doing no harm."

Kathy swallowed. "You gave my brothers wine."

"So? Good for their little stomachs. Besides, with a snap of my fingers I can clear all three of their heads."

"You said you'd get me. Back there with my uncle."

"And I will, but in my own wicked time. Don't wish that my revenge be hurried—you won't like it when it arrives."

Such candor was unsettling! "But you plan no immediate harm?"

"No."

"I can get my uncle."

"Do that. I haven't given up on him."

Kathy took a step. She was back with Kelvin. Kelvin was massaging a foot, and she suspected he had been saying things he wouldn't have wanted her to hear.

"Uncle Kelvin, she's with them. The witch. Zady. She's with my brothers."

Kelvin looked startled. "What's she doing?"

"She fed them. She gave them wine."

"I don't know that I like that. Boys their age shouldn't have wine." He shrugged. "Still—"

"Uncle Kelvin!" she exclaimed, shocked.

"She's not hurting them, is she?"

"No, but she might. Get moving! You're a hero, for gods' sake!"

"Don't swear, Kathy. Give me the boots."

"I want to go with you. I want you to carry me."

"I will. The boots."

Kathy took them off and handed them to him. He put them on and stood up as she put her feet back into her own boots. They seemed much less satisfactory than they had before she tried the magic ones.

"You want to play piggyback?" He bent over.

She climbed aboard his back, grasping his shoulders, her thighs clasping his middle. She realized that she was no longer a child; this would now be improper, were it not for special circumstances.

"Uh, Kathy, where do I go?"

"It's not really far. There's this big tree where the boat is tied and—"

Kelvin stepped across the river, carrying her. He had picked a spot not out of his line of sight. Immediately he stepped again, further back and on the side of the river where she had found him. Four more steps and they were by the boat and then by the boys and the now—only temporarily, Kathy thought—beautiful Zady.

Kelvin looked and looked at Zady's dress as Kathy slid from his back. He seemed under her spell again. Maybe she should have left him back there or not gone for him at all. Unfortunately he still had the boots, and all she had, should a fight develop, was the weapon her mother had used to help destroy Zoanna. Kathy knew that the sling was a tool and a weapon in their hands, but facing Zady she would rather have had a crossbow or a sword.

"Hello, Kelvin," Zady said. Her barely covered breasts bounced as she took a step and turned toward him.

Kelvin actually blushed. He seemed more like one of the boys than her middle-aged uncle. Truly, it must be a love spell the witch had cast. Maybe it made him react to any young woman. After all, he had even kissed her, Kathy. A generalized spell would account for the trouble he had gotten into after the long-awaited wedding declarations at the twin palaces.

"Zady, my niece told me where you'd gone. I'm sorry she was so rude to you back there."

Rude! What about Zady? What about the way they had been acting? She'd saved the old fool, that was what she had done! Now she was coming to understand what was meant by love being blind.

"Unwise children eventually get punished," Zady said. Her mouth was that of a temptress, her voice soft and caressing. She might have been speaking of being unclothed with Kathy's uncle. Maybe she was, on another level.

"Zady!" Joey piped. "I thought you said your name's Shady."

"A mild deception, little lad."

"But—"

Long white fingers made a motion. Joey opened his mouth, looked surprised, and grasped his throat. Clearly the boy could now not speak.

Kelvin took no notice. His eyes were locked with the eyes of the temptress, and not with the appearance of hate.

"It was nice of you to feed them, Zady. Boys need nourishment."

"As do girls. Not all of one kind."

Kelvin stubbed his toe on the ground. He acted just like Will Shranks, the dumbest boy in school—the one always trying to look up some girl's dress. That was one reason Kathy preferred shorts or boys' pantaloons. Now Kelvin was wilting like a summer weed, ready to fall into Zady's arms.

Kathy wondered about her best course. The boots had helped before, but this time the witch might be aware that he wore them and be prepared to counter. A rock in the water and one to the head had worked before; could they again? Kathy tried easing her sling down from her shoulder and into her hand. Throwing stone. Throwing stone. She at least needed ammunition.

"What are you looking for there on the ground, as if I don't know?" the witch asked her. Her voice was soft, but there was a hint of old-crone meanness in it.

Kathy desisted. If that smooth arm came up to make a magical sign, she'd swat it with the sling. A futile gesture it might be, but maybe it would delay the witch and snap Kelvin to his senses.

"Oh, now, Kathy," Kelvin said, "you're not going to start that again!"

"I'm not going to start anything, Uncle," she said with an innocence every bit as feigned as that of the witch. "It's already started."

"You mean the past. But she's changed. Can't you see that?"

"You've changed, Uncle. You're under the same spell that Zoanna cast on Grandpa. You're being just as big a fool now as he was back then."

"Don't," Zady said, making it a hiss, "take Zoanna's name in vain! She was the rightful ruler of Rud before this upstart—"

Kelvin's expression changed. It was as though icy cold water had been thrown on him. Was he thinking now about being tormented atop that cliff? In a mental flash was he seeing his daughter Merlain, then the age of Joey, walking to what should have been her death by falling?

"ZADY!" Kelvin cried out. As a madman might he lashed out at her with an open hand. He struck her chest right where the nipples stretched the fabric. Zady went down, falling backwards over Joey. Joey grunted; the boy had been crawling on the ground, searching for something probably imaginary.

Kathy grabbed Zady's right arm, determined she would make no gestures. It was hard to hold. The witch's strength was that of a strong horse. Kelvin grabbed the left arm as well. The witch's head changed, becoming hideous with its warts and filth.

"A sword," Kathy heard Kelvin whisper desperately. "Oh Mouvar, do I ever need a sword!"

CHAPTER 12

Aborted Plans

*P*rofessor Devale scowled at the scene in the crystal: Zady, with beautiful new body, being held down by Kelvin. To the side of the struggling pair, the young girl held Zady's arm with all her weight and strength. The young boys, well confused with magic-spiced wine, stood with open mouths, unable, even if they had been older, to take sides. Zady's ugly face, now so much like that of a wrinkled snake's, raised on her strong, young neck. The ugly old head struck like a snake, sinking sharp and hideously yellow fangs into Kelvin's hand. Kelvin screamed with pain as blood welled from the hand, but held on.

"Well, at least he's not wearing those gauntlets!" Professor Devale remarked.

But he was wearing the boots. Propelled by necessity, programmed as they were to protect the host, they slammed one of Kelvin's knees into the witch's groin and at the same time punched the other knee hard into her stomach. Zady vomited, having been caught unprepared.

"Smart, Zady, smart! Let them get the better of you! I knew you were unwise when you tried corrupting them! Nice try, but pitifully performed."

The young girl was screaming and lashing Zady with a strap. She knelt on Zady's arm and held with her left, meanwhile bringing the sling up and down in a frenzy. Zady rolled her head from side to side, having given up for the time being on biting.

"An engaging show, but really, magic is supposed to do

more than entertain. What have Kelvin and the girl got, anyway? Nothing but those silly boots." However, Devale did note that the young girl was pretty. There was something about beauty when it was innocent that even the most practiced illusion could not match.

Zady transformed into a serpent and threw Kelvin from side to side as he held on to her. She tried getting past the flailing sling to bite the girl, but the boots did not let her. Something about Kelvin's position changed, starting with his legs, and he was able to just grab the back of the head. The snake opened its mouth, revealing large, dripping fangs. Kelvin must have got a breath that dizzied him, but he pushed the head back, held on, and strained.

"I didn't know you had it in you, Kelvin. Of all the heroes Mouvar ever picked you have to be the least. But courage—I'll grant you have courage."

Zady became Zady the beautiful, complete with sensuous lips and a skin that was alabaster white. Her eyes rolled back. Her tongue protruded. Her lips begged, and Devale didn't need to hear in order to know that they also promised. Still Kelvin squeezed and held on.

"Oh, spare me! Zady, you must know that that pity-me bit won't work, even on Kelvin. He's wrestled you before."

Zady transformed again. Now she was the big, ugly bird that could either fight or flee effectively. Her beak snapped near his face, but Kelvin held the feathered throat. Her talons tried to rake and geld him, and would have except for the boots. Ever alert, the boots brought his knees down with magical strength that jarred his entire frame; the knees pinned the talons, preventing their reaching their objective. The girl had her weight on the right wing of the big bird, pressing down hard, right arm beating her with the strap. The bird shrieked, trying to use her left wing to beat Kelvin, but his right shoulder and blood-smeared right arm pressed below the wing joint.

"You might as well desist, Zady. Mouvar's hero and his helper have you pinned. Keep up the farce and one of the little boys will eventually think to bring a knife and cut your head off. Twenty years, Zady, and you haven't learned a thing!"

Kelvin forced the ugly bird's head back on its scrawny neck. The bird's eyes rolled back. Its tongue protruded. It squawked. The *CRACK* sounded loud through the crystal.

The bird's head drooped back; to all appearances it was dead.

"Just think of what he could have done if he'd worn his gauntlets! They would never be fooled into thinking that supple bird's neck could break. But don't worry, Zady, I don't think he's smart enough. He's letting go, the fool! He's trying to get up but the boots are resisting him. Get out of this yourself—I've interfered enough."

Zady became Zady, made a superhuman effort, pulled free, and leaped up. Kelvin made a grab for her and the girl swung her strap at her, but again she was the bird. She snapped her ugly beak, shot into the air, and flapped her wings.

Before Kelvin and the girl could fully react she was circling them. She dropped a dropping in Kelvin's face, mockingly fluffed her rump at them, and started to fly away.

That was a mistake. The girl moved like lightning. The rock hurled from the sling caught Zady's avian rump and sent feathers flying. The creature plummeted from the sky, then splashed.

The bird disappeared. Zady's ugly human head appeared on the surface and her arm raised a fist and shook it at the shore. As they watched she vanished from the water. She did not reappear.

"Zady, with that clumsy performance you've set magic back at least a thousand years! I know you'll be back here begging me to help you more. What a pitiful excuse for a playing piece! I don't know whether Mouvar or I picked worse!!"

Zady was back in Professor Devale's office at the university in record time. She'd flown directly to the ruins of the former Rud palace, along the underground river to the correct spot, and had dived, still in bird form. Standing dripping naked in his study she was all ruffled feathers, though now in her human form.

"Professor Devale, you just have to—"

"You're incompetent. In fact you're a disgrace!" Attack was best with her kind.

"I was trying to corrupt them. I was doing fine until that niece interfered."

"You didn't take precautions. If you were going to seduce the lout you should have taken him to an isolated mountain. And how stupid to let him wear the boots. Wasn't one defeat by boots enough?"

"I didn't know he had them! I thought he'd flown."

"Flown? Like a bird? You think he's a warlock?"

"I . . . forgot. I'm so accustomed to changing to bird form myself that I forgot he couldn't. Besides, he could have ridden a horse or walked. He could have had his flying belt. Or for that matter, a boat."

"It's a pity you weren't smart enough to find out."

"Why? Once I had the attraction magic going full strength I knew he'd get there. I could have waited for days."

"But you didn't. That should have suggested something to you. Haven't you crystals and powers that work?"

"Mine work. I just don't use them."

"Why not?"

The rheumy eyes looked at his carpet, the red spots draining from her sagging cheeks.

"I say you were stupid and incompetent. The lowliest apprentice could have handled a seduction."

"After his niece interfered I thought it would be fun to corrupt his entire family. I wanted to get to him through them and make him think he's an ally."

"You really thought it could work?"

"I thought it would be fun."

"It wasn't, was it?"

"It could have been."

Devale shook his head negatively and raised his right hand to polish his right shiny horn. "Zady, Zady, Zady," he lectured, "you are such a disappointment to me. You had every opportunity to use your magic training and your brain, but instead you let emotion take control of you."

"How's that?"

"Don't be coy and dumb at the same time." Exasperated, Professor Devale snapped a finger and sent a fine pink powder expanding into a cloud. In the heart of the cloud Kathy Jon Crumb was facing the seductress and her uncle. Kelvin had just suggested that Zady had changed. In reply the girl berated him.

"You've changed, Uncle. You're under the same spell that Zoanna cast on Grandpa. You're being just as big a fool now as he was back then."

"Don't," Zady said, making it a hiss, "take Zoanna's name in vain! She was the rightful ruler of Rud before this upstart—"

The professor snapped his fingers again and made the cloud vanish from his study. Left were only a few wisps of pinkish smoke that rapidly disappeared.

"Now wasn't that smart. You, a witch of centuries of experience, supposedly the strongest witch around, and you let this mere girl-child trick you. Oh, she didn't know she was tricking you, but you should have known. You probably said the one thing that would enable Mouvar's hero to break an attraction spell. How did you think he'd react after you mentioned Zoanna and his father and called her the rightful ruler of Rud? Then, as if that wasn't enough, you called him an upstart. That was dumb of you."

"He was an upstart!"

"Of course, but that hardly suggests that you have changed. You were right at the point of berating him for everything he had done, and you would have if he hadn't broken the spell. How do you explain that?"

"Helbah gave him some protective conditioning."

"And you never thought of that, did you?"

The beautiful body hung its ugly head. Slowly a tear leaked out the right rheumy eye, acknowledging his accuracy.

"I wanted so badly to corrupt them," she sniffed. "The children are young enough to be turned bad. I could have recruited them, gotten Kelvin to turn against his children, to leave his wife. Maybe I could have had him kill Helbah for me; possibly even Mouvar."

"Now on that last you're dreaming. I'm not saying it wouldn't be pleasing to me if it were possible. But Mouvar and I are harder to kill than mere witches and warlocks. There's a way, but not for you to know and not to be used by Kelvin."

"He could work against him, at least."

"Oh yes, if you had properly seduced and corrupted him. Witches aren't supposed to lose their faculties and grow senile, but I fear that you have. Therefore I think I'll get a replacement for you from among my brightest students. As for you, I'll just wave you out of existence, and—"

"No, no, no!" Zady was plainly scared now. "I'll do your bidding. I always have done your bidding and I'll do it now. Give me a chance to serve you and I swear I will not fail!"

"Why should I?"

She indicated her body, nude and glistening. Her smile suggested things that only she would think to offer.

"That's getting a little thin, you know."

Her body immediately became buxom, with valleys and depths that hadn't been there. Her gesture indicated what she had done and invited him to explore.

"I didn't mean your body needed upholstering. That slender niece of his is just as appealing, partly because she doesn't know it." Though it was sort of interesting the way Zady's breasts had become near-udders and her lower parts grosser and more tantalizingly haired. Firm and smooth was arousing, but fuller and grosser was inflaming to his senses. Still, he had to be stern with her or she'd assume that he was no more than a warlock with oversized glands.

She gave him a look. It suggested that he would be foolish to deprive himself, as very possibly he would.

"All right, I'll give you another chance. But you'd better not come whining to me again. This time I want results!"

Instantly her warm pillowy arms were about him, her eager body smothering his in flesh. Her superior weight bore him down, and he let her, only signing as they dropped, converting the desk with its books and papers into a soft, open bed.

Zady might not be a whiz in modern necromancy, but in the more ancient magic she was superb!

Kelvin rowed the boat. His niece watched him from her seat in the bow. His nephews lay like three veterans of dissipation nursing man-sized hangovers.

"I could kill her for what she did to them!" he swore.

"You will someday."

"Yes, if Helbah's right I suppose I'll have to."

"They're not really hurt, are they? I mean they're just sleeping." She indicated the three bodies in the bottom of the boat.

"Helbah will know if they've been poisoned with some foul substance. I think it's just the wine."

"She seemed so nice, they said. I really think she was trying to make them like her."

"Yes, the way she tried with Merlain and Charles when they were kids. She almost succeeded with them, too, and would have if it hadn't been for Helbah."

"I know the entire story, Uncle Kelvin. You've told it so many times."

"Yes, yes, I know I have. I've been living in the past. I have to get over that."

"Living in the past?" Kathy seemed puzzled.

"Sort of thing my father says. He's never forgotten Earth expressions and I've adopted most of them."

"Like 'hell' and 'damn,' as St. Helens says."

"A little like that, only those are swear words."

"Oh. You know this Yokes who has the new boat rentals?"

"I think I knew his grandpa. The old man got us boats whenever we went to use the transporter; he helped Jon once."

"I know," Kathy said in a weary way. "Mom is going to be surprised at how early we've come home."

"Will she? I thought she knew your brothers."

Kathy smiled. "Maybe we should give them wine to drink more often. I never saw them so good."

At her words, seemingly propelled by them, Alvin sat up, hung his head over the gunnel, and heaved up all he had eaten and drunk. He made disgusting vomiting sounds.

"That's why not," Kelvin said, nodding. "One of the reasons."

"Ohhh, I'll never trust a witch again!"

"Tough, Alvin, but you'll have to trust one witch: Helbah."

"Helbah never gave me wine."

"And she won't. Nor will I or your mother or sister."

"Dad might," Teddy said, not stirring from the floorboards.

"He won't either," his sister said.

"Why? I'm not sick," Teddy bragged.

"You will be when you get home."

Kelvin looked down at Joey, sleeping like the proverbial lamb in his father's expressions, then maneuvered the boat into the pier. The young man with the boathook didn't look a thing like the Yokes Kelvin remembered, but the old man had been old when Jon first met him, and this was the old man's grandson.

"Why, you're the Roundear!"

"These are my sister's children."

"And you spent the day with them! You really are a hero!"

Kelvin found himself whispering "Drop dead" under his breath, another of his father's Earth expressions. He helped his niece clear out the boat, putting first the tackle and then the boys on the dock. He helped her up, got up himself, and felt, despite his new streamlined form, weary as he had seldom been.

"You anxious to get home, Kathy?"

"Yes!"

"So am I. Suppose I carry you and the boys to your place and then I step home to mine?"

"You mean—"

"Of course."

He picked up Joey, thought of the Crumb cottage and where he wanted to step there, and stepped. The fields and the roads blurred by. Joey, who was now very wild-eyed, voiced his astonishment as Kelvin put him down. Kelvin waved at his sister coming out the door, stepped back, got suddenly miserable young Teddy, stepped back, and got Alvin, who seemed less miserable now that he had been properly sick. He made another two trips with fishing tackle. For his final trip he picked up Kathy Jon, hugging her to him like a daughter. But she was not his daughter, and she was no longer any child, as he had become aware recently. She was a good and lovely young woman. She had saved his unworthy and most unheroic hide this day, and he could never repay her, badly as he wanted to. He took the step, and was beside his sister's house for the last time. Now Jon was inside, getting her sons in order.

"Thank you so much, Uncle," Kathy breathed, and kissed him on his cheek.

"Don't do that!" he exclaimed, embarrassed.

"I'm only play-acting," she said, hurt.

Should he explain? No, she would catch on soon enough on her own, if she hadn't already. Then he thought of something else. "Kathy, were you at my house, in my room this morning? With the stuffed fish?"

Her mouth dropped open. "I dreamed I was, Uncle! How did you know?"

She had dreamed it, but had not done it. So that, too, was the mischief of the witch. "I dreamed it too," he said.

Then his sister appeared. Kelvin fended off Jon's invitation to come inside, and stepped home.

Heln was there at the door before he could open it. Before she could speak, he did. "Heln, whatever I did last night, I'm sorry. I beg you to forgive me. I'm sure I was an awful fool."

Her eyes widened. "You really *don't* remember!"

"I really don't. But I've been under an evil enchant—"

"It's all right, Kelvin. I've had time to cool down. I must

admit it was sort of funny when she sailed up in the air like that, screeching."

"Who?"

"Danceye Nellie. She had been putting her flesh under your nose all evening, in the guise of serving others. Then when she bent over in front of you, her rump almost in your face, and you goosed her—"

He was appalled. "I did that?"

"You must have. Because she almost leaped over the table. Served her right. After that she behaved with more decorum."

"So you're not—"

"Not anymore. Just don't do it again."

"I won't!"

She frowned. "Not unless—"

Oops. Had he done something else? He didn't dare ask. "I—"

"Unless she pokes her rump in your face again."

He stared at her. Then she started to laugh.

Relieved, he grabbed her around her full, middle-aged waist and hugged her for all the little he felt he was worth.

"Heln, Heln, Heln, I had the most terrible experience today of my life. But now it's over with. Now I'm right."

"You were wrong before?" she asked, clearly puzzled by this.

"Heln, you will never, never know how wrong I was."

Nor would he be, he vowed, the one to tell her. Helbah might know, Kathy Jon certainly did, but he hoped that neither had fully seen the lust in him that he now so thoroughly wanted to forget.

CHAPTER 13

Preparations for War: Zady's

*T*he young fellow with the mincing gait didn't look like any king or prince the commander had ever seen. As the slicked-down dandy with his purple pantaloons and nattily sequined shirt flounced up to the door of Recruitment House, every old and young veteran was at the windows, staring at him.

"Commander Roarer," the young recruit with the new sword scar across his right cheek whispered, "that can't be from Rotternik."

"Not from Rotternik," the commander said. His left arm, missing except for its stump, was throbbing painfully. That was always a bad sign. "I don't know where it can be from."

"As long as it has gold," the recruit whispered.

The commander shook his head. Though they were all mercenaries, there were some things even more important than gold. "Possibly a tourist."

"But from where?"

"Another frame, maybe. Let's hope it goes back there."

Everyone moved away from the windows as the door opened. The stranger stepped inside, doffed the fancy tall hat sporting an eagawk's plume, and bowed from the waist. His hair was a rusty color, a shade redder than well-dried blood. His eyes, when raised, were of a yellow color belonging in the face of an unreasonably maddened feline. Clearly not the usual visitor to Recruitment House.

"Commander Roarer, let me introduce myself," the apparent fop offered. "I'm Master Jade and I represent a power. I'm in need of an army. I'm prepared to pay well and offer a bonus in conquered territories to everyone who fights."

"To whose victory?"

"That has to remain a secret, Commander."

"Not if you want to hire mercenaries. We have to know that you can pay and the chances of your success."

"I assure you, Commander, that victory will be ours. As for the ability to pay—"

The dandy held out an open hand and on it appeared a gold coin. The likeness on the coin was of Zoanna, a former queen of Rud overthrown by the Roundear. The hand closed and reopened, and the coin was two identical bright and shining coins. Three times the hand opened and closed and on the third opening the hand had become impossibly filled with Zoanna's shining images.

Men from around the room gathered round them, looking greedily at the coins. The dandy turned his hand over and the coins fell to the hard wooden floor, clinking. They continued falling, continued clinking for an unnaturally long time. Men grabbed the coins as they fell, picked them up, put them on tables and unobtrusively into pockets. Still the coins rained.

"I believe, Master Jade, you have made your point." The stump burned now like fire.

"I thought I would. Can I have my army assembled and ready to ride in three days?"

"Three days? Impossible."

"Nothing is impossible, Commander. Consider for instance these coins, which can become valueless unless earned." A slim hand turned over and made a pass as the gold coins stopped falling. As the pass was completed the coins took on a dull appearance and each, whether in pocket or hand or on table, collapsed into a pile of sand. The warriors, seasoned and unseasoned alike, stared with opened mouths and rounded eyes at what had seemed a fortune.

"Very, very impressive magic," acknowledged the commander. "Magic can help with a war but seldom win total victory."

"Right, Commander. My side needs troops."

"You haven't declared war yet?"

"A simple precaution."

"You would march against the Alliance?"

"Yes."

"Insane, even with magic. The orcs—"

"Haven't magic to match ours, Commander. I assure you ours is the more powerful."

"You come from out-frame?"

"Of course."

"You would buy an army to help you defeat our past customers?"

"Our victory is certain. Afterwards there will be a new order composed of seven kingdoms, and those who helped establish it will be lavishly rewarded."

"It would mean an end to Throod, as well as other kingdoms."

"Oh, Commander, armies are always needed. Throod will have to supply troops to put down uprisings, collect taxes, arrest and slay malcontents. There will always be those who have to be repressed, tortured, and slain."

"Yes, I suppose there will be. But you are malignants."

"However did you guess? Yes, I represent malignant power. Malignants after all have the strongest forces."

"Not in this frame. Here malignants have been kept down in numbers. Zoanna of Rud was such a malignant, and she was defeated by a mere boy."

The dandy hissed loudly. It was more like a serpent's hiss than that of a feline. His eyes grew larger and somehow even more predatory.

"Commander, enough of this chitchat. I want my army!"

"You're Zady."

The dandy raised his arms and there was a poof of yellow, sulfurous smoke that quickly cleared. Gone was the dandy. In his place was a beautiful redhead in a slinky red gown. She put cat's eyes on him and they seemed almost to smoke. Her face was as beautiful as the rest of her.

"Yes, I am Zady." She looked around the room, first at one warrior and then another. "I am Zady, and I am malignant. Follow me and the gold will all be yours. Each man who enlists in my service will have a palace, and—"

Her hand gestured, and now she stood totally nude, displaying all the natural hollows and contours. She twirled around, making certain every man saw all that he wanted to. Remarkably beautiful women there had been in Throod, but never one so instantly inflaming to the senses. Commander Roarer feared for his men.

The dress was back. Her beauty would remain a part of every man's memory. Every man was now staring at what was almost as startling. She smiled a wet-lipped smile.

"Each of you can have me, or others magicked to this form. This is only one of the little marvels that a malignant's magic can bring to you. How many of you are willing to follow me?"

"I am!" one brash youngster said, coming forward.

"I too," said another. Two more would-be soldiers joined the first. Their minds, Commander Roarer understood, were now subservient to their glands.

"Zady, I understand your head is not always so young," the commander said. "I understand it is quite old and ugly."

She turned her face to his, and of an instant it was ugly, and old, with large warts, rheumy eyes, and stringy hair. A stench came from her that was overpowering.

The commander blinked back tears. Seeing and smelling had to be believing, but a hag's face on the lovely body and smelling her without magic deodorant was a very hard experience.

"Yes, Commander, this is me," she croaked. "But I don't have to look like this. That is the advantage we malignants have over ordinary mortals. With the right magic"—the hand waved away the strong scent of decay and banished the ugly hag face and restored, after the smoke dissipated, the breathtakingly lovely creature—"I can be anything or anyone I

wish," she continued dulcetly. "I can make any woman a
warrior takes appear to him and others as I appear now. Or
at the man's request I can make any woman or girl or puling
infant look any way he wants her to. I can make the object of
lust struggle, or not struggle, weak or strong. The choice can
be yours. How many of you like the idea?"

Not surprisingly, several, including four fairly decrepit
old vets, moved forward with the others. Each looked rather
uncomfortable with his own choice, but determined nonethe-
less. It was exactly what the commander had seen in men he
had been forced to execute.

"Excellent! And you, Commander?"

"Go to your Devale!" the commander said.

"Oh, Commander, I intend to do that as it becomes necessary. But surely you would like that arm fixed? And surely
you want to be young and strong and virile? I can give you
what you secretly want. After victory—everything."

It took a supreme effort, but he managed it. "No."

The beautiful creature looked sad. "Oh, Commander.
You won't pick the men for me? Isn't that your job?"

"I won't ask men to serve a malignant. Some will join
you; I can't help that. But as for me, I want no part of it."

"Not even"—and her gown again vanished—"a little
part?"

"Not anything! Be gone, damned witch!"

"Oh, Commander, I'm so disappointed!" The slim hand
waved and somehow dispatched a powder that produced a
greenish cloud. The cloud drifted to his face and enveloped it.
He took a breath despite himself, sneezed, and the cloud dissipated.

The commander felt himself to be old—incredibly old. He
could hardly stand. Looking down at himself he saw that he
had shriveled as though with extreme age, and that he now
had not one arm ending in a stump but two. He felt an itch on
his head and back that cried out for fingers, and his fingers, he
was appalled to realize, were gone. The itching immediately
became maddening.

"Poor, poor commander, aren't you sorry now?"

"You!" a big burly warrior-type snapped at her. "Restore the commander!"

"Or what, big boy?" She made a gesture, and a cloud formed and cleared, leaving the dog-faced veteran as a small, ugly-faced canine. The puppy tried to bite her ankle and she gestured again, and there was the warrior on all fours. Another gesture and he was out of uniform. As he stood amid astonished stares trying to cover himself and failing, one of the Zady recruits laughed. In a moment someone had stood up and challenged the laugher, and then, the commander knew, a fight was imminent. But Zady, always ready it seemed, made some quick passes and tossed another powder. He sneezed. Smoke cleared. He raised his hand and looked at it. The soldier who had challenged Zady was now clad as he had been in full uniform.

Zady smiled a malignant's smile. "What you have had, warriors, is a demonstration. I need an army and you know that I will pay. I will expect troops to be assembled here for me in three days."

"No!" the commander surprised himself by snapping. "Any man who signs needn't return to Recruitment House!"

"Why, Commander, they don't intend to return. Are you certain you won't join yourself? I can promise you all the rape and rapine you've ever wanted, before, during, and after battle."

He shook his head.

He wanted to say something stronger, but remembering how weak he had been and what it felt like having two stumps, he desisted. He did want to order her out.

Poof! A puff of smoke and she had vanished.

Alas, looking at the eager faces of the readily convinced, the commander knew that she had won against him. In three days' time she would return and her army, without his approval, would be waiting.

Lucernia, president of the malignant Witch and Warlock Society, was a little taken aback at Zady's sudden appearance in her bedroom. The old hag with her lovely new body had appeared just as Lucernia was about to demonstrate for a group of teachers the latest means of breaking students. She had the young future warlock in a contortion spell and had herself stripped to the fundamentals. In a moment more she would have shown how with a little imagination they could make a living knot that would not first involve their transformation into serpents. Lucernia was fond of this particular feat she had perfected. Alas, Zady had to appear right between the red-faced witch and the green-faced one, interrupting her and breaking her concentration.

"All right, Lucernia, get these out!"

"What? Zady, do you forget who I am?"

"I'm trying not to remember. Out!" With a wave of her hand and a puff of smoke Zady returned all the other visitors to outside the apartment. "I've got business."

"What business can possibly be more important than corrupting?"

"Destroying. Destroying mundanes."

"You tried that, Zady. You failed. The Roundear of Prophecy scorched your feathers, and I believe you lost your head."

"Shut up," Zady said nastily. "What has been doesn't matter. I need an army of malignants as well as the army of mundanes I'm getting."

"Dream on, Zady. No one will serve you after your last debacle. You've been the laughingstock around the university since you let that uneducated bumpkin slice off your head and his brat keep you from reattaching it. Some Grand Witch you are! Even an apprentice could have done better."

Zady gestured, and Lucernia choked on the resulting purple-and-green-slashed cloud and became an ugly thing in a corner. "Very funny!" she gasped, finding that she had neither mouth nor lips but was speaking with a sphincter not normally used to produce words. The humiliation of doing what she had formerly been accused of doing was tremendous.

"Lucernia, you look good without bones. Maybe you'd like to stay that way for a while—say the next century?"

"What do you want, Zady?"

"I told you. I want total victory, and I'm going to need the most accomplished of my former classmates. That includes you, which shows the lamentable lack of standards."

"See Devale. He knows the alumnae."

"But you're the president of the guild. Devale doesn't keep up with the activities of the graduates. Some have gotten themselves burned. Others have gotten involved with—if you will excuse the word—benigns. I want the current best and I will have them."

"So you want me to pick."

"And persuade. With the benefit of a little magic if necessary. You *do* know magic, don't you?"

"Oh, very well. Change me back."

Zady tossed a smoke that filled all Lucernia's senses and overcame her and brought her upright, boned out to her usual large proportions.

"Zady, I don't know why you are so bossy and impolite with your colleagues."

"You want me to be polite? What's malignant about that?"

Lucernia rubbed her wattled throat that a moment ago hadn't existed. There were several things she would have liked to do to Zady that were malignant, but she knew her skill was inferior to that of the Grand Witch of Malignant Magic. Besides, even more than most of them Zady was teacher's nasty little pet.

"All right, Zady. I'll get your malignant practitioners for you. But you lost before. Do you really think that now you can win? Kelvin beat you proper!"

"Yes, I am going to win!" With those words, Zady vanished.

The wizened apothecary turned from taking inventory of his aphrodisiac and love potions to see a shapely female body materialize in front of him. He was savoring the astonishment that he wouldn't need one of his own powders when he recognized the nude witch by her less-than-beautiful head.

"Zady!"

"The same, Smedlic. I've come to give you an order. I want enough changing and confusing powders to stock an army—a real army. I want communication crystals, phials of shape changers, wizard wands, materialization and transformation materials, elixirs of malignant nature, and invisibility cloaks."

"Only one invisibility cloak in stock. They take time to materialize. If you witches weren't always losing them—"

"I'll take the one you have, and everything else that will prove useful. I'm taking over the dragon frame."

"Against—Mouvar?" he inquired dubiously.

"Mouvar's hero. Mouvar doesn't cheat. Devale will if he knows that it's necessary."

"Zady, you've got a job ahead of you!"

"And you've got an order! Get on it immediately or face my wrath."

She vanished, leaving the apothecary weak and shaking and alone in his shop.

Zady materialized with a loud poof directly in front of Devale's big desk. She had perfected her appearance and disappearance until it would seem to mundanes that she had the magic opal. Oops, that was a thought—she'd have to go back to the apothecary and tell him she needed a faintheart powder powerful enough to reduce a dragon to a coward. That would be tricky, because dragons weren't normally brave or unbrave—they simply were.

"Zady, you have been doing well," Devale remarked, looking up from his desk's viewing crystal. The horns on his head glinted in the overhead light. "But you will have to nullify that dragon. Have you given any thought as to how?"

"I planted an abundance of passion weeds and get-on flowers for him and his mate. They're in and out of that little lake in dragon territory all the time—they won't notice a few unfamiliar plants. They can be locked in passion while I'm beating and destroying the Alliance. I can keep Kelvin from going there and spoiling their fun. Of course Kelvin's brats can mind-talk to it, but they have to be within range. The opal won't be of help to them if it's not used, and it will be one of my prime objectives to see that it's not."

"After the battle you'll have to destroy the dragon."

"No problem there. I'll first reduce him to cowardice and while he's cowering I'll do an inside-out spell. Once the dragon's copper scales are on his inside and his gizzard and guts on the outside, I'll take the gem."

"You have it all planned, then? You won't expect me to break the rules and help?"

"Professor, I'm not going to need your help. With only Helbah and an old hero to defend the Alliance, my victory is assured."

"That's what I like to hear, Zady. Confidence."

CHAPTER 14

Preparations for War: Helbah's

Kelvin felt foolish standing in front of Recruitment House with the old witch on his back. Helbah had pointed out that there was no reason why they should ride so far when with his Mouvar boots it was just a step. Accordingly he had reluctantly stooped down, waited until she and her familiar were in place, straightened, and stepped—from the twin palaces to Throod, right where he had visualized.

Helbah slid off, carrying her familiar. Kelvin sighed and felt along his spine. It wasn't that Helbah was heavy, but it felt as though his back had been punctured in eight separate places. Since Katbah and Helbah were in some sense one, perhaps some bizarre transformation had taken place.

Helbah stretched, as though she really had been on some long, fatiguing journey. "There! I'd say that was much better than flying!"

Of course! She could have flown in bird form. Why hadn't she? Was he just here to keep her company?

Grizzled and young faces were looking out the window at them. Someone must have seen their arrival. A middle-aged man completing one enormous step with a hag—a nice old hag!—riding on his back.

"I do hope Captain Mackay remembers me," Helbah said, adjusting her wrapper. Always she wore the same old dark dress. In her own clothing she displayed neither interest nor imagination.

"Helbah! You know Captain Mackay can't still be living! Not unless he's a warlock!"

"Now I wouldn't put anything past the captain! He was a real charmer in his day. But I keep forgetting that most people are only human. It gets harder and harder as the centuries slip away."

They walked in and it was almost the same inside as it had been when he had come to buy mercenaries to fight Zoanna. There were tables and chairs, bottles and cards. In the corner a gray-haired man stood up. The man had one arm missing, but it wasn't Captain Mackay.

"Welcome, Helbah. Welcome, Kelvin. I'm Commander Roarer."

So he was a different man, but similar in appearance. Except for the light greenish eyes he could have passed for a Mackay duplicate.

"You know why we've come," Kelvin said, echoing Morvin Crumb's words spoken over a quarter of a century ago. "You received Helbah's message."

The commander nodded. "It came floating down from the ceiling. That's a neat trick. Captain Mackay, my predecessor, used to get messages from a witch that way."

"Ahem," Helbah said, clearing her throat with unaccustomed loudness, "we've business."

"Yes, yes, I quite understand, and I'm sorry that there wasn't some way for me to make an immediate reply. Please sit down. I've some information for you."

They took their chairs, sitting at a round table still damp with mug rings. Recruitment House smelled more like a drinking establishment than did Lomax's. Kelvin suspected that in a moment they'd be offered refreshment and that this time he'd not be passed over because of his assumed tender age.

"Refreshment!" the commander called to a man carrying a tray. The man wore a stained apron and had a scar across his face, but clearly here he was a waiter. He came over and put down mugs and poured an amber liquid that didn't quite smell like wine.

"I never imbibe," Helbah said. Katbah appeared uninterested. Kelvin picked up his mug, sniffed, then tasted. Something bit his tongue and he set it down again. He'd wait until he was home and could have real fruit wine. Soldiers always seemed to feel that drinking went with the uniform.

Commander Roarer drank, then wiped his mouth on his uniform sleeve. He fixed Helbah with a gaze.

"She was here, wasn't she, Commander?" she inquired, knowing the answer.

He nodded. "I'm afraid she was, Helbah. It wasn't my choice. She sent no advance message."

"Typical. What did you do for her?"

"Personally, as little as possible. But she persuaded some men. She'll get her army."

"And that will leave mine short?"

"Of men you're better off without. But there's more—many men now say they won't serve the Alliance. It's the stories they've heard that the witch is now unbeatable."

"We beat her once," Helbah said. "That's why there's an Alliance."

"Technically, you lost, since your side surrendered to the orcs. As for Zady, she may be better equipped this time. Magic is something no fighting man wants to chance."

"I cut her head off!" Kelvin said, coming to his courage. "My very young son kicked it off a cliff, deflated her body, and unmagicked the girl who grew up to become his bride."

"That's very commendable, Kelvin, but the fact is that today Zady's back. This time she's not neglecting to hire mercenaries and buy war supplies. I'm sorry to tell you that my kingdom is more greedy and corrupt than others. They agreed to sell her all the war supplies—catapults, harness, war-horses, armor, swords, lances, bows, arrows, crossbows— the lot. They agreed to let her hire all who will take her gold. I'm sorry to tell you that there are more who will take her gold than those who won't. There are a few of us—a very few—who want to fight on the side of the Alliance. Gold isn't neces- sary—we'll fight by your sides for our lives. There are only a handful of us, but we will serve you, each of us, until our deaths."

How cheerful, Kelvin thought, but he knew the aging veterans had no choice. It was like that Earth saying his father was always repeating in arguments with his father-in-law: "Those who live by the sword, die by the sword."

"Thank you, Commander," Helbah said, pushing back from the table. "Your help is accepted. Come, Kelvin, we've got business with the orcs."

"But—" Kelvin started, then shut his face. Helbah knew better than he, prophecy or not. Helbah, after all, had lived to see many wars over the centuries.

Outside he leaned over and waited while his passengers climbed on his back. It had been a good deal more fun when his niece Kathy Jon did it. He made certain Helbah had a good hold, then took his long, long step.

Brudalous was at the rebuilt land palace once destroyed by human brats. That had been a long, long time ago, and Merlain and kings Kildom and Kildee had been helped into incredible mischief by Zady. The children had actually gotten away with the magic opal Zady had coveted, but the subse- quent war had had a beneficial outcome. Today the orcs gov- erned themselves through the Confederation under the

Alliance. The Alliance itself had its figurehead ruler accepted by orcs and humans alike: Horace, keeper of the opal.

Kelvin stepped onto the sand where his two human children had once been, and Helbah let go of his shoulders and slid off from his back. Brudalous, a fish-faced giant to them, was watching his grandchildren, or taddlings, at play in the surf.

"Helbah, Kelvin, I got your message," the fish-face boomed. The skin, if anything, seemed scalier and greener than Kelvin remembered. No protocol for orcs—they got down to business.

"Brudalous, you're prepared to fight for the Alliance?" Helbah demanded.

"Of course. We have no choice. We're part of the Alliance."

"You have trained warriors and equipment?"

"We're always prepared, Helbah. Orcs have their traditions to keep."

"Your magicians?"

"Krassnose, our resident wizard, and Phenoblee, my dear wife, are now reviewing spells."

"You do know who Zady is, don't you? She's more than just a witch."

"We know. Once she tried to use us to destroy the Confederation."

"Have you heard that she now has powers greater than mine? Perhaps greater than Krassnose's and Phenoblee's and mine combined?"

Brudalous waited, his face as impassive as always.

"Then there will be no pulling back? No leaving the Alliance?"

Brudalous showed his daggerlike teeth. "Orcs do not surrender easily. Perhaps this time we will die, but if we die we die as orcs."

"That's all I wish to know, Brudalous. There have been rumors and I wanted to check on them myself. Inform Krassnose and Phenoblee that I will have some witch and wizard allies as before and that this time they will work with orcs against a common foe. Come, Kelvin!"

"But—"

"The old palace ruins. You can wait there for my return. If Horace was available to us I'd take him instead of the transporter."

"The dragon," Brudalous intervened, "still has the opal?"

"Yes, but he's newly mated in dragon territory and on his sunnymoon. I don't want to interrupt until it's necessary. You know how dragons are. Bend down, Kelvin; you expect me to jump on your back?"

Kelvin leaned forward and Helbah almost, it seemed, did jump on his back. Once she was properly seated with Katbah digging his claws in, he straightened and stepped.

The old palace ruins—the very rocks and masonry that his father had brought down years ago with his Earth weapon—never seemed to change. Weeds and other vegetation didn't grow high here, possibly because of the hordes of tourists. Today being a workday, there were no tourists here. He waited while Helbah changed herself into an ungainly swoosh and Katbah into a batbird. The transformed cat attached itself with tiny wing-claws to the transformed witch's slick feathers. Helbah took off and he watched her fly across the ruins and, he knew, down the ancient stairs, along the river, and then underwater to the air-filled dome with its transporter.

Good luck, Helbah! he thought after her, and wished that he, like his offspring, could project it to her.

Helbah wasted no time but flew straight to the hotel, where she joined Wizard Whitestone and Zudini the master illusionist at a secluded table. They had been waiting for her— impatiently, she gathered.

Whitestone said, "Well, Helbah, she's starting again, right?"

"Just as you told me, Whitestone. She grew a new body somewhere in dragon territory."

"Reminds me," Zudini began, "of my greatest offstage escape. I was set upon by malignants, dismembered, and my parts suspended in a bag inside the rim of an active volcano. Well, my brain still functioned, so opening my mouth I—"

"Not now, Zudini," Whitestone cautioned. "Save it for those memoirs I know you are writing. We've got business. Helbah's frame is facing peril of another sort."

"Actually it's the same sort, just as you predicted. She's going to stage a war so as to kill and damage as many humans and orcs as possible. Then she's going to get Kelvin and his relatives and me and everyone who helped us and—"

"Now, now, Helbah, we're not going to allow that to happen. Some of us have been planning ever since the convention."

"Yes," Zudini added, "even if you hadn't our sympathy for what you endured at her hands we'd still want to get Zady. She never can pay for the insult she did to our convention."

"And me," Helbah added.

"That," Zudini said, "goes without saying. You were the guest of honor. Zady interrupted your speech."

"Actually she did quite a bit worse," Whitestone reminded. "The insult to Helbah and the convention was great. But great as the insult was, she did still worse."

"Yes," Zudini agreed, "she tried to steal the opal."

"More than that. She tried to destroy Helbah's home frame. The damaging of a frameworld until it is malignant-dominated cannot be tolerated."

"Agreed." Zudini's head bobbed. "Oh, I quite agree."

"Then you can get help?" Helbah asked. "You can get some of the conventioneers who were with me before? It's going to be harder this time. I know she'll have practitioners of malignant magic with her. She'll attack the Alliance, but no one can say where. Precognition doesn't work for anybody these days."

"Yes, yes, that's a bad sign," Zudini agreed. "But if bad

comes to worse, escape is still possible. Even if your frame is taken over by her, you and your favorite humans may come here."

"I don't want to escape with my favorite humans! I want to lick Zady proper! I want her out of my existence and all existences! I want her to burn and make a complete ash of herself! I want the Roundear of Prophecy to stand up and be a hero, and—"

Zudini and Whitestone exchanged pitying glances. They would be remembering the hero who had been tricked by Zady all through the convention. Kelvin had in effect entrusted his children to her, though he hadn't known she had switched identities with his sister. Such mistakes were not treated forgivingly by those with more than a smattering of the art.

"What we've done," Whitestone interrupted in his turn, "is contact all former convention members who were there. More than half have agreed to work to punish Zady for the humiliation they suffered. And there are newcomers who have earned their pointed hats who have volunteered. Zudini's daughter, Zally, and her husband, Frederich, will come. Then there's very young warlock Ebbernog who has developed a latent ability along with his quick mastery of the art. Ebbernog was frightened by Zady as a child. He was innocently bouncing his ball in the children's suite when this other child appeared—one of the four who were missing. He told the attendant, bounced his ball again, and struck Zady, who was wearing an invisibility cloak."

Yes, Helbah thought, and it must have been Ebbernog's latent ability that had made the ball move with unusual speed. Merlain's thought to him to throw the ball there had evidently triggered his ability. Telepaths like Merlain and Charles were rare, but those gifted with the ability to think-move objects were almost as rare. A warlock with psychokinesis ability would be an asset of great worth.

"Yes, I remember Merlain telling me of Ebbernog's experience." She did not say that Merlain had described him as a "dumb little fat kid." Even today Merlain was often weak in

empathy, as when she condemned her father for being a
dragon-killer way back in his youth. Her father, of course, had
had no choice; nor had Ebbernog.

"Wizard Whitestone, Warlock Zudini, I appreciate what
you've done, but now I have to be getting back."

"But my dear lady," Whitestone urged, "surely you can
have a cup of brew with us first?"

"No, I have to be leaving. War may begin at any moment.
She may choose to attack anywhere, and I haven't troops and
protective spells in Aratex and Hermandy. There's no time to
spare."

"But Helbah," Whitestone persisted, "we're coming with
you. The others I mentioned will soon follow."

"Come on, then," Helbah ordered. "It's back to the
transporter station and then home to the twin palaces."

Not bothering to stand up, she changed into a swoosh in
the chair and changed Katbah into a batbird clutching her
feathers. She hopped out of the chair, beat her wings, and flew
past startled waiters and waitresses, including one waitress
with very spectacular cleavage she dimly recognized. She flew
through the hotel lobby and out the door, which the doorman
just managed to open for them in time. Out in the street they
flew high above the floating platforms, past the shops and the
police station and into the familiar terminal. Straight to the
nearest empty booth she flew, pecked the proper coordinates
on the controls, and transported, not even bothering to
change.

The nanosecond of time that seemed to the traveler a
longer time was no different for a bird than for a person.
Cometing stars, twisting sensation in the stomach, an explosion of lights. Then she and Katbah were back in the dome.
Not wasting time, she dived out the airlock, swimming for the
surface with strong swoosh wingbeats. She exploded from the
water, circled just a moment in the air, and was joined by two
ruffled swooshes bursting from the water. Together, side by
side, they flew to the ancient dock, then elevated their bird
selves above moldering stairs and the broken masonry and
statues and junk of a onetime glorious palace. Now it was out

to where the ruins ended, wings beating steadily, to where a plume of dust floated above a departing horse and rider.

Kelvin was waiting here. He looked up at them, a little bit startled by their sudden appearance. He stood his ground while they landed and changed into their human forms, his expression a bit less confident than befitted a hero.

"Helbah, Whitestone, Zudini—I remember you from the convention! Something's happened! Something terrible. I've just received word. Hermandy and Aratex are under attack! Zady attacked first and then declared war. The war has started!"

CHAPTER 15

Return Engagement

*I*t was hot on the battlefield. A different location than before, but almost the same situation as the last time Zady had made war. The one big difference was that rather than a war between orcs and humans it was a war of malignants against benigns, with humans and orcs expendable by both sides. Another difference was that both sides were better equipped—especially Zady's.

Kelvin stood feeling like a fool with the equipment Mouvar had somehow given him throughout the years. He had on two belts: his sword belt and the belt holding his antimagic weapon. On his hands were the gauntlets, and on his feet the boots—his last gift from Mouvar—that made the levitation belt unnecessary. In his hands, but firmly in contact with the ground, was the chimaera's copper sting. He looked to Helbah, who was staring out over the ground like a seasoned strategist; on her shoulder, sharing her staring, was Katbah, her familiar, also known as the creature called a cat.

"Not yet, Kelvin. I'll tell you when."

"I wish Horace was here," he complained. Actually if Horace had been present he would have feared for him. Dragons were not among the most vulnerable of creatures, but they were as susceptible as humans to magic attack. Even with all the will he could muster Kelvin doubted Helbah could counter the spells Zady would throw at Horace.

The human army in the dung-colored uniforms emblazoned with blood-red tridents began their advance. Zady had somehow obtained both uniforms and men, probably through magic. There might be dead people reanimated in that line, Kelvin thought with a shudder, or even look-alikes from other frames. How would he feel if he met his own brother—or someone who appeared to be his brother—out there sword to sword? He knew he would not feel good, and as never before he hated that there were wars and that he, very much against his desire, was a hero of bloody conflicts.

General Knight, Kelvin's father, was conferring with General Sean Reilly, known in more normal times as St. Helens, father-in-law to the Roundear. Neither man had worn a uniform for well over twenty years. Now, looking at them from the relative safety of this ridge, Kelvin thought them both the very picture of professional soldiers. Both men were clad, as was he, in the grass-green uniforms bearing Helbah's sun-and-moon symbol. His father, and undoubtedly St. Helens as well, would be wishing they had lasers and jetpaks instead of swords and horses. Alas, the lasers and jetpaks had long vanished, and would never have held their power over the years. Kelvin wondered about science that was limited and magic that lasted until the power was ended by a spell. Of course Mouvar's gifts to him were of science origin, but then magic and science at some point merged. Mouvar's weapons would not have lost their power, he hoped, and according to popular theory they never would.

Now the two generals for the Alliance were riding in

different directions, each to his own troops. In the meantime
the enemy was creeping forward. In the advance were men
with swords, followed by men with bows and spears. Behind
the light artillery were the wheeled catapults, already cocked
and loaded and ready to move up. At the rear were witches
and warlocks and major officers. At any moment hostilities
would begin.

The dung army's advance halted. The troops divided
neatly and the catapults rolled forward. Men chopped ropes
with their swords and great rock missiles rose high into the air.

Helbah and her magic-wielders acted as their green-clad
troops charged out to meet the foe. The missiles became fireballs and exploded, showering the troops of both sides with
white-hot pieces of rock. Some of the men fell; others staggered and ran with flames on their backs. Kelvin wondered if
he shouldn't have used the chimaera's sting; the benigns' tactics had hardly stopped the missiles, though they had kept
them from exploding over the ridge.

Now the witch's fire started in earnest—glowing balls of
flame from Zady's side that had to be countered and stopped
by Helbah's. Some of the fire got through, burning men and
horses, striking and injuring and even destroying defenders.
Return witch's fire went out, scoring some hits but mostly
being stopped by the defenses of the intended targets. Kelvin
looked to Helbah, and finally she nodded.

Placing his hands on the chimaera's sting, he concentrated, and the great electric bolt shot out, drawn from the
ground, and scored a hit among witches. They were running
with tattered, smoking clothes, putting each other out as best
they could, while fireballs continued. Kelvin tried another
bolt, this time directed farther to the rear, hoping to strike
Zady. He wished again that his weak eyes were stronger. He
had only a vague notion of where she might be.

His bright blue bolt stopped before reaching its target and
curled upward. A superior magic was stopping the natural
force of nature. Kelvin swallowed, remembering that Zoanna
had not been able to defend against the bolts. Yet Helbah had
warned him that Zady would be watching for the sting to be

used and would have developed a method of countering. As his bolts curled back on themselves he belatedly saw that there were large coppery shields floating where he had intended to strike. Of great size, the disks resembled saucers.

Kelvin tried a bolt closer to their ridge. He blasted a catapult and sent the survivors scurrying into green-clad soldiers. He tried another, and a copper disk was there, just above the catapult he'd tried to get. His bolt sizzled harmlessly on the shield, curled up slightly, and was gone.

Kelvin tried some unmagical swear words that his father-in-law had taught him. It didn't help, though surely there had to be some practical reason why soldiers on Earth learned such words. If damning could really damn, he saw no signs of it. The shields were defending against the bolts at least as effectively as the invisible barriers were defending against the sizzling balls of witch's fire.

In the meantime the fighting was getting furious. Men were being killed out there, and Kelvin didn't like it. It wasn't just that warfare seemed to be a brutally inefficient way to settle differences, or that the bloodshed sickened him. Helbah had warned him to stay out of the hand-to-hand combat at least until Horace arrived. But Horace was somewhere in dragon territory and otherwise occupied. The worst of it was that Helbah had declared him needed here. Without her command he might have employed the belt or the boots to take him and Glint into dragon territory. But dragons being dragons, could even Glint convince Horace to leave Ember and come here?

"Desist with the sting," Helbah ordered, and he did desist, realizing that his efforts were now wasted. He needed his strength, he was sure, and using the sting continuously was, as he had found out before, as tiring as doing battle with a sword.

"Helbah, I'm going out there!"

"No! You mustn't. You'd be her natural target. Zady would use everything she has to capture you. Remember how she pulled you through the air?"

Kelvin remembered all too well. She had pulled him out

of a battle with the orc leader while he was wearing his levitation belt.

"Maybe she's out of that spell," Kelvin said. It was an illogical hope and he knew it, but somehow he had to try.

"And maybe you're out of sense! You see how strong her magic is. It's going to take everything we have to contain it."

"But I want to do something! All this equipment, and I can't do a thing!"

"Wait for Horace."

I don't want to wait for Horace, he thought, but knew better than to say it. Helbah was testy enough normally, and now with her hands full she was worse. He thought about stepping out with his boots and right onto Zady. Unfortunately he didn't know where Zady was and Helbah and the others couldn't locate her. For that matter each of them would have wanted the witch pinpointed so that they could attack her instead of her minions. But Zady was keeping concealed. She might be anywhere wearing an invisibility cloak. She could even be among the benign, though Kelvin trusted in benign defensive magic better than to suppose she was.

"Damn!" Kelvin said, using one of his father-in-law's minor expressions. "Can't you tell me to do anything?"

Helbah gestured offhandedly and he suddenly found his lips were sealed. She'd shut him up, in her fashion. That was what she had for him to do! And him a hero!

"Witch Helbah! Witch Helbah!" The boyish-faced, chubby young warlock was at her elbow. "Now, Witch Helbah?"

"Now, Ebbernog. Kelvin, get ready with that sting—this may be a onetime chance."

"Ready," Kelvin wanted to say, but Helbah had his mouth shut. His hands were on the sting in bolting position. He hadn't the slightest idea what Ebbernog was going to try.

Ebbernog rolled his boyish brown eyes back into his head until only the whites were showing. He placed his fingers against his forehead and the color in his cheeks gradually vanished. Suddenly the young man's eyes rolled down to where the pupils showed, now much smaller than they had been. The eyes glowed, stabbed out across the battlefield.

Very impressive, Kelvin thought, *but I could have gotten something done with my boots and sword while you're—*

The floating shields above the enemy shot skywards, traveled a way through the air, and dropped.

"Now, Kelvin! Now!" Helbah ordered.

Kelvin shot his bolt. The witches and warlocks he hit flamed and sizzled, and some were reduced first to skeletons and then piles of ash. It was like his taking of Zoanna all over again. Almost he could imagine Zoanna and the wicked impostor king resurrected here in order to again die.

"Keep it up, Kelvin! Keep it up!"

Bolt after bolt sizzled. He got witches, warlocks, wizards, and ordinary mercenary fighting men. The flung-away disks crashed down onto catapults and onto enemy soldiers, inflicting more casualties.

Helbah was rapidly giving orders. She and her colleagues were throwing fireballs at a faster and faster pace.

"OOHHHH!" Ebbernog dropped over, landing on his face. Kelvin hadn't seen what hit him, but something must have.

Helbah swiveled, her eyes darting left and right.

"So, Helbah, you would fight me, would you?" The voice was close. Helbah flailed her arms and got red in the face. She made a choking sound, clawing at her throat.

"Your protective spells aren't as good as you thought, are they, dearie!" Definitely it was Zady's taunting voice. Kelvin could see finger marks on Helbah's neck and knew that she was being throttled. A moment more and there would be no Helbah to defend them, for once she dropped unconscious Zady would surely use witch's fire to destroy her. In this situation Kelvin felt worse than worthless. He wanted to help Helbah, but this was in the midst of battle and to drop the sting now might prove to be equally disastrous.

His boots and gauntlets acted simultaneously without his help. The gauntlets used his hands and muscles to wrench the sting from the ground, held it out, and swung it like a flail. The boots carried him forward.

The sting struck something invisible that emitted a shriek. Before his eyes the bare seat of a woman's anatomy appeared with a red, lurid line scratched across it.

Kelvin gasped. He wasn't used to such sights, and it had been a long, long time since he had attended a convention. Now the gauntlets grasped the sting at its middle and base and started a fast, upward drive.

Kelvin closed his eyes. He didn't want to see what would happen when Zady got what would have to be the severest sting of her witch's life. Mentally he braced himself for the geyser of blood. Zady would not only get the point, she'd be impaled on it!

The sting struck nothing. Kelvin snapped open his eyes to see a serpent wriggling on the ground and to feel his body being pulled by his gauntlets as they took a different hold and used the sting as a spear. The sting darted, but the snake was suddenly a bird flying in midair. The gauntlets, not waiting for him to think of it himself, swung the butt down and made contact with the earth. The gauntlets moved up the shaft, positioning the tip to point at the wildly flying bird.

Kelvin waited. His gauntlets tingled, a signal that usually meant danger.

Helbah made croaking sounds, her eyes bugging at him. Her finger pointed sternly at the bird.

Oh! He had to think! He had to send the bolt out himself with his own mind. The gauntlets could control his hands and the boots his feet, but his mental impulse was needed to send the bolt.

Kelvin wished up the bolt, but by then the bird, achieving a remarkable flight speed, was out over the benign human army. If he released it now, his father or Lester or someone he knew might be struck. The bird was swooping low, deliberately, keeping out of reach of thrust-up spears and swords, but too near to present a safe target. Kelvin did not dare to take the risk.

"Hurry! Hurry! She's getting away!" Helbah shrieked at him.

The bird was now darting down and then climbing up—momentarily concealed behind a horse, and then right in line with a horse's rider. Kelvin held his fire.

The bird dipped down, then darted behind the shell of a burned-out house. Kelvin waited. Now he'd get her! He'd blast her the moment she came out.

"Shoot, Kelvin! What are you waiting for?"

Of course she was really beautiful, he thought regretfully, and willed the bolt to destroy what was left of the house. The bolt shot outward with a terrific crack, as of pent-up anger and hatred directed at a proper enemy. The house exploded in a fiery flash. Balls of witch fire scorched the grass immediately after.

Helbah made a quick sign and released Kelvin's lips.

"Did we get her?" Kelvin gasped.

Helbah glared at him. "Thanks to your delaying, no. She had her cloak and she had the instant she needed to become a woman and don it. You waited too long!"

"I'm sorry," Kelvin said. "I didn't want to harm the men, and then I didn't think of blasting the house—I was waiting to see her."

"And then you'd probably have held your fire because she'd have been naked!" Helbah said accusingly.

Kelvin, try as he might, could not deny Helbah's charge. Still, he wanted Zady destroyed—the safety of his children and his home and all their lives depended on it.

"EEEEEK!"

Helbah's head snapped around at the younger witch's cry. A trembling Zally was pointing at something that appeared to be an army of grayish ants. The ant army was well within camp, and behind and to either side of it lay the bodies of men in green uniforms.

Helbah drew a glass globe from beneath her voluminous gray skirt and threw it. The ball exploded on the ground, covering the ants with smoke. As the smoke cleared, villainous full-sized soldiers were revealed, coughing to clear the smoke from their lungs.

"You," Helbah said, "mercenaries and fools! I can destroy you now or I can send you home. You choose!"

The officer with a houcat's face said hastily, "We surrender! Send us home! Send us home!"

Helbah indicated a small box that had held some magical goods. "Get in there, then. All of you!"

"What—?"

Helbah drew a sign with her fingers and tossed another transparent globe. More smoke, and the mercenaries emerged from under it again the size of ants. She pointed to the box and the antmen marched in. She sealed the box with a gesture and motioned to a warlock Kelvin had seen but did not know.

"Parcel for the king of Throod. Deliver it."

The warlock changed immediately into a large eagawk. It landed on the box, sank its talons into its sides, and took off with it. In a moment the bird was high in the sky, and then a cluster of fireballs came sailing across the sky from the enemy side. It was what was called a shotgun emission and was designed to stop messengers and fleeing foes. Kelvin shot a bolt at the cluster and half of the small fireballs vanished as the others spread out. Additional fireballs flew from benigns and one by one the attacking fireballs were stopped. Only one fireball had not been quickly targeted.

One was enough. It engulfed the startled warlock before he knew it was there, and warlock and box of Zady's army burst into tattered red sheets of flame.

"Poor Yorick," Helbah said, watching floating feathers turn to ash. "He was a good warlock. I should have seen that coming. Zady had her sniper waiting. She probably thought he was going for reinforcements. I wish we *had* reinforcements— we don't. What we need is some intelligence!"

"You mean spies?" Kelvin asked, and then he was thinking—his children were telepaths, and who could possibly be better as spies? Perhaps they should be here instead of waiting for Horace? No, no, he would never forgive himself if they got hurt.

But Helbah had read his expression. "Of course! Merlain, Charles, and Glint! Bring them here, Kelvin, and we've got our intelligence!"

When, Kelvin wondered, would he remember not to think?

CHAPTER 16

Reconnaissance

Well! What are you waiting for—for me to turn you into a bird?"

"No, Helbah. I'm leaving right away."

Kelvin loved Helbah as he would his old witch granny, but the sharpness of her tongue cut harder than he thought she realized. He concentrated on the twin palaces and the spot by the swimming pool, and stepped.

Behind him he heard sizzling fireballs and several popping sounds, and felt a blush of heat on his back. Then he was stepping down, down, down, into the courtyard and to the side of the pool. Merlain and Charles were there, having just stepped from the water without a stitch. They would have made a perfect couple, were they not brother and sister; he was a handsome young man and she an attractive young woman. But their matching copper hair gave them away: they were siblings, as similar as they could be, in body and attitude. Glint seemed nowhere about.

"Oh, Daddy!" Merlain exclaimed annoyedly, grabbing a

towel and wrapping it around her hips. Though not without modesty, neither twin had ever shown hesitancy about changing clothes or lying nude in the presence of the other. Their concern was for the thoughts of people other than themselves, which could only be because for years they had mind-peeked. Kelvin knew that Merlain had no concern about him seeing her body, but she must have mind-peeked enough to know that he thought it inappropriate, particularly since the witch's curse had enhanced his awareness of just such bodies, so she was expressing the appropriate aversion.

Kelvin shifted his weight from foot to foot, adjusting to his surroundings. He still saw no one but Charles and Merlain, now both putting on soft blue robes Helbah had provided for them. He had somehow expected to see Heln and Jon and her brood, as well as Glint. Helbah had cast many protective spells over the palaces and their grounds and had deemed this the safest place.

"Where is everyone?"

"Glint's gone to find Horace," Merlain said.

"What! You know Helbah asked him to stay!"

"He'll be back," Charles said confidently. "The dragons aren't the only ones on their sunnymoon."

That was right: they were married now. How could that have slipped his mind? "Come to think of it, young man, where's your wife?"

Charles shrugged, as might a man long accustomed to matrimony. "She's on the grounds. Probably with Mom and Grandma. We stayed here waiting for Glint and Horace."

"Grandma has never really seen the palaces," Merlain explained. "Then the royal pains were with her too, and you know how well Charles and I get on with the pains."

How well he knew it, Kelvin thought. All their lives they and the two kinglets had seemingly been natural sparring partners, despite the adventuring they had shared. Would that his children were normal and fought with each other the way he and their aunt Jon always had. As far as he knew Merlain and Charles never even had words.

"The pains never miss a chance to show off!" Charles

opined. "They can't do magic or read minds, so they make a big thing of pretending to know more about Helbah's business. They'll be showing Mom and Grandma all her books and her paraphernalia for casting spells. All they've ever had to do with magic was getting born."

"That's all any of you should have had to do with it," Kelvin reminded him. Since their long-ago magic-filled adventure they had, as far as he knew, left spells to the experts. But secretly it made him a little proud to remember how well his six-year-olds had used bad magic to eventual good ends. After Glow's disenchantment, performed by Charles with proddings from Helbah, he had feared they might dabble. "And come to think of it, they did help you with your spells and drank the Alice Water to become giants."

"Only because we let them," Charles said. "We had to work together—there was no other way."

"There may not be any other way today, either. Where's Jon and her children?" He hoped his own children had *not* mind-peeked about his recent impressions of Kathy Jon.

"They'll get here eventually, Dad."

"You mean they're not here yet? Haven't you been searching for them?"

"Helbah told us not to leave."

"With your minds! Haven't you tried to reach them?"

"Well, gee, Dad, we can't reach all the way out to their farm. You know how stubborn Aunt Jon is—she probably didn't want to come."

Kelvin felt like tearing out handfuls of his newly regrown hair. Sometimes it depressed him that for all their smarts and special abilities his offspring demonstrated no more responsibility than had he and Jon. He had worried about them using their telepathy too much, and instead they had used it too little.

Jon paused after handing the heavy travel sack up to Alvin. The boy sat in his father's place on the front seat of the buggy as if he were already a man. Only the bickering going on between Teddy and Joey and big sister Kathy Jon made her mindful that they were still her children. She looked back at the house, wondering what she had left undone.

"I have to go back inside. I've forgotten something."

Their carriage horse, Old Hobbin, chose that moment to defecate, saying in effect what Jon's favorite and only husband would have said. Always impatient when younger, Lester was becoming more unmanageable every year. Their having had the children late in the marriage might account for some of it. Not that their children weren't darlings, but as Kelvin's father-in-law had said, they did try the patience of a saint. Many they encountered were not close to being saints, which made it that much worse.

Jon walked back to their cottage, unlocked the door—children weren't as trustworthy these days as they had been when she and Kelvin were brats—and went back inside for the second time. She could imagine Lester fuming at her, and she wouldn't have blamed him. She tried all the windows and found she had remembered to lock all of them. What was it that had compelled her like an aching tooth to come back inside?

"Hello, dearie, remember me?" The voice came from nowhere.

Jon flinched, but there was a vial of something under her nose, a fist hitting her in the stomach, and an ugly floating head with a lot of warts.

Zady! Zady with her invisibility cloak! I mustn't breathe. But then she did, for she was gasping.

"Well now, dearie, we're just going to change into birds and fly away from here. Won't that be fun?"

Bluish powder rained on her from midair and something rounded touched her cheek. A window she had just checked unlocked itself and raised. She tried but couldn't stop fluffing her feathers, then springing out the window and flapping her wings. Beside her flew an unusually ugly, dark swoosh. She was flying with Zady, not willing it herself but powerless to prevent it. Down below was the carriage and Hobbin and the children. Neither horse nor children looked up. Zady dropped a wad of excrement, and the dark stain appearing on the newly washed buggy top showed where it had landed.

As they flew across fields and farms only one thought sustained her: Zady, perhaps remembering how Jon had escaped her at the convention, had chosen her and not her daughter on whom to enact first vengeance.

Glint looked down at the greenery beneath his feet and manipulated the control on the belt with practiced fingers. Kelvin had shown him how to use the belt only yesterday and sworn him to secrecy before leaving it with him as a precaution. Helbah would have disapproved, he knew, but Helbah wasn't telepathic and what the old witch didn't know could surely not hurt him. It had taken him all morning to reach dragon territory and then get up into the upper highlands. He landed now on a tall mountain and projected his thought: *H . . O . . R . . A . . C . . E!!!*

The answer came, but the thought was irritated rather than glad. *Glint! Busy! Go away!*

Horace. You have to take me home again. Into that swimming pool at the palaces.

Go away, Glint! We're having our sunnymoon.

He addressed his dragon sister. *Ember, you don't have to take all day and night every day and night! What's gotten into you?*

Horace has, Glint.

Her literal nature would have amused him at another time. *I know, I know, but I need him.*

You've got Merlain! Horace thinks she smells nice for a human.

I need him to take me home to her! I need him now, Ember.

Ember need him now too.

And Merlain needs me! Horace will come back to you. He won't mount any girl dragons on the way home.

He'd better not! Ember would scale him!

Why was he arguing with her? Obviously dragon passion, when not solely for procreation, was awesome. They must have been at it continuously these past days, and both acted as if he had interrupted them during preliminaries. Truly there were things he hadn't learned about dragons. And to think that without his aid Ember would have been a spinster!

Oh, very well. Pest! Horace was suddenly in front of him, crouched belly down. *Get on!*

Glint climbed up on the coppery scales and settled down with a hand on either undersized dragon wing. He was thankful that Horace didn't know about the belt. If the unquestionably male dragon knew that Glint could return to Merlain without his help, he'd go back to what he'd been doing and redoing and doing some more for days and nights on end. Some sunnymoon that dragon had! Glint could almost envy him.

Go, go, go! Horace thought impatiently.

Glint visualized the swimming pool at the twin palaces, and between one of Horace's *go*s and the next they arrived.

SPLASH!

Glint emerged sputtering from the pool and grabbed Charles' extended hand. His father-in-law was there, and now, glory, glory, glory, there was Merlain talking to the two Mrs. Knights and the two fiery-haired kinglets. Some of Horace's and Ember's passion must have stuck to him—he could hardly wait to be with his own wife.

"Horace, you're going to have to help us," his father-in-law was saying, coming rapidly with a quick step that had carried him all the way from inside the nearest palace. "The Alliance is in trouble and now's the time to justify your title. You have to—"

Later, Horace thought, though Glint doubted that Kelvin got the thought. *Horace help Alliance later. Horace has to help mate now.*

"Horace, are you listening to me? Horace, don't turn your head away from me! Horace—"

The dragon vanished. Water rolled back into the spot he had occupied and the swimming pool went GLURP! Waves rose quickly in the pool and splashed each side.

So much, Glint thought, for putting too much confidence

in a dragon who wasn't your only child. Kelvin obviously hadn't instilled parental discipline. If Merlain bore him a dragon he knew he'd teach it to obey.

"All right, Glint," Kelvin ordered his son-in-law, "climb on my back. You could fly with the belt, but I think it's best left here in the event of a sudden emergency. You didn't by chance teach Merlain?"

"I know how," Merlain said quickly, taking the belt from her husband. "We stayed in mental contact while he was flying. Until he got too far away."

"Well, don't you use it! Not unless I come back and tell you to. No going after Horace again until Helbah gives me a spell to cool him down! There has to be something that will do it—I'll ask."

"Good-bye, Daddy. I'll take good care of Mom and Grandma. Oh, and Aunty Jon and the niece and nephews. Glow can use the crystal if we need to reach Helbah."

"Fine." Glint settled, and Kelvin made a mental note to suggest to his son-in-law that he get Helbah to reduce his weight. The young fool had been stuffing himself with cooakes and pies and other fattening foods ever since his marriage. When, Kelvin reminded himself with a fatherly wince, he wasn't making love to his beautiful young wife. He took the step.

Exploding fireballs dazzled the eyes and deafened the ears as his boot soles made contact. Helbah and the other witches and warlocks were still busy countering spells. The human armies still fought as seemingly mindlessly as they had. There were still phantom soldiers on that field, appearing and disappearing at various spots. The difference in the real and unreal was that the real soldiers bled as they were injured. Where magic was involved it was always impossible to know the actual number of the enemy. Even the fake soldiers caused injuries and death by appearing and then disappearing in precisely the wrong places. Thus soldier clove friend rather than foe, and the arrow aimed at the heart of a phantom ended by piercing a fighter wearing a green uniform.

"Glint," Helbah said quickly, "I want your help! Can you think out there and learn their plans?"

"Mind-snoop?" Glint said the words as though they were scandalous. "I can try. It's going to be hard because there are so many minds thinking at the top of their thoughts—really blasting it out."

"I don't want excuses, I want action!"

"Right!" Glint saluted Helbah, whether in mockery or respect it was hard to tell. He closed his eyes and sat down between two fatigued witches holding their heads and moaning over the surfeit of spells they had cast.

Kelvin waited. Though Glint appeared simply to sleep, he knew that his mind was awake and moving outward.

Glint reached out, entering minds at random, searching. *Gonna pull her down! Gonna rip off her clothes! Gonna—*

It was like a mental maggot pile of unsavory thoughts coming at him wherever his mind sought to penetrate. He wanted not the minds of the soldiers fighting in the field but the officers and malignants who planned the strategy.

Don't know what the witch is up to, but she's sending in more phantoms. I hope the men don't count on them! Need an ally to stab a goodie in the back and you may get chopped by him as the phantom vanishes. I hate magic warfare! This will be the last of it ever. When this fight is over I'll have all the drink I want and a palace. I'll march those women inside, make them strip, lie down in rows on the floor, and then I'll—

So much for the superior minds of officers! If any of them had tried full indulgence, as he himself had after marriage, they would know that one woman was more than enough.

There had to be a warlock behind the officers. If he could just reach to that distant ridge and keep the minds separated.

Old Zady's really got us humming! I'm so weak now from making her fireballs and ejecting them that I could sink into a hundred-year sleep! How long does this go on? I'm tired of it! I should be home casting sophisticated love spells, not wasting my talents! If I wasn't afraid of her I'd—

There had to be a witch or a warlock who was planning!
Those simply working weren't worth investigating.

*—froog-eyes, with tails of newts and a dash of maggot-
wood—*

NO.

*Devale, I worship you. And your apprenticed pupil whom
you yourself taught evil! Come now to the spell she is casting and
enter it as you once entered her newly defiled self. Devale.
Glorious Teacher, I ask in the name of all that is foul that—*

Definitely not! But close. Closer.

*So after the vomit spells hit them on the left flank and the
phantom giants storm through we'll bring on the real giants.
Won't they be surprised! We'll mash them down into puddles,
and then we'll bring in more phantoms, only these will be phantom dragons. Inside the phantoms will be armed fighters on
war-horses. When the dragons seem to kill, it will be the men
inside the illusion doing the slaughtering. The old toady dragon
trick, with new variations. Some of the phantoms won't just
conceal fighters, they'll conceal warlocks with death-wish powders and coward vapors. We'll decimate their entire force! Helbah won't be able to keep up with it. We'll win with this tactic,
and then there will be rewards aplenty as we go to raping and
torturing. Only the roundears must be saved for Zady! The
Grand Witch of Malignancy has malignant plans for her enemies!*

That's it! he could not avoid thinking. *That's the information Helbah wants!*

The mind he was in blanked. He knew the malignant had
caught on to his presence and would be calling to Zady. He
had to withdraw his mind and take the information to Helbah.

*Oh, Kelvin, I hope you know what you are doing! I hope
you're really the hero they always said! I don't know how long
I can hang by these ropes without losing consciousness, but she
will wake me only so I can see the slaughtering. Oh Kelvin, oh
Kelvin, don't let her get my children! I always tried to believe in
you, I always really did! Oh the pain, the pain, the sick, terrible
torment—*

Kelvin's sister—here!

His right cheek stung suddenly, and then his other one.

"Wake up! Wake up! She almost got you! If I hadn't seen the spell she was casting she would have!"

Glint opened his eyes to look into Helbah's concerned face. What was the old witch talking about? Was it then all illusion? Had the thoughts of Jon Crumb been bogus, designed to keep him occupied while some terrible fate was witched?

"THE ORCS ARE COMING! THE ORCS ARE COMING!" someone shouted.

There was cheering all around, and Glint was finding what he had to tell Helbah was already becoming clouded. He had to tell Kelvin, though.

"Kelvin, your sister—she's got her!"

"NO!" Kelvin said, immediately stricken. He looked to Helbah, his eyes searching hers.

"It's true," Helbah said. "Zady had her before you fellows got back from the palaces. Why didn't you hurry, Kelvin? I told you to."

But the hero's sickened expression was the only answer Glint knew she was ever going to get.

CHAPTER 17

Battle of Giants

*T*he orcs are coming! The orcs are coming!" The cry went up and down the lines. Kelvin looked up from his despondency, feeling a dim ray of hope. The orcs, he remembered, were reputed to be better versed in magic than Helbah or any of her helpers; they were also strong and magnificent warriors.

"Krassnose," Helbah greeted the orc wizard, distinguished by a darker-than-usual green face, "it's so good to see you again."

Krassnose opened and shut his gills once, an orc acknowledgment. Like all orcs Krassnose could breathe perfectly with the lungs nature had given him, but underwater he changed over to gills. Nature had been more generous with orcs than with other creatures in that respect. Kelvin's father had said that they might have evolved from Earth's lungfish, whatever they were.

"Krassnose, I hope you've tricks the rest of us haven't thought of. Our defenses are strained already. What magical strategies do you suggest?"

"Strengthen defense barriers," Krassnose said.

Helbah frowned. "I know you orcs are stronger in every way than the rest of us, but can you really—"

Krassnose raised his webbed fingers and above them a fireball that had gotten through their barrier detonated. Sparks rained down, snapping and sputtering and winking out before landing on those below. Now a faint glimmer appeared, showing where the orc had made a superior magical barrier or wall to halt further fireballs.

"Well, Krassnose, that is impressive, and I'm sure it will help. But we were hoping you orcs would have attack plans. What do you think our army should do?"

"Get out of orcs' way," Krassnose said. "Orc army will handle puny invaders."

Helbah looked crestfallen. Kelvin sympathized with her. The orc wizard was not only disparaging their magic as weak but also their army. Remembering how it had been twenty years ago, he had the feeling that quite possibly the orcs might be strong enough. Twenty years ago the combined might of the Confederation had not been enough to turn back or defeat the orcs; there had been no way short of a superior magic by which the Confederation could have won.

"Krassnose," Glint began, looking up at the giant in awe, "when I spied into their minds I found—"

"He knows," Helbah told him. "I've been in crystal contact with Brudalous all morning. He knows what you found."

As though on cue the orc leader came forward. To see a band of orcs grouped together was almost like looking at a grove of trees. When one of them moved away it had to be startling.

"Helbah, Roundear," he said, opening and closing his gills twice. "My orc army is about to launch its attacks. As my warriors march out, have yours fall back."

"As backup?" Kelvin suggested.

"No, to keep safe. When an orc warrior swings his sword he cuts a wide swath. Swords and clubs often do not distinguish between friend and foe, especially in the heat of battle."

"Oh." He knew the orc leader was right, though it rankled. An orc could step back and if a human happened to be there the human was likely to be kicked back into eternity. In size orcs resembled trees and windmills more than men.

Helbah relayed the orc messages to the generals via crystal. St. Helens looked out as if he were ready to explode at the insult; on the second crystal Mor didn't look much better. Yet they were good soldiers, as St. Helens often said. If the orcs wanted the humans to retreat as the orcs moved up, they would. First John Knight, then Mor Crumb, and finally St. Helens issued orders to their nearest officers. Helbah widened the images with a pass of her hand, giving them a second view of soldiers in green uniforms before them.

Kelvin looked to Helbah, hoping she'd tell him to do something to help. He wanted to help; he wanted to lead things. Heroes were supposed to lead, not cower way behind the action. To his surprise he found that now he desperately wanted his heroship; now that it was too late, he wanted it. When he thought of his sister he wanted more than anything to rescue her. His gauntlets did not yank him forward into action and his boots did not move his feet and force him into a long, long step. Alas, he was just a man after all, and in every way that counted, less than the giants surrounding him.

On Helbah's battery of crystals Kelvin watched the battle; he imagined himself a little like the human couch-potatoes

his father had described as spending their lives watching a
distant people, sometimes dead people, doing things in boxes.
Those vision boxes of Earth must be a lot like the viewing
crystals, magic or what his father insisted was science. In the
long run it mattered little how a thing was accomplished, used
or misused, so long as it was. With others who possibly had
eyes no better than his, he settled down to what he felt would
be a long viewing.

Men on the left began vomiting. The orcs, better protected by stronger spells, walked on past their green-uniformed allies. The men were clutching their middles and
staring in awe at the great bulging muscles. They must have
been glad enough that the orcs were here and that they had
been ordered to fall back.

The orcs marched on and in great strides. No horses for
orcs, since an orc was far bigger than even the largest war-
horse. Each orc had a large knobby club swung over his scaly
shoulder. Each carried an unsheathed sword the length of
three men in his right hand, and a shield the size of a rowboat
in his left.

Marching trees, Kelvin thought. *Trees marching to destroy the woodcutters.* Only the fish-faces of the amphibian
creatures spoiled his analogy.

Suddenly, astonishingly, giants of even greater dimen-
sions came striding up over the top of the greenish hills in the
background. These new giants appeared to be men, but with
dark, sinister faces. Dressed as they were in the dung uniforms,
complete with swords and shields much larger than the orcs',
they seemed in every way a greater force.

The orcs paused not at all but marched on. The facing
giants charged down the hills, huge swords raised high, emitting guttural barks and growling sounds that were audible way
back here. Kelvin shivered, seeing the orc army about to be
crushed.

"Watch this, Kelvin," Phenoblee said, bending low to
whisper to him. The orc witch and wife of Brudalous looked
horrendous, but was actually a decent person in her fashion.
She raised her webbed hands and made a downward sweeping

motion. Instantly a wind began blowing out there, out past the orcs. The giant apparent humans were blown backwards, breaking against the hills and scattering as separated whiffs of vapor. Illusion they had been, but an illusion subject to magic.

Kelvin felt like giving a rousing cheer, but just as he drew breath to change desire to action, a second column of giants came over the hill. These appeared to be much the same as the first wave, but just a bit smaller. Their faces were definitely as mean looking as those in the first wave had been. They brandished swords, spears, axes, and clubs and came at a loping run.

Phenoblee raised her hands and repeated her earlier action. The wind rose up, raising dust and denuding trees. Still the enemy came on. "These aren't the phantoms," Helbah remarked unnecessarily. "Can you do anything against them?"

Phenoblee shook her head. "Zady has her protective spells. If there's an opening maybe Krassnose or I can help."

In the crystals the two armies had almost reached each other. Kelvin hated to look. It was like two great beast herds about to crash.

"Zady must have gotten some Hagus Water," Helbah remarked. "That's the malignant's equivalent of Alice Water."

Kelvin remembered the use his two human children had made of Alice Water. They had grown big and later bigger using it on that trip Zady had sent them on. Fortunately Merlain had had the water or neither of his twins or the royal twins would have survived; neither would they have gotten the opal.

Thought of the opal made him wonder: when, if ever, would Horace come to his senses? He was going to have to look for him. Drag him back by the tail, if necessary. Mating might be a delight for dragons as it could be for humans, but Horace had a responsibility. If the orcs had the opal now he had the feeling Zady's forces would be running in the other direction.

The armies merged. The carnage commenced. Great

swinging swords. Great chops. Cries of rage; cries of pain. Just another battle, but larger, more impressive because of the size of the combatants. Green orc blood flowed and orcs died, but red human blood flowed also, and dung-uniformed soldiers died and shriveled down to what had to be their natural size.

One thing gradually became apparent: though they were now larger than the orcs, the enemy warriors were lighter. Kelvin recalled his father talking about that once: the magically created giants would have to have the same mass as their former selves. The enchantment might enhance it some by bringing in mass from elsewhere, but it wasn't feasible to bring enough. That meant that for all the fury of their blows they just hadn't the weight behind them. Time after time a blow that should have decapitated an orc was turned aside by his neck scales. Equally impressive was that the orcs, who had their natural weight, sometimes swung hard and sheared through armor that should have stopped even their blows. Evidently Zady had increased the size of men, uniforms, and weapons together. If she had had the weapons forged rather than enlarged they would have been more deadly and the armor more protective. But then if the armor and weapons were of denser mass, the bodies of the warriors could not have handled them. Truly, magical enlargement did have its drawbacks.

As the aggressors died, they and their uniforms and weapons shrank to normal human size. Such was the nature of magic, as experienced by Merlain and Charles many years previously. If they had lost their clothes and traveling packs whenever they enlarged their Alice Water could not have saved them.

Kelvin was thinking that the orcs were at the start of mopping up. At that moment a dragon came charging down the hill behind the dung-clads. Horace! But no, this dragon was bright gold in the sunlight and had large, swordlike teeth even bigger than Horace's. Kelvin shivered as the beast displayed the teeth and emitted a roar that was freezing to all who heard.

The dragon charged through the fighting men, ignoring

the human fighters but slashing with claw, snapping with teeth, lashing with tail every orc within reach. It was a formidably large dragon, and repeated sword thrusts did nothing to stop it. Time after time an orc's oversized sword swung right through the golden scales. Kelvin wondered that the beast showed no wounds and emitted no cries of pain.

A second dragon came to join the first. Then a third dragon, a fourth, and a fifth. Now the dung-uniformed giants were fighting between and at the sides of the dragons, and everywhere the dragons scuttled, orcs were flung dead and dying to either side.

"Oh, this is terrible!" Phenoblee cried. Her crest rose on her head in an extremely agitated manner. "They're only dragons! What's the matter with our warriors? Why don't they fight?"

More and more dragons came charging over the hills. They were the full length of the orc army, attacking only orcs. Kelvin saw one big orc leap at a dragon's snout as the snout was down on a wounded orc. He had the impression that the orc's feet went through the snout as through a phantom, but the snout moved so quickly and the orc died so fast that he thought he must have been mistaken.

Now the orcs were backing up. Some threw away their weapons. Heedless of wounded comrades and the few brave and foolish humans who had moved up to help them, they were running. Orcs in retreat? Unheard of!

"Phenoblee, that must be the death-wish powders and coward vapors! And those dragons are phantoms!"

"Tell me something I don't know, Kelvin."

"Can't you stop it? Can't anyone?"

"No."

"I'm going to try!"

"No you're not, Kelvin." Helbah made a move of her own and Kelvin realized she had him held in a spell of immobility. Well, boots and gauntlets would overcome her spell! He willed for them to do something for him—to leap from safety and into the midst of the enemy where his gauntlet-activated sword would cut down concealed wizards and warlocks and dung-clad fighters. Nothing, try as he wished, happened for him.

"Now," Helbah said.

Phenoblee raised her hands and made the downward sweep. Instantly a wind was blowing. It tore the dragons to shreds, exposing the wizards and warlocks and fighters who had been their magic guts. The orcs, astonishingly, were still running.

"Can't you do something, Phenoblee?" Helbah asked. "I knew that I didn't have the power, but I thought that you—"

"No protection against death-wish powders and coward vapors. Pharmaceutically the malignants are ahead of even orcs."

"Then we're doomed."

"We would be without a hero. Wait until they start up the rise, then release him. Kelvin, you blast the malignant army without exposing yourself. Just point the tip of your chimaera sting over the wall and give them a shock that will stop them. Ready, ready, NOW!"

Kelvin found he could move. Now his gauntlets and his boots were moving him. He had the sting under his hands, butt firmly against the ground. In the crystals he could see the eager, inflamed faces of the enemy. He concentrated on drawing forth the planet's energy through the sting—of exploding it out in one big crackling lightning bolt.

In the crystals he saw it—the blackened, screaming faces amid the charred and burning corpses. It was like that expression his father had—shooting fish in a barrel. Only this was no barrel with fish—this was impending doom outside the wall. Orcs, shivering and trembling, were climbing over the barrier. Orcs were throwing themselves flat, screaming, webbed fingers over their eyes. Obviously Zady's power had been great, but not, as it turned out, as powerful as the chimaera's.

"Kelvin! Use your Mouvar weapon now!"

Helbah's voice hardly penetrated as his body responded. Moved by the gauntlets more than by his own thought, he whipped out the bell-muzzled weapon and pointed it just at the wall. His finger triggered, and—

On the other side of the barrier there was an explosion. Bits of cloth and flesh and metal rained all about them, pieces of something that would give him nightmares landing and sticking on his face and arms and head.

"Well, at least the old buzvald had good aim!" Helbah remarked. "You countered that warlock's magic but he did hit you—with himself."

Kelvin wanted to vomit. He turned his head aside, ready to empty his stomach. At that moment Helbah grabbed his arm.

"Some still coming. Another shock, hero."

He knew he couldn't, but he did. The gauntlets knew just how to raise the sting and point it, and possibly helped him fire its bolt of energy. The energy exploded with charred bits of flesh as the lightning arched up over the barrier and down with a resounding crack.

"That did it! Now they're retreating! Give them a few parting bolts!"

Watching the crystals he saw the lightning strike retreating dung-clad soldiers and destroy them. Mercenaries never to gain the rewards promised them. He saw their bodies fly in all directions even as the dazzle came and went in his eyes.

Lightning, lightning—Master of Lightning, he thought. But it wasn't him exacting revenge and retribution in defense of those he loved—it was something far greater than himself.

"Kelvin, Kelvin, snap out of it!"

Dazed, he realized that he had just about wiped out the enemy, and then he saw it, there in the crystal—even more enemy than there had been, coming with the floating copper shields above their heads. Experimentally he fired a bolt and watched it sizzle and leap in a blue line from shield to shield before striking the ground to one side. Zady had reinstated her sting defense.

"Ebbernog," Kelvin suggested.

"Oh, Kelvin, the lad's burned out! Didn't you see the way he looked? He'll never be able to move things with his mind again! He won't be able to use his mind at all unless we finish this battle and Phenoblee can cure him. Kelvin, you must get

Horace, or if not Horace, the opal! Get it now, immediately; it's our only chance!"

"I'll try," Kelvin said, and took a long, long step. As before he heard imploding fireballs and felt heat singe his back, and then a blur of green and brown continuing on and on and then his foot coming down, down, down to rest.

He stood dizzily, hearing a dragon roar. He was at the spot where he and Jon had been when they had first adventured. They had slain a dragon, and then—

But now was not the time for reminiscences. Hastily he sidestepped a golden dragon's maddened charge. It wasn't Horace, and he knew Horace had to be up in those mountains. He took a sight on a distant peak and stepped there. Clouds floated by on either side as his dizziness returned and his lungs fought to adjust to the height.

So now where was Horace? That ledge over there—could that be the one Glint had talked about? He wished now that he had paid more attention. He stepped over to the ledge he had chosen, down to it, and standing, adjusting to the transference, he thought that yes, it did indeed look right. Down below him was a winding road where Horace might have come, where Glint and Ember had watched him in Ember's astral form. If that was the road and this the right ledge, he just had to go up mountain to find Glint and Ember's cave.

He stepped up the mountain and he searched and searched until he did in fact find a cave. As he stood before it, looking inside, a smell drifted out that had to be of a badgunk, a creature noted for its ferocity and stink. Could Glint and his foster sister have lived here?

"Skeeunk." The little cub looked up at him from glistening black eyes, then elevated its hips and broad tail and danced toward him on its front legs. A stinking shower was coming fast, and if baby was here at the entrance, could mama be far behind?

He stepped, not quite fast enough. The spray from under the cub's raised plume caught him on the chest and stomach and partially on the face. He put his foot down on the ledge he had recently left, bent over, and was sick. A bit later his boots took him to a pond of water and plunged him repeatedly into its icy grip.

Many steps later Kelvin had to concede to himself that he wasn't finding Horace. All he was doing was stepping on mountains, stepping on cliffs, stepping in water. He was sopping wet most of the time and he still stank. He was stepping, stepping, stepping, and discovering nothing that could in any way help.

Worst of all he was now lost. He was wasting his time while his sister was suffering. Because of his inadequacies Zady was going to win her battle and subject all those he held dear to unspeakable torment.

CHAPTER 18

In Search of Horace

*M*erlain sat between Charles and Grandma Knight watching the faraway battle. It was almost too much to bear, all this killing. She and Charles and the royal pains had seen similar things when they were children, and then not in crystals. They had lain in the woods, fire all around, watching a soldier die. They had seen with wide, scared eyes dying horses and men. There had to be a different way, she had thought then, and thought so now.

Charles, she thought to her brother. Carefully, she did not look at her grandmother or the pains. *I think one of us should go get Horace.*

Charles' eyes remained on the action. Fireballs were zooming again. Thanks to the orc witch the Alliance had their defense. It was a standoff. But those advancing dung-clads with the copper disks levitated above their heads appeared ominous. She hoped her daddy had that handled.

You know what Helbah said, Merlain. You know what Daddy said too.

Charles, are you always going to listen to your father? We're grown-ups! We're smart!

Smarter than Helbah? he asked, willing to believe.

Yes! Just because she knows magic and has been around for centuries doesn't make her brilliant. Certainly we're smarter than the kings!

Charles moved his eyes sideways to check. Kildom and Kildee, as if responding to a cue, were bringing fresh glasses of lemmieaid and a big bowl of magically popped corbeans. They sat there now, stuffing themselves, smearing butgen over their faces with every crunch. They watched first one crystal and then another, focusing on the killing. In theory they were studying strategy, but in fact they were enjoying the excitement.

What do you want me to do, Merlain?

I want to get Horace.

Your husband tried that.

But it's me Horace will listen to. He won't say no to me, Charles. To you, he might.

So how will you do it? he asked.

Take the belt. You know I can use it as well as Glint. I can be over in dragon territory and to the right place before you know it.

I doubt that, Merlain.

Doubt it all you like, I'm going.

What do you think Grandma will say, not to mention the royal pains?

I'll take the belt out of the cupboard and pretend I'm going to the privy. Once I'm outside, I'm gone.

You're gone in the head, Charles opined. It was that sibling rivalry they had inherited from Kelvin and their aunt. *You just want me to sit here and pretend I don't know?*

You don't know a lot of the time. But yes. All you have to

*do is keep your mouth shut. Grandma won't think about me
being gone for a while. If she does mention it tell her I went for
a swim. She won't be suspicious.*

*You must not know Grandma—she's been suspicious of
something ever since I remember.*

*Oh, Charles, you know how snoopy women are. She's not
quite a witch, but she does read the cards. Besides, it's just a
grandmother's way to be protective.*

*If you're going to go, Merlain, go. I'm tired of arguing with
you.*

And you will keep your mouth shut?

Don't I always?

Merlain stood up and made a point of stretching. She
started out to the kitchen, where she intended to grab the belt
out of the cupboard and dart out the back door.

"Where are you going, Merlain?" one of the redheads
asked. She was like a big sister or cousin to them now, though
once she and Charles had been physically the younger. Typical
young brats when they were adventuring together, they still
were.

"Out."

"Going to swim?"

"Maybe later." How nice of them to suggest it for her.

"I'm coming with you." The leer was naughty.

"Not where I'm going, you're not." The suggestion of
what she would be doing was perfect. She couldn't have
planned it better.

Royalty snickered. "I thought you were fidgeting. You
sure you don't want help?"

"No, I'll be right back." She went on, knowing that she
would not be followed. What was it in boys their physical age
that made them so crude? Of course Kildom and Kildee had
been crude and bothersome enough when younger. How those
freckled faces had lit when they had a chance to pinch a
shapely bottom or look up some unwary woman's skirt!
They'd had the time of their kid lives at the convention. Wearing the invisibility cloaks Zady had given them they had
pinched bottoms, spied upon, and otherwise behaved grossly

to their hearts' content. Thankfully the cloaks were past history, otherwise not a girl or woman in their kingdoms would feel safe.

In the kitchen she opened the cupboard and took out the belt. She wrapped it up on itself, slipped it under her blouse, and held it there as she walked to the privy. Once she was inside she slipped the belt on, exited, and went around the building to the back. There were trees shading the necessary structure and a walk paved with half blue and half white flagstones; like all else here, the division was up the middle—two white stones on the left, two blue on the right.

She put her finger on the belt's red button and mentally rehearsed the steps. She pushed the button, nudged the rise lever, and rose to just under the branches. Then forward along a path, then up above the trees.

Learning to use the belt had been far easier than learning to ride a horse. Besides, the belt was faster. The only problem was the occasional bug colliding with her. Other than that, flying was, as her grandfather Knight said, a real breeze. She would have been enjoying the trip if it hadn't been for the circumstances.

What had gotten into Horace? She just couldn't believe he would behave so irresponsibly. Could Zady have put a spell on him? Why hadn't Helbah or someone thought of the possibility? Maybe old Zady put a spell on them so that they wouldn't think of her putting a spell on Horace? If that were the case Zady had missed thinking of Merlain and Charles. The old witch might not miss many chances to plot evil, but she'd proven herself vulnerable when she lost her head.

Faster than she had realized it would happen, the terrain changed. It started as farmland and occasional patches of wood crisscrossed with roads to wilderness. Soon the wilderness grew dense, and the land more mountainous. Ahead was dragon territory, and high in the territory's roughest mountains was where Glint had found Horace and Ember. Merlain knew the spot well, having been deeply into her beloved's mind. Being telepathic, as her grandfather called it, had its

advantages. If Daddy and Helbah realized how many were her
advantages they would have sent her here themselves.

Sooner than she had expected she saw the big rushing
mountain stream, and the quiet pool shaded by trees and
bushes—almost a garden with its flowers and ferns. It was like
seeing it again, this time through her own eyes. She flew overhead, easily spotting the couple on the bank. She slowed,
pushed the descend lever, and gently landed on the opposite
shore.

HORACE! HORACE, WAKE UP!

Huh? Who's that?

Merlain.

Who's that, dear? the other dragon's thought came.

Shut up, darling. It's my sister.

We need you and the opal, Horace. NOW!!!

Why? Ember needs—

Horace, this is important!

Nothing more important than Ember. She passionate mate!

*Horace, do you remember the ugly witch? Do you remem-
ber how she made me fall? Then Daddy cut her head off and
stepped after me, and you swallowed the opal.*

"GROOMTH!" Horace said. Most dragons had poor
memories and didn't need to remember much, but Horace was
her brother. He remembered, and the remembering made him
angry.

*Horace, that old witch is back! She's got a new young body
and her old, ugly head! She's come back to get the opal! She'll
take it from you! And she'll make me walk off the cliff again!
Only this time she won't let Daddy come after me!*

"GROOMMTH! GROOMMTH! GROOMMTH!"

*Yes, Horace, I knew you wouldn't like that. That's why I'm
telling you. Only you and the opal and maybe Daddy can save
me. Help me, Horace, help me!*

Instantly Horace was by her feet. He looked down at her
with concerned red eyes, his tail wagging nervously from side
to side. Truly, she had him now. He would return with her the
way she wanted.

"GROOMTH! GROOMPTH!" Ember protested. From
across the pond she seemed far smaller than she actually was
and as forlorn as an abandoned kitup. She must have become
used to Horace's opaling, but she wasn't used to his leaving
her.

Don't go, Horace! Don't trust sister! Humans are for eat-
ing, and some of them are tough! Stay, Horace, stay!

Shut up, beloved! This is family.

But Horace, I need loving! It's only been a couple days and
a couple nights! What kind of lover are you, anyway?

Merlain had been wondering about that herself. She and
Glint had had quite a time after their marriage, but continuous sex had turned out not to be practicable. By all accounts,
dragons were less inclined than humans. How was it that these
two had been so constantly avid? It was evident that it wasn't
just Horace's desire; Ember was just as eager. Something more
than romance or telepathy was operating here.

Suddenly she had her answer. Dueese were mating on the
water, raising and lowering their wings and beating the water
to a frenzy. Across the pond two mustters, their oily coats
gleaming, were locked in an embrace of lovemaking. She herself, she recognized, had an urge that only her husband could
satisfy.

Ember, she thought quickly, *the old witch made plants*
grow here to keep you passionate and occupied. She did this so
that Horace would not come to kill her and she could kill all the
rest of his family.

I'm family now! Ember insisted. She was glaring across
the water as though she might charge.

Of course, Ember, of course! But making love for many
days and nights will weaken him.

He sleep, be strong later.

Yes, Ember, yes, but when he's very, very weak the old
witch will come for the opal. She'll turn him inside out and take
it from his gizzard. Then she'll leave him. What'll you do then?

Tickle his insides?

He won't be able to eat or to pleasure you. Don't you want
him to pleasure you?

The female dragon's golden head snapped up. *Go, Horace! Go kill old interfering witch! Kill everyone sister say to, then come back! Hurry back! Don't delay!*

Thank you, Ember! Merlain thought to her. *Thank you for being sensible. When this war is over I'll bring Glint here and we'll sunnymoon as well.* And how! she thought to herself without sending it out. Glint would be thrilled.

Kelvin paused on the third ledge he had found that looked right to him. This could be the one, but there were so many ledges in so many mountains. He hadn't realized the size of dragon territory. It must cover an area as large as Rotternik, most of it up and down. Someday he'd have to look at a map.

If this were the mountain and the ledge, there should be a river. There should be a wide place screened by trees and bushes, and there, Glint had assured him, he would find the dragons.

His weak eyes just weren't up to the task. He had to step carefully and not miss any rivers. That blue ribbon—that had to be another river. He stepped off from the ledge, to the bank of a pretty mountain stream. It was rushing right along, fish leaping in the rapids, and he thought the water too swift. But then just in case this was the river, he should pace its length. With his spanner boots each stride would take him as far as he wanted.

He stepped out, visualizing a place he could see where the rapids started. He came down a little too fast and stumbled, tripped in the water, and got wet. In a moment he was more than just damp and was being pulled along by a current.

His gauntlets, almost angrily, it seemed to him, reached out and grabbed a boulder and held on while the boots pulled on the calves of his legs and pulled his legs against the boulder. His gauntlets found a vine and he pulled, and the boots pushed and he stumbled up on the boulder, wet but free. This wasn't going to work unless he took shorter steps. From a distance he had seemed to be stepping where it was dry. Ignoring the water soaking his clothes but somehow not in his boots and gauntlets, he stepped carefully to a log lying midway across the stream. He landed almost right, so that his feet only slipped but did not slip all the way off. He stepped from the log into a clump of bushes and got scratched. Then he stepped onto a big rock and next onto a clear stretch of shore. The following step took him to the start of a sharp bend.

"WHOOF!"

Kelvin rubbed some remaining water from his eyes to see a golden blur coming at him. A dragon! He sought to pull his sword, but his gauntlets didn't help.

"NO, EMBER, NO! THAT'S DADDY!"

Merlain's voice! She was shouting the words from somewhere close or else his mind amplified words she had both spoken and thought. Somehow words that were spoken loud and thought strongly at the same time came through deafeningly.

"WEOOMTH!" There was now a copper-scaled dragon between him and the golden-scaled one. The golden-scaled reached the copper and lifted front legs, circled its throat and squeezed.

"Horace, this is Ember?"

Who else, Father?

Kelvin was stunned. "Horace, you can mind-talk! Like Charles and Merlain!"

Always could. Ember and I mind-talk together. Glint taught her. Merlain and Charles and I always mind-talk.

"Merlain, how did you—?"

His daughter lifted from the opposite bank and flew to him. She landed beside him and gave him a hug that seemed to be influenced by Ember's. She had become more demonstrative with the years, but never before had she hugged him so hard.

Kelvin looked at the levitation belt as soon as she let up on him. He had known she must have it, and now that this was confirmed he should speak. Parental disapproval needed to be voiced. He opened his mouth.

But she didn't wait. "Daddy, I know how badly you need

Horace and the opal. He'll take you to the battle and you can
kill that old witch! I could see what was happening and I
couldn't stand it. I knew Horace would listen to me even if he
wouldn't listen to my husband. That's why I disobeyed you
and came here, Daddy—to help you."

He swallowed, amazed at how well developed and fast-
talking his daughter had become. He felt for her as a devoted
father should feel, but now he felt an additional unasked-for
urge. He could wish for her mother to be here with him and
for their daughter to be safe with her husband at home.

"Daddy!"

She had gotten up on Horace's back. Horace was squatting and she was reaching out her hand.

Kelvin grabbed a wing and yanked himself up, almost
going over his son's neck. He straightened, took a good hold
on the opposite wing, and felt more the fool than he had in all
his years of heroing. "Don't worry, Daddy, I can hold on to
you. Besides, I've got your belt. Horace is taking us to the
palaces' swimming pool."

SPLASH!

Water got into his nose and mouth as he bobbed to the
surface. There was no one about that he could see, but Merlain
was already flying to the blue palace.

"Charles! Grandma! Glow! Kildom and Kildee!"

Everyone came in answer to his daughter's call. "Bring
out a crystal!" he called.

In a moment Glow brought a crystal out to him. It
showed the battle, or part of it. Dung-uniformed Zady-fight-
ers were battling and sweating and suffering from the heat
under the floating copper disks. His allies and friends hacked
away at them with swords. Now and then a sword connected
and an enemy went down. Then a green-uniformed man Kelvin vaguely recognized took a sword in his vitals; his guts
burst forth as his attacker ripped, and with the ripping Kelvin
lost the contents of his own stomach. In a moment rage replaced his sickness.

"Go there, Horace!" he shouted, tapping the crystal.

"Kill those wearing that putrid uniform! Take me with you! Now!"

And suddenly there was a sword swinging at him and he was ducking it and Horace was bellowing and lashing out with a taloned forefoot.

CHAPTER 19

Unexpected Allies

Kelvin discovered that Horace's undersized wings made excellent handholds, or in his case gauntlet-holds. He and his boots and his gauntlets now seemed attuned to Horace's sudden moves, including his opal-leaps. With no trouble at all he would brace himself at just the right time, and the hard scales of his mount remained practically glued to his pantaloons.

At first he used his sword as though he were on horseback, or rather the gauntlets did. But practice made perfect, as his father often said, and Horace was quickly done with practicing. Horses and riders fell and rolled to the whipcrack of the dragon's tail. Great pointed teeth speared through armor and man, and a flick of a forefoot pulled them off again. Roundhouse sweeps of forelegs took men from mounts or down with mounts. Whenever the enemy had them surrounded and seemed to Kelvin about to pull them down, the enemy vanished as Horace opaled them to a more congenial killing spot.

Soon the enemy got wise to their tactics and became less prone to attack. This left Horace attacking group after group of dung-clad men. Kelvin was thinking that they would win despite everything, and then he saw the sorcerer with raised hand and curved bony fingers making a hurling motion.

The Mouvar weapon was out of its sheath and triggered before Kelvin realized it. The sorcerer caught the rebound of his own hostile magic and collapsed as a mewling, unsupported mass of flesh.

It had been the notorious gelatin spell that turned the strong weak by liquefying their bones. Horace was moving them around so fast now and the enemy was so thinned that they were bound to come more and more into the range of magic-hurlers. Helbah and her crew would be working to protect them, but Kelvin knew that he and the gauntlets had to remain alert.

In a short while Kelvin was using the Mouvar antimagic weapon almost exclusively. Horace was so efficient at grabbing, slashing, and gnashing, then being elsewhere, that there was little need for the sword. Once one of his boots kicked out and caught a dung-uniformed killer in the face. A little later the gauntlet not holding the Mouvar weapon grasped a sword blade, twisted it from a hand, hurled the sword, and skewered the attacker.

Kelvin knew he was a perfect picture of a hero. He knew there was a hero fighting here, but that was his offspring. Even in the midst of battle he had to marvel that he and Heln had produced such a magnificent, enviable son. In a short time Horace's mouth and claws were red with men's blood and his tail smeared as well. Still the enemy was there in surprising numbers.

Trust old Zady to reanimate the dead and fill in with phantoms, Kelvin thought, and knew that this was happening.

"She's doing it now, Helbah," Glint said, closing his eyes to the crystals and concentrating on what was in his head. "She's sending Lucernia to Rotternik."

"You ready, Whitestone?"

"Ready, Helbah."

"Krassnose, Phenoblee, keep watch."

The orcs opened and closed their gills, acknowledging.

Helbah made a gesture and a smoke, and two white dovgens flew up from behind the wall. Immediately fireballs sped to destroy them, but were shattered against the orcs' magical barrier.

The smooth-backed Master of Rotternik stood on the balcony looking down at the beastmen: oranguillas, gortans, babkeys, and monoons. All were hairy, unlike Strongback himself. All were considered ugly by smoothskins outside the border. In actual fact the nature of the population was Rotternik's greatest strength. In the past Rotternik's terrain and less-than-friendly life-forms had been protection. But Zady's coming altered that.

The ugly old witch with the now-beautiful smoothskin body had come straight to him with her ultimatum: Rotternik's population must swarm out at her order and attack the survivors of the Alliance. Since she had demonstrated remarkable powers, Strongback had reluctantly agreed to assemble the citizenry and await her messenger.

Overhead an ugly bird was circling in slow, ominous patterns. Strongback had an urge to call for an archer, but considering Zady's power he knew it would be unwise. He waited as patiently as he could for what was really no surprise. A warty-necked buzvul landed in front of him with a plop. Smoke puffed around the bird and a smoothskinned woman with stringy hair and sunken light eyes stepped out.

"Strongback, I'm Lucernia, sent by Zady. You have all your population out of the trees?"

"Down to the smallest babkey," Strongback mourned. He didn't like what Zady had demanded, but he saw no way of defying her. Rotternik had had its share of magic practitioners, but unfortunately long ago. There had been a choice then.

The population had chosen to return to the trees and lead happy contented lives rather than build cities and war with other kingdoms. It had seemed a wise choice then, and certainly it was popular with the general citizenry. Protecting their kingdom and their way of life was the magical border that shut out the gaze of intrepid explorers from other lands. Magic from afar would not work past the border, not even the magic of communication crystals.

"Then you'll order them to swarm and I'll add magic to aid in the recognition of the enemy. If the magic doesn't take and they destroy some of our mercenaries, no problem."

"I believe in Zady's ruthlessness," Strongback said. Could his people expect better? The chattering babkeys and long-armed oranguillas and their cousins, the very powerful gortans, were beasts to the outsider. Wouldn't all be destroyed when Zady's battle was won? Of what use would they be?

Two small dovgens lit on the balcony railing behind Lucernia's back. There was a poof of smoke, and the smoke cleared immediately to reveal a small woman and a small man. The woman he recognized.

"Hel—" he started, then gulped. "—bah!"

"And Whitestone," said the tall, robed man. The wizard gestured, and fire snapped from his fingers and coiled around Lucernia's puffy ankles and stout, bowed legs. At the same time Helbah made a move and the malignant was stiffened with a spell.

"Strongback, you've a choice to make. Serve Zady or serve the Alliance." Whitestone did not quite make it an ultimatum.

"Zady said the Alliance can't win. She said serve her now or she'd wither all of Dreadful Forest." He pointed to a large yellowwood's drooping leaves and dead branches. "Like that."

"Zady lied." Helbah made a pass, tossed a powder, and the tree straightened up, healthy and bright. "If she wins, the world will get sick and eventually die. Trees, plants, birds, animals, people—to her they have no value."

"What can I do?" Strongback felt hope, observing the tree. "Can I fight for the Alliance? Can my people?"

"Yes. Your populace can fight, and you can fight personally. Zady is the enemy, not the Alliance."

"Helbah, as you know the magic crystals do not work

within Rotternik's borders. It was a precaution taken long ago by my ancestor. But when you go back, tell your people that Rotternik's people will indeed swarm. We will fight to save our forest. Rotternik together with the Alliance."

"Done," Helbah said.

Kelvin couldn't believe how tired he was getting. He was hardly striking out with anything other than the Mouvar weapon, but the continual fighting was exhausting in ways other than physical. All had become just a blur of noise, dying screams, crunching bones, and horror. When he was younger Kelvin had sometimes found relief through fainting and vomiting, but now his spell-strengthened body would not allow it and there was never a chance to do it anyway. The dragon's strength and stamina were truly marvelous: kill one bunch of foes or be mobbed by overwhelming numbers, and he paused not a moment before opaling into a new fray. It seemed a continuous fight to Kelvin, regardless of the scenery that changed. It seemed to him that they had traversed the length of Hermandy's border and were not far from Rotternik. That glowing border might be close.

A big man disappeared from beneath Horace's left forefoot as they opaled. Now a thin man's corpse was in the big man's place. Horace, pausing not for breath, shook a man with a yellow beard, then quickly and daintily wiped the garbage from his teeth. Now the remarkable child was grabbing new foes, his slapping, slashing tail creating further havoc on either side. Mouvar's weapon darted in Kelvin's hand, his gauntlets triggering it. Wizards and witches who served Zady burned or screamed or otherwise suffered what they had intended to be his and Horace's cruel fate. Kelvin tried focusing on just one bit of action, but all blurred. The gauntlets moving his hands and the boots sometimes swinging his feet were not in the least dependent on his eyesight. Time after time his hand destroyed attackers he never saw. Less frequently a boot yanked him to the side in order to kick a mounted enemy or deflect a weapon while the gauntlets were otherwise occupied.

Oh, what an impression he was making! And he knew

that he was completely undeserving. He just wanted to get out of here so he could be suitably sick. Without the boots, gauntlets, weapon, and dragon, he was just a country bumpkin.

Now there were giants before them—orc and human. The orcs had been cleansed of their cowardice and were back in action. An orc and a human of slightly larger size were grappling. The orc was trying to get its teeth into the man's throat, but the man had a large dagger barely held back from the orc's heaving breast. The orc was losing green blood, and surrounding him were many dead men who had returned upon their deaths to normal human size.

Kelvin didn't know how Horace knew that the enlarged man and not the orc was the enemy. One quick snap at the man's ankle and the giant looked down, and in the distraction the orc snapped his teeth deep into a neck vein. Blood showered them, very, very red. Then they were away, in nearly vertical position, Horace's claws and tail wrapped around the throat of another human giant. The second giant twirled, and the orc he had been about to slay slew him instead with a deft sword thrust through what seemed an exploding torrent of the giant's bowels.

Now they were on a hillside where they had been before. Kelvin could see many dead former giants lying in dung uniforms partially dyed with red. There wasn't another human giant in sight—only orcs searching with narrowed eyes and ready swords and clubs.

Horace snorted as the scenery changed. They were now facing a second dragon, this one with golden scales. The dragon lunged for them, mouth open and ready to grab. Kelvin felt terror, but his gauntlets thrust the Mouvar weapon into the open savage mouth and triggered. Instantly the illusion of a dragon was gone, and in the spot the illusion had occupied were two charred wizards turning rapidly into ash. A swish of Horace's tail went through the former wizards and dissipated them into particles and sparks that would never revive to cast destructive spells.

Kelvin sighed at the nearness of their own destruction. Horace had been preparing to fight another dragon, not seeing through the illusion. Only the gauntlets had recognized the magic and reversed the spell in time.

Now they had opaled to a different spot. Here were men in green uniforms. He recognized his father and brother-in-law before him. His father had a wound on his arm and Lester was trying unsuccessfully to stanch the abundantly flowing blood. Instantly Kelvin was unwary, and alarmed for his father.

"Father! Lester! It's me and Horace!"

There was no answer.

His gauntlets tingled. This meant danger, but look as he might he saw no enemy. Could his father and Lester be an illusion, as the dragon had been? If so why didn't the Mouvar weapon lift in his hand? Because the illusion concealed enemy soldiers and not enemy magic-wielders?

Horace was starting toward their apparent kin, accepting them as genuine. Kelvin knew that if he didn't act now it might be too late, and if he did act and he was wrong, the mistake would always haunt him. He drew his sword, though he feared there was no reaching down to them; otherwise the gauntlet would have drawn it for him.

Horace, these people aren't who they appear! It's the enemy: DESTROY!

There was no one at all in front of them and Horace's tail was striking and splintering with stunning force. They were to the side now, many dragon-lengths from where they had been. Behind them and scattered all over the ground were slithers of wood and pieces of rope and a large dragon-lance with its tip smeared with a dark-green paste. Far from the wreckage, thrown there by the destructive whip, three men in enemy uniform lay smashed.

It had been a catapult set to skewer Horace! A trap Zady or one of her wizards or witches had thought up. Without his gauntlets he would never have guessed.

They were on a new hill, and here there were only scattered dead. A second hill, equally devoid of apparent life. Now a third hill with Alliance soldiers and orcs. Kelvin drew a breath to hail them, but Horace was not wasting time.

They were in a glade. Heln was here, rushing to them. His mother was standing back, smiling.

His Mouvar weapon jerked in his hand. An old hag clutched her face and screamed. A second hag opened her arms before reaching them and dropped something that produced a big green smoke.

They were on a plain. A howling wind, unslowed by trees or rough terrain, tried hard to separate them. Kelvin held on while he and Horace were lifted and carried by the wind. They were being drawn up a wind funnel, to be slung out and dashed in a moment. Kelvin stopped his breath.

They were on the top of a hill he had briefly glimpsed while whirling. Whatever witch or warlock had hit them with the wind had taken the gauntlets by surprise. That didn't happen often! But now they were free, and—

They were in an almost familiar place. Alliance fighters and benigns were here and the gauntlets were not tingling. Why were all the faces turned skyward?

A great smashing, crashing wave of water roared through the hills, bearing down on them. Boulders and logs and torn-up trees and houses rode the crest. An illusion or real? Real, he guessed.

Horace was squatting. Hastily Kelvin motioned for the people nearest to climb on. Three people grabbed his outstretched hand and climbed up to join him. Then there was no time—the water was falling on them.

They were on a facing hill. Below, people wearing green uniforms were being tossed and drowned. There was no going back to make further rescues.

The man holding Horace's tail tight in his fighter's hands started to say something and at that moment the hill began to shake. "QUAKE!" the man screamed, and disappeared as he dropped off, and—

They were at a different place where there was fighting. Green and dun uniforms swirled about, seeming not to notice them. No shaking ground here, no monstrous flood, no destructive wind blowing. Behind the tangled, fighting knots was the glowing border of Rotternik.

The battlers stumbled across the magic barrier and disappeared. Kelvin knew that those men would see nothing behind them if they looked back—only the glowing border. As a deterrent to unwelcome visitors the border had long served its purpose. But now Rotternik was being invaded by fighting men as more and more unintentionally crossed the border.

As he watched from Horace's strangely still back, two Alliance soldiers stepped back into visibility. Gone were their foes—living or dead they had been left behind. One of the men screamed words, and then hairy arms and legs and beastly faces appeared just behind them. Hairy folk, big and small, were leaping, running, almost flying across the legendary barrier.

Kelvin heard a groan from one of the two men they had rescued. "Gods," the man said, clutching Kelvin's shoulders, "isn't it enough that we have to fight magic! What can we do against babkeys?"

"We can run from them," the companion in escape supplied. "If they keep pouring on out, we'll have to!"

"You don't mean that," the first soldier said. "You'll fight them, even if they're meaner and stronger than Zady's mercenaries. We—" He paused, staring. "Did you see that?"

"Yeah, that babkey's got a dung-clad! Eating off his face! Doesn't know its colors. Unless Zady cues them they'll attack anybody!"

"They aren't now! Look!"

The newcomers, apparent beasts all, were attacking with unparalleled violence only the dung-clads. They ignored the phantoms, possibly cued in by the lack of smell.

"Well, I'll be cursed! They're helping us! They enlisted on our side! Come on, let's help them as well!"

The two flood escapees dropped from Horace and ran with quickly drawn swords to attack five dung-clads battling one large gortan swinging a tree branch at their swords.

Soon Alliance soldiers and hairy folk were battling a common enemy.

CHAPTER 20

Retreat

Zady and her minions had been preparing spells all morning, but there seemed to be something unusually complicated in the spell she was working on now. Jon had to wonder about it. Hanging by her wrists, suffering little more pain than that of her swollen wrists and aching body joints, she had nothing to do but think. It was good to think about things that might later help. The old hag was up to something new, and it was best to concentrate on that. Instead of on the pain.

From the first moment that she had been tied here Zady had insisted that she watch the magic crystals lined up in front of her. There were three, each the size of a small table, and in each horrifying scenes occurred. Men were disemboweled with full sword sweeps, horses beheaded, limbs hacked off living bodies while blood squirted and the victims screamed their last.

Constantly Zady would interrupt her spelling to attend to Jon. Tapping an image of a suffering man she would toss a powder in her face, and Jon would inhale the powder every time. Under Zady's influence she felt the unspeakable pain of the one Zady had chosen. This had gone on and on, and only the fact that the hag was now involved in other mischief was giving her respite. Jon was grateful that there was nothing worse happening to her than sweat getting into her eyes and insects crawling on her face. She hadn't screamed for probably an hour.

It would be pleasant to sleep, Jon thought. But Zady

would not allow it. To sleep would be to awake to another's agonizing fate.

Zady was reciting what seemed gibberish while making gestures with her young arms and hands and twisting and turning her young body in a macabre dance. Before her on the ground was what seemed a child's toy: a catapult of no great size with a man-sized spear loaded on it. Zady was dancing around the catapult and giving it her attention.

Jon wondered why the witch put all this time and effort on one spell. It had to be that the toy catapult brought here by soldiers in a cart was of some real importance, but of what importance she couldn't tell. With the full-sized military catapults she had at her command, why the toy? There had to be a reason.

Zady stopped her dancing and came over to her while her minion Lucernia smirked. She looked up at the ropes, making certain they were cutting off circulation just enough to maximize the pain, not enough to kill the limbs. Dead limbs didn't hurt. Then, smiling from her hideous warty face, she gestured at the object of her labors.

"You are wondering why, aren't you, dearie? Watch!"

With a wave of her hands and a sprinkling from a vial, Zady made a sulfurous cloud that sent Jon to coughing. When her eyes got unwatered there had been a magical transformation. The catapult was now large—several times bigger than those wheeled out to battle. Fast to the large central timber, the spear was now by itself as big around as a respectable tree. The witch pointed two fingers at her and brought her shapely arm around, ending in a finger snap and pointing at the catapult with a commanding forefinger.

Dragon Horace was there before the catapult, her unlikely brother riding on his own son's back. Magically, undoubtedly through the use of the opal, they had suddenly appeared. The copper scales of the dragon flashed in the bright sunlight, and Kelvin's jaw dropped as he looked with bugged-out eyes at her, his sister. In his right hand Kelvin held the Mouvar weapon she had seen him use so effectively, but the sight of his sister had to be distracting him.

WHACK!

The great timber shot forward, propelling the oversized spear with the speed of magic. The spear entered Horace's back and came out his belly, burying its cruel forged head deep into the hard ground. Horace's legs and tail spasmed; his head jerked in a shower of his own human blood. The dragon was pinned there, through his backbone and torn vitals, and in time he would expire. In the meantime a blood-soaked Kelvin was scrambling from the victim's side. One of Horace's hind feet kicked in reflex and struck Kelvin.

Jon blinked. Her only brother, broken and bloody and undoubtedly dying, was lying almost at her feet. He raised a smashed face and looked up at her from the eye not hanging down his cheek. His mouth opened and dark blood gushed out between broken teeth.

"KELVIN!" Jon screamed.

The witch's fingers snapped.

Reality was restored. Kelvin and the dragon son were gone. The catapult was again small. Zady's warty face was gleeful and Lucernia was dancing as though from joy.

"Did you enjoy the show, dearie? It's only a preview."

Jon struggled with something she knew was not right. "They'll see! They'll have to see! Horace will even if Kelvin doesn't!"

"Wrong, dearie."

Zady sprinkled some more vile-smelling liquid, made a twirl, and pulled out a nothing from under her dark wrapper. She spread the nothing and her body vanished, leaving only her head. The head floated over the catapult. The body reappeared and then disappeared as she stepped up on the catapult's platform. The catapult vanished by degrees until it seemed gone. Zady reappeared, gesturing at nothing and obviously very pleased with herself.

"You see, dearie? No, you don't, do you? Nor will the lizard see, nor your brother. I will restore the size and when they come here, drawn in part by my magic, they will arrive at this spot. It won't be long now. I suggest you resume screaming."

Zady's long and beautiful fingers snapped, drawing Jon's attention to a crystal she could not avoid seeing. In the crystal Kelvin, covered with his son's blood, was sliding off the copper scales. A great scaled foot swung, caught him across the lower back, lifted him, and flung him hard.

Jon screamed as pain exploded in Kelvin's body, as his face struck ground and smashed. She felt it all as his mangled features lifted, one eye hanging by a thread on his mashed cheek. There was no way she could deny she felt the agony.

She screamed and screamed, uncontrollably. Zady listened, pleased, savoring it.

Kelvin saw the lone light-colored swoosh circling, somehow avoiding the fireballs imploding all around. It had to be one of his side, he hoped; this seemed logical since his side's magic-makers were giving it protection. He'd better warn Horace, since to Horace the big, ungainly bird would look like lunch.

Horace, I think that bird's a friend. Don't eat it.

What's the matter, you think I'm stupid?

As a matter of fact Kelvin *had* thought that until fairly recently. Dragons were, after all, dragons, and though dragons were known for strength and ferocity, no one ever had credited them with brains. Horace of course was different, but it was all too easy to think of him as a typical dragon.

The swoosh landed between them and the three hairy people pulling apart a dung uniform with the unfortunate malignant mercenary wearing it. Blood and intestines soon burst, but in the meantime smoke puffed where the bird had been and cleared to reveal a handsome young blond man without armor.

"GLINT!" Kelvin exclaimed. He hadn't expected his son-in-law.

"Helbah sent me. There's a mission for you, but I have to help. She knows where Zady is, but she wants me to reconnoiter first. I have to get close to find out what defense she has planned. After I find out I tell you, and then we move in and attack."

Kelvin considered that reconnaissance hadn't helped them much. Glint had only confided what he had learned to Helbah, and Helbah had revealed nothing about any of it to him. At the time Kelvin's being left out had rankled, but now he knew there had to be a reason. Helbah wanted Zady destroyed at least as badly as he did.

"Where is she?"

"Help me up, Kelvin." Glint held up his hand.

Kelvin's gauntlets clasped Glint by the wrist and easily lifted him up and behind him. Glint locked his arms around Kelvin's chest, clasping his hands in front.

"Don't go where I tell you first—Helbah warned against it. Zady's with her main minions atop that mount, in where she can keep watch. There is an outcropping about halfway up that will give some protection from fireballs. If Horace can focus on it and take us there, that's where we go first."

They were. The rocks above them were almost a roof. Behind them was a cave mouth and the remains of something's kill.

"Well?"

Glint closed his eyes. Kelvin felt him slump and reached back to brace his elbows. He knew the telepath was trying for minds up the mountain. If Helbah had let him take the dragonberry as he had wanted to, he would have done the reconnaissance himself. But the dragonberries were dangerous, as witness the time his brother and sister-in-law-to-be had been trapped in astral form in the world of the silver serpents.

Glint lifted his head. "It's going to be tricky. She's got Jon tied by the wrists to this tree limb before an array of crystals, and she wants to use her to bait you and Horace. She knows you won't like the way she tortured your sister."

"Tortured? She tortured Jon?"

"Mentally. Illusion stuff, but bad. She has a trap set for us. I don't know what it is, but I got a little of it from Jon. The problem is that Jon's in so much agony that her thoughts are mainly of what she's feeling. She's trying to think a warning, but all I get is 'Don't come! Stay away, Kelvin! Please, please

stay away!' I think she's tried to believe that one of your
children or I would read her."

"Jon's in agony! We have to stop it! Horace—"

They were surrounded now by trees. Horace had jumped
them further up the mountain.

"Slow, Horace!" Glint urged. "I don't know what the
trap is, but Jon's warning us away. I think I should—"

They had moved. They were on a narrow ledge, Horace
clinging to a slope. They moved again.

A plump, middle-aged woman hung from her wrists and
screamed uncontrollably. Her eyes were wide with horror and
focused on where they now were, though there had been no
instant's time to notice their arrival.

WHACK!

A spear of unlikely size had buried itself in the ground, at
the spot they had momentarily occupied. But now, thanks to
Horace's sudden thought, they were only close. Somehow the
dragon had barely touched the spot and then ordered the opal
to hop them to the side.

Thinks I'm stupid! came Horace's thought. At the same
instant he launched himself physically, possibly with the help
of the opal, to an apparently empty spot between trees. Wood
splintered invisibly beneath them, and wood and bits of metal
and broken ropes became visible beneath the dragon's weight
and fury. Suddenly all the device's remains were visible, and
even to Kelvin it was clear that the dragon's instincts had
carried him to the logical spot to set up an invisible catapult.

Kelvin would have drawn a sharp breath, but his Mouvar
weapon snapped up and triggered. To their side a fireball
changed course and swooped on a plump, wide-mouthed
witch who had been its sender. The witch burned, screaming.

Zady was standing directly facing them, her hands raised
to throw a magic spell.

No. Horace! It's a trap! was Glint's thought, so desperately strong that it was dizzying.

Zady vanished as Horace's weight broke through a thin
covering revealing a pit lined with large, piercing spikes. Kel-

vin had time to notice the dark green smears on the points almost touching Horace's copper belly scales, and then—

They were back where Horace had been when he pounced for Zady. The witch's evil minion burned brightly now, not getting help, her form turning into ashes.

"I don't catch Zady's thought," Glint complained. "She's blocking me. Where'd she go?"

"Take me to Jon!" Kelvin ordered.

They were in front of his sister. Horace stretched and Kelvin stood up on him, pulled erect by the gauntlets and balanced by the boots more than by athletic ability. The right-hand gauntlet drew his sword for him and sliced through the ropes holding Jon's wrists.

"Oh, Kelvin," Jon said, sinking into his arms and reminding him unavoidably that she wasn't a slender girl any longer. "I knew you would come! I knew—"

He positioned her in front of him, ignoring her senseless chatter. His left gauntlet pulled her hand over to a vestigial wing and cramped her fingers to it.

There she is! Glint's warning thought stabbed at him.

Yes, Kelvin thought, *if it's really her this time. Careful, Horace; it may be another trap!*

Before he could focus his eyes properly the trees had again changed positions. Horace was clawing at something. When his eyes did adjust he saw a serpent squirm out from between Horace's talons; then a bird of great ugliness, dropping its feathers as its wings beat in frantic takeoff.

"WHOOOF!" Horace huffed, and they slammed to the ground as the bird evaded his pounce.

"I'M NOT DONE! I'M NOT DONE!" the bird called down, circling.

"You'd better get, Zady," Kelvin said. He wished he had the copper sting now, or Helbah to hurl a few fireballs.

The bird made an obscene fluff of its rump and dropped a big and evil-smelling dropping.

Horace roared. His eyes fixed red and glowing on the escaping witch.

Kelvin saw air beneath them and ground far below. Horace was bent over, jaws snapping, and a loud squawking came from under him.

Let her go, Horace! Opal us down, Glint urged.

They were falling, and then they weren't. Trees and grass blurred and they were at the spot where Jon had been. Horace was holding something under his talons, and then his jaws were down, snapping. Jon was sitting up, watching.

Kelvin wanted to help, though not exactly through biting. He had been ready to make love to Zady once, but that had been a consequence of magic and was now unreal. He felt as he knew Horace must, that killing her was necessary.

Horace lifted his head. Hanging from his mouth was a snake's tail. He opened his jaws and turned, permitting Kelvin to see the serpent's body and head.

The serpent was a bird, flying from Horace. Horace's tongue shot out, lassoed the bird by the neck, and yanked it back. His throat worked; he made a sound like water flushing down a nearly clogged drain. "Gur, gur, glug."

End of Zady. Or was it? Kelvin had always heard that a witch had to be burned. What happened if one was eaten?

Horace settled back on his tail and burped. His stomach rumbled. He rolled his eyes wildly, then started gagging uncontrollably. His neck extended and ejected from the depths of his throat a wet and smeared bird. Horace couldn't have helped it; had he been able to stomach her, he would have. The bird flew off.

Horace looked after her, a puzzled and annoyed dragon. He communicated his feeling to his father.

"Never mind, Horace. Keep after her and maybe Helbah can burn her."

Then he had a horrible thought. Could Zady have gotten the opal that was inside the dragon? Could she have allowed herself to be swallowed, for that?

Horace spat out bird feathers and snake scales. They were now not on the flat-topped mountain with its sky-forest. They were down on a plain where a battle had been fought, amidst dead and dying men. The battered bird was flying ahead of them.

That was a relief! Horace was still opaling, which meant he still had the opal. If the witch had tried to get it, she had failed. Maybe she had discovered that she would be digested before she found it in there.

Wizards and witches and warlocks and magicians of the malignant kind were changing to birds, flying, flocking. All just ahead of them and the ugly bird that was Zady. They all flew ahead, and Horace opal-hopped across the battlefield, keeping Zady's wings beating.

Now they were in farming country that had to be Rud. Ahead flopped the birds, now pursued by wild beastmen and soldiers in green uniforms, and orcs and enraged citizenry. They hopped over and through fleeing herds, pausing only long enough for Horace to slap down a few dung-clads who had not yet changed or who were in fact mercenaries. Still the birds flew on.

They couldn't use magic in bird form, Kelvin thought, seeing a fireball. The birds scattered, but not quickly enough. Some were caught and burned; some fell smoking and squawking even as they turned black and incinerated. Pursuing soldiers and citizens screamed approval.

Now the terrain was even more familiar. They were past Rud's present-day royal palace and rapidly approaching the ruins of the former palace. Kelvin began to feel a hope that they were actually driving the malignants home.

They were in the ruins, broken masonry and what remained of statuary all around. Ahead of them a diminished flock flew with rapid wingbeats.

They were at the head of the ancient stairs leading down to the underground river. *Now we must stop,* Kelvin thought deliberately to Horace.

"Whoof!" Horace said, hardly sounding as if he agreed with his dad.

They were in the water and Horace was paddling with all four feet and switching his tail. He seemed not to be thinking of his riders. The birds were flying just ahead of them, many squawking in terror, almost within reach of Horace's avenging snout.

They rounded the bend, Horace not pausing. Here, lighted by the glowing walls, the dimple in the water marked the installation. Birds dived, their wings and webbed feet flying them underwater.

"WOOF!" Horace said. His back muscles tautened for the long dive.

No, Horace! No! You'll drown us! Jon is weak from all that was done to her! She'll never survive going underwater! Horace, take us back!

They were back on the landing. Ahead of them lay the underground river with its glowing rock walls. Above the water flopped birds that were not birds, fleeing for their home.

"Why'd we stop?" Jon asked.

"Shut up, Sister Wart," Kelvin told her affectionately. He raised a finger to his lips and indicated Horace.

A white dovgen lit on the newly rebuilt dock and became Helbah. The good witch raised her hands and between them materialized a ball of witch's fire. The fireball went hissing up the river and around the bend in pursuit of the last dark straggler.

Kelvin slid down Horace's back and helped Jon down after him. Glint slid down as well and the three of them walked out on the dock to join Helbah. The water lapped almost angrily beneath the dock. The two excursion boats, left here under royal sanction for use by the Yokes Tourist Guides, rose and fell on their mooring ropes. Had this been a weekend the boats would have been on the water and filled with tourists and guides. How fortunate for the employees of that agency and the young and old people who would have been touring that Zady had warred on a weekday. Sometimes by chance alone a thing did work out right.

Helbah shook her head. "We almost had her—almost," she sighed. Around the bend light flashed and the fireball's implosion signaled its expiration. Kelvin wondered if the fireball had caught a malignant and crisped it, or at least singed its feathers. He glanced around. There were no birds in the sky now; they were alone.

"Jon, give me your hand," Helbah said. "I will give you strength to throw off the effects of Zady's magic."

"There are no effects," Jon said. "What she did to me was all in my head."

"That's real too," her witch mentor said. "Here."

Old hands took younger hands and held. Watching Jon's face Kelvin could see her brighten. She was so brave, was his sister, that she pretended her hurt had all vanished. She had been that way as a child, refusing to cry where an ordinary girl would have been hysterical. Even when the evil dwarf and the wizard Zatanas had been draining her blood she had done little more than ask him to save her life. In all the years since, she had hardly changed.

So intent had Kelvin become on Helbah's healing of his sister that he had all but forgotten his son. He owed Horace so much more than he had ever expected he would. He must find a way to make it up to him. Too many years he had dismissed the dragon as a beautiful, worthless novelty who was little more than a dutiful pet.

Behind him he heard a wet smacking sound that did not sound menacing. He turned to see what it was.

Horace had his head down. The dragon was devouring something in great haste. Considering all the energy the dragon had used today he must have been ravenous, and if dragons had nothing else they did have enormous appetites.

As he looked back at his son Kelvin was only mildly curious. A dead animal or a slain mercenary was all the same to Horace. But as he watched the copper-sheathed snout come up stained with red, he was aware of a rumbling.

Horace was looking back at him with eyes narrowed in a way he had seen them narrow on the battlefield. Unbelievably, the dragon gave every surface indication that he was about to charge.

CHAPTER 21

Friend or Foe?

*H*orace saw the enemy soldiers confronting him and prepared to destroy them. Two males, two females. The females
must be witches come to use destructive magic. He should bite
them first, then gut the males with a couple hard kicks. As a
final gesture of his contempt and anger he would turn his back
and pound all of them with his tail. When he got done there
would be no enemy, only a hearty lunch.

He reached out his head to the old woman, and her eyes
stared into his and reflected him.

Where was his father? Where his aunt? Where was his
new brother-in-law? Where was Helbah, the witch he knew
had protected them?

Questions, questions, questions! Dragons should never
ask. He opened his mouth over the woman's head, the better
to engulf her. If she was going to turn into a bird she'd better
be quick!

Horace! Don't!

Glint's thoughts? Where was he? Here were three enemies.

Horace, that's Helbah!

This wasn't Helbah. Couldn't be. But there was something different about this malignant. He sniffed. This didn't
smell like a malignant; it smelled like Helbah.

*Horace, you're under an enchantment! I'm standing with
Kelvin—watch and I'll wave my hand. That's Helbah you're
about to bite. Jon is beside Kelvin.*

Another trick! He wouldn't believe what his eyes knew
were false. Yet the enemy was waving his hand.

Think to me, Horace! Think to me! I'm Glint.

Hard to think, Glint. Why you look like enemy soldier?

I don't. It's magic. You see me as Zady wants.

Magic, yes. As when he had thought the enemy to be his
grandfather and Uncle Lester. He sniffed again. It still smelled
like Helbah.

The enemy soldier who claimed to be Glint turned to the
witch he claimed was Helbah. The witch's eyes did not flicker,
merely reflected his great teeth and the scales on his chest.

"Tell him, Helbah. Tell Horace he's bewitched! I know
that you can help him."

The witch's mouth opened and without other movement
she said, "It's an identity spell, similar to what Zady once used
on Jon. She must have had an invisibility cape. She may be
here now, watching, hoping you will destroy us."

Horace remembered that he had briefly lost sight of Zady
and gotten her mixed in his mind with the other flying birds.
There had been too many birds, though he had tried never to
take his eyes off her. But every time he opaled she had a chance
to drop back or move ahead of the others. Not enough chance
to do magic, but to change position slightly,, and all those birds
looked alike. Besides, he'd had to look to where he was opaling, or he might have killed a friend.

Can she rid me of the spell, Glint?

"The spell is hard to undo," the good witch or bad witch
pretending to be good said. "I haven't a key ingredient.
There's a certain herb, but the plant is unknown in most
frames and rare in others. I may have to travel to other frames
searching for a cure. Kelvin will have to care for you while I'm
gone. He'll have to bring you food and you'll have to stay
away from people."

I can kill my own food, Horace thought, annoyed.

*No you can't, Horace. You listen to her! The meer you kill
and eat could be me or Merlain.*

Horace thought of eating a meer that was actually his sister. Not good for either.

Horace, remember that cave midway up Flattop Mountain? That was our first stop. Go there. It is a big cave and people won't be stopping by. Kelvin and I can bring you food, letting you know we're us. Anyone else who comes could be Zady.

Horace knew he didn't want to go to that cave. What he wanted to do was return to Ember. Thinking of their pond, he was there.

He splashed into the water right where he had thought, to the side of a great tree trunk. He ducked his head, sucked water up, and spewed it out through his teeth. He still had a foul taste from that bird! Now where was Ember?

Horace, you're back!!!

Hiding, playing their game. He searched the shore from where he floated. In a moment he'd surprise her. There—a flash of gold behind the appleberry bush!

Horace opaled to the spot and onto a smaller dragon's back. The dragon under him turned its head and hissed loudly in his face. This wasn't Ember! This was a dragon of his own sex!

Horace bit angrily for the intruder's throat, wanting to kill it. The sanctity of the mated state demanded extreme measures. What this intruder had been up to he didn't care to think.

His teeth pushed hard through overlapping golden scales, searching for the softer hide and pulsing vein that held life. He could taste the gold on his forked tongue; soon he'd taste blood. He opened his jaws a little to take an even harder and renewed bite.

HORACE! You're too rough! That hurts! Get off me, big copper lump!

Ember! He could hardly believe it was she. He sniffed hard and detected her fragrance.

He opaled back into the water where he had been. He had to explain to her somehow. But how could she be expected to understand? Ember was the delight of his life, but she was a dragon and a female. Dragons and females, his human brother had once explained to him, are quicker to anger than to accept excuses. Sometime maybe he would think to her and she'd understand, but for now he'd better do what a human would under similar circumstances—run.

Unhappily he opaled to Flattop Mountain's cave.

"Do you think he went where you told him?" Kelvin asked Glint. The dragon had disappeared so fast that there had been what Kelvin's father called a sonic boom—air rushing in to fill the space Horace had occupied. He hadn't been aware of the phenomenon while riding, but it occurred to him that both friends and enemies must have been startled by the noise of Horace's sudden exits.

Glint shook his head. "I don't know, honestly. He was a pretty confused dragon. If I hadn't thought to him and Helbah fixed him with her stare . . . I hate to think."

"Why don't you step over to the cave and find out?" Helbah demanded of him. As usual she made him feel it was obvious and he should have thought of it himself.

"Yes," Kelvin managed to say. "I'll step back there and see. Wait."

He stepped, concentrating as well as he could on the cave entrance where he and Horace and Glint had recently been.

He came down on the ball of his right foot, directly in front of the cave, just as visualized. He looked up at the overhang, then inside. The dust was undisturbed except for the pad marks of a large bearver and the partially eaten carcass of a mountain goeep. He looked at the golden-colored fleece the bearver had left, thinking how its shade matched that of the typical dragon. There would be batbirds and piles of dried batbird excrement further back. In the front there was an ancient painting of sticklike hunters pointing to a flattened dish with circles around its rim. The pictured disk had flames coming from its rearmost edge, and definitely it was supposed to be above the hunters' heads in the sky.

What an imagination those ancients had! Kelvin thought, and stepped back to the entrance.

Almost into open jaws. The dragon breath almost

knocked him off his feet, and in an instant he knew why popular superstition had dragons breathing fire.

"Oops. Sorry. Son. Just your old man this time. It's right that you keep alert. I'll be back with food, and maybe I'll bring along Merlain."

He wasn't certain how much Horace understood under the enchantment, but now was definitely the time to make his exit.

He waved almost in Horace's face and stepped back to Helbah and Glint on the waiting dock.

Lester stared. There was Jon, preternaturally beautiful. "I thought—" he said.

"Oh, Lester, I escaped, of course," she said. "You should have known I couldn't be kept anywhere against my will."

"But Helbah said—"

Jon said some bad words—very bad words. Lester had heard her say some pretty rough things before, but never like this. It must have been the influence of the malignants, he thought, and resolved to make things right for her.

He squeezed her tight against him and placed his un-shaven cheek up against her hair. She was just so attractive. She had lost some weight and gained a good deal of sex appeal. Maybe that was just his fond perception; still, it was exciting.

"Where is the old . . . benign?" she asked.

Lester held his wife back at arm's length, looking her hard in the face, unable to believe the way she had asked that. Something about her just didn't seem right. But of course she had been held captive; he had to make allowances.

"Helbah may be in another frame," he explained. "She's going to have to get a cure for Horace."

"A scaling would cure the lizard best."

Truly, this wasn't like Jon at all! Could there be magic at work on her yet? Hadn't Helbah or one of her helpers checked on the possibility? Or—he hated to think of this, but had to—the way Jon had so suddenly gotten free—that just might be suspicious. Kelvin had mentioned things that—no, impossible!

Jon smiled in an unusual manner, and drew up her shirt to show an amazingly well-formed young breast. "Well, dearie, I suspect that now you want a little sex. Maybe a little more than a little, hmm?" She showed the other breast, as breathtaking as the first. "Maybe you'd like to have me tie you up and whip you a little first?"

This wasn't Jon! There was no way that it could be, and not just because of the physical improvement—uh, correction, physical change. This was Zady or one of her minions! "You are not my wife," he said grimly.

Lester forced his hands to close on her throat. Immediately he found he was holding a squirming serpent. The snake hissed in his face, spitting drops of spittle that he moved his face to avoid. In avoiding the spittle he let his grip slip on the snake.

Wingbeats. Lester made an anguished grab.

"I'll be back! I'll be back!" Zady called down to him. She hovered a moment, and something smelly plopped on the ground.

Amid a flurry of faster and faster wingbeats, pursued by a fireball released by Zally, who had been guarding the Crumb farm on Helbah's orders, the nasty witch flew on her evil way.

But Lester remained chagrined. How could he have been fooled by that creature, even for a moment? Not only fooled, but tempted. He felt unclean.

A carriage pulled up and Jon stepped out. She was covered with blood spatters and dust, and had large purplish bruises on her wrists and arms. Lester thought that she had never looked more lovely.

But was it really Jon, this time? It was supposed to be, but after the witch's ruse, he had a nagging doubt. Suppose . . . ?

But Lester couldn't contain himself. He ran to his wife and threw his arms around her. "Oh Jon, Jon! I thought we had lost you for sure!"

"Kelvin broke me out as quick as he was able." She hugged him as she hadn't hugged for years. "Where are the children?"

"At the twin palaces where they're supposed to be."

"Let's go get them right away! I don't know why Kelvin dropped me here since he knew they are there."

The first thing she was concerned about was the children. That was Jon, all right! Lester's doubt faded. "I do," he said, sniffing her hair. "It's what I'd have done for him and Heln given reversed circumstances."

"Oh, Lester!" But she wasn't displeased, only concerned as a mother. "I'm certain they're safe, but I want so badly to hold them."

"Me, too, I hope. We can start for the palaces, but I know that soon they'll be here. Now that the war's over, Helbah will want our children to be home."

"Lester, is the war really over?"

"I hope. Only there is what happened to Horace."

"I know. I was there with Kelvin and Glint."

"Do you think Helbah has the cure?"

"I know she'll try to get it. But she says it's one of the ultra-rare herbs."

"Do you think—I know this sounds crazy, Jon—but do you think that Zady may have planned on Melbah leaving our frame to seek Horace's cure?"

"You don't think it's over, do you?"

He shook his head. "I do wish that I believed it's over." He held her, telling her without words how very much a respite from fighting meant to him.

By and by they went into the house together. Jon stripped and cleaned up. Her body was her own, and her own age, but it seemed perfect to him. By mutual agreement they did not come out until much later in the day.

Helbah turned to Whitestone and said what she had on he̶ ̶d: "I can't go."

̶itestone patted her shoulder. "I know you can't, Hel-
̶understand why. Zady might not be able to raise

another army or find more malignant helpers, but until she's burned to ash she's a menace."

"Yes," Zudini added, "and that means watch and don't get caught unprepared. You have friends, Helbah. We'll search all the frames in existence if we have to, but it's going to require time. None of us now knows an apothecary in any frame that carries the herb."

"Not only that"—Whitestone continued the pessimistic note—"but that very herb may not exist any longer. Zady may have taken especially vengeful steps to see that it doesn't."

Helbah looked down at her feet. "I know you'll do your best. I just don't know that any of us can help Horace."

"Keep him isolated," Whitestone advised. "And don't let others near him since he can't tell friend from foe."

"He's smart for a dragon," Helbah said, "but if the herb can't be found his frustration could turn him into a rogue. Can you imagine what a rogue dragon could do with the opal?"

"Worse than the battle," Whitestone said. "And since the dragon is his son it would be hard for the Roundear to slay him."

"The dragon is the head of the Alliance, after all," Helbah said. "How could the Alliance function without its unifying safeguarder of the opal? If he were to turn rogue we'd be finished."

"I'd suggest a reading of the cards," Whitestone said, "but I understand the cards here don't show a future. Possibly the reason is Horace."

"Possibly," Helbah said. But privately she believed the fault had to do with Zady and not with their unfortunate copper-scaled ally.

"Well, we really won that one," Kildom said to Kildee.

"Yes we did, brother," the identical king replied.

"You two did nothing!" Glow said, hugging the just-returned Glint and eyeing them over his shoulder. "You did just what I did—you watched."

"A king can say no wrong," Kildom retorted.

"That's can *do* no wrong," Kildee corrected him.

Glow sighed. She was so happy she didn't care how they teased her. She knew that Merlain and Charles and Kelvin's mother all felt as she did. Who wouldn't feel elated after such a great victory?

The word she didn't want to hear came round to her by way of Charles. Gently Charles took Glint's place and Glint went to Merlain.

Don't let them know, Glow, but Helbah's worried. Horace may not be able to defend us again. Zady may only have started her fight.

Glow wondered what he meant, and immediately had her answer. She allowed her face to show nothing to the kinglets and to Mrs. Knight. It was possible, all too possible, that the terrible fighting that she had thought ended in victory was but a preliminary.

It was enough, Glow thought to herself, to make a girl wish she had never grown up and married but had remained always just a dreaming, hardly feeling, enchanted sword.

St. Helens and John sat at their familiar chess table. One of them was winning and one losing. One of them was waiting for the other's move. St. Helens had to admit to himself that he hadn't the faintest recollection of who had moved last and who had made the best moves. It wasn't just the unaccustomed third glass of dark red—it was the way things were happening.

"John, what do you think will become of your grandson?" There, he had asked it! Now it would come out.

"Charles will do fine. A mind-reader just about has to."

"I mean the other one. His litter mate, so to speak."

"Horace? He should do fine. I don't like to think about it."

"I don't either. Seems I have to."

"I don't think we can help. I'm not certain anybody can, except possibly Helbah or her witch and warlock friends. If it were a matter of a blood transfusion or a replacement part . . ."

"Kelvin takes him his food. What does he say?"

"He says that Horace sniffs him, each and every time. Has to. Zady or one of her minions could fake his appearance."

"Hell of a note, ain't it, Commander?"

"It is, and don't address me that way. You know I haven't succeeded you in rank since the day we got exploded from Earth."

"Wasn't that a gas, though? You know that there's no logical way that we should have survived. As for our being here . . . that's nuts."

"I know it well, old friend." John moved a knight—appropriately.

St. Helens studied the board, momentarily interested in it. So it had been John's move, not his.

"Commander, you think it could have been the doings of Mouvar?"

"Possibly. Something saved us."

"Perhaps then it can save Horace? I mean if saving's, as your wife used to say, in the cards."

"She doesn't say that anymore."

St. Helens moved a pawn. He couldn't have said why. His thoughts were now on cards, not chessmen.

John studied the board in his turn, or seemed to. St. Helens suspected that his thoughts, too, were of predicting cards.

"You've become a master tactician, St. Helens."

"How's that?"

"Your move places my king in check."

"Oh." He hadn't noticed. "I forgot to say check, so by the rules it's your move again."

"I wonder about Mouvar. Maybe he's a player. Maybe he used my son and grandson for his own purpose. Maybe he's accomplished what he wanted to and now—"

"Moving your queen there will put you in check again," St. Helens said.

"In that case I concede the game. I couldn't have won without a Mouvar stepping in. I wonder about my son and grandson. Mouvar doesn't do big things like piping down the walls of Jericho, but he gives indications that he knows what's going on. He left those boots for Kelvin at the right time, and a personal message for him."

"You think maybe it's a game that's been played for centuries?"

"Our centuries, perhaps. By Earth time we could have existed here for minutes or seconds. That relativity thing we used to discuss."

"I get what you're suggesting, Commander. If Mouvar's a god—"

"He's not. Or if he is he's not all-powerful. My other son in the different frame has a wife who believes she spoke to Mouvar as a child. Sounded more like something from a UFO than a god."

"That robot talked about him too, didn't he? That robot on the chimaera's world."

"Yes, it talked about Mouvar and claimed it visited different frames. The tin man also talked about major worlds and minor worlds. Worlds of science and worlds of magic. Mouvar, according to the robot, came from major worlds run through science."

"I've never understood it, Commander. Mouvar may have used science in building transporters, but then didn't he use magic? He left the gauntlets and then the boots, and don't forget the opal that may or may not have been his."

"As my unfortunate daughter says, maybe science and magic blend. At some point of development maybe the two are indistinguishable from each other. To our ancestors, yours and mine, the inventions we grew up with would have been seen as magic. When I consider what the transporters do and what the gauntlets and boots do, I'm not sure if they're magic or if they're—"

"Science?"

"If we were Neanderthals how would we comprehend computers?"

"We wouldn't. We'd call them magic."

"Right. Magic or science, to us Neanderthals there's no

practical difference. The big question is, are we or are we not more than chess pieces to beings such as Mouvar?"

St. Helens dutifully considered the matter. After several long minutes of difficult thought he concluded that both he and his old commander had had more than a sufficiency of dark red. As for the answers, from where they sat there were none that made sense.

CHAPTER 22

Help Me, Devale

*T*he faintest of clicks sounded in the silent room, and the beautiful young woman with the old and warty face stood before Professor Devale's desk with her head down. Not now was Zady the arrogant witch she had been. Now she was properly repentant and humble.

Devale smirked. He knew this last defeat would break her. He knew what she wanted.

"Professor Devale, Master, your eager but failing student has again returned."

"I see that, Zady. Do something about your head."

The young arm flipped an invisible fabric and the head disappeared from the neck up. Standing before him was a usable body without any unfortunate accessory.

"Hmmm, that might be interesting, but bring back the red hair and green eyes."

Brilliant red hair, an exact copy of Zady's long-ago destroyed niece's, floated above the neck.

"The entire head, Zady."

Now the head matched the rest of the body in seamless, enticing allure. A whole woman now, and wanton beauty deserving the word witch. She stood there silently, awaiting whatever humiliation he should choose to inflict.

"You may speak, Zady."

"I did my worst. The dragon still has the opal but doesn't know friend from foe. I intended that it destroy Helbah and the Roundear in big, unfriendly bites."

"But that too failed, didn't it, Zady? Just like your gold-bought fighters and your former classmates."

"I tried."

"Of course you tried. But that didn't do it, did it?"

"No. Blind luck enabled them to win the battle, but not the war."

"Blind luck favors the most intelligent and forceful plan of action. Your bumbling mishmash didn't deserve to succeed, if it depended on luck. Your course of action should have been so sure that victory was inevitable." Oh, it was pleasant teasing her with a lecture on elementary strategy!

"Surely true," she agreed tightly.

"What will you do now—hide?"

"I haven't surrendered yet."

Devale let his eyebrows climb toward his horns. He was getting it out of her a little at a time, savoring his revenge. She had been sassy to him, and now she would suffer. "What, then, is your plan?"

"I need your help, Professor. I can't handle it alone."

"But you weren't alone. You had your army and your underlings."

"Not enough. You have to help me."

"But I *have* helped you. I have given you gold. Will more gold enable you to meet your ends?" He put just the right degree of uninnocent perplexity into his voice.

"I want to make an example. Your powers are much greater than any witch's or warlock's. You can do what I never could."

"Yes?" It was wonderful when he could reap compliments without even fishing for them.

"I'll demand surrender of the Alliance. To prove that they dare not resist me I will make an example. I will take something from their world that has been there for a long time. The entire Alliance must be impressed."

"You can do that, Zady?"

"I know that *you* can. Let the Alliance think that it was I. Will you do it, Professor?"

"I prefer the appellation Great One rather than Professor. It better defines our positions."

She didn't even blink. "Will you, Great One? A mountain or a city? Why not a city?"

"Why not a kingdom?" he asked grandly. "A kingdom from outside the Alliance? That should impress them for a start."

"A kingdom from outside the Alliance? There's only Rotternik and Throod."

"Which will it be, Zady? Which of those two do you wish removed forever from the frame?"

Zady's eyes glowed as she looked up at him. "Oh, Great One, if you will do that I will be so grateful—"

"Of course you will. Which?"

"Rotternik should have fought on my side, but they fought with the Alliance. Helbah got to them after my visit."

"Then it's Rotternik?"

"No. Throod failed me with its arms and its armies. Can Throod be destroyed?"

"Throod can vanish completely, never having been."

"You can do that? You can take it from the frame?"

"You doubt my power, Witch?" He was showing off, of course, but he indulged himself. The fact was that she had come up with a notion that would truly impress the folk of the frames, and so he would follow up on it. For his own aggrandizement rather than hers. Everyone would know the true power behind the magic.

"Oh, no, Great One! No!"

"I will wish to watch the reactions of your enemies as you work at destroying them. I may add embellishments and assist with refined torments. You will need a large communication crystal that will give you access to my wisdom and accord me the pleasure of viewing. I will stay here, in this office, but my eyes will watch and my senses be gratified."

"Oh, Great One! Oh, Great One!" The witch leaped and clapped her hands in anticipated joy. How eager she was to promote his notoriety! "We will destroy the roundears and the lizard that holds the opal, and everyone and everything that they hold dear! We will destroy Helbah and her ilk and bar them forever from what will then be our frame! We will succeed as only you and I can!"

"We will, Zady. Gradually, artistically, as befits my kind and yours."

"Of course. Oh, Professor, the pleasure of it!"

"It's Great One. And speaking of pleasure—" He made a gesture that converted his desk to a bed. "Time for mine."

"How do you want me, Great One?"

Pitifully subservient and foolishly grateful, as she was now. The attitude was more important than the form. But naturally he did not tell her that, because she could pretend attitude as readily as form, and he preferred at least a bit of reality along with the pretense.

"The present form will be satisfactory." He made a smoke and changed his own form to that of a large snake. Moving quickly, he struck and buried his long fangs in her left breast.

She screamed delightfully, slapping him, flailing his body with her frenzied jerks.

The venom he had injected was taking immediate effect. He released her nipple from his snake mouth, dropped onto the bed, and became a large, goatish creature reeking of lust.

"Do your damnedest," Zady gasped. She crawled onto the bed beside him, shaking from head to toe. The left nipple had turned black and the blackness was creeping into her breast. She could have concealed it with illusion, but had the wit to realize that he didn't want that.

Pleased with the evidence of his potency, Devale bit her right breast, butted her in the stomach, and hurt her wherever he could with quick blows of his front hooves.

After he had broken several of her bones he mounted her, not neglecting to break her back. His passion pounded at its cruel and demanding height.

Not lightly did he take a witch's invitation to do his damnedest. Before he healed her she would learn exactly what his damnedest really meant.

The dark-visored warlock, though a stranger, stepped boldly into the Cryptgreen Drugs and Potions Shop. Just as though he belonged here he went right to the shelves holding antidotes and spell reversers. He searched there, shaking his head from time to time.

"You wish a certain product?" an apothecary with bald head and pallid complexion inquired. "Name it and we will order it."

"Dandlecat fluff."

The apothecary appeared to wilt. "Honored warlock, that is extremely rare!"

"I know. It seems I was misinformed."

"Perhaps—a shop specializing in—"

"Yes?"

"I hate to suggest it, but one of the shops serving benign clientele."

The stranger exited, as though properly offended.

On his way to the transporter station Whitestone had to reflect again on the advice he had been given: "Try the shops serving malignants, if you dare. No shop serving benigns has the fluff or can obtain it."

It had been an exhausting and fruitless search.

The pharmacist at the Rexmall stared in disbelief at the oddly dressed person who had negotiated the soda and lunch counters, passed by the aisles of stationery and toys, and come right to the back. Orange hair and a zoot suit right out of the 1940s: this fellow was weird!

The customer reached into a pocket, brought out a coin, and put it on the counter. The pharmacist examined what was surely a gold coin, without touching it.

"What can I do for you, sir?"

"I have more of these coins. You may have what I want under a trade name. It's an herb that has been known to grow naturally. What I want is dandlecat fluff. It has been used successfully in restoring certain conditions of damaged sight."

The pharmacist knew a nut when he saw one. He knew a gold Krugerrand as well, he thought, though he had never actually been shown one. If he could have sold the mental case something he would gladly have accepted the South African coin. Alas, he would need a prescription to sell the head case something that might benefit him. Dandlecat fluff indeed! He might as well have asked for unicorn horn.

"Sorry," the pharmacist said.

The customer left, buying nothing and inspecting nothing on the way through the holiday shoppers. If he had been dressed as Santa Claus it might have made a little sense. Maybe he was a Hollywood actor on a television stunt show? Possibly the pharmacist should have been more cagey and gone along with the stunt.

Mourning the loss of a possible free trip to Hawaii or some other bounty, the pharmacist busied himself filing prescriptions for more normal customers. Someday, he thought disgustedly to himself, there would come a time when he'd have his wits about him.

After leaving the drug shop, Zudini simply walked. "If they don't have it there they won't have it anywhere," he had been told by the man he had asked. Zudini believed the man, though the gentleman had acted strangely about the suit he had on. Waste a lot of effort on an authentic disguise and that was what happened!

He was walking in a residential district. The sun was beating down on him a bit too warmly. Strange white houses were bordering the street, each with a square of green grass decorated attractively with bright yellow flowers. Zudini hardly noticed, though later he was to regret not picking a bouquet.

"What a waste!" he cried aloud, ignoring a blue-uniformed man with a bag on his back, and a child on some sort of wheeled board. "My greatest escape ever! To the strangest world across the Flaw! Without the fluff they'll never believe it happened! Without a new pinch of opal powder I'll never be able to repeat! I've lost an entry in *The Guleless Book of Magical Records.* What an incredible, humiliating sacrifice!"

Horace saw his father stepping down in his boots before the cave. He had a dish of chopped meat, which was strange because before Kelvin had brought the meat in a bucket.

Horace wriggled close, allowed Kelvin's hand to pat his head, and savored the rotten aroma. Black and maggoty, just the way he liked meat best. He was about to take a bite when he wondered why Kelvin hadn't thought to him the way he had before.

Horace knew that something wasn't right. He sniffed at the dish appreciatively, and moved his nostrils until they touched the dish-holder's hand.

His nose wrinkled to the witch's smell, and instantly he remembered that his father did not look like himself these days. If this were really he, he would appear to be a warlock or a soldier.

"WHOOF!" Horace said, and snapped at the hand, causing it to drop the dish. The dish shattered, producing a dark-green stain that smoked and ate into the solid rock.

Now he was certain! But the witch had become a grotesque bird, and the bird had started flying from the cave even as the dish dropped. He leaped after her, determined to chase her all the way to the underground river and beyond. His jaws clicked and she was further ahead, and then he was under her and she was flapping her wings wildly. He followed with opal-hops, landing on trees, houses, barns, in fields, on roads, anywhere that kept her in sight.

He opaled above and tried catching her. She wriggled out

from under. Below was a dung-uniformed soldier aiming a
bow—a big, rough fellow hardly worth a good bite. Ignoring
the puny danger of the arrow, he put down his talons and
prepared to drop all the way to the ground to rip off the man's
face.

NO, HORACE! NO!

Merlain's thought? Or a trick?

That's our brother, Horace!-Our brother Charles!

He couldn't chance it. He twisted in midair and opaled
into some bushes, landing hard. Overhead the bird was an
ugly speck.

*Oh, Horace! Go home to the cave! She'll trick you if you
don't. Helbah was watching—she knows the bird is Zady. She
won't let her get to you again. Go!*

Grab bird! Tear out feathers! Pull apart!

*That won't destroy her, Horace. Not unless somebody is
there to burn up the parts.*

*Chew off head, squeeze and tear body, scatter feathers.
Won't come back.*

*Helbah says she could, given time. Her astral self would
survive and find a way. That's why she has to be burned.*

You and Charles come with me. You burn her.

We would like to, but—

Come! Never before had he tried commanding her.
Before he had always done what she wanted.

An enemy soldier stepped from the bushes. Horace shot
out his tongue, tested the air for the scent.

It's me, Horace. Merlain. See how hard it is to tell?

Climb on my back.

She did, taking hold of his wings. *Now, Horace, where is
she?*

He searched the sky. There were better eyes than those of
a dragon, but he could still see better than a mere human
person could. He saw birds, many birds. He did not see one
particular bird.

Oh, Horace, she's gotten away!

Horace hung his head. He had been so busy thinking to
her and she to him that the prey had escaped. Doubtless Zady

had landed and resumed her human form, in which case she would again be dangerous.

"Whhhhhoooofff," Horace cried softly. "Whhhhhhoooooffff!"

I know, Horace, but you must wait your chance. Daddy or I or someone needs to be there so that if you destroy her she won't be coming back.

The thick-muscled soldier scratched behind Horace's ears as Merlain knew he liked. It was comforting, knowing that the hand was really hers.

And beware of anyone coming near you. Anyone at all.

Merlain, come to cave with me. Stay with me.

I can't. I'm married now, and— The soldier's hand stretched down and wiped up a drop of moisture. *Why, Horace, you're crying! Oh, very well! I'll come stay with you for as long as I can.*

Horace opaled them. But once back at the cave, eyeing the ugly soldier, he knew he might awake suddenly from sleep and do her harm. That must not happen.

He thought to her about it, and by and by he returned her where he had found her. Then, a sadder and no wiser dragon, he returned alone to his lonesome cave.

St. Helens moved a bishop, watching John's face. His old commander's mind wasn't on the game. He'd better help him talk it out and then maybe he'd remember how to concentrate.

"Two wines," St. Helens ordered.

The wines were brought by Nellie, who was busy with other orders from other men still wearing uniforms; she patted his hand quickly but didn't stay to chat. John took his glass—a new affectation replacing mugs and jugs in the wine and chess houses—and gulped it in one quick draft. No leisurely savoring or commenting on the bouquet.

"Commander, you think Zady's coming back? I'd thought we had her whipped."

"Never underestimate a witch—especially her."

"Ummm, you're right there, Commander. I learned that from the old days. Specifically from old Melbah in what was then the kingdom of Aratex. You just can't believe their power sometimes."

"I was thinking she might come back strong. Maybe with an army from another frame. Maybe she'll have something new and horrible that none of us will know how to deal with."

"Like an atomic weapon?" The thought of those still gave him nightmares. In the world where he and the commander had been born, atomic weapons had been in a sense an all-destroying magic; to a majority of people it probably made as much sense.

"Hardly an atomic weapon, you Irish tale-spinner. But I was thinking maybe something could be the equivalent and be magic. Helbah sounded so pessimistic last time I saw her. She didn't say what she feared, and I'm not sure she knows."

"Hmm, I think Zady's done, Commander. What she did to your grandson was her last play. At least I'm hoping that was her last."

"I just wonder what kind of gesture she could make." John made circles on the tabletop with the bottom of his wine glass. "If she has an atomic equivalent she could destroy a city as an example—the way the United States destroyed Hiroshima and Nagasaki. I dreamt about Zady having the bomb, crazy as that sounds."

"Don't even think it, Commander. She has to follow the rules of magic, whatever they are. I thought back in Aratex I was beginning to understand magic. Old Melbah commanded earth, air, fire, and water, and that sort of made a little sense. Elemental magic. In her hands as powerful as bombs."

"I remember. I thought the same way then. But of course that wasn't the limit of magic. It may have been Melbah's, but it wasn't Zady's. I've no idea how her spells work. You've any ideas?"

St. Helens had to wonder if the commander really expected him to answer. It was good that he was at least talking.

"I've been pondering," John continued. "Old Zatanas used sympathetic magic and that had a logic. The part is equal to the whole; the likeness to the object. As when he used lizards to control the movements of dragons—or tried to."

"Wasn't that something, though! But wasn't there more?"

"Yes. Made a laser beam bend once; I've no idea how."

"Likewise these phantoms and the shape-changing and making people big or small like something in a child's story book. Most of these effects have only temporary duration, but then so does a speeding bullet or the fissioning of an atom."

"Tough, ain't it? I stopped trying to figure it out back in Aratex. Only thing I know is that Zady ain't got no bomb, normal or atomic."

"And that," said the commander, "is the one truth about warfare here that I actually like!"

CHAPTER 23

Atom Bomb

Kathy! Kathy! Kathy!"

"What is it, Joey?" Kathy Jon looked up from the stringpeas she was shelling to see her little brother waving frantically outside the kitchen door. "I'd like to play with you, but Mother said get this done or there'd be trouble. As if it wasn't enough I had to hoe these things and carry water to them when it was dry! I don't like stringpeas anyway!"

"Come look up in the sky!" Joey cried, not even agreeing, as he usually did, with her estimate of the vegetables. He was red in the face as he alternately pointed and called out.

"Oh, very well! I guess I'm entitled to a break." Kathy put the large pan of stringpeas back on the table beside the dishpan filled to heaping with the green-and-black-striped pods. It wasn't that she hated the work so badly; it was just that it was boring. Left to her own devices she would have been catching fish or bringing down a ducoose with a throwing stone from her sling. Fish and fowl tasted better to her and were a lot more exciting to get. Given a choice she would rather clean fish she had caught herself. And as for eating, as far as such good-for-you vegetables as bruselbage and cabsprouts went, there was no comparison. Give her a nicely browned fish every time!

And sometimes unusual things happened out by the water. Such as nude naked bare witches appearing. Such as her uncle Kelvin lying on the ground. Such as him kissing her when she went to help him, and telling her she was pretty. Uncles could kiss nieces if they wanted to, since it was all in the family, though it had been a shock at the time. But pretty—no one had told her that before. Her head had spun pleasantly ever since. She wanted very much to know if it could be true. She had never thought of herself in that way, and never wanted to, but now, oddly, she was intrigued. Maybe there was, after all, more than outdoor adventure to life.

Still, she should not be thinking about such things. Not while great evil threatened.

She wiped her hands leisurely on the apron her mother had made her don, though they weren't in the least damp. It was sort of fun to keep Joey waiting and dancing outside the screen. The brat should have been helping his brothers and poor dad. Thank the gods, as Grandpa Crumb was always doing, that she was here for them.

As she looked through the screen door she saw her father and mother looking up at the sky. Her father had been pushing a big wheelbarrow filled with dirt-encrusted potabers he had dug that morning. Her mother stood beside the wheelbarrow, still holding a dull-red pumpquash in either hand by its stout stem. Kathy liked pumpquash pie as well as baked squakin, so she approved of her mother's harvesting the vines. But what *were* they looking at?

Suddenly it seemed to Kathy that she had the answer.

They had to be watching a flock of wild geeucks flying west for the winter! Immediately her thought turned to golden roasted fowl cooked by her in the absence of their mother.

Her sling and rocks were, as usual, not far away. She grabbed them up from the shelf, shoved the screen open, and leaped, rather than ran, outside. So it wasn't ladylike; well, ladyhood could wait another minute.

She looked up, stone already in its leather pocket, ready to twirl. Her first reaction was disappointment. There was no flock of waterfowl overhead, only streamers of white cloud. But the streamers had a peculiar shape, and as she strained her neck to look upwards it dawned on her that they formed words. The longer she looked at them the more they made sense.

CITIZENS OF THE ALLIANCE, YOU MAY THINK YOU HAVE WON A BATTLE BUT YOU HAVEN'T WON A WAR! I, ZADY, MALIGNANT WITCH EXTRAORDINARY, AM ABOUT TO TRIUMPH! YOU WILL SHIVER AND SHAKE AND MOVE YOUR BOWELS WHEN YOU SEE THE EXTENT OF MY NEW POWER. WATCH AND BE WARNED!

"Now what does that old hag think she's doing?" Kathy's father rumbled. Her mother put down her vegetables, took her father's face in her hands, and kissed him. The two were a lot more demonstrative than they had been before Jon's capture by the witch, and Kathy was not about to object. She was just so glad to have her mother back! Others might not ever know what love was all their lives, but Mom and Dad did.

Then Jon motioned her and Joey close. Not knowing what to expect, Kathy gave Joey a shove with the back of her hand and moved over.

Her mother put her arms around them, all three. It was as if she expected the sky to open and a giant foot to stomp down. Always her mother had been so brave, so what her father called feisty. Kathy couldn't understand it. Had her mother's capture and torment changed her that much?

"Look! Look!" Alvin and Teddy were running, shouting at them as if they hadn't eyes. Jon desperately motioned for them to join the rest of the family in its huddle in the backyard.

The boys came close and dropped their mouths open, looking alternately upward and at their mother.

"I know it's going to be something bad!" Jon said. "Look down at the ground! Look down at the ground, not at the sky!"

There was a look on her father's face that had never been there before. It was as if he expected something even worse than before was about to happen.

"I know it's going to be something disastrous," Lester Crumb said in a hoarse whisper. "Look down at the ground!"

Kathy remembered the tall tales told by Grandfather John and St. Helens. She had known that her mother believed the stories, but she hadn't suspected it of her father. Even if the stories had been true, this wasn't Earth. The sky wasn't going to flame. Neither would the flesh melt from their bones as St. Helens had described. But she looked down, wondering, and waited, expecting that nothing would occur.

A great light flashed and the ground became bright. She closed her eyelids, and still she saw the light. The ground shook as from the tread of a heavy giant.

BARRRRROOOOOMMMMM!

"What's she up to?" Kelvin demanded of Helbah. The witch had summoned him and his father to her early this morning. Something was going to happen—something unprecedented, she said. Now they stood out on the royal grounds with the two little kinglings, quiet for a change, sober-faced, even. They were all looking up at the strange message Zady had magically spread across their sky.

"I don't know, youngster, but it's going to be something bad."

Youngster! She had never called him that before. Not even when his youth might have justified it. She was really worked up over Zady's reappearance in their frame and now these mysterious letters above their heads.

It had to be a bluff, Kelvin thought. The old hag had lost her army and her malignant helpers. How she had gotten back into their frame, if in fact she had left it, he didn't know.

"There are benign powers and there are malignant powers, and I've never heard of either taking over the entire sky. This isn't just illusion, Kelvin! Everywhere, in all the kingdoms, everyone is looking up at the sky as we are doing! Everyone is seeing the same letters! Everyone is getting her message!"

"Hardly the Rotterniks," Kelvin said. He was trying to reassure her a bit. "Babkeys can't read."

"That's right, go on, boy, make jokes! You've been a happy, carefree person too long! You don't know what it's like out in the real, cruel world!"

She sounded, Kelvin thought, as he might have sounded had he an ordinary son who was idling. He resented that. He knew he was no idler and never had been! Admittedly he and his family had lived on the king's bounty for a long time, but that was the reward for heroship. As for the heroship, he'd never wanted—

"Do you think we should keep looking up?" Kelvin's father asked. "It could be a trick. She may be intending to blind us."

Kelvin immediately recalled his father's and father-in-law's fantastic war stories of people's melted eyeballs running down their cheeks and men's shadows etched permanently on walls and pavements. The strange thing was that they seemed to believe those stories, though there was no magic capable of that kind of destruction. Of course Earth, his father always insisted, utilized science.

"I don't know what is going to happen," Helbah whispered. "Your wife can't see in the cards, can she, John? In that we're blind already. All of us are blind to the future."

"Meow," said Katbah on her shoulder. The animal, or Helbah's animal half, whichever interpretation was preferred for a familiar, did not seem worried. That was normally a good sign.

"I'm going to keep watching," Helbah said. "You can watch or not as you prefer."

Kelvin decided to keep watching too. He couldn't believe there was a chance they'd all soon be stricken blind. Unfortunately there was now nothing to see except those cloud letters. Some of the sights he had glimpsed recently had impressed him far more. After seeing giants and friends who suddenly vanished to become enemies, the sky message was tame. He saw that his father was still watching.

Light flashed, or rather the sky did. The entire region overhead was flooded with a dazzling brilliance. Just for a moment it lasted, and then the cloud letters vanished as mysteriously as they had appeared, and the sky split apart like a torn envelope. The ground shook, just as from an implosion, as when Horace opaled and the air rushed in and made a tremendous:

BARRRRROOOOOMMMMM!

Kelvin's ears hurt, but overhead something miraculous was happening. Having split apart, the sky was now filled with mountains and a jungle and rolling farmland. It was so very real, and seemed so very close, that Kelvin almost felt he could touch it. Not like a crystal image, though those appeared to be real enough. This had the same solid three-dimensionality as seen through an ordinary window.

Now the greenery blurred and the jungle was closer and closer, and there was a cairn. The cairn grew larger, as with diminished distance, until finally it was as though they were standing before it. The metal plate on the central rock read: "Dedicated to the Memory of Throod's Fighting Men Killed in the War with Rud, 1824."

"I'd thought it was Rotternik," Kelvin said, letting his breath out.

The cairn slipped by and the road came nearer as the familiar monument was left behind. Then, suddenly, a large building not unlike a barracks. Above the door: RECRUITMENT HOUSE.

"That's Throod, all right," Kelvin's father said.

As though responding to his voice the scene grew close and narrower. They could see the men in front of the building—battered warriors for the most part, though a few were fresh-faced. Kelvin wondered how many of them had been in Zady's army and run home once they had been accorded the chance. There was fear in these men. They were one and all looking up at the sky. Were these men seeing themselves there? If so, this must be an even weirder vision for them than for everyone else!

"It's like a zoom lens on a camera," Kelvin's father said. Again he was contrasting a magic that was new to him to the science he had accepted as natural. Kelvin had to wonder once again why his father and his father-in-law thought that putting a name to something and explaining it in nonmagical terms made it manageable.

A voice came loud and clear from the sky itself: "LOOK, YOU OF THE ALLIANCE! LOOK AND TREMBLE AT ZADY'S POWER!"

CRRRAAACCCKKK!

The loud splintering sound, like the voice, came from the sky. The men there trembled and fell down as their ground shook. Recruitment House collapsed from the shaking, its shingled roof coming down as the walls crumbled and split apart.

"Earthquake," John said, giving it a name.

"Magic," Helbah corrected.

The scene moved back, back, leaving prostrate men, some of them screaming and reaching imploringly up as though to touch the sky. Now they were seeing the road and the cairn that had been knocked over after having stood for two centuries of time. Shying horses; running, falling men and women; and—though there were few in this soldier's paradise—lost, crying children. Fear was panicking them, and who could blame them? Great trees were being uprooted and felled. Wild animals were emerging from the jungle. Beautiful orchards and crops of waving grain were dimming along with parade grounds and houses and windmills and all manner of man's conceit; statues and plaques and monuments to those who had died and afterwards been termed great. It was a haze coming between them and the sky.

It was also one hell of a vision. What could it mean?

CCCCCRRRRRAAAAACCCCCKKKKK!

Another horrendous sound from above, and Throod was missing. In its place, and Kelvin had to rub his eyes, the borders of Klingland and Kance and Rud now joined—forest, only forest, spreading far and wide. The scene moved downward, closing with the treetops. Babkeys and other forest dwellers chattered and scattered there. It was like a land reborn, or as Throod might have been before it was a kingdom of mercenaries and had human inhabitants.

Kelvin swallowed. "What? What? Where?"

The voice from the sky boomed loud, almost answering him:

LOOK, PEOPLE OF THE ALLIANCE, AT WHAT ZADY HAS DONE. THROOD IS NO MORE. IT DOESN'T EXIST. IT HAS NEVER EXISTED. ANYTHING YOU HAVE THAT CAME FROM THROOD, WHETHER WEAPONS OR HARNESS OR HUMAN BEINGS, IS NOW GONE, NEVER TO RETURN. ZADY CAN DO THAT WITH ALL YOUR KINGDOMS, ONE BY ONE. ORC OR HUMAN OR BESTIAL HUMAN MAKES NO DIFFERENCE TO HER. PEOPLE, BEG YOUR GOVERNMENTS TO SURRENDER NOW TO ZADY AND SUBMIT TO HER OVERWHELMING AND OMNIPOTENT MIGHT. I WANT A DELEGATION FROM THE ALLIANCE TO COME WITH AN OFFICIAL SURRENDER AND I WANT IT WITHIN THREE DAYS. MY NEW HEADQUARTERS FOR POSSIBLE FUTURE DECIMATION OF THE KINGDOMS IS NOW

IN DRAGON TERRITORY, ROUGHMAUL MOUNTAIN: SEND YOUR DELEGATION THERE. FAILURE TO DO SO IS UNTHINKABLE AND WILL NOT BE TOLERATED. EACH DAY AFTER THE THIRD DAY ANOTHER KINGDOM WILL DISAPPEAR. UPON SURRENDER, EXECUTION OF MY ENEMIES WILL BEGIN AND END UPON MY DISCRETION. I HEREWITH DECLARE NO MERCY FOR THOSE I HATE AND IMMEDIATE OR EVENTUAL DEATH FOR ALL THOSE WHO DARE TO OPPOSE ME. THINK ABOUT IT, BUT DON'T THINK FOR LONG.

BBBBBLLLLLLIIIIIPPPPP!

Another horrendous noise and the sky was the sky once more. Kelvin found himself staring at a fluffy white cloud that had somehow assumed an obscene shape. Other clouds were normal and the sky bluer than he remembered.

"It's a trick, isn't it, Helbah?" he asked the witch, though inside he feared the answer.

"No trick," Helbah said, looking stricken. "It's just what I would expect her to do if she had unlimited power. She now has such power. I don't know how she obtained it, but she has. Throod is vanished, and according to Zady it's never been."

"That's nonsense!" Kelvin's father said, obviously annoyed. "We were there. We got mercenaries and weapons to free Rud and then to fight other wars. We saw the Flaw. The Flaw! What can have happened to it? Where—"

"Come inside and we'll see." Helbah led the way, followed by clearly scared Kildom and Kildee and then by Kelvin's father. Kelvin brought up the rear, fearful that he was going to see that what he had just experienced was no lie.

Inside her war room Helbah gestured and lighted a crystal. The swirls started inside the square hunk of semitransparent rock, then merged and formed a picture as her hands made passes. In the crystal was jungle, looking as it had in the sky. The jungle grew closer under Helbah's manipulations and a river appeared, but no signs of habitation and no people or livestock. Helbah followed the river and then the river and the jungle ended abruptly. There was a great, open tear or emptiness that extended through the jungle and became lost to sight at either side. No fences surrounding it now, naked stars gleamed in what was permanent, unyielding blackness. The river here, as it did underground in Rud, swirled past the awesomeness, making a bend and sharp turn as if aware of what would confront an unwary traveler. Part of the river did not make the turn but instead fell downward, as a waterfall, into the great emptiness. From their apparent position above the river they could see the falls thin as it dropped and vanished.

"That's the Flaw, all right," his father said, just as he had commented on the sky scene. "Only it's not as I remember. No barriers. The river wasn't this close to Throod. It's as though the river is misplaced."

"The river was moved long ago, when Throodians cut a new channel for it," Helbah said. "This is the river in its natural wild state. It will flood from year to year and carry unfortunate trees and creatures into the Flaw with its higher waters."

Kelvin shivered. The Flaw always had rather scared him. His father and his father's companions in war—or 'was it maneuvers in practice for an eventual war?—had come to this spot from Earth and impending destruction. Only then there had been barriers along the edge of the Flaw, and tourists gazing through the peepholes, and not too far away Recruitment House and its soldiery. Kelvin often wondered what it was like for his father and those who were soon to perish despite an escape that couldn't be accounted for. They had been in or near an atomic explosion, his father had said, and then something twisted in their minds and bodies and almost instantly, as it seemed, they were at the Flaw's edge outside the barrier. It had been, to Kelvin's knowledge, the only time anyone had traversed the frames without resort to either transporter or opal. He would have thought such a transference impossible, but his father and his men had undoubtedly arrived physically and mentally intact.

"Seen enough?" Helbah asked.

Kelvin nodded. His father nodded. It was compelling just to look on that eternal blackness and those distant stars. Somewhere other people might be looking up at those stars, seeing them not in a Flaw but their own sky.

Helbah snapped her fingers. The awesome scene vanished, and in its place was nothing more than a chunk of very light, pinkish crystal cut into a box shape and now supported by a stout stand. Kelvin's father had remarked on the similarity of a magic viewing crystal to what he called television; however, his descriptions of living and dead people appearing in the entertainment box gave his son—and most sensible people, Kelvin felt certain—a cold fear.

"Throod really has vanished, hasn't it?" John said. "I don't understand it, but it happened. It's like the atomic bomb all over again."

"Really, John, you and your comparisons!" Helbah was annoyed with his slowness and his habitual references to things nobody in this frame had witnessed or cared about. If he persisted in it he was in for another of her tongue lashings.

"No, really. St. Helens and I were talking about it. I didn't know what was coming but I remarked that Zady might come up with something overwhelming that no magic could deal with. I was thinking of atomic weaponry, since that's the most overpowering force I ever experienced. When the first two atomic bombs were used they ended immediately what would otherwise have been a much longer war."

"Nonsense!" Helbah snapped. "Such power would be beyond that of any witch or warlock!" Then she became more sober and less certain. Her seamed face worked as though she were about to cry.

"As is," she finished in a husky voice, "what happened this morning in this frame. You are right, John, Zady really has an overwhelming force. Whatever she has, it violates everything I thought I knew about magic. If there's a defense that's possible I'm sure it's one that has never yet been conjured."

Jon was flying. The earth wheeled below, looking prettier than it ever had before. She felt exhilarated, freed. But how had she gotten here? When had she again become a bird?

Oh—she was dreaming! So in a moment she would wake up and be home. Still, she could help the process along, because she remained nervous about being away from her family, even in a dream.

Home was back the way she had come. She tried turning.

Her wings beat steadily on, refusing to obey her. This wasn't a nice dream anymore; this was turning ugly.

"Wake! Wake!" she tried to cry, urging herself to the necessary course. But all that came out were two squaks. This was a nightmare!

As she thought the word nightmare, a dark shadow passed between her and the overhead sun. She heard a screeching. Turning her head upward on her bird neck she saw it dropping on her: an eagawk with extended talons.

Nightmare? No, this was worse! *This was reality!* The evil witch must have left a residual spell on her, so that she had not truly escaped. Now she was being recovered, at the witch's convenience.

She tried to scream. In this she succeeded, as the cruel talons caught her.

CHAPTER 24

Trip to Roughmaul Mountain

Kelvin, Heln, his parents, both his human children, and their respective mates were gathered with Helbah and the nominal kings of Klingland and Kance in Helbah's headquarters. They had done the crystal searchings for an extended length of time, or at least Helbah had, and neither Horace nor his mate had made an appearance. They weren't at the cave where Horace had been told to wait, nor at their retreat where they had sunnymooned. They just weren't anywhere that Helbah could find.

"Do you think she's got them?" Kelvin asked. After seeing what had happened to an entire kingdom he could well believe that Zady could magic them from existence. It was painful to think about. Horace had seemed a monster to him and his wife, but then Horace had saved the other siblings and stood by him the day Zady lost her head. He, and he thought Heln too, had come to love Horace as a son—a little like a retarded human son—ever since.

As though thinking the same thing, Heln suddenly buried her face against the brownberry shirt covering his newly muscled chest and began crying. A loss of a kingdom was bad, but the loss of a child and the child's mate was disastrous.

"I don't know if they exist in our frame anymore," Helbah said. "Any luck yet, Charlain?"

Charlain looked up from the table where she had spread the cards. "It's always the same, Helbah. All the cards show is danger and uncertainty for anyone I ask about. The death card never shows, but that doesn't mean they're safe."

John patted Charlain's shoulder. "At least you don't see disaster."

"I'm not certain, John." She looked with violet eyes from her astonishingly still-beautiful face. Now those eyes were wide and frightened in a way that Kelvin could not remember them ever having been before. He didn't like the tremble on her lips as she whispered, more than spoke, to his father. "The cards are worthless."

"Darling, you've never said that before!"

"I've never felt this way before! Maybe it's something Zady's doing—preventing me from reading the future."

"The future you read always has been ambiguous," John reminded. "That uncertainty card showed up a lot in the past, didn't it?"

"Yes, but before I could always find the right questions to get around it. Long ago Lester was wounded and the cards wouldn't tell me if he would live or die. But then I asked about specific medicines, and finally I found one that the cards told me would save his life. They had been unable to answer until I made the decision on the right or wrong medicine."

"Ask them if there are questions that will remove the uncertainty," John suggested.

Charlain almost absently shuffled and laid out the cards. She closed her eyes in concentration, then raised her hand above their backs. Her fingers made a circle over the cards, her forefinger pointing outward, then down.

Triumphantly Charlain opened her eyes and picked up the card her pack had chosen. She looked at it, and promptly burst into tears.

Kelvin didn't need to see the card to know that it was what she called the chaos or uncertainty card. What it meant, or had meant in the past, was that any outcome was possible. The cards had as much as proclaimed their own impotence.

"Helbah," Kelvin said in agony, "isn't there some magic you can use?"

Helbah looked around at them, her eyes lingering longest

on the two unmatured kings whom she had nourished and trained over a span of time equal to Kelvin's own life.

"You know, hero, that there isn't. I've told you before—the magic Zady is now using is beyond my ability. I don't comprehend it in terms of magic any more than your father comprehends it in terms of science. The power Zady's displaying isn't comprehensible."

"Then it comes from beyond the stars?"

"Kelvin, the questions you can ask! You're as bad as Kildom and Kildee. Do you really know what you just asked?"

"No," Kelvin admitted. He had just asked the first question that occurred to him.

"I will tell you, then. The answer is I don't know. There is power all witches tap or harness, but we don't think of it as other than magic. Whether what we do or command comes from the planet or the stars or somewhere else is of no consequence. Your father's science worries about things like that, not practitioners of magic. Zady may have found a new and more powerful source than that from which is derived either benign or ordinary magic. But if she has, does its origin matter?"

"If we could find the source we might destroy it," Kelvin's father said.

"Oh, John, John!" Helbah chided him. "You're thinking science. If a source exists it probably isn't in our frame and there's no way of locating it. On Earth could you locate and destroy the source of electricity?"

Kelvin's father hung his head. Charlain held him close, trying to comfort him. He had said a foolish thing and Helbah's words made him realize it. To not believe in magic was bad, but to be forced to believe in it and then to have to acknowledge to yourself that you had no idea how it worked was demoralizing. As always, Kelvin sympathized with his father. It was all the consequence of his miseducation—an overemphasis on cause and effect and denial of even the possibility of magic.

"Are we going to go to war again?" one of the royal twins

asked in a squeaky little voice. They had been sitting there so quietly, so well behaved, that that alone seemed magic.

Helbah said, "I don't know." She didn't bother to box their royal ears. It was a defeated witch standing in this palace room, not a disciplinarian.

Suddenly the largest, most impressive crystal Helbah owned flared, and then the lesser crystals brightened as their inner markings swirled. When the swirling stopped Zady's ugly face, which seemed to have grown even more warts, looked out at them and around the room.

"All my enemies together!" Zady enthused in her crackly voice. "Kelvin of the round ears, father of the Roundear, Mama, and the two who were born with the help of a chimaera!"

"We're here too!" one of the kinglets said.

"Yeah, we're your enemy too!" his brother echoed him. Katbah, perched familiarly on Helbah's shoulder, as befitted a familiar, spat.

"Yes, all my enemies," Zady reiterated. "And now I have some orders for you. But first, would you like to see your sister, Kelvin?"

Before he could answer the scene changed in the big crystal. It showed Jon, apparently unharmed and by herself. Behind her was a stone wall. Overhead, open sky with dark clouds scuttling through it.

"Come closer, dearie. Come look in my crystal."

Jon stepped closer, moving as one drowned and dead. "Kelvin!" she said, bumping into something invisible. "Kelvin, don't come here! Stay away from her! Stay away!"

Jon vanished from the crystal and Zady's warty face reappeared. She began a cackling laugh and continued it far longer than seemed possible. Finally her eyes fixed on Kelvin, chilling him to his depths.

"Kelvin, I want you in dragon territory with the Alliance's official surrender and I want you here in three days. Failure to arrive will cost the Alliance a kingdom. With you I want"—her eyes roved the room—"your father, your two grown-up brats, and of course your dragon brat. Incidentally, your sister will suffer what will be your future punishment until you arrive."

The searing eyes turned away from them. Zady spoke and apparently gestured at an unseen Jon.

"Dearie, a spear up your derriere, perhaps?"

Jon began screaming. She screamed loudly and piercingly in a way Kelvin had never heard her or any woman scream.

"Stop it, Zady! Stop it!" he pleaded and ordered in the same breath.

"Why, what do you want to do about it, little boy?"

Jon's voice broke in over Zady's, though she hardly stopped screaming. "It's not real! It's not real! Kelvin, it hurts! It hurts!"

"Yes, dearie, the spear isn't real but it hurts anyway, doesn't it? The pain is excruciating for you, just as it was for that war-horse. After I tire of this one, I'll cut your breasts off again. Then you'll be stepped on by an orc and squashed but still conscious. After that—"

"NO! NO!" Kelvin shouted.

Jon continued screaming.

"Many, many innovations I've thought up. Come join the fun, Kelvin. You won't enjoy any of it."

"No, Zady, no! Don't torture her! I'll come there. You can torture me if you must!"

"Spoken like a true hero." Again the insane laugh.

"I'm coming to find you! I'm coming!" Kelvin said.

"Of course you are, dearie, and don't forget to bring your rejuvenated old father and your mind-reading grown-up brats."

"Zady, Zady, don't go! I want to keep talking! Zady—"

The crystal blanked. Kelvin felt that a part of his mind blanked with it. It wasn't until Helbah spoke that he even thought again.

"You have to go," Helbah said. "With or without surrender."

"We must never surrender, Helbah!" He was pleading, wanting her to contradict him and yet knowing that she couldn't.

"No, not even if all the kingdoms vanish one by one."

Kelvin swallowed. "I've got my boots on. I'll just step over into dragon territory."

"Not without me," Glint said. "I can read her mind if I get a chance."

"I'm coming too!" Charles said. "I want to do more to her than I did last time. Cutting her head off will just be the start!"

"Me too!" Merlain echoed. "She made me walk off a cliff. I haven't forgotten that! I still have nightmares!"

"And don't forget your father," his father said. "She wants me as badly as she wants you. After all I was married to her niece."

"I have to go alone," Kelvin said, faking bravery. Possibly the rest could escape to another frame. He wished he could believe it and somehow make it happen.

"No, you can't go alone," Helbah said. "You need these others, just as they each said."

"But the danger—"

"We're all in danger."

"She'll do horrible things to—"

"To all of us if she gets the chance. Don't you let her get the chance!"

"But I can't take all the others! I've only one pair of boots and one levitation belt!"

"Make more than one trip. Carry them into dragon territory with you, Kelvin, one at a time."

"But—! But—!"

"Son," his mother said, coming close to him, "do as she says. Helbah knows best."

"But they're my children, Mother! They're young, and I'm—"

"A hero, Son—a prophesied hero. You've got all your past to prove you are a hero, and you know that Mouvar favors you."

"Who is Mouvar?" Kelvin had to ask. "Is he a god or a wizard or a green dwarf? If he favors me so much, why doesn't he come here and help?"

"Because that's not his way, Son."

His mother held his face in her hands and looked as beseechingly at him as she had sometimes done when he was a small boy. Now, as then, her mother-magic was doing its work. He did understand that it didn't matter what Mouvar was—what mattered was that Mouvar had foreseen him and had provided weapons for him. The gauntlets and the boots and the levitation belt, not to mention the antimagic weapon, were all Mouvar's gifts. So, in a way, was the chimaera's sting. And come to think about it, it might have been through Mouvar's maneuvering that he met the chimaera and that eventually his own remarkable children were born. Mouvar might have foreseen or arranged everything that happened in his life, but it was he, not Mouvar, who was the designated hero.

It all rested with him, and all he could do was hope that Mouvar knew everything and would push him to be a hero in spite of himself. But could he win? Could any human or nonhuman win against a power that could take kingdoms right out of existence? He would do what he could, but he hoped that Mouvar had more knowledge of the future than did his mother or Helbah. If Horace with the opal and he with Mouvar's gifts couldn't defeat Zady, then Zady must be undefeatable.

"Do you want me to come too, Charles?"

Charles kissed Glow. "No, dear, you stay here with Helbah. With Dad's help we'll win. We'll burn Zady to ashes and scatter them. After that we'll come back to you."

Kelvin was touched by his son's confidence in him. He wished that he had that much confidence in himself. It was time, high time, that he started acting like the hero everyone said he was.

"Dad, you take the levitation belt as a precaution. Merlain, I want you to carry the Mouvar antimagic weapon and keep a sharp mind out for hostile magic. Son-in-law, you strap the chimaera's sting on your back and hope to use it. Charles, here's my right-hand gauntlet—I fought a war with the left one and won. Now we're all armed. Everybody ready?"

There were nods of real or feigned eagerness as his small

band buckled on and secured their weapons. Kelvin knew that they had no choice. He stooped down, visualizing the place in dragon country where, as children, he and Jon had encountered their first dragon. The old debris piles would long have washed away, but the river would still have its bend and that ancient rock and big tree would still be there. He'd step well away from the water, at approximately the spot where he and Jon had once tethered their long-gone but never forgotten donkey. He indicated his back with a jerk of his thumb.

Glint took hold of his shoulders and threw a leg over his side. Kelvin lifted him, glad now that he could do so as he couldn't have before Helbah had made him exercise and lose weight. Glint was heavy. But it was only for one step. One step and his son-in-law would slide off and he would leave him there and step back.

Kelvin took the step he had tried delaying. Glint dismounted and looked about. It was a tamer section of dragon country than where he had dwelt with Ember. Wild enough for Kelvin. He hoped Zady would not pull a surprise raid on his little party before all of them were delivered. Glint would be searching with his mind, and Helbah would be watching by crystal, but the possibility was evident.

He stepped back and got his father, who was even heavier than Glint despite his rapid loss of weight. Now he had to fetch his children, and the necessity pained. He waved at his father and Glint. He could count on his father to check on anything Glint sensed by rising into the air as high as was necessary with the levitation belt. He hoped that Glint wouldn't sense Jon in horrible agony from Zady's torture.

He stepped to the palace, bent over, and his son Charles got astride his back. Charles, good boy that he was, could use the sword at his belt with the skill of a master swordsman, with the aid of the gauntlet. He stepped over and down on the riverbank beside Glint and his father. Charles slid off. Kelvin hated worst of all that he was now required to fetch Merlain.

She was waiting, and wasted not a moment. She had pulled on a rough brownberry shirt that would be warm high in the mountains and that covered the Mouvar weapon. He straightened up, took one last look—it might really be his last, he knew—at his mother, at Helbah, at his wife, at the beautiful girl his son had married, and at the two apparent boys. All looked back confidently, including Helbah's familiar. The magic crystals showed his father and Glint and Charles awaiting him and Merlain.

"GO!" Helbah ordered him.

He straightened up and took the step. Countryside blurred as it had before.

"Whee!" Merlain said. "This is more fun than riding Horace!"

Fun! She was still a girl in some respects, and here was her father taking her into more peril than she could imagine. Her mentioning her dragon brother did, however, spark a thought.

He put his foot down, right beside Charles. Merlain slid off and he carefully felt his vertebrae. All he really needed was for his middle-aged complaints to come back!

They were looking at him expectantly, and he had to act as if he were the leader he wasn't. Merlain had given him the clue.

"We have to find Horace," he announced. "We have to find him now, before we go to Roughmaul Mountain. With Horace we'll have opal power."

They looked at him as if they respected what he had said, as he himself did not. Belatedly he realized that if Horace encountered them he would see them as Zady and helpers of Zady and would attack them. Or, and this was an equally terrible thought, if Horace encountered Zady he would see in her only a friend.

CHAPTER 25

Return Visit

Horace was a very unhappy dragon. Not knowing whether to eat someone was frustrating. A mistake might deprive him of relatives. An equally bad mistake could deprive him of his life. As for Ember, the best reason he had yet found for living, he dared not return to her. The last time he had been there he had seen her as a male dragon filled with the mating urge and had been within one jaw snap of killing her.

Yet there has to be a way, he forced himself to think, using his inherited human faculties. Helbah had said she would try to remove the curse Zady had put on him, but to him it seemed that she was helpless. Maybe someone else could help. Should he find Zady and ask her to remove the curse? No, no, she'd never do that, and besides he'd bite her first. Zady after all would hurt Merlain and Ember, and in all the existences there was nothing worse than something that would hurt Merlain and Ember.

It was very, very hard work, this thinking. It just wasn't natural for a dragon! Perhaps if he remembered everything he had ever done he would discover something that could help.

For days and nights Horace paced the area in front of his cave. He'd eat the meat that was brought to him daily by someone who seemed an enemy but whose thoughts were those of an ally. He always investigated the thoughts thoroughly, and so far he hadn't been wrong. Sometime he might be wrong, and the thought bothered him. After eating he'd resume his slow dragon pacing, his tail now and then lashing out in frustration. Somewhere in the past there was an answer.

One morning as he paced and hurt his head Horace noticed that the sky was changing. White clouds were assuming peculiar shapes. He had never seen them do that. The shapes strung all across the sky and did not appear to be moving.

The sky flashed a dazzling bright. Horace blinked and the strangely shaped clouds vanished. The sky cracked into halves. The ground shook and rock fell and bounced and slid from higher up the mountain.

BBBBBAAAAARRRRRROOOOOMMMMM!

The sound was louder than any dragon roar. Louder even than thunder. His head hurt and rang and did nothing good for his disposition. Overhead the sky finished cracking to reveal a land of trees and streams and farms. Horace hadn't known that there was a land beyond the sky—Merlain had never mentioned it.

The sky-land came closer. There was a road, now a big pile of rock, now a building with soldiers in front of it looking up into the sky. Did they see him? Were they enemies of his? Should he opal onto them and destroy them?

A voice came from the sky: "LOOK, YOU OF THE ALLIANCE! LOOK AND TREMBLE AT ZADY'S POWER!"

Zady! It was Zady's voice! He tried to find a thought coming from the sky. He tried sniffing scent from the sky. Nothing! It was some sort of trick!

CRRRAAACCCKKK!

The sound was like a breaking tree. Men fell down as the ground in the sky trembled and shook. The building fell, its top coming down and its sides splintering.

Now the sky-land was receding. Men were screaming at their sky—reaching out hands as though to pick fruit over their heads. The road was in the sky and the pile of rocks. Woodland, shying horses, men and women running, screaming. Children running—and now Horace felt a pang, remembering when Charles and Merlain were like these in size. Trees were falling. Wild animals were running, but no dragons or hunters were chasing them. Trees filled with fruit, grasses higher than Horace had ever seen, long stretches of green with

men in uniforms prostrated in a line with weapons scattered
by their hands. All was growing dim, dim, dimmer.

CCCCCRRRRRAAAAACCCCCKKKKK!

The land in the sky changed with the sound. There were
now no men or farms or buildings. Only trees and a stream
and hairy creatures not quite like humans. This was an improvement! This sky-land Horace liked!

"LOOK, PEOPLE OF THE ALLIANCE, AT WHAT
ZADY HAS DONE. THROOD IS NO MORE. IT
DOESN'T EXIST. IT HAS NEVER EXISTED."

Horace ceased to listen to Zady's unpleasant voice. It was
shouting nonsense: things to be understood, if at all, only by
humans.

"I HEREWITH DECLARE NO MERCY FOR
THOSE I HATE AND IMMEDIATE OR EVENTUAL
DEATH FOR ALL THOSE WHO DARE TO OPPOSE ME.
THINK ABOUT IT, BUT DON'T THINK FOR LONG."

BBBBBLLLLLIIIIIPPPPP!

The sky was now the old, familiar sky—very blue with
white fluffy clouds moving across it. Had it been some magic
that had made him see the sky-land? Had it really been there?
What about Zady? Where was she? He knew he had heard her
voice, croaking as a froog's voice, loud as a dragon's first roar.
Had she been up in that sky-land? Should he go up there and
destroy her?

Horace wasn't too good with words but he recognized a
threat when he heard one. Zady intended to kill her enemies.
Zady's enemies were his parents, his friends, his brother and
sister and himself. The only way to stop Zady killing them was
to destroy her. Merlain said by fire. Horace understood fire; he
had been burned by it after lightning struck. He had to help
his father—it was a son's duty!—but he had to be able to
recognize his father and to identify Zady.

Old problem right back again. But now he might not have
time. Zady might start killing them. She might kill Ember.

Fright at the thought of losing Ember made him opal-
jump. He was back at their spot. A big, ugly male in heat
confronted him there.

HORACE! came Ember's thought.

The big male rushed at him. Horace crouched defensively, protecting his belly from a possible upward strike. The male dragon stopped.

Horace? Horace, don't you want me anymore?

It was her! Cautiously he eased up and stretched out a forefoot to her. Her tongue came out and licked at him.

Could he leave her again? Did he dare?

With the opal in his gizzard he could go anywhere. But Ember hadn't an opal in her. She could only move at a dragon's customary dragon pace, and there was no way at all that she could go some of the places he had been. No way that she could have gone with him and Merlain and Charles and those other two child humans.

Merlain, then hardly more than a hatchling, had held the opal then. The children had got on his back and held on and she rubbed the opal and it took them to a place where there was this big chimaera creature with its two human heads and one proper dragon head. Merlain had explained later that this beast was their godparent who had helped them and their father, though Horace failed to remember how. Merlain had said that the creature had given their father a magic birthing powder that had made Horace a dragon and her a girl and Charles a boy and allowed them to live. He hadn't liked the chimaera the one time he had visited, but that had been because it tried to take the opal from Merlain. He had delivered the woman-arm a sharp slap with his tail, and Merlain had rubbed on the opal and taken them home and away from there.

Ember put her forefoot affectionately across his big back as she teased at him, wanting him to do his masculine duties by her. At another time he would have been pleased to oblige, but now he saw her as a male, and no male was going to clamber on his back! He wouldn't allow that, even if—even if it were really Ember.

Merlain and Charles and those hatchlings he had been told were kings had ridden on him. His father and Glint had ridden on him. Might not his mate ride?

Suppose he was to take her to see the chimaera? The chimaera had somehow saved his and Merlain's and Charles' lives before they were born. Might the chimaera be able to help him now? And suppose he had Ember with him? If he saw Ember as he knew her to be and not as a male dragon in excessive rut, he would know that he was truly helped. Then, with the curse lifted, he could return and find his father, and together they could go and find and burn Zady until she was nothing but a pile of ashes.

It was worth a try. The alternative to trying was to be frustrated indefinitely.

Ember, he thought forcefully, *climb upon your lord and master's broad and willing back!*

Mervania had been tending her garden all morning, shoring up drooping green and yellow corbean plants and patting dirt up around the bright-orange pumpquashes. She'd have to speak to her captors about better controlling her island's weather. Mertin and Grumpus were asleep on their necks, nodding and snoring as she eased their mutual body down the row of plants.

Mertin woke with a loud snort. He twisted his neck stalk to look at Mervania, his fellow head. He belched in typical Mertin fashion and stretched their carapace to the extent that that was possible. "Mervania, we've company!"

"Don't be stupid, I would have sensed—"

She stopped, having turned slightly, and was now looking at two adult dragons, one on the other's back. They were right across her cabsprouts and ruttabeets. The dragon on the bottom was of a dimmer color—copper—than the shiny golden-scaled dragon on top.

"As if gophmice and molphers weren't enough! How can a poor chimaera get her gardening done? How'd they get here?"

"Gwoomth!" said Grumpus, studying the creatures from its dragon eyes.

"Copper good!" said Mertin. "We always need copper to supplement our diet."

"Mertin, we are not going to eat one of our godchildren! This one has to be—the one that should have been a nice head like Grumpus without that ugly—"

Horace raised his head and hissed.

"Ah, so you're sensitive, are you, little beast!" That was not an insult, or at least no more of one than to refer to a creature as human or dragon. Everything was inferior compared to a chimaera, of course.

Compared to the chimaera, the two dragons, one atop the other, were not tall. They barely came up to Mervania's neck stalk. In all the worlds the three heads of the chimaera had explored in astral form they had never encountered an intelligent creature that towered over them. Dragons were large, orcs tall, and the chimaera largest and tallest of all.

You tried to take the opal from my sister!

Oh, that! But I saved her later, didn't I? Helped her, at least.

Maybe did.

Why are you here? She was really curious. To have come here as it had, the dragon must have swallowed the opal. It or the one on its back.

You help Merlain?

She needs help, does she? Can't humans do anything right!

Humans not problem. Witch.

Zady, I suppose. I don't know what Kelvin was thinking about, letting her escape! I really don't know if he can think.

Horace gnashed his jaws. *Don't insult Father!*

Don't you take that tone of thought with me! You're just a dragon! You could have been one-third of a chimaera, but stupid Kelvin wanted his mate to survive the birth. I don't see why—she never was other than human. His Heln isn't in the Mouvar prophecies and she can't even read minds.

Don't insult Mother! The female dragon on his back hissed loudly, giving support to her mate.

If you aren't the most ridiculous creatures! Dragons are intended to eat humans, not defend their pitiful honor.

Father and Mother not ordinary humans. Horace not regular dragon.

I'll grant you that. But what's Zady doing that made you come here? No, don't bother to strain. I'll get the answers.

She sifted quickly through Horace's recent memories. The first thing she discovered was that Horace saw his mate as a large male while the mate saw her and her fellow heads as just what they were. The poor dragon had been spelled and spelled properly. It took but a moment to learn the rest of his story, and then she cautioned him to stay while she scuttled to her herb patch, where she plucked several silver-headed flowers from among bright yellows. She brought them in front of Horace's face and held them before his nostrils.

Horace sniffed just as she blew out a breath and disturbed the tiny feathered seeds.

The dragon opened his mouth, probably to roar, and she tossed the bouquet inside and almost down his throat. He choked, blinked, coughed. His eyes got big and he hiccuped.

Ember, you're you again!

Well, who did you think I'd be?

I can see right again! I can know friend from foe!

Of course you can, you ridiculous creature! Mervania thought to him. *Your curse is lifted.*

I will go back and kill Zady!

Not just yet. I want to mind-talk.

You help kill Zady?

Now why would I do that, Horace?

"Guuuuurrrrrrrr!"

Oh, very well, I won't tease you anymore. Don't go back— not just yet. I need to take an astralberry and go see what's happening. I can't help until I know what Zady plans. If your father can't handle it and Helbah and Katbah can't, then maybe I can advise them.

Help Merlain!

That's the idea. Ember, aren't you uncomfortable perched atop him? Why not get down and stretch your legs? I can't offer you anyone to eat, but maybe you'd like to gnash a pumpquash or a couple ripe zellons?

No. I like being here. You got carrion?

No carrion, Ember. Sorry. Grumpus ate the last we had.

We weren't expecting company. Actually we mostly eat company. Family's the exception.

Glad we mated. Not want to be meal for human-headed crawly thing.

Mervania half-raised her sting in intended reprimand, but forbore shocking their guest. It would be difficult to shock one of the dragons without shocking the other, and Ember had intended no insult but simply described in her terms the scorpiocrab body of a chimaera. Simple minds had simple concepts.

Swallow that astralberry! Horace ordered.

Mervania sighed. So impolite, but she ignored it. The berries were growing in the shade of a big wilpuss tree. She crawled over to it, plucked a ripe white berry, and held it in her human hand.

Swallow it! Horace ordered her again.

Very well. But you guests stay here until after we return to our body. Otherwise we might have to chase you down and eat you, to teach you manners. With that gentle admonition Mervania popped the berry into her mouth and swallowed.

Aw, what did you do that for?

Shut up, Mertin. It's only a short trip.

But I wanted to eat them.

Gwroomth!

You too, Grumpus.

They were now floating over their island. At her urging they drifted on over the swamp and the trees and the desert and into the cave of the transporter. The square-ears were not there now, Mervania not having bothered to mind-communicate with them that they were coming. The transporter, though, was set on the same coordinates it had been set on since Kelvin's last visit. Wanting to go where they needed to go, they drifted their consciousness into the booth, through the Flaw rupture, then out into the chamber intended for roundears. The chimaera had nearly round ears on her Mervania and Mertin heads; not so on Grumpus', but astral was not physical and so the trap was not sprung and the molecular structure of the installation was not instantly destroyed.

They drifted out of the chamber, along the underground river, up above the ancient stairs, above the old masonry, across country to where the dragons had started their journey. Here there were mountain crags and spires and an abundance of rough. Where was Zady? That was what they had come for.

They drifted at thought-pace, speeded by being chimaera and astral. To the highest, darkest, most forbidding mountain in this whole mountain range. Along the way they saw dragons and sheoats and goeeps and other denizens of the mountains. Grumpus commented twice, having spotted living or dead creatures that appeared appetizing. Then they were where she was, and even to a chimaera she had the ugliest of human faces. The rest of her was bare and what Kelvin and his father would have considered beautiful. Were they not in astral form Mervania saw no reason why Grumpus and Mertin should have been denied. One reason only—the head was excessively unappetizing and would make them sick.

The old witch was doing something with lighted crystals and bottles and retorts and powders piled around her. On her biggest crystal a face loomed, and it was a face that Mervania recognized.

Mertin, do you see it?

I see it!

Whimper. Whimper.

Don't be afraid, Grumpus. It won't get us. It can't.

What's it doing with her? It must want this world. It's cheating. Mouvar won't like it.

Of course it is cheating, Mertin. What else would you expect?

Do we dare advise Mouvar's hero? Will we if we can?

It's cheating. It's proper that we help Mouvar.

It may go to our frame and destroy our square-ears.

Not until the end of the game. It doesn't know we are here. If Mouvar wins, we're safe.

If. Mouvar loses sometimes.

Many times. At least as often as he wins.

Whimper, whimper.

Yes, Grumpus, we go back.

They went back the way, all the way, that they had come. They were in their chimaera body, which had remained untenanted. The two dragons waited, munching on Mervania's prize plants.

You have to return, you dragons. Horace, you must not delay helping your father. We'll watch what happens. We'll help when we can.

Horace squatted down and Ember reached up with her foreclaws, hooked his small, worthless wings, and pulled herself up and back into place. The two visitors abruptly vanished.

Poor dragons, poor humans, Mervania thought. *Even if we could go there physically there would be no protecting them.*

CHAPTER 26

Disappearance

That's Forbidden Mountain," Glint said, pointing at the mist-covered peaks; with the sun behind them they seemed almost to float in the sky. "I can show you where her old nest used to be."

Kelvin grunted. He had studied the maps, such as they were. Sons-in-law were supposed to get pushy, but Glint was overdoing it. Yet he did need someone to help him lead.

"We can go there together and leave the others here," Glint said persuasively. Out of politeness he was making no attempt, Kelvin hoped, to read his mind.

"I don't think we should break up," Kelvin said. He had no clear idea why he said it; the danger was so obvious. He looked in turn from Glint to Merlain and finally to Charles. "You haven't been able to catch any thoughts, have you?"

"Just a few dragons," Glint said. "None of them ours."

"Then we'd better get over to the right mountain. Rough-maul is that set of high walls and jagged teeth to the north of Forbidden. If Horace and Ember aren't near your old cave and they aren't where they sunnymooned, they have to be in one of the other of those mountain ranges, assuming they're in this frame." But they could be anywhere, and as unlocatable to Zady and Helbah as to him and Glint.

"Let's try that ledge, about halfway up the big dragon's tooth with its point concealed by mist."

Kelvin leaned over. "Hop aboard, Glint. You others had better wait here." Contradicting himself again; he was doing that lately. The truth was he would gladly have left the search entirely to Glint.

Glint threw a leg across his back. Kelvin found him no lighter than before but made no protest. He straightened the best he could, took a sight fix on the distant mountain range, and stepped.

The step carried them. Up, up, up, forward, forward, forward, and, as a cliff loomed, to his considerable terror, down to a firm footing on a narrow ledge.

Glint slid off his back and stood beside him, young and strong and heroic looking. In the morning mist Kelvin could now barely see the surrounding spires; as for Forbidden, it was here entirely lost.

"That one held the nest," Glint said, pointing. Following the direction of his son-in-law's pointing finger he could make out a collection of rubbish balanced precariously atop a spire. Zady had chosen a location for regrowth protected by facing mountain walls and overhang, yet according a clear view in every direction. Any dragon or human on the ledge they occupied or a nearby peak would have been spotted; undoubtedly she had seen Glint when he had spied on her and put a spell on him to keep him from coming back.

It had been a big step for nothing, then. He strained his never-more-than-adequate eyes but saw nothing interesting around or near the surrounding peaks. Glint had the eyesight and the mindsight as well, so why had he yielded to him? Could there have been some slight mental urging? Had leaving the others alone, even for this short a time, been entirely wise?

Fearing that they had wasted enough time and placed the others in danger, Kelvin stooped and motioned Glint to resume his back. Glint gripped his shoulders and put his legs around him as though he were now an accomplished Kelvin-rider. Kelvin straightened, thought of where they had left Merlain, Charles, and his father, and stepped.

Breezy mountain air, green-growing smells with a hint of carrion, blurring trees and rocks. His boot touched down, its step completed. Glint slid off his back, quicker than a squirbet leaping from a branch. This was where they had left Charles and Merlain and his father, but now the place was deserted. He looked around in desperation, willing that it were not so—that what he had most feared had not in fact happened.

The others were missing, and probably in Zady's cruel hands. Glint, his forehead furrowed, was trying desperately to reach them.

Zady's ghostly, mocking laughter broke into their discomfiture. "Kelvin the strategist!"

He looked at Glint's stricken face and then spoke to the empty air: "What do you want, Zady? Where did you take them?"

"Wouldn't you like to know?" Cackling followed, either to mock him or in enjoyment of her own nonanswer.

"You want our surrender, don't you?" It seemed a fair guess, assuming she wanted anything.

"You aren't ready to give it. Besides, I want your most precious child present—I've a little plan for the lizard that none of you will like. Besides, Zady wants to have a little fun first."

"You mean—" Kelvin swallowed, imagining what had almost been. In his mind he saw the beautiful, shapely body, and it still called to him.

"Wrong, Kelvin, though I may give you the desire. You didn't think I'd let you possess me, did you? If I had favored you it would have been to bind you to my wishes forever more."

Kelvin felt as though a wind left his stomach. He had realized the truth of her words ever since his niece had helped release him from her spell. The denial had been complete in his mind except for the part ruled by his masculine ego. Only a good woman gave of herself, and there was nothing good about Zady.

"I want to know where they are, Zady! Tell me!"

"Of course you do. I won't tell you."

"Glint?" His son-in-law's powers had to be good for something; Kelvin's certainly weren't. Let him read her and tell.

"I can't see her thoughts," Glint said in a tone of agony. "She blocks."

"The others?"

"Unconscious or taken away from here. As my wife sometimes says, Mouvar help us!"

My son-in-law the telepath! Kelvin thought disgustedly. How did Helbah expect them to defeat this old hag, anyway? And what had Mouvar to do with it? He had never fathomed Mouvar or his plans in the past and certainly didn't now. Apparently Mouvar moved among frame-worlds more easily than Kelvin moved along these mountains wearing Mouvar's gift. Why would Mouvar, a seeming god in power, be interested in what happened in one unimportant frame!

Because it isn't unimportant, Kelvin, a thought broke in on him. *Not while they play the game.*

Mervania? It's you, isn't it? I recognize your thought as clearly as I could recognize your voice. You're here! You're going to help me!

I'm here astrally. You know I can't be here bodily. There's no way I can leave my island prison except in immaterial form.

Where are they?

Safe for now. She has them but has not yet started to do them real harm.

You can advise them?

Some. I can't do a lot. I'm limited, by being as I am. I have to keep taking astralberries, and that means that I can't stay.

Yes, you have to keep taking them. Your superior chimaera system can—

Take only so many without risking permanent harm to myself. Too many, too close together, and I could never claim my physical body again.

I don't care about that, Kelvin thought hastily, *I just want your help.* Immediately he felt ashamed of his stupidity and selfishness; the chimaera, after all, could once have eaten him.

Oh, now, Kelvin, Mervania teased as in the time of his youthful folly, *you don't have to apologize to me. I know you feel bad because you hadn't the wit to trick me.*

No, that had been Stapular the robot who had tricked her, he remembered. But there was someone else alert for trickery now. It was time that he resumed speaking to Zady before she discovered the chimaera was actually here.

"Zady, what is it you want of me?"

"Why, to torment you, of course. To give you suffering." There was no indication that she knew of the chimaera's presence. Though Zady might be able to block thoughts, she wasn't much good at knowing them.

"You want to fight me with or without magic?" It was as bold a challenge as he had ever thrown at anyone during his entire life.

"Why should I? You're already in my power. You've already lost. The official surrender will be but an acknowledgment."

He knew that she had to be right. All that she left out was that there was no way that he or anyone dare acknowledge her victory. As Helbah had put it, not even if the kingdoms all were to vanish one by one. The finalization of a Zady victory was something no sane person dared to contemplate.

"Zady, let me know that they are alive. Let me hear their voices."

Silence. A silence that stretched for longer than Zady would need to answer. Had she heard him? Was she still there?

"Zady, speak to me. We have to talk." He was sounding desperate and he knew it, but then what was his alternative? He was desperate and Zady had to know it as well as he.

Mervania? Mervania? The chimaera might be his only chance. If she couldn't advise him, who in any of the frames could?

The chimaera head did not respond to him. Had she returned home to her own frame? Was she even now at work in her garden or preparing to cook some luckless visitor? Or was she here, searching for Zady or the dragons in her astral form?

"Glint?" He turned to the last spot where he had seen his son-in-law. Glint was not there! A meer path led up through the forest. Perhaps he had taken that, having to answer a call of nature. Yes, that was probably it.

"Glint! Glint!" he called loudly.

Silence, seemingly of an eternity. Finally in a nearby tree a tiny greenish bird began to sing. A dragon bellowed in anger or lust. A tree branch snapped as a bearver descended from what had been its perch.

He was alone in dragon territory. Alone, and like the fool he undoubtedly was, he had distributed all his Mouvar gifts, with the exception of his boots and his left gauntlet.

A dragon roared very close, and he turned quickly, knowing that he hadn't time to take a step or draw his sword.

Glint had never felt such an overpowering urge to defecate. His feet, almost of their own accord, had found the meer path and walked him up it and past a large boulder. He wasn't certain why he wanted to be out of Zady's invisible presence, but Merlain's mind had let him know all about expected modesty, and at the moment his wife's views seemed to apply.

"Zady, what is it you want of me?" he heard Kelvin say after a lengthy cessation of talk. He had tried probing the old witch's thoughts and it was like trying to shove through a tough elastic wall. There was no probing *that* mind, and considering Zady's nature that would ordinarily have been very well.

He felt the boulder and prepared to do what he had come for. Oddly, he did not seem to have to now. Suddenly a pain deep in his chest, and then a hand—a very pretty woman's hand—holding a vial beneath his nose. Involuntarily he breathed.

He felt that he was shrinking, and then he felt that he had feathers on him. He turned his head on his ungainly neck and saw his wing tips and his tail.

"Come, dearie, come. It's time to fly to the nest," a woman's soft, seductive voice whispered.

He couldn't help himself; he was flying. It was like a dream. His wings were flopping but he put forth no effort. Now beside him, flying by his side, was the ugliest bird he had ever seen—an apparent cross between a swoosh and a buzvul. The bird flew ahead of him and he followed right behind its tail. There was nothing to do but follow. Treetops, feeding dragons, meer, a stream, then higher, higher. A spire—a lone spire between mountain walls. On the top of the summit was a pile of sticks.

Glint remembered Zady nesting there—growing a lovely new body from her ugly old head. He was landing where she had once been. Again the pain hit him.

He blinked his eyes and he was a man. His clothing was open, just as it had been back at the boulder. Magic did things like that—converted the enchanted back to their original state with all their clothing and weapons intact.

Zady was perched on the far side of the pinnacle. She was herself with beautiful body and ugly head.

"Here we are, dearie. You wanted to spy on Zady when she was but a head. Now Zady has brought you here and will leave you for as long as it pleases her. If you get tired of the view, try looking at the show I'm providing for you."

Glint looked at where her finger pointed. At the edge of the rough nest was positioned a large, irregular cut of crystal. In the depths of the crystal a face—a very frightened, pain-filled face. The face was that of a woman of unusual beauty with reddish, almost coppery hair.

"Merlain!" he cried, recognizing her at last. "Merlain, my wife!"

"Guess what's being done to her. Notice the perspiration on her forehead. See the way her eyes blink."

Glint lunged. At the old hag with the lovely young body. He meant to do her violence of a fatal nature. His grasping hands closed on the neck where the wrinkles started and there was a poof of grayish smoke. As his eyes cleared he saw a sheer drop below to distant rock. He was right at the very edge of the pinnacle, his fingers digging into crumbly rock.

"Jump! Jump! Jump!" he heard from overhead. He wrenched his eyes away from the compelling drop and looked up to see the big bird hovering on an updraft. As he did, it dropped a dropping that lit on his face, almost in his eyes, and splattered on him.

He moved back on the ledge, backing carefully on hands and knees. The bird was circling, circling, and then flying toward Roughmaul Mountain. He watched it flop out of sight.

Something took his breath away. It was the nest. The old twigs and sticks and ancient feathers were covered and well soaked with the foulest of excrements. He looked at his hands and clothing and found that he was well plastered.

"Phew!" he said, and feared he tasted something. It really stank, and after that there was little more to be said.

Something occurred to him. The weapon Kelvin had given him and helped him tie securely to his back. The polished, spearlike, copper object that he had said came from the scorpiocrab tail of the chimaera.

If that bird should come back or he should see something of her from this height, maybe then he could use the weapon. It was a forlorn hope, but it was worth a try. He tugged the leather thong that held its tip tight to the back of his belt and pulled it round to his front. The thing felt smooth and cool, as a weapon should. He shrugged the strap from his shoulder and, standing at his fullest height, pushed its butt down in the excrement. Kelvin had just placed his hands on it so, he thought, placing his own hands on the shaft, and then had concentrated.

Glint tried thinking of a lightning bolt. The shaft under his fingers remained cool.

This wouldn't do if he had a chance to singe Zady's feathers! Kelvin had said that the butt had to make contact with the earth. By "earth" he knew the place where Kelvin's father had originated was not meant, but rather the ground. Beneath the nest there must be rock. Would rock work? Kelvin had never said and he had no way of knowing.

He pushed hard on the sting, giving it the best effort of his arms and back. He pushed until his legs hurt and the thing sank no deeper. Beneath the rain-softened dung were years of dried excrement.

He sighed. There was only one thing to do. He hesitated over the sword and the knife on his belt. He had never used a sword in his life, but he had used the knife a lot. The blade had been with him since he was a boy. When his sister and he were released from Zady's spell he had been the age he had been at enchantment, with everything on his body that he had had then. In addition to a young boy's clothing he had been outfitted with a deadly sharp, sheathed knife. His mother had provided for him as best she could. That was the way of magic—one day an enchanted sword, the next day a child restored.

It had to be the knife, though the task he faced he hated. He got down on his belly, almost overcome by the fumes, and pushed the blade into the top layer of excrement. He made a sawing motion. Dried dung, sticks, and old eagawk feathers came away with his application of the knife; he pushed these in a pile and finally, as the pile crowded him, rose to his feet, picked up an armload, and tossed it off the pinnacle. An updraft interfered. He coughed, rubbed his smarting eyes, and went grimly back to work.

For a long, long day he labored. He chipped and hacked and got thirsty and hot under the blazing sun. He was afraid his blade might be damaged, but it was a magically conditioned knife his mother had strapped on him. As he worked and sweated he sometimes glanced involuntarily at the crystal with its horrid view of his wife's face.

She was suffering terribly and Zady allowed no clue as to how. He had tried reaching his wife with his mind, and that had gotten nowhere. What he must do, as soon as possible, was get down. With wings or spanner boots or the belt worn by John Knight getting down would have been no problem. Climbing down was impossible—there was just no way.

He went on trying to ignore the crystal, but time after time his head turned involuntarily and he widened his eyes to stare at it. She was suffering, really suffering, and there was no way of reaching her or of adjusting the crystal to show more than her face.

Finally it became too much. He climbed out of the hole he had dug, wrenched the crystal from its spot, and tossed it over the side. He watched it tumble, turning end over end, then dwindle in the distance. Far, far below he imagined that he saw it smash.

Now, holding to the edge of the nest support, Glint regretted his action. She had been in torment, and that was dreadful to see. Zady had cursed him by making sure he saw only his wife's torment. Now, thanks to his rash action, he still could not see. Worse still, he could not know for certain that Merlain was alive. With the crystal showing him her pain at least he had had that assurance. Now he knew nothing at all about her and could see nothing if Zady decided to relent.

Much, much work and his tough, callused hands became torn and bloody and hurt. Still he chipped away, now and then wrenching out a large chunk of petrified ordure and tossing it. The heavy stuff at least didn't fly back. He imagined it exploding far below, wishing that it was landing on Zady.

Finally his knife scraped rock. He hastily scratched away until he had a bare spot as wide as his two hands. Triumphantly he rammed the sting down to contact, held his hands in position, and thought of lightning.

PIFFF!

A tiny blue spark appeared at the tip of the sting and vanished.

This was lightning? This was what he had worked so hard

for? Why? What was the matter? But he knew, even as he fought his own rage.

Bare rock was not a close enough contact. It had to be solid, untainted dirt.

CHAPTER 27

Hell

John Knight stood with his daughter and grandchildren, Merlain and Charles, in what was to his Earth-educated mind a large cage formed entirely of invisible force fields. They could not get out; they were as much prisoners in here as though there had been material walls and bars. When he approached either side of the square he had paced off, an energy pushed him back. In the large crystals arrayed just outside the square he could see scenes that had to interest him. Mentally he numbered the crystals and alternated his viewing of them.

Crystal one: Kelvin all alone now, looking down a path and seeming bewildered. It had to be some spell Zady had cast on him that Helbah hadn't been skilled enough to counter or quick enough to avoid.

Crystal two: Charlain, his unpredictable predicting wife. Beside her on a couch sat beautiful Glow, who had once been a sword and was now his grandson's loving, telepathic wife. To the side of Glow were the slowly maturing kinglets, Kildom and Kildee, her charges of the past twenty years. In a chair all by themselves sat Helbah and her familiar. Helbah was moaning as though in great pain, and the cat was staring into her face as if to give her some of his feline strength. Considering the linkage of witch and familiar, the cat might have been in fact helping her.

The third crystal showed an apparent man with polished horns growing from his forehead. John only now saw the face where before there had been a swirl of darkness. He saw and he recognized.

"The devil?" he whispered, questioning only himself. "Old Nick? Satan? I thought you were myth."

"Mythtaken, weren't you?" the imaged creature replied. The words took John mentally back across the years, to when a robot in another frame had used those words under appalling circumstances. Had the horned one access to his memory?

John blinked his eyes to clear them of what had to be illusion. He was going mad, he had to be. He hadn't felt so overwhelmed by anything for years. There was just no way, his rational mind assured him, that this could really be happening.

It couldn't be, even though in this frame and others there was magic, and though witches and warlocks and wizards and necromancers did exist here. Even though here there be dragons, he thought wryly, and even though his son had started an incredible career by killing one.

Even though he had traveled to worlds almost identical to this one. Even though he had encountered doubles of people he knew who on similar worlds had almost opposite characters. Though he had met a chimaera and a robot, both with advanced superiority complexes.

Though he remembered all his previous adventures, starting when he and his men had been ordered out on maneuvers where they had somehow survived an atomic explosion. Or had they? Could his entire life after the explosion have been bogus? Could all have been a dream in a mind as the mind disintegrated? Could all have happened in the instant of explosion?

"So you remember me from my Earth visit?" the creature asked. Its tone was rasping, as of the points of iron nails scraped across mortarless flagstones.

John shuddered. Old Testament imaginings and the ignorant posturings of those who insisted they believed everything. Mythical creature, mythical terrors. But suppose it wasn't quite. Suppose—?

"Oh, hell," the creature said, "allow me to introduce myself. I'm Professor Devale here."

"Professor of—"

"Necromancy, of course. I train all the witches and warlocks—the ones you call evil."

"Of course. Very logical."

"You want to see hell?"

"Not particularly."

The creature snapped its fingers. In the crystal were flames and rivers of lava and people he had killed and people he had seen die and had wept over.

"No, no, no!" John cried, though he knew it for illusion. "I don't want that."

"Then I'll move it closer." Devale, alias the devil, alias Satan and Old Scratch, double-snapped his fingers: *snap, snap.*

Instantly flames sprang up around them. Everywhere on him, on his grandson and granddaughter, on Jon. The air was choking and sulfurous. The heat was blistering. He was burning, he was burning. Merlain and Charles and Jon were—

"Granddad, what is it?" Charles' voice.

"The crystal! The crystal!" Couldn't the boy see?

"You mean Dad? Helbah and the pains?"

"The other."

"There's nothing in it."

His eyes saw them burning, twisting, ghastly. His mind knew that reality was different.

Grandfather! Charles inside his head.

See it, Charles, see it? See him there in the crystal?

Yes. Maybe—

Charles, no, no, don't!

Charles reached for a mind and encountered one. Instantly it was like being in a quagmire of unpleasant feelings and lusts. He felt himself swallowed by the maelstrom, spun, tossed. He reached out, trying for a mind-hold.

Welcome, little telepath!

You are going to vanish me? Like Throod?

No. I find you amusing.

You did what Zady took credit for?

Of course. She was one of my successful graduates.

You let us go!

Why should I do that?

Because of Mouvar.

Mouvar? You know nothing about Mouvar.

Don't I? I know plenty!

Let me see.

You can't! I won't let you.

Don't be absurd.

It was like a steely rod driving deep into his consciousness. Charles tried to push it out but it only penetrated the more mercilessly.

Stop! Stop! Stop!

Oh, quit your noise! The rod withdrew, leaving him feeling drained. Before his mind's eye as well as his corporeal eyes Devale's horned head appeared.

Just as I thought, nothing. A few hints, a few superstitions, nothing more!

Helbah told me, and before that the chimaera—

The chimaera. Oh, yes, Mouvar was clever using it for his purpose. But what was produced? Only you and your sister and your dragon brother. What kind of success is that?

You'll find out! You'll find out when Mouvar wants you to find out!

I doubt it. Whatever foolish notion Mouvar may have had he didn't confide. As for you and your sister and your aunt and your grandfather, I can destroy all without effort. You know I vanished a kingdom. I can do the same with you.

Why don't you, then?

Why should I? I can have fun yet.

Charles, what's it doing?

Out Merlain, out!
I want to help!
You can't!
Welcome, young unbelievers, came the thought of the creature who called himself Professor Devale, *to the boundless pains and agonizing torments of your grandfather's self-created hell.*

Jon had never suffered such pain in her life. It had been bad enough back on the battlefield when Zady made her experience the pain of terrible wounds inflicted on others. That had been ghastly, worse even than having her blood almost drained when she was a child. But then she had been alone in her sufferings, though thanks to the wizard magic her brother had felt some of her pain and horror. Now—

She burned! She burned! She burned!

Now her father and her nephew and niece suffered with her. They were suffering, all of them, and there was little comfort in knowing that it was illusionary and that their bodies were not really being consumed by fire. The flames crackled all around. The smoke choked her and brought tears to her eyes with its strong smell of sulfur. She could see the others suffering as she was suffering, and that made it worse, far worse.

Her father was staring into the big crystal even as he appeared to her to burn. Inside the crystal a face was wrapped in apparent flames and seemingly enjoying it—part of the illusion, surely. The horns on the creature's head seemed like goat horns. Something her father had told them in childhood but warned them not to believe as he had believed in his own childhood. A dark, fallen angel, whatever that was, with horns and a tail. A creature responsible for evil thoughts and deeds on Earth, living as it did beneath an imagined shell of Earth. Her father had envisioned such a creature and such a place. It had shocked her childish mind to know that even as a child her father had believed in its reality. Now the reality seemed here. A part of her father still believed the source of his childhood torment was real. His parents and their parents had believed it real as well.

She burned! She burned! She *burned!*

Horace looked about at the familiar surroundings of their sunnymoon spot as Ember slid from his back. She emitted a high squeal of pure delight at being here again. Creatures with one dragon head and two human heads and a copper-sheathed body were not her idea of fit company.

Now, Horace? Now we can love again?

Not now, Ember. There are things I have to do first.

More important than me? Her thought pouted as it came into his. In this her thinking pattern resembled one of Merlain's.

Have to. Have to. I'll be right back.

That's what you said before! She was so appealing, now that he could again see her in her true form, that he wanted nothing so much as to clasp her and forget all that had happened. But Zady, terrible being that she was, could not be forgotten so easily.

Ember turned her tail to him and lay prostrate in the sand. Her head turned to look back at him, and it was all the enticement any male dragon should surely need.

Merlain had told him about hate. It was something people had and dragons hadn't. Dragons killed and destroyed because it was their nature. Humans, who were supposed to know better, killed and destroyed because of hate.

Horace had never understood what Merlain had been talking about. Rage he understood, but the longer-lasting, all-commanding hate? Merlain had believed there to be a difference.

Zady had caused him to see his kin as enemies and his mate as a competing male. He would have followed Zady and killed for her because he would have seen her not as herself but as Helbah, or Charles, or their father or mother or even Merlain.

Ember's slim tail swished. *Come on, big boy! Come! Mama's ready for loving!*

After all his waiting and yearning he dared not take the time. That was the cruelest bite of all! He had to remember what Zady had done to him and the chimaera's warning that he dare not delay helping his father.

Horace, recipient of human emotions, was beginning to feel hate.

"Please, Helbah, please," Lester begged. "She's suffering so—you've got to help her!"

"I would if I could," Helbah replied. In the main crystal Jon's drained face with the sweat glistening on it was hardly bearable. She was screaming again now, screaming for what relief it afforded. Beside her young Charles and Merlain and even John Knight were suffering and screaming as well.

"Be thankful that we can't hear them," Charlain said. Kelvin's and Jon's mother was holding Lester's hand, inviting him by gesture to cry on her shoulder. Lester, not untypically, would have none of it. He appreciated his mother-in-law's intent but he wanted only to get at those causing his wife's torment. There was nothing that he could have done, and that made it worse. A fighting warrior in one revolution and three wars, he was as powerless now as an infant. If only it could be something man-to-man, with swords and shields and maybe spears.

"Please, Lester," Glow urged him in turn. The lovely young blond who had once been a sword and was now Charles' wife looked at him beseechingly from the opposite side of the couch. She and his mother-in-law had taken turns at Lester-calming all day. If he only had a way of going there! If he only had a weapon that would work!

If only that idiot dragon was around! But in the crystal that showed Kelvin there was no dragon, only a bewildered middle-aged man who had protested all along that he didn't want to be a hero. What kind of an Alliance head and keeper of the opal was the dragon! If Lester could have transformed into a dragon he would be there now, rescuing his beloved.

"Don't ask," Helbah said, seemingly reading his mind, though she didn't. "I will not transform into a swoosh. Yes,

I could change you and yes, you could fly, but you couldn't change back into a man unless I was there. I'm not going into dragon territory. Together the two of us could do nothing. We're better here, watching and waiting."

"For what?" It was petty of him, but he couldn't help snapping at Helbah. The dear old witch had given her best, and he knew it, but still this waiting helplessly was getting on his nerves.

"For whatever develops," Helbah said.

"Maybe we could ride there," St. Helens suggested from where he and his not very small waitress friend filled a large chair. "We could round up some troops and—"

"Hush," St. Helens' waitress friend said, pressing her lips near to the old warmonger's best ear. "Hush, you know the worthlessness of that. The Roundear of Prophecy will soon make true all that has been predicted about him, or else—"

St. Helens looked at her puzzledly, his arms not changing position where they held her. Lester felt as puzzled, watching them.

"—or else, dear Sean Reilly, we and the world will vanish as did Throod, as surely as any of us are sitting here."

"It's like something Grandfather used to say," young Kathy Jon said from across the room. She looked so much like a younger version of her mother that looking at her now Lester almost had to pinch himself. "You remember, don't you?" she asked her brothers.

The young scamps nodded energetically, though Lester felt certain that none of them had the faintest idea of what their sister was getting ready to spring on them.

"Speaking of the wars he had experienced and almost experienced he used to say that the people at home had it hard. They had to wait and watch and look at their televisions and read their newspapers. That's all they could do, ever, and still the popular saying was that those who waited still served."

"Wartime propaganda," St. Helens said. "It hardly applies here." His affectionate waitress friend shut his mouth with her hand, then pressed it into unresisting silence with the application of her own. Tomorrow might after all never come.

Lester admired the little show and thought that, like Charlain and Glow, the girl was taking their minds off their pain. But what of young Kathy Jon? Was she just speaking to be heard?

"We can't help them, so we just have to hope for them and wait," his daughter continued. "I know I'd like to pop that witch again with a rock—a bigger rock! But we all know how powerful she is. It will take a really strong hero to overcome her."

"I'll say!" one of the boys said. It was Alvin, the eldest. Lester wondered if he too had once always looked upon any disaster as a challenge and thought that perhaps he had. Boys would be boys, as the saying went, and it was a boy's nature to think that all could be solved with determination. Unfortunately he didn't quite feel that way anymore. Fighting an army or a monster maybe, but being confronted by Zady was considerably worse.

"I wish I were Kelvin!" young Teddy Crumb said. "I'd take that old sting of his and ram it up—"

"By the way, where is the sting?" Lester found himself interrupting. "Come to think of it, where's Glint?"

Helbah sighed. "I was afraid you'd ask that. Glint went into the woods when Kelvin was talking to the air. Kelvin's looking for him now. Zady must have been there in an invisibility cloak and she may have vanished him."

"Vanished? You mean like—"

"Yes. I didn't have a crystal tuned to him. Now I've tried and tried and I can't tune to him anywhere. We may have lost Glint already. Merlain may be a not-widow because his vanishing means he really never was."

"I don't believe it!" Glow said. "I believe my brother still exists and is alive."

"I hope you're right, Glow. But we have to accept the possibility. Whatever Zady did with him, she didn't take him to the others."

"Maybe he's doing something with the sting?" the oldest scamp suggested.

"I hope you're right, Alvin, but I can't imagine you are. He disappeared too fast."

"Kelvin disappears fast," the scamp argued. "So does Horace."

"Alas," Helbah said, "Glint hasn't either Kelvin's boots or levitation belt and he certainly hasn't Horace's opal."

"Oh! Oh, yeah. I guess."

The boy subsided into gloomy, embarrassed silence, as did the rest of them.

In the crystal the painful-to-watch ordeal continued on and on. It seemed to Lester that there could never be an end to it, Kelvin or no Kelvin.

CHAPTER 28

Dragon Rage

Kelvin turned, wanting to do battle or flee but knowing there was no time. Facing him was a dragon, all right, but of coppery scale tone and a familiar expression.

"Horace! I'm so glad to see you. Where's—"

A second dragon emerged from the bushes. Golden-scaled, with unnaturally twinkly dragon's eyes, it had to be Ember.

"Your bride is very attractive, Horace. You're a lucky dragon."

Horace rubbed his snout on the ground and snorted appreciation. Ember actually pulled her head back, as if coy.

"You seem not to be under the spell now. You're not, are you, Horace?"

No spell now. Chimaera fix.

Chimaera! So that was what he had been up to! Mervania had not forgotten the child whose birth she had assisted. Without her powder, Merlain, Charles, and Horace would have been one enormous creature, if alive. As for Heln—there was no way a human woman could have survived the birth of a chimaera.

"We've been searching for you. You're needed, Horace. The fate of the Alliance is at stake."

Horace looked toward the river. He seemed to be but a dragon. Of what interest human and orc problems? Dragons lived but in the moment, the same as wild creatures everywhere.

"Merlain and Charles are in deepest peril. Zady is hurting them."

Instantly the dragon raised his head higher. His toothy mouth opened and he roared a dragon's roar. Clearly he did not like the idea of his brother and sister being hurt.

"Yes, Horace, I quite agree. But we have to be careful. Our enemies are other than dragon or humans. They have powerful magic that can destroy—"

Horace raked his claws on the ground, leaving furrows and the torn-up roots of grass. He was ready even if Kelvin wasn't.

"I'll have to ride on your back again, Horace. You'll have to locate them in the mountain range over there, and then—"

GET ON!

The order startled him. Definitely Horace. Definitely the dragon had been learning. And really, he was an intelligent offspring, though of an unusual nature. He had had Merlain's thoughts and Charles' and later Glint's and Ember's. There was no reason, really, why he shouldn't think directly to his father.

Horace held out a forefoot, almost like a talon. Kelvin took hold of the leg, stepped on the foot, and was lifted up to where his left gauntlet pulled him by grasping a wing. The gauntlet and the boots did his thinking and moving for him. He rested now between the small wings, holding one securely in either hand. Clearly his gauntlet was anticipating a fast move from Horace.

Horace snorted loudly and Kelvin imagined his brow wrinkling. Absurd thought, a dragon with a human brow. But Horace had to be searching—think-calling for Merlain.

Merlain burning. Charles burning. Your father burning. Great horned face in center of large crystal, laughing.

Even filtered through Horace the pain and the terror were overpowering. Kelvin was made dizzy by their suffering. Without his gauntlet holding on to the wing stub he might have slid off as his right hand weakened. But Horace, through the agony and terror and the shrill mental screams of his sister and brother, pulsed with a large and hideous strength. He would go there and he would save them.

Something occurred to Kelvin. Zady wasn't blocking! Zady had to want Horace to find Merlain!

"NO, HORACE! NO!"

Kelvin's shouted words were lost. The trees and the river were gone. Now high on a mountain they were between a large crystal and four tortured people writhing and screaming in imagined flames. The creature in the crystal raised fiery red eyes to the dragon and smiled.

"Welcome, Horace. Welcome, Kelvin. You can now become a part of history."

Clawed hands raised above the creature's horns and its eyes glowed even more brightly and somehow wickedly.

Horace pounced on the crystal, ignoring the crystals that showed him in the act and Heln and the others at home watching him. His claws raked the surface, producing a screeching noise. His tail cracked repeatedly with bone-jarring blows against the faceted sides of a magically hardened mineral.

The creature in the crystal showed no fear. Its too-human mouth opened and it shook with cruel, hearty laughter. Clearly, as far as it was concerned, Horace was entertaining.

Could Kelvin and his boots and single gauntlet be anything more?

* * *

Merlain and Charles saw their father and brother and tried with all the mind power they had to push back the agony of what felt like very real burns. Their breaths were searing, their eyes watering. There was no way they could hold back the screams accompanying their brother's roars.

Dragon Horace and Merlain's father were on the crystal, Horace attacking the image he saw there. Both had appeared together, her father on Horace's back. Now the dragon attacked with all his bravery and strength. The dragon claws made screeching sounds on the impenetrable surface; the dragon tail pounded the sides with powerful slaps that sent the crystal to vibrating. Inside the crystal the horned creature laughed.

Merlain saw the clawed hands raised above the horned head. In a moment her father and brother would be destroyed or captured and made to suffer in the flames. Her right hand grasped desperately for nothing and scraped against something long concealed beneath her oversized shirt. The Mouvar weapon that reversed hostile magic! Could it help? Could it ease their intolerable pain?

Hardly knowing what she did, certainly not thinking through her pain, Merlain pulled the bell-muzzled weapon and touched its trigger. Just as she squeezed it through the cloth, the flames appeared on Horace and her father. Horace attacked all the harder; her father retained his seat as the creature laughed.

The Mouvar weapon buzzed. The flames were gone from around her and her brother and father. The flames weren't on her and Charles and their aunt and grandfather. The flames were all over the large, hideous face!

The creature screamed—a scream both mental and physical.

"Pain, pain, I can't stand pain!"

The crystal blanked. The crystal turned the color of ash. The crystal crumbled, becoming a light-gray powder as it disintegrated. The pile shook, and Horace crawled out of the heap, still carrying his father. The dragon shook and cracked his tail twice. Powder flew, leaving dragon and father of dragon uncoated.

Kelvin dismounted and took several long strides. Nothing stopped him or seemed about to.

Merlain knew instantly that the barrier that had held them imprisoned was no longer there. She rushed to her brother and father. She hugged each in turn and rejoiced in her father's return hugs and her brother's forked-tongue kisses.

"Oh, Daddy! Oh, Daddy! Oh, Daddy!" she cried.

"My little girl! What happened? What saved us?"

"Oh, Daddy, it was this!" She held out the weapon. "Take it! I'm afraid of it!"

Kelvin took the antimagic weapon as though she had extended something very ordinary, patted it absently, and stuck it under his own overlarge shirt into the band of his trousers. It didn't show against his recently flattened stomach any more than it had against hers.

"Daddy? Where's Glint? Where's my husband?"

Kelvin's face instantly lost all its redness. The guilt sweeping over it told her what she least wanted to know.

Merlain's father had failed to keep proper watch on her husband! At the very least he had lost him!

"I'll bring him back," Kelvin said. He grabbed one of the wing stubs and pulled himself up and resumed his place on her brother's back.

Jon watched as Merlain handed the Mouvar weapon back to Kelvin. After such a long time she could hardly believe that she wasn't feeling agony. She checked the skin on her hands and arms—not even blistered. Those protective spells of Helbah's might not have been entirely useless! Kelvin had done it again! Or at least with his son's and daughter's help he had. For the last eternity or so of the torment she had not retained the slightest hope that any of them were going to be rescued.

She looked at their father standing by himself and wiping his brow. She felt sorry for him, and not just because of what they had all suffered. He was older than his children and grandchildren, though he scarcely looked it. Older people had less stamina and had a way of dying suddenly when the pain mounted. Men had less resistance to torture than women because only women experienced childbirth. How fortunate her father had been that Helbah had made him exercise and regain the strength and musculature he had known at an earlier age. Watching him check his hands and arms as she had been doing, she knew that like herself he was going to be all right.

She wasn't so certain about her niece and nephews. Telepaths must find it hard if they felt the pain of others as well as their own. She knew about that now from experience, having been made to feel the agonies of the terribly wounded. But perhaps being telepaths they could control the pain impulse better? She hoped that was the case. Merlain must have had some presence of mind to zap the devil the way she had.

"Jon," her father said, coming to her with widened arms, "Jon, we've been rescued."

"Exactly what I was thinking, Father." She hugged him as he closed his arms. She could feel his heart beating strongly in his chest. He must really feel an emotion, she thought, because her father never had been a demonstrative person. She had even heard her mother remark on it at times, more with sympathy than misunderstanding. It all had to do with his having grown up on Earth. How could a people be expected to feel for one another if they didn't accept even the possibility of magic? She wasn't certain why that was, but her father's hardheadedness had eased with the years and his gradual, grudging acceptance of magic.

"I'd like to get old Zady now and wring her neck!" So strong and determined, with only a hint of hesitancy in his voice.

"Me too, Father. I'd like to get her with a stone, the way my daughter did."

"You have a lovely daughter, Jon, and good boys."

"No fault of mine, Dad. It had to have been their heritage."

"The heritage, my flattering daughter, was not entirely mine."

He released her, feeling uncomfortable, she knew, with the realization that he was actually showing tenderness. It was his Earth upbringing telling him that men were strong and tough and didn't cry and didn't show emotion, except possibly when securely at home with their wives. Such madness, that, and it was all part of what he believed was the difference between masculine and feminine. You'd have thought that his life would have taught him how tough and strong women could be, and how strong didn't mean not showing that you cared.

As these unaccustomed thoughts flooded her mind, she looked over past Horace and saw something that instantly plunged her into terror: Zady!

Wordlessly she pointed and screamed.

"WHAT HAVE YOU DONE? WHAT HAVE YOU DONE?" The words were so loud that they had to be magically amplified.

Kelvin raised his eyes to the stone peak, all thought of his son-in-law vanishing. She must have flown there as a bird and concealed herself with invisibility. Now she clearly intended to wreak havoc.

"You don't assault a god! You don't do that!" Zady chided in an aggrieved voice.

"Zady, what have you done with my husband?" Kelvin's daughter shouted back. As usual her mind was on one overriding subject and she had guessed that something had happened.

"Wouldn't you like to know, dearie?" Zady's tone was now taunting and threatening at the same time. "I'm going to burn him and I'm going to burn the rest of you. For years and centuries and maybe until the end of time!"

The hag raised her hands and began spelling. Kelvin knew that her gibberish words would draw forth the power from somewhere, and then something unpleasant would happen.

Kelvin drew a breath, thinking instantly of fireballs. Now

that she was aware of the antimagic weapon she would take care to insure her own protection; if a fireball came back at her it would be stopped by a shield of magic. It was going to be so unpleasant to burn. He had had quite enough of a taste of it.

GARRRWOOF!

With Kelvin still on his back, Horace was on the pinnacle, on the witch. Because he was other than a magically produced fireball, her barrier did not exist for him. His great powerful claws sank deep into the lovely woman flesh, producing a scream and runnels of blood. He lifted the apparent woman to his mouth and opened wide to bite off her horrid head.

The woman was a bird, torn and bleeding, falling from Horace's claws, falling through space, then tumbling. It righted and began to fly. It circled, climbing higher.

"I'll get you! I'll get you!" the witch-bird screamed.

Horace was in midair where the bird had been, grappling, then falling as the bird flew on. Kelvin hadn't time to react before they were swaying on some treetops, directly below the flying bird. It seemed Zady and Horace were repeating themselves.

Zady's dark wings beat faster as she tried for distance. Horace was in the river under the flying bird, on a hill under the flying bird, on a road under the flying bird. He was taking large opal-hops and keeping up with her.

They were on a rooftop as the people inside the house screamed, then on the roof of a covered bridge with a snorting, prancing horse beneath. They were on hills, in open fields, in water, on ruins. The ruins were those of Rud's onetime royal palace, where wicked Zoanna had ruled. The bird flopped down a stairway. Horace was under her as she flopped above the dock and the excursion boats. The bird flew down the underground river, and Kelvin knew where it was headed. This time he was afraid that there would be no stopping him.

"No, Horace! No! We can't!"

Horace and Kelvin were underwater, and in front of them was a desperately swimming bird. The bird's propelling wings beat steadily.

Kelvin remembered not to breathe, and then they were coming up inside the installation. Zady, already her proper self, was ready to step into the transporter.

As the dragon and its passenger arrived in the airlock, Zady raised her hand. If she only had time she would cast a spell, but that was not the main danger as Kelvin saw it. The transporter here was for pointed-ears only, and if Mouvar's warning applied here it would be destroyed if they tried using it.

"NO, HORACE! NO! NO!" But Kelvin's cries were as they had been all along, futile efforts to stop an enraged dragon.

The dragon was suddenly on the woman and taking her with its great momentum and weight into the too-small transporter.

The paneled sides of the transporter booth vanished in a pinkish, soundless flash. Still their momentum continued.

Down, down, down through a bewildering sea of twisting, turning blackness, twinkling stars and hissing comets.

"He's got her! He's got her!" Kildee cried excitedly.

"Dolt," came his brother's instant reply. "He and Kelvin were killed! It was her plan, she tricked him!"

"Helbah, tune the crystal!" Charlain demanded.

Helbah looked crestfallen. "I can't tune it to where they're going—where they may be going if they're not destroyed."

"*Are* they destroyed?" Glow's question came quickly.

"I don't know. My magic goes only so far. Charlain, can you try to see?"

Hastily Charlain dealt out the cards. "Kelvin," she said loudly, and lifted the first. Uncertainty. Well, at least not the death card. A second card, Possibility of Death.

"Please, cards," Charlain whispered, "tell us something we don't know."

Hesitantly she turned up the third card in the sequence. Possibility of Success. The cards had said that the possibilities were equally balanced. Kelvin might live and Kelvin might die and there was no getting past the question.

"Try Horace," Glow suggested.

Charlain picked up and shuffled the deck. She knew what they were going to tell her—precisely nothing.

She dealt out the cards. "Horace," she said, and picked up the Uncertainty card, followed by the Possibility of Success card, followed by the Possibility of Death card.

"Does the order make a difference?" Glow asked. "When you asked about Kelvin the second card was the Possibility of Death."

"Normally it makes a difference," Charlain said wearily. "In this case it may mean that Horace's chance of succeeding may not be canceled by his death."

"How—how could that be?"

"Horace's idea of success is to destroy Zady. The possibility is that he may succeed in that even though he dies. For his father death would seem to be a shade more likely and the chances of success a bit less than Horace's."

"I don't like that," Glow said.

"Try asking about Zady," Helbah suggested.

It was as good an idea as any. Almost uninterested now she laid out the cards.

"Zady," she said, and turned over the first. Uncertainty.

Second card: Possibility of Success.

Third card: Possibility of Nothing.

Glow tapped the last card with its depiction of an empty box. "Is that different from a death card?"

"For a witch it may be," Charlain said. "All the cards really mean is that she may or may not succeed in her wicked plans, and that after she does or doesn't, she may or may not continue as an existing witch."

CHAPTER 29

Devale

Helbah was more startled than anyone in the room as her warning spell was activated. The slab of crystal reserved for the warning blinked on and off several times and a voice, actually Helbah's own, said, "Visitors."

Helbah glanced at Katbah. The animal's fur was lying down, certainly a good sign when one expected enemies. Possibly it wasn't Zady or a Zady helper outside; she'd ask.

"Who's there?"

The crystal crawled with lines and circles and produced a mirror image of what was outside: Strongback, the king of Rotternik, and three of his furry court.

"Look! Babkeys!" one of the twin kings cried out.

"Rotternikers," his brother corrected him. "I wonder what they want."

"They're not hostile," Helbah said. "But what a time to come here!"

She watched until the delegation was at the blue palace door. The blue palace was actually used more than the white, as everyone knew, even citizens of Rotternik. However, the palaces were connected, blue Klingland's to white Kance's. When they reached the doorstep she made the entrance sign and went forward to meet their guests.

"King Strongback! What a pleasant surprise! Is this an official or unofficial visit?"

"Official," Strongback replied. He merely glanced at the human visitors and the lighted viewing crystals. "Most official."

"Then you have business with Klingland and Kance?"

"With the Alliance."

"Oh." She could not have said why but that surprised her.

"Rotternik wishes to join the Alliance as a member. We do not wish to disappear as did Throod."

"Well, that certainly is good news," Helbah said. At any other time it would have been cause for rejoicing. "I will tune in the titular heads of Rud-Aratex, Hermandy, and Ophal."

Helbah made a gesture and three crystals stopped their swirlings. In the smaller crystal appeared King Rufurt's aged face. In the largest crystal appeared the fish-face of Brudalous, king of Ophal. Finally, after a brief wait for the king to get to the throne room, King Hadanhowler of Hermandy. All three of the kings would be seeing this room in their own magic crystals.

Helbah motioned to Strongback.

Strongback pulled himself up stiffly, not bending forward as much as his ministers, and said, "Rotternik seeks membership in the Alliance. Is our membership accepted?"

"Confirmed," said King Rufurt. "Welcome to the Alliance."

"Ophal confirms membership," said Brudalous. He was trying to push back a strand of seaweed that had gotten caught on his headcrest. As was almost always the case, he was underwater and his gills were opening and closing in typical orc manner.

"Confirmed," said King Hadanhowler. Unlike a former king of Hermandy he was quite young and handsome and wasn't reputed to be at all sadistic.

"That leaves Klingland and Kance," Helbah said. "Kildom, what do you think about Rotternik joining the Alliance?"

The young redhead swallowed. He and his brother had seldom dealt directly in matters of state, but that was changing as they gradually matured. In earlier times Helbah had decided for them and spoken for them, as was her nonofficial but practical right.

"I think it would be nice to have some babkeys around," he said. "Klingland confirms Rotternik's membership."

"Forgive His Highness for an immature observation," Helbah said. The ministers would not have been offended, but Strongback could have been. Babkeys were after all hardly representative of Rotternik's most intelligent inhabitants. Yet in his own mind the mischief maker was only complimenting the kingdom for having something the others didn't. Helbah understood and she knew the others would as well.

"King Kildee, you have the deciding vote. Speak up."

"I, King Kildee, Sovereign Almighty King of Kance, think it appropriate that Rotternik be in the Alliance. I say confirmed."

Helbah felt like cheering. Kildee had to outdo his brother just a bit, but the title, grandiose as it was, was legitimate.

"Now you take an oath," King Rufurt prompted unnecessarily. The roly-poly king of easygoing days was definitely becoming senile as he continued to pile on unneeded weight. Helbah made up her mind to slim him and find him a magic cure if the danger of Zady ever passed.

Strongback was already raising his hand: "I, Strongback, King of Rotternik, hereby swear allegiance of my kingdom to the Alliance. My ambassadors will visit each of you in request of foreign aid."

Typical, Helbah thought, but also practical. Of all the kingdoms Rotternik could use the most help. The great forests would always be retained, but the hairy inhabitants would visit the ground regularly and some would start to live there. Soon there would be hairy tourists, some of them with tails and manners foreign to the inhabitants of other member kingdoms.

In short order the Rotternik delegation left the palace, and the crystals lost their kingly faces. Things were back to normal now as they awaited their nonexistence or the dawn of a hard-won new life.

"Does this mean," Glow said, speaking up timidly, "that Kelvin's prophecy is fulfilled?"

"Until from Seven there be One/Only then will his Task

be Done." Charlain recited the familiar near-verse. She sighed, giving Helbah an uncomfortable look. "I only hope that his task will all be done. If Zady gains control it won't matter if we say there's one kingdom or ten."

"There should be a line that says, 'When Zady's done, then all the kingdoms come,' " Kildom offered.

Helbah approved the young monarch's sentiments, though surely not his attempt at verse. But future hopes aside, the situation here hadn't changed.

As young Kathy Jon had remarked previously, all any of them could do was sit here and wait.

"We have to find him!" Merlain wailed. They had to concentrate on that. Now that her dragon brother and her father were off chasing Zady they had to deal with what was most important to her: her husband.

"Don't worry," said Charles, being brotherly once again. "We're certain to find him if he's alive. You know how Zady loves to torment people. She may have done something painful to him that won't have killed him outright."

"You're such a comfort, Charles." Strangely, he was, his unpleasant suggestion aside. "I've been searching with my mind, but either he's far away or—"

Dizziness afflicted her. Almost too late she realized that Glint was projecting his thought to her. She hadn't been able to reach him because he was high up in an eagawk nest. As she looked up, where she had not thought to search for him, the height of the peak with its precariously balanced nest was overwhelming.

Zady got me, Merlain. It was my own fault. From the projecting cliff in Forbidden Mountain I watched her growing her new body. I watched the eagawks bringing her nourishment, and then it was as though I never wanted to come here again.

She spelled you, Glint. Are you hurt?

No. But the surroundings here aren't the most pleasant.

Neither are we hurt. Horace and Daddy rescued us and are after Zady. This time they're going to fix her proper. Can you get down?

*Not without Horace. Merlain, it's really hot here with the
sun beating down. And the air—*

"Grandfather," Merlain said aloud, "do you think you
can use your belt to get my husband? He's up there, in that old
eagawk nest."

Grandfather Knight looked upward, straining his eyes,
she knew, in the sun's bright glare. Then he activated the belt
and lifted. She watched him soar high and higher until he
seemed with distance to become first the size of a bird and then
an insect. She saw him hover near the top of the spire, then
descend. She knew he was in the nest. She waited and waited,
now and then giving Charles a nervous look. What was keeping him?

"Grandfather will fetch him," Charles said. "Unless of
course Zady set a trap. That could be why she brought Glint
here—to act as bait."

At that moment the insect, now larger, lifted. It flew at
them, coming lower and lower, finally becoming Grandfather
Knight carrying her husband. They landed in front of her and
Charles, and Glint immediately let loose of her grandfather's
shoulders and slid off his back. A moment later Glint was
rushing at her in the most incredible charge.

Merlain hardly caught her breath as he hugged her, pressing her tight. He hadn't seemed so passionate since the night
of their wedding, and Lord, but he had tried.

"Oh Merlain, Merlain, Merlain!"

"Oh Glint, Glint, Glint!"

Grandfather was being disgustingly sick and Charles was
holding his own nose and pointing first at Glint's rescuer and
then at Glint. Merlain sucked in air through her nostrils and
immediately knew the reason for her grandfather's sudden
illness and her brother's mental affliction. She had, in that one
breath, a good reason to be sick herself.

She had to be diplomatic, she supposed. Like her dragon
brother Horace and her human brother Charles she knew how
to appreciate a good stink. But an eagawk nest that had held
a stinking witch for twenty long years had a stench not to be
appreciated.

"Husband, Grandfather," she gasped, "you're just going to have to take baths, both of you! Even Horace wouldn't come near you smelling like that."

Another too-small booth exploded outward, and Horace was so startled by where they were that he let Zady loose. In his mouth were the remains of her dark-red dress. She ran screaming down a long marble corridor, pushing startled students aside; leather-bound books hit the floor in her wake, spines cracking and emitting smoke. Fallen would-be witches and warlocks scampered to get up and save their lives by any means possible. Accepting this strange confined place with its dark wood paneling and twisted, tortured artworks done mainly in blacks and reds, Horace opaled after.

"Save me! Save me!" Zady screeched. She yanked open a door and ran inside. "Professor Devale, I can't stop it! Help!"

Horace opaled into the office, smashing doorway and room furnishings. A shred of red dress remained caught on a front tooth.

"Incompetent!" Devale said, and hurled Zady's naked, bleeding form back at Horace. Horace shot out his forked tongue, lassoed her throat, and yanked her partially into his mouth. He clomped his great jaws with sickening crunch and spat out her head at the master enemy.

Devale ducked the missile, and Zady's head was neatly skewered on his left horn. He lifted the head on his own, meanwhile gesturing with his hands and blowing a bluish powder. The light-blue dust enveloped them and entered Horace's and Kelvin's nostrils. Kelvin thought to blow off the powder but found immediately that he could not.

"You fools," Devale said with the rasp of triumph, "you've fallen into my trap! You are both too dangerous to play with, so I'll do with you what I did with Throod. I am going to finish this spell I have started, and when I am finished neither dragon nor hero will ever have existed. Thus in one move I will have finished this game and won!"

Kelvin had to wonder what Devale had won and what the game was. His father had talked a little about a game Zady's protector and his own might be playing. Unfortunately Kelvin had thought his father was talking nonsense and had paid it scant attention.

Devale began mumbling, oblivious to Zady's head, speared through its cranium and bobbing with his. Drool came from Zady's open mouth and ran down his forehead; Devale ignored it.

Horace ignored the mutilated body of the beautiful young woman under his raised foot. He seemed never to be going to put down that foot to render and tear her and to lower his jaws to bite. His great tail remained still, not clearing the room of broken furniture in one fast sweep.

Kelvin knew that he and Horace were done. He couldn't move and he knew that Horace couldn't. Devale must have started his magic while they were chasing Zady. Kelvin had been motionless and helpless before. First he had been held by Zatanas, Zady's wicked and somewhat untalented brother. Next he had been paralyzed and held motionless by the stare of a great silver serpent, then again by a Flopear intent on splitting him on an oversized sword. In every instant of complete helplessness something had intervened. In the three incidents now remembered so clearly it had been the gauntlets.

He wore but one gauntlet now, and Devale was out of reach and far too big to strangle. The gauntlet could act by itself and save them only if it had a weapon. He had given away his weapons. Glint had the chimaera's sting that might have saved them. His father had the levitation belt that might have hurled his body into the monster's face. Charles had the right-hand gauntlet, and even if they could reach Devale it would certainly take both to choke him. He had given his daughter Merlain something else, and—

And she had given it back!

The gauntlet acted before his thought was finished. With one motion it dragged his hand under his loose shirt, grabbed the weapon with his fingers, and activated it.

Devale was just flinging out his own fingers in a triumphant gesture. The bell-shaped muzzled weapon beneath the cloth took his attention on the last syllable he spoke. He could not retract it, though he seemed to try. It was also during his final thrust of commanding motion. Too late now to change the spell and prevent its effect.

In an instant it was over. All over.

CHAPTER 30

Mouvar

*T*he weapon in Kelvin's suddenly reactivated hand jumped and hissed under his shirt, and with the sound and the restoration of his nervous system Devale and the remains of Zady vanished. Not only Devale and Zady's severed head were gone, but every drop of blood and spittle and other bodily fluids were completely and cleanly vanquished.

Kelvin moved the gauntlet now, placing the muzzle of the antimagic weapon more firmly in his belt. He withdrew his hand and looked at it, wondering as he did so why he wasn't shaking. His hand was all right. He was all right. Horace was all right. Only Devale and Zady had been affected by Mouvar's weapon.

"Horace, we've won! We've defeated them!"

It materialized slowly in front of them: a dwarf with a very large head and skin the color of pale-green grass. The creature had pointed, not rounded ears, and hands that were webbed between the fingers like a frog's.

The creature blinked light-orange eyes at them while transparent eyelids opened and closed sideways. It did not speak to them, but thought.

I am Mouvar, Kelvin, and I am not what you see. What you

see is the way I have chosen to appear to people in this frame and in others. The large head, the webbed fingers, even the pointed ears were typical of ancestors that your people would find most acceptable. As for my messages: I had to leave something that you would identify with and that would exclude those not meant to use the transporter. As for my pointed ears, look carefully.

Kelvin blinked, and in the course of the blink Mouvar's pointed ears changed to round. He looked better with pointed, Kelvin had to think, but possibly that was due to an early preference.

My kind gave up a dependency on bodies. We now roam the cosmos and the frames without form or in any form we feel like. I am what you must consider truly alien, and yet I am of your essence, of the essence of many races, some of them human. In this way I am similar to but otherwise unrelated to a race that is your enemy as well as mine. The creature who called himself Professor Devale was of the enemy—a reverse polarity of mine.

"But I never knew any Professor Devale! I fought against a dark warlock with horns!"

You knew his nature. If Devale the creature exists anywhere it is on a world not much different from Earth or the world you grew up on. To you as to your father, your world was all there was, all there could ever be. If Devale is anywhere, there also will I be.

"But why was I the hero?" Kelvin protested. "You provided me with gauntlets and the boots, the levitation belt and this weapon. Why couldn't you use them yourself?"

It was your battle, Kelvin; your fight. You were what your people needed. What you call my magic wasn't really that. Yours was the true necessary magic after you were properly forged.

"You worked on my . . . essence?"

You did that, Kelvin, as necessity determined. All I did was give you what you needed and could then apply.

"My children?"

Needed and therefore were.

"Everything in my life—everything planned?"

It was your choice. Always your choice.

"But I never chose to be a hero!" Kelvin protested. "I never wanted it! I just wanted to live my life as what I was, an ordinary ignorant farm boy!"

The Mouvar image frowned. *That was the point. You were ideal.*

"How could I be ideal? I was the worst possible hero!"

I see I must clarify another aspect for you. Devale and I have been playing a game, over the millennia. The winner of each round then accepts a handicap for the next round. It is the sporting way. Devale won the last, so this time he had the handicap. He lost his awareness of the point. Because of that, I was able to win this round.

"Round? As in roundear?"

The image smiled. *That, too. We regard it as a cute touch, round ears and pointed ears. But mainly it is that the point of the game is the game itself. It is an entertainment, and it remains interesting as long as the issue is in doubt. Once it is settled, one way or the other, the game is over, and there is nothing to do except start a new one.*

"I don't understand. What issue? What point?"

We take turns assembling and dismantling the empire. When Devale succeeded in fragmenting the last empire into seven or eight smaller kingdoms, the victory was his. Now I have succeeded in assembling a new empire, using the least likely of heroes. Needless to say, the less qualified the hero, the greater the victory. Anyone can make an empire with a superhero, but real skill is required to do it with a bumbler. Devale was sure I could not succeed with you. You weren't even an ordinary yokel; you were to be the son of a soldier rescued from a foreign world who refused to believe in magic. What a farce! But I did succeed, amazingly, and I never interfered directly, and so this is my greatest coup yet. Devale will have to try to dismantle this empire with someone even less likely, and that will be his greatest challenge yet. I look forward to interfering with it. I will of course be allowed to break the rule against direct interference, since I won't know the point, this time.

The meaning was percolating through Kelvin's mind. "All this adventure—the Prophecy, the Roundear Hero, all the battles and carnage—a game? Only a game?"

Mouvar shrugged. *It does relieve the boredom.*

"But this is callous beyond belief! To toy with the lives of real people, to make and destroy kingdoms—"

This is the stuff of history, Kelvin. Real people are always the victims of empire making. We merely manage it for some diverting purpose, instead of allowing it to be normally chaotic. You hardly have cause to complain; but for this, you would indeed have been unremarkable, and would probably never have met and married Heln. You would have had to settle for a loutish village girl who would soon have grown callous and fat. Your children would have been as dull.

"But you say the game has ended!" Kelvin exclaimed, horrified. "Are you going to destroy my family?"

Mouvar smiled. *By no means! It will take Devale at least a generation to fashion a new prophecy and set up a new hero. "A Pointear there shall surely be, Dividing One to Two and Three . . ." Doubtless you and yours will be gone by the time that manifests. After all, this time Devale will be aware that the joy of the game is in the playing, while I will be the one who thinks that preserving the empire is important. He will be the one to make some deliberate errors, merely to prolong it a bit more, as I did this time. So live in peace, hero; you will probably be happier if you do not tell the others about this, and manage to forget it yourself.*

Kelvin was disgusted, but had to agree. What good would it do to let the others know that they were merely pawns in a game which was now finished? At least they could live out their lives in innocence. "What now?"

A parting. Do it, Kelvin; don't think about it. End the game. Deprive me of my knowledge of the point.

With dawning comprehension Kelvin saw the green dwarf start a by-now familiar gesture. Mouvar was smiling, but no words had ever been clearer to Kelvin.

This time it was he, not the gauntlet, who pressed the trigger.

Dwarf, gauntlet, and weapon were gone. He was alone in an empty place with Horace.

But what of the orc's opal? The opal was not a Mouvar gift. The opal, like necessity, existed where it had to exist, just as did the required courage and basic goodness. It should still be inside the dragon. They could use it.

Kelvin wanted to be home with his loved ones, and so did Horace. The dragon's copper-colored tail swished and they were there.

EPILOGUE

*I*t was a great day for a picnic. The children were running and shouting and taking delight; the birds were whistling and singing. The dragons, kept away by Helbah's magic and the presence here of Horace and his family, were roaring lustily in the distance. Kelvin's young grandson hugged his dragon cousin while Ember, a worried mother, looked on as if wondering if she could trust them.

"This is one heaven of a place!" St. Helens enthused, his arms tight around Nellie's now incredibly bulging waist. They had gotten married, finally, and now progeny was to follow; thus was always the way.

"I think it's too good for dragons alone," the still-blushing Mrs. said. Then, probably thinking she saw a stab of disappointment in Ember's atypically gentle dragon eyes, "I mean it's better than anything elsewhere. The mountains, the water, the air—the flowers! It's the perfect place to share."

"Agreed," St. Helens said. "The only reason I'm not making a fortune selling this place to sunnymooners is that I don't own it and I wouldn't want it crowded."

Kelvin knew what he meant. He and Heln, Glint and Merlain, Glow and Charles, Ember and Horace, and now decrepit old father-in-law and his shockingly young bride had shared exquisite moments here. There was something in the air—something Helbah had said she had reduced in intensity but not entirely nullified.

"Dear," his beloved said, taking his hand, "do you think that our grandchildren and our great-grandchildren will someday come here? It could become a family tradition—a sort of reward and remembrance for what you've accomplished. Kathy Jon may be next. She's so pretty and mature for her age that I expect—"

"Kathy's just a child!" he said defensively. "She doesn't even like boys! She told me herself that—"

"How old was Jon when she and Lester wed?"

"Too young," he grumbled. "And so were we."

"Really?" Her eyes widened intriguingly, forcing him to remember.

"No," he admitted. "No, we weren't. We were just young. But you know what I mean—Kathy's a tomboy."

"As was your sister."

"Yes. Very much like her, in fact."

"Only the two of you were adventuring."

"Yes, it seemed as if we had no choice."

"Let me see it again, husband."

"Right here? Right in front of everybody?"

"Yes."

"It's so embarrassing. Doesn't seem proper, even."

"Please."

"Oh, very well."

He reached in his left rear pocket and brought out the small box he had been awarded ceremoniously amid cheering hordes both present and watching via crystal. He flipped its top, revealing the Alliance's specially struck medal with its single word: Hero.

Heln touched the coin-shaped medal almost reverently. Her eyes grew misty looking at it. "Do you remember, dearest, how it started? You and your young sister adventuring? It was like something from a storybook."

"We used to talk about Mouvar. The legend, myth, story character. We pretended that he was real and that we were fulfilling some great, planned destiny." And he would never tell the truth about that: that even when it became real, it remained pretense, on another level. Mouvar's game. Mouvar and Devale were real; their worlds, the worlds Kelvin and others had visited, the Flaw, all reality as they knew it and perceived it to be, existed as but a greatly expanded chessboard. He, his companions and friends, witches and warlocks, dragons and chimaera were but playing pieces or accessories in a game he never would comprehend.

"But dearest," Heln said earnestly, "it *was* real—your adventures. You defeated the royal Rud army and freed Rud from a tyrannous woman. You defeated her a second time when she reappeared with a helper from another frame and more magic. You defeated the witch who held me captive in Aratex. You defeated Zady twice. Because of what you did we're united, all of us. All seven kingdoms, including the orcs' and Rotternik."

"I don't deny it," he said, forcing back the madness. "But you know I'm not certain how I accomplished any of it. It's selective amnesia, I guess. I remember doing it, I know it happened, but I don't know how I managed it."

"Tell me again, lover. Tell me how you broke free of your bonds and saved your sister from Zatanas and Queeto."

"I don't know how it happened. I don't know. It was as though I had magic."

"Are you certain that you didn't?"

"No. And when I pointed at Melbah and she somehow flamed herself—I don't know, it was as though I returned her evil to her. The same thing happened later with Zoanna, and—"

"But do we have to understand? You did it. It was through you that it happened."

"I'll never understand, never. I believe I used my father's

laser weapon and jetpak at one time, but I can't honestly remember using either. It was as if I flew when I needed to fly and reversed magic when I needed it reversed. Zoanna, and later Zady, obligingly made ashes of themselves."

"You did it. You did it, hero."

"Yes, I have to accept that, but the circumstances, the handling of what happened—I simply don't remember. It was as though there was a goodness and a badness, and as though the goodness had to be reached and the badness put down. Does that make sense to you, Heln?" He hoped it did, because maybe then he could begin to truly forget.

"Yes," she said. "It happens. It's necessary."

"Yes," he echoed her, perplexed as always. Mouvar had played a game, but there was much that couldn't be explained by that. Such as Kelvin's father's appearance in this realm. Perhaps things were not quite as Mouvar believed. It would be nice if that were so.

He watched his grandsons circling, the two-legged one holding the four-legged one's copper tail. There was so much joy in the world that was possible, with or without magic. So much goodness when badness was kept vanquished or at bay.

It was, most obviously, a wonderful time for young and old and those in between. A near-perfect time had dawned for those present and the many not present.

It was a great fine time for the Alliance.

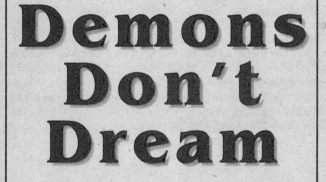

SCIENCE FICTION FROM PIERS ANTHONY

☐ ☐	53114-0	ANTHONOLOGY	$3.50 Canada $3.95
☐ ☐	53098-5	BUT WHAT OF EARTH?	$4.95 Canada $5.95
☐ ☐	53125-6	DRAGON'S GOLD with Robert E. Margroff	$3.95 Canada $4.95
☐ ☐	53105-1	THE E.S.P. WORM	$2.95 Canada $3.95
☐ ☐	53127-2	GHOST	$3.95 Canada $4.95
☐ ☐	53108-6	PRETENDER with Frances Hall	$3.50 Canada $3.95
☐ ☐	53116-7	PROSTHO PLUS	$2.95 Canada $3.75
☐ ☐	53101-9	RACE AGAINST TIME	$3.50 Canada $4.50
☐ ☐	50104-7	THE RING with Robert E. Margroff	$3.95 Canada $4.95
☐ ☐	50257-4	SERPENT'S SILVER with Robert E. Margroff	$4.95 Canada $5.95
☐ ☐	53103-5	SHADE OF THE TREE	$3.95 Canada $4.95

Buy them at your local bookstore or use this handy coupon:
Clip and mail this page with your order.

Publishers Book and Audio Mailing Service
P.O. Box 120159, Staten Island, NY 10312-0004

Please send me the book(s) I have checked above. I am enclosing $ _____
(please add $1.25 for the first book, and $.25 for each additional book to cover postage and handling.
Send check or money order only—no CODs).

Name _____
Address _____
City _____ State/Zip _____
Please allow six weeks for delivery. Prices subject to change without notice.